NARCOSIS ROOM

LOUISE CYPRESS

OWL HOLLOW PRESS

Owl Hollow Press, LLC, Springville, UT 84663

Narcosis Room
Copyright © 2019 by Louise Cypress

Library of Congress Cataloging-in-Publication Data
Narcosis Room / L. Cypress. — First edition.

Summary:
Ellie Savage's dermatologist dad and psychiatrist mom run the Narcosis Clinic, a medical facility where disturbing issues are resolved while patients are beautified. Ellie is her parents' most ardent supporter—until her dreams become a nightmare and the only way for Ellie to remember who she is, is to forget everything she thinks she knows.

ISBN 978-1-945654-19-0 (paperback)
ISBN 978-1-945654-20-6 (e-book)
LCCN 2018961100

To my in-laws, Marc and Lynn

BOOK ONE
BEFORE

CHAPTER ONE: ELLIE

3:09 P.M. | JUNE 3RD

The little girl looked like someone had taken her to the butcher shop and ground her face into hamburger. One of her pigtails was crooked, making her scars appear even less symmetrical. She looked up at me from where she was coloring in a book on the coffee table. Her crayon broke.

"That's quite a grip you've got there." I crouched down and gazed into her dark brown eyes. "Could I color too?" She hesitated. "Please?"

When she pushed the box of crayons over, I gave her my electric smile.

"Ellie." Mom's voice had the professional tone she always used around prospective clients. "I'm so glad you're volunteering in the clinic today because I'd like you to meet Katie."

"Nice to meet you." With a contented sigh, I plopped my butt on the floor right next to Katie, and the little girl giggled. I selected a brown crayon the same shade as her skin. "Maybe you could give me some pointers?" I inspected Katie's depiction of a princess attacking a dragon. "You look like you know what you're doing."

Katie smiled at the compliment, but her parents didn't notice. They both sat in wooden chairs in front of Mom and Dad's double-wide desk on the other side of the room from where Katie and I colored. Katie's father clutched a brochure with an iron grip. His wife stared at the wall of diplomas and medical degrees that dominated the room.

Mom smoothed her French twist. Her red hair was the same color as mine. "Ellie's highly trained at counseling new patients and making them feel at home."

"She's the Narcosis Clinic's version of a candy striper," Dad added. "Aren't you, sweetheart?"

"Yeah, except you never let me eat candy." I pretended to scowl and leaned against Katie. "Does your dad let you eat sugar?" Katie froze at the contact. I rushed on. "My dad's a dermatologist. That means a skin doctor. He thinks ice cream and candy are bad for my complexion." I sat up straighter and did my best Dad impersonation. "'Modern medical miracles are no substitute for proper nutrition.'"

My parents both chuckled, and then Katie's parents laughed too—with the wheezing sound of people who had held their breath too long.

I chose a green crayon from the box. "You have no idea how many vegetables they make me eat."

"I don't have to eat vegetables," Katie whispered. "I used to, before the raccoon, but now I can eat anything I want. Even ice cream for breakfast."

The adults stopped laughing, eyes trained on Katie.

I turned my body to shield her from view. "Ice cream for breakfast sounds delicious." I shaded in the tail of her dragon. "If you come here, you won't need to worry about breakfast for three months."

"That's what they told me." Katie set her crayon down, forehead furrowed. "But I still don't understand."

"Want me to show you?" I glanced up to Mom, seeking her approval.

"That would be excellent." Mom leaned back in her chair. "Ellie can show Katie what a narcosis room looks like while we go over the paperwork."

"Come on, Katie." I held out my hand. "Let's go."

Katie's tiny fingers sweated in my palm as I led her into the hall, through the locked doors, down the glass staircase, and into the heart of the public lobby. Since the Narcosis Clinic was only a few blocks from the Space Needle, we often got tourists who wandered over from the Seattle Center curious to take a peek at the medical facility famous for making dreams come true.

A seven-minute documentary played on repeat in the foyer. *"Narcosis rooms have been around since the 1960s when Dr. William Sargant first used them in London to treat depressed housewives. Despite the dutiful attention of Nightingale nurses, Dr. Sargant's early experiments in narcosis sometimes caused death and insanity. Thanks to the pioneering work of Doctors Belinda and Warren Savage, narcosis is now safe. If you struggle with any of a variety of health issues, the Narcosis Clinic can help. Patients wake up three months later thinner, happier, and with smoother skin. And they don't remember a single painful surgery."* I'd heard the spiel so many times it was seared into my mind. *"Sleep for three months and make your problems go away. At the Narcosis Clinic, dreams really do come true."*

"We don't need to watch that," I told Katie, hurrying her through the metal doors into the staged narcosis room that tourists viewed. "I've got something better to show you." The scent of lavender greeted us, and light filtered in through clouded windows.

"It's beautiful!" Katie skipped over to the brass bed piled high with silk cushions. When she turned to look at me, her maimed face gouged my heart. "Can I jump on the bed?"

"Of course you can; just let me move these sensors out of the way first." I slid some tubing aside and made sure the machines housed in stainless steel boxes behind the bed were disconnected. It was real equipment even though it was just for show. "Go for it!"

Katie leaped into the center of the pillow-top mattress and vaulted herself like it was a trampoline. Squealing, she bounced up and down until the comforter tangled and all of the pillows fell onto the floor. When she finally collapsed in a heap of exhaustion, I pulled over one steel container with a small monitor sticking out the top.

"See this computer?" I flicked a switch on the side of the box and the monitor turned white. "It monitors patients while they sleep." I pointed to a smaller box next to it that had headphones attached. "And that's the computer for psychic-driving."

Katie sat back up so she could see. "Like driving a car?"

"More like driving a brain. If a person comes in here feeling sad, my mom plays a psychic-driving tape that says, 'I love my life. I am happy all the time.' Or something like that. Then, when the patient wakes up, she's all better."

Katie wrinkled her scarred forehead. "What will the tape say for me?"

"I don't know. What do you think it will say?"

Katie looked down at her hands. I hadn't noticed before, but a chunk of flesh was missing from her left elbow. Mom could heal that too. In addition to being a psychiatrist, she was a plastic surgeon.

"Maybe the tapes would say something about the raccoon," Katie whispered. "About how not all of them are bad and I don't need to be afraid all the time."

I swallowed hard. "Hold on a sec. Your pigtails are crooked." I reached over and adjusted the offending hairdo. *If only everything were so easy to fix.* "Much better." Katie's smile made me glow inside. "Do you have nightmares?"

Katie nodded. "It's hard to sleep. The other doctors said the only thing they could give me was medicine."

"Well, those doctors don't know everything. My parents are brilliant."

"Really?" Katie looked up at me under a fringe of long eyelashes.

"I promise you and your beautiful eyes that you've come to the right place."

Another smile burst across Katie's face even as her brown eyes welled with tears. "Nobody says that word about me anymore."

My eyes became wet too, especially after I kissed Katie on her hamburger cheek. "Don't worry, Princess Katie. Three months from now, everyone will say that you're beautiful."

A couple of hours later, my parents and I were upstairs in our residence making an early dinner. "You're remarkable," Mom said to me as she stood at the kitchen counter grating carrots for a salad. She'd traded her heels for slippers and wore an apron that said "SURGEONS KNOW HOW TO SLICE." "You're so poised and helpful. Every day you make your father and me proud."

I flushed at the praise and took down some plates so that I could set the table.

"No, really." Mom dumped the veggies into a bowl. "The way you handled that patient today was exceptional. By the time you brought Katie back into the room, she was begging her parents to sign the papers."

"I can't believe they were nervous in the first place." Dad adjusted the burner, where he pan-fried salmon. "If Katie were my daughter, there'd be no way I'd let her live like that. Ninety days of treatment will fix everything."

"Now, Warren, let's not judge." Mom rinsed lettuce over the sink. "Subjecting your child to elective surgery is scary."

I shook out the placemats. "I don't think reconstructing Katie's face counts as elective."

Dad nodded in agreement.

"And I hope they killed that raccoon."

"Ellie!" Mom chided me.

"You can't honestly hope the raccoon is still alive?" I set three plates on the kitchen table then sat in my usual chair.

"The only thing we can control is what happens inside the clinic."

"Always the objective scientist." Dad kissed Mom on the top of her head on his way to bringing the salmon to the table.

"I can't help what I can't help." Mom took off her apron and hung it on her chair before sitting down. "So I don't bother worrying about what's beyond my control." She picked up her napkin and placed it on her lap. "Speaking of which…"

I stared at my empty plate. "I'm not sure what I want to do."

"We could still send you to camp this summer like you told your friends you'd be doing." Dad broke off a piece of fillet and slid it on my dish before serving Mom and himself.

"Archery and canoeing sound like a blast," I said sarcastically.

Dad shrugged. "Starting another round of narcosis is entirely your decision."

"I'd psychic-drive all the AP prep directly into your head," Mom said with a tempting tone. "Wouldn't that make senior year easy? But there's nothing wrong with studying the old-fashioned way too. We could send you to camp with flashcards instead."

"The school bit would be a nice bonus, but that's not the reason I would do narcosis."

Dad set down his wine glass. "Your nightmares might go away with time."

"I'll find you a new therapist," Mom offered, "to help you with your phobia."

"But what about my lost memories?" I accidentally dropped my fork, and it clattered to the table. "How would I get those back?"

"Even with narcosis, there's no guarantee," said Mom. "Retrograde amnesia is hard to cure."

"But you said if my brain can rest and feel safe for three months, there's a good chance my memories will come back on their own."

"Maybe." Dad twisted his napkin. "We never should have sent you to boarding school. I wish I knew what happened that is making your brain forget."

"At least I came back speaking French."

"Not worth it." Mom's voice shook. "I'll never forgive myself.

"Me either," said Dad.

I hated when they beat themselves up like that. "Guys, it wasn't your fault. Dad didn't go wacko when he went to Remington Prep."

"Don't say that!" Mom slapped the table. "Not only is it politically incorrect, you're doing great now. When your brain is ready to remember, it will. Another summer of narcosis might help you remember faster, but I can't make any promises. That's why this is your decision." Mom took my hand in hers.

"Thanks, Mom." I squeezed her hand. "I think I want to go for it, but I'll let you know in the morning for sure." I looked at Dad. "Okay?"

He reached for my other hand. "Absolutely."

CHAPTER TWO: DEAN

3:09 P.M. | JUNE 3RD

I was bored brainless. I woke up in Boise, stopped for a mall appearance in Spokane, and was now inching toward Seattle. The tour bus smelled like armpit even though the backup dancers rode in the van. The bus was reserved for equipment, my stylist Maxine, my manager Gary, the bus driver, and me. Nobody climbed aboard unless they were trustworthy.

Not that Gary was loyal. If his 15 percent cut of my earnings wasn't enough to keep him in toupees and Corvettes, he'd dump me. That's why he'd followed me instead of Sam when the Heartacres had broken up. Sam last's album had dropped like a turd, but I was in a new city every night selling out stadiums across America.

"Would you look at all those trees!" Maxine pressed her nose against the glass. Her hair was frosted pink this week, and she looked like an aged wood sprite. "Did you know they call Washington the Evergreen State?"

"Tho I've heard," I lisped.

Maxine glanced up at me. Even sitting, my six-foot-two frame towered over her barely five foot one. I loved her like she was my grandma. Learning facts about each state we visited was one of Maxine's favorite things about being on tour. She sent postcards to her grandkids from every town we stayed in. I taught her how to FaceTime them on her iPad too.

"I hope our hotel is by the Space Needle," Maxine said. "I read that—"

My phone buzzed, interrupting Maxine's latest bit of trivia. When I saw the notifications scroll across the screen, my heart dropped into my stomach.

SAM ANDERS AND PANSY WILLIAMS ELOPE. SEE PICTURES OF THEIR VEGAS WEDDING.

What the heck were they doing getting married? Sure, Sam was twenty-one, but Pansy was the same age as me—nineteen. When we were together, she could barely commit to dinner reservations. Now she was all "'til death do us part"? Sam might have been in love, but Pansy was using him, just like she'd used me.

"Did you see the news?" Gary burst into our sitting area from the back of the bus.

"What news?" Maxine looked at me accusingly until I held out my phone so she could see. She slipped her rhinestone glasses onto her nose. "Oh. My. Gosh."

Gary bounced on the balls of his feet like the bus floor was lava. "I can spin this to your advantage. If anyone asks, you're focusing your angst into your solo career."

"For sure," I answered. Painting me as a lonely boy sold records. But the truth was, Pansy had done more than unleash a torrent of celebrity gossip. She'd shaken me up from the inside and done immeasurable damage. Case in point, my lisp had returned with a vengeance.

I'd met Pansy on the set of *American Dance Party* when I was sixteen. It had been love at first sight—at least for me. Sam had been there too, of course, flirting with every groupie he could. Six months later Pansy and I had still been going strong, until one day I'd boarded the tour bus and discovered her and Sam playing tongue hockey. Breaking up the Heartacres had been her ticket to fame. Now instead of Pansy begging for bit parts in movies of the week, Hollywood jumped at the chance to cast the girl who'd broken up the most popular boy band in decades. She'd left me with my heart ground to bits by the spike of her stiletto shoe.

"You know," Gary said. "This could be perfect. It's a ready-made excuse for why you'll be out of the spotlight all summer. Instead of that bit about the ashram in India, we'll say you're holed up in Bermuda writing songs about being dumped."

I tapped my foot to a melody stuck in my head called "Soul Crusher" that I was still in the process of composing.

"Oh, honey." Maxine's pencil-thin eyebrows knitted together. "That girl was no good for you. I knew it the first time I met her. How she kept that little yippy dog in her purse and let it crap all over the place. It wasn't right." Maxine patted my hand. "Why don't you call your mama? You know she'd love to hear from you. In fact, I wouldn't be surprised if she called you right now."

As if on cue, my phone started ringing.

"No way." I chuckled.

"See?" Maxine winked.

With a little wave to Max, I answered the phone and carefully walked to the rear of the tour bus. The blue curtains on each bunk bed swayed with the movement of traffic. I climbed into my berth just as Mom's worried voice blasted my eardrums.

"I saw the news, honey. How are you holding up?" I could hear Mom's concern all way from the big house in Toronto that I'd bought for her and my little sisters.

"I'm fine. And I told you not to call."

"I wanted to hear the sound of your voice."

"You heard it. I'm hanging up." I swiped the screen closed and opened up my messages.

MUCH BETTER, I texted.

THIS IS RIDICULOUS, replied Mom. JUST TAKE YOUR TIME LIKE YOU DID WHEN YOU WERE YOUNGER.

I'M NOT A KID ANYMORE, I typed back. I NEED TO HANDLE MY LISP MY WAY.

BY LETTING THEM CUT YOU OPEN?

NOBODY'S CUTTING ME OPEN. I decided it was better not to tell her about the doctors removing those weird lumps on the bottom of my foot. I'LL LISTEN TO SOME TAPES WHILE I'M ASLEEP FOR A FEW MONTHS. IT'S CALLED PHYSIC-DRIVING.

I KNOW WHAT IT IS. I READ *PEOPLE*.

SO WHY ARE YOU FIGHTING THIS? YOU KNOW IT WORKS!

BUT IT DOESN'T LAST, **Mom texted.**

IT DID FOR A YEAR AND A HALF, **I answered.** AND THIS TIME THE DOCTORS HOPE IT WILL BE PERMANENT.

JUST TELL THE WORLD THE TRUTH ABOUT WHO YOU ARE.

NO!

PUT IT IN A SONG, **Mom pressed.** YOU NEVER LISP WHILE SINGING.

I'M TURNING OFF MY PHONE. WE'RE DONE HERE.

LOVE YOU! Mom's words flashed across the screen, and I waited longer than I probably should have before I replied.

LOVE YOU TOO.

Ten minutes later I was sitting in the styling chair as the bus lumbered past Walla Walla.

"About what Gary said," Maxine began, waving her rat tail comb back and forth. "I don't want you to let him bother you." She pointed the comb at me. "You got lucky if you ask me."

"I don't think that'th what getting lucky meanth."

Maxine harrumphed and grabbed my hair by the roots. I grimaced as she teased it into place. "High school romances never last."

"I didn't go to high thchool."

"Don't be smart." Maxine teased my hair higher. "You know what I mean. You started dating that girl at sixteen and haven't seen anyone else since she broke your heart."

"Who am I going to date?"

"Anyone!" Maxine reached for some gel. "There are girls lined up outside of your hotel every night who'd be happy to spend time with you."

I rolled my eyes. "You want me to have a meaningleth relationship?"

"I want you to have fun. I want you to enjoy being nineteen instead of being this mini-adult who takes care of everyone else."

"I don't take care of everyone. I bankroll them."

"Same difference." Maxine worked a dollop of gel through the back of my hair to achieve the fullness the audience expected. "Gary, the dancers, the tour company, me—we're all living off of your talent. But what about you, Dean? Can you honestly say you're living?"

I shrugged underneath the hairdressing apron.

"So mix it up," Maxine coaxed. "Kiss a girl. Ride up to the top of the Space Needle. Go for a joyride. Be everything that you are: young, handsome, successful, and the kindest entertainer I've ever had the privilege of working with."

First Mom and now Maxine. It was like they were tag-teaming me to tell me what to do.

Maxine whizzed the can of hairspray all around me in a cloud. Then she set it down with a definitive *clink*. "Be free, kiddo," she told me. "You earned it."

"After thummer."

"No," she insisted. "You deserve to start living right now." Maxine set down the canister and spun the swivel chair so that I could face the mirror. Dean Mathews, pop star extraordinaire, stared back at me. And he looked miserable.

CHAPTER THREE: COLE

3:09 P.M. | JUNE 3RD

I'd rather clean the head than work the ship's galley, but Dad rotated my sister and me through all the possible workstations on *The Royal Racer*, the high-speed catamaran our family owned that shuttled tourists back and forth from Seattle to Vancouver Island. He insisted that grunt work built character. All I knew was that any job that involved interacting with the public was torture. Marley knew how shy I was, which was why she manned the register while I assembled the food.

"Two Fisherman Lunches and a Skagit County Special," Marley called over her shoulder. Her sandy-blond hair was tied up in a ponytail, and her *Royal Racer* T-shirt hung loosely over jeans.

I lined up three baskets in front of me and tossed packets of crackers, tins of smoked salmon, chicken salad, and tiny wedges of cheese into each one. We didn't cook anything on *The Royal Racer*. Instead, we picked up ready-made sandwiches from Pike Place Market and filled in the rest with locally sourced snack food. I added cups of water to the tray and brought it out to the counter.

"Here ya go," said Marley, sliding the tray over to a father with a six-year-old yanking on his arm. "Have fun in Seattle."

"Thanks," the man said. He was walking away when his son stomped on his foot. The father turned back to the counter and looked past Marley to me. "Do you have any straws?"

"Sorry." I shook my head. "Straws are bad for sea life."

"Save the whales and all." Marley smiled brightly, and the customer shrugged. As soon as he left, her cheery expression vanished. "What is the holdup? If we don't get home soon, we'll miss the concert."

"I think we'll still make it. We won't have time to stop at home first, though."

"I can't go to a Dean Mathews concert looking like this."

"You look great."

"You're such a liar." Marley reached for the metal sign that swung above the counter and flipped it to CLOSED. "Let's clean up early."

I eyed the clock. "We're supposed to stay open for five more minutes."

"I know, but if I hurry and change right now, then I won't have to go home. We can head straight to the zoo as soon as we dock." She tossed me a wet rag and picked up her huge purse. "I'll be right back."

"Okay." I grabbed the bottle of disinfectant and started spraying. Maybe Dad would let us take off early before all the passengers had disembarked. He and Mom were cosponsors of the concert after all. Every summer the zoo brought in a new lineup of performers, and this year Marley had begged and pleaded for Mom to use her weight on the zoological board of directors to get Dean Mathews to come. Then Marley had used her position on student council to turn it into a full-on school event.

"Ladies and gentlemen, this is Captain Evans speaking. Please return to your seats." Dad's deep voice piped over the loudspeakers. "We will be arriving at Pier 59 in twenty minutes."

Twenty minutes? Man, we were cutting it close. I double-knotted a bag of trash and put a new liner in the bin.

"Please tell me the dirty stuff is done." Marley reappeared in the galley wearing a sundress and cowboy boots and sporting smoothed hair.

"You'll freeze your tush off in that outfit. I'm not giving you my sweatshirt."

"I don't need your stinky sweatshirt. I won't get cold." Marley twisted and turned in the reflection of the stainless steel refrigerator. She wasn't stick thin like some of her friends, and I knew that bothered her. "Liam says I should do CrossFit this summer."

"Yeah, well, Liam's an idiot, and I don't know why you date him."

Marley adjusted the spaghetti strap of her dress and sighed. Then she walked over to the register. "Have you tallied up yet?"

"No." I reached for scouring powder and a sponge. "I'm almost done cleaning, though."

"Wonderful." Marley's fingers flew over the cash register buttons entering in the code to print out the day's sales. The purser would cash out the till once we were docked. "I heard that Ellie is going to the concert too."

I felt my ears burn red. "Yeah, so?"

"So, maybe we could bring an extra chair and see if she'd like to sit with us, and then invite her to our party tonight."

I gave the sink an extra vigorous scrub. "Are you trying to torture me?"

"Of course not." Marley pulled out the register tape. "I'm just giving you a nudge. You've been crushing on her forever, and I've seen you stalk her Instagram account."

A prickle of sweat broke out across my back. "I don't need my sister's help getting girls. You might run Emily Carr High's student council, but you're not the boss of me." I squeezed the dirty sponge with both hands and tossed it into the sink.

"I'm not trying to boss you around, and I know you don't need help getting girls. But the question is, can you get the right girls?" Marley arched her eyebrow at me. We were twins who looked remarkably alike. When her tan face stared back at me, it was like a reflection of myself with better shaped eyebrows.

"How can you say they aren't the right girls? They're on *your* student council."

Marley rolled her eyes. "Yeah, but do you like any of them? As much as you like Ellie?"

I looked away from her. "They're all right, I guess."

The truth was I'd had my heart glued to Ellie ever since sixth grade when she'd gotten kicked off the school bus for jumping on the benches and pretending to surf. Her red hair hung to her waist and the way she wiggled her hips made me tingle in places I was just learning could tingle.

Or maybe Ellie had first caught my attention in fifth grade when she'd stood on the stage in the middle of the lunchroom and given the whole cafeteria the Hunger Games salute.

Or maybe my crush had started in fourth grade when Ellie had stuck a recorder up her nose and played "Mary Had a Little Lamb" at the school concert. I thought being forced to learn to play the recorder was lame too, but Ellie had been the only person brave enough to do something about it.

Or maybe I'd liked Ellie since second grade when she came over to our house to play with Marley, and they'd gotten into Mom's makeup and spilled bronzer all over the white carpet.

Or maybe, if I was honest, I'd had a thing for Ellie ever since kindergarten when she'd showed up on the first day of school wearing a full-on princess costume, with a tiara and everything, and her pockets had been full of earthworms.

"Hello," Marley said. "Earth to Cole?"

"What?"

"I said if you really liked any of my friends, you would do more than just talk with them."

"You make me sound like a loser."

My sister pursed her lips.

"I'm not, you know," I said, trying to defend myself. "I have plenty of experience with women."

"Stop!" Marley plastered her hands over her ears. "I do *not* want to know the details."

I pulled her arms down and tweaked her nose. "Ellie doesn't like me."

"You don't know that for sure!"

Now I was the one rolling my eyes. "Ever since Ellie came back from boarding school, it's like she's a different person."

Marley grimaced. "Boarding school turned her into a robot."

"She is not," I said immediately. "Ellie's just… more reserved."

"And she's totally forgotten who her friends are."

"It's not as if she and I were ever friends." I took off my apron and hung it on a peg. In the distance, I could see the dock approach. We were almost in port.

"I was good friends with her." Marley slung her purse over her shoulder. "I thought she was my best friend, and then she went off to Connecticut and didn't answer one letter. For two years!"

"Maybe she didn't get them," I offered.

"Then why did she totally ignore me when she came home for ninth grade?"

"I don't know," I mumbled. All I could say for sure was that Ellie had come back more gorgeous than ever. When she'd left for seventh grade, she had been pretty. When she'd come back to Seattle, she had been the hottest girl at Emily Carr High. There had been no way freshman-me could talk to her. Two years later, I still couldn't string together a sentence in her presence.

Marley uncapped a tube of lip gloss and smeared it on. "Just because Ellie and I aren't BFFs anymore doesn't mean you can't date her. I've forgiven Ellie for your sake."

"I don't need your permission."

"Sure you don't." Marley slid black sunglasses down on her nose. "But I'm giving it to you anyway."

CHAPTER FOUR: ELLIE

5:30 P.M. | JUNE 3RD

Olivia Chen was running late, but I'd expected that. I sat on a bench on the steps of the clinic and scrolled through my Instagram account. A stack of books, my striped tights, a cup of clam chowder from Ivar's, a crow watching me from a telephone wire, the Pacific Science Center at night. When I concentrated, the memories clicked into place. Selfies, pictures with Olivia, the cafeteria. The images were my daily record of existence. One photo a day helped me fight my retrograde amnesia. Mom thought social media was a waste of time and that I should keep a journal instead, but Dad said I shouldn't listen to someone who still had a flip-phone. I was so engrossed in my Instagram feed that I didn't hear the Subaru pull up.

"Are you ready?" Olivia hollered from the driver's seat. Her cheeks were slightly sunburned, and her dark hair was wet, like she'd just gotten out of the shower.

"You bet." I stashed my phone in my purse and opened the passenger door. The heat wafting out felt nice. Even though it was June, it was sweater weather. "Thanks for cleaning out your car for me." I scooped up some sweatshirts and a water bottle from the floor and tossed them in the back. Then I scooped Olivia's collection of lip balm off my seat and into the center console, where they belonged.

"Watch out for the papers! Those are important."

"You drive around in a dump." I carefully placed fliers for Olivia's kayaking club in the backseat until finally there was a place for me to sit down.

"I was on the water all day. You're lucky I showed up at all."

"Like you would miss a Dean Mathews concert."

Olivia grinned. "Never. I have all of his songs." She turned on her blinker and headed into the traffic that swirled around downtown. "I still can't believe the parents' group arranged this. If I had known that a private concert with Dean was in the works, I wouldn't have raised a ruckus about them canceling Winter Formal."

"I wasn't going to Winter Formal anyway, so this is ten times better as far as I'm concerned."

"There are lots of guys who would have asked you."

"Yeah, but…"

"You were holding out for Mr. Perfect."

"I'm not sure if he exists," I lied.

"You're telling me you don't think Cole Evans is perfection? I saw how you were looking at him in chemistry yesterday."

"That was an accident. I had something in my eye."

Olivia grinned mischievously. "Then why are you blushing?"

"I'm not blushing!" As soon as I said it, I felt my cheeks burn red. "Besides, it doesn't matter what I think about Cole. He never says two words to me."

"Cole never says two words to anyone. If you get a head nod from him, you're lucky."

"Well, he's never head-nodded at me either."

"Marley probably wouldn't let him. I've never seen a guy so loyal to his sister."

"They have that twin thing going on," I agreed. "And Marley pretends like I don't exist, so there's no way Cole Evans could be my Mr. Perfect."

Except, of course, that Cole sat next to me in pre-calculus, so I knew he was smart. He always lent me a pencil when I forgot one—sometimes on purpose—so I knew he was kind. He was captain of the lacrosse team, which meant he was in exceedingly good shape. And I once saw him reach into the garbage, pull out an empty can of soda, and toss it in the recycling. So yeah, Cole was not *my* Mr. Perfect, but he was, in fact, perfect.

Something smooshed under my foot, and when I lifted up my ankle, I spotted a granola bar wrapper stuck to the sole of my boot. "Yuck!"

Olivia glanced over. "Oops! Sorry about that."

"If you kept a trash bag in here, your car would be a lot cleaner."

"But then I'd never be able to find anything."

"Like garbage?"

"Like an extra fleece or a raincoat. It might be cold at the zoo tonight. Did you think of that?"

I pulled my windbreaker a bit tighter. It wasn't insulated, so if the temperature dropped, I'd be screwed. The concert was being held outside in the grassy amphitheater of the Woodland Park Zoo. "At least it's not raining." I looked out the window to the gray clouds above. "Yet..."

"A little precipitation won't stand between Dean Mathews and me." Olivia changed lanes.

"Hey, wait a second." I suddenly noticed where she was going. "Why are you taking the Aurora Bridge?"

"Because I-5 will be packed right now."

My heart picked up rhythm. "But..."

"We'll be on the bridge for like ten seconds. It's not a big deal."

My lungs stopped working as the bridge approached. All around us, Lake Union stretched out as far as my eyes could see. *So much water.* "Olivia! The lake!" I couldn't stop the hitch in my voice. Total hysteria crept over me like a choking vine of poison ivy. "What if the bridge breaks? What if we plunge over the side?" Gasping. Hyperventilating. Losing all control of reason. Water everywhere.

"Ellie?" Olivia's hand on my back brought some sanity back to my thoughts—but only some. "Put your head between your knees and take five deep breaths. You can do this."

"I can't do it! You know I can't!" Panic strangled my insides as I brought my head to my knees. "What if we go underwater? What if I have to swim? I'll drown!"

"Nobody's going underwater." Olivia pulled her hand back, and my head bumped into the dashboard when she slammed on the brakes.

I kept my head down, terrified. "What was that?"

"Nothing. The car in front of me made a sudden stop, that's all. We'll start moving again soon."

"You mean we're stuck on the bridge?"

"Only a few minutes more." She didn't sound convinced.

"Why is this happening?" I wasn't sure if I was asking the Lord Almighty or the girl sitting next to me who was supposed to be my best friend.

"I'm sorry." The car started moving again, crawling along at a slow speed. "I didn't think this would bother you so much. You can barely see the water from the bridge."

I squeezed my eyes shut, and tears spilled out.

"It's not as if I brought you to a beach," Olivia continued. "I'd never do that."

A sob bubbled up from my chest that I couldn't hold down. I wasn't sure if it was from terror or humiliation.

"There." Olivia rested her hand on my back again. "We're across the bridge. It's all over now."

I looked up from my knees. "But it's not over, is it?"

As soon as she could, Olivia pulled the car over to the curb and parked. Then she turned off the ignition and gave me a hug. "What if I taught you to swim?" she murmured into my shoulder. She pulled back and looked at me. "Stay home from French Camp this summer. I'll take you to the pool every day."

I shuddered. "I couldn't."

Olivia gave a fierce nod. "You could. We're turning eighteen this year. You've got to learn to swim and stop being afraid of water."

My stomach felt woozy. I sniffed, and my nose dripped.

"Here." Olivia rummaged around in the driver seat door and handed me a tissue. "Will you at least think about it? Look, I know this is awkward to talk about, but you need help."

I twisted the tissue to bits.

"It's not just your fear of water, Ellie. Sometimes you get this faraway look like you're not paying attention." Olivia reached into the back seat for her purse and pulled out her phone. "I've been doing some research on ADHD. Did you know that for girls it can make them appear—"

"Stop. I don't have ADHD." I didn't want Olivia to know that something had happened to me at Remington Prep that was so traumatic, my brain made me forget. She already thought I was enough of a freak show. I took a deep breath. "But I do have a problem. It's this fear of water thing. Sometimes I have nightmares and I don't get enough sleep. That's probably why I zone out at school from time to time. You're right, though. I do need help. I can't keep living in fear."

"Good," said Olivia. "So that's yes to swimming lessons?"

"That's a no, thank you." I straightened the baseball cap over my curly red hair. "I have another solution in mind." *One that I don't have to be awake for.*

We drove the rest of the way to the zoo in silence and barely said two words as we unloaded the car. It wasn't until we set up our blanket on the grass in front of the stage that Olivia must have felt like it was safe to speak again.

"This is a great spot, but I'm glad I brought this old quilt to sit on." Olivia's small frame was buried in a North Face fleece. She rummaged through her wicker picnic basket. "Would you like a sandwich? I brought extra."

"No thanks. My parents and I had an early dinner."

"I envy you and your family meals. Mom doesn't get home until late." Olivia peeled back the brown paper wrapper from her hoagie. She had the type of metabolism that burned through carbohydrates. She ate like a trucker and never put on weight. Even my parents noticed it. Dad joked that if he could culture Olivia's gut bacteria Mom wouldn't need to do lipo on patients anymore. They could infuse patients with Olivia's stomach bugs instead.

Around a mouthful of sandwich, she continued, "Of course, every time she comes home from a business trip, my dad morphs into Martha Stewart."

I smiled, trying to ease the tension. "I love it when your dad goes on a baking rampage. I hope you brought double dessert." I helped myself to the picnic basket and pulled out a plastic container of cookies. "Double fudge macadamia nut?" Olivia nodded and my mouth watered. The cookies were still warm. "I can't believe we're seeing Dean Mathews live," I said between bites.

"What a great way to end junior year, huh?" Olivia untwisted a thermos of coffee. "The only thing better would be if Sam Anders were here too and the Heartacres got back together."

"Yeah." I held out a spare cup and kept my hand steady while Olivia poured me a cup of coffee.

"Do you remember the time in ninth grade when we were in world history, and Mrs. Carson posted a picture of Dean on the wall as an example of a famous Canadian?" Olivia asked.

I nodded and smiled, pretending like I knew what she was talking about—my default for when my missing memories caused problems.

"There was a picture of Alanis Morissette too." Olivia smiled and her sunburnt cheeks shined like apples. "Marley made a big deal about how Alanis Morissette had sailed on *The Royal Racer* when her tour went to Vancouver Island. And you said…" Olivia looked at me expectedly.

Shoot. "I don't remember." I tried to laugh it off.

Olivia's smile faded for just a second, but then she continued. "You said, right there in the middle of class, 'My mom *loves* listening to Alanis Morissette!'"

I laughed. "I bet that annoyed Marley."

"She's touchy. And if I hear her brag about how her parents' catamaran service is a Seattle legend one more time, I'll hurl."

"Me too." I helped myself to more cookies.

A silence lapsed. Olivia dug her toe into the grass. "Are you still mad about the bridge? I'm sorry for that. That was my bad."

"It's okay. I'm the one who's a weirdo." *So weird that I can't remember much before ninth grade. And even chunks of that are missing.*

"You're not weird. But I think you might have ADHD. For girls, it can make them appear spacey sometimes." She pulled her phone out of her pocket. "I found this website and it says—"

"For the last time! I don't have ADHD!" I grabbed the concert program, which sported a close-up of Dean's face. "My parents have screened me for that, okay?"

Olivia's thumb passed over her phone like she wasn't quite ready to give up.

I shoved the concert program into her lap. "Would you say Dean's eyes are turquoise or more of a maritime blue?"

"Um, I don't know. Is maritime blue a color?"

"Of course it's a color."

Olivia looked back down at the program and slid her phone back into her coat. "I can't get over Dean's cheekbones," she said, allowing me to change the subject diplomatically. "He looks like Edward Cullen's twin brother."

"There's a resemblance," I agreed. I wasn't that impressed by Dean's beautiful face because I knew who'd made those eyes and crafted those cheeks. The plastics work was pure Mom, and the smooth skin had Dad's signature in every pore. But if I'd heard it once, I'd heard it a thousand times: "Clients who come to the Narcosis Clinic deserve privacy." So though I wanted to tell Olivia the truth about Dean's good looks, I didn't say one word.

"Oh, it's you," said a voice behind me. I turned around to see Marley shivering in a sundress and boots. She peered down at us. "This is the last piece of good grass left."

Cole stood next to her, holding three beach chairs. He was close enough that I smelled the scent of Juicy Fruit on his breath. I couldn't stop myself from looking into his hazel eyes. As soon as our pupils met, Cole looked away. My insides turned to mush. For some reason, the fact that Cole never spoke to me made me want to talk to him so bad, I could hardly stand it.

"Hi, Cole and Marley," said Olivia, who must have noticed how flustered I was by Cole's sudden appearance. "We got here early to get a good spot. You guys can join us if you want."

Marley looked down her nose at the grass. "There's not enough room for all of us."

Olivia and I scooted closer together, clearing space on the sod. If it had just been Marley, we wouldn't have bothered, but the thought of watching the concert with Cole was tempting enough to tolerate his bossy sister.

"Um…" Marley pointed to the chairs her brother held. "I know everyone else is sitting on grass, but we have commemorative seats they gave us since my mom's on the zoo's board of directors."

"That's great," I said.

Marley looked at me. "But there's no room for our chairs here."

Olivia shrugged. "Sorry about that." She looked back down at her program, but Marley didn't move.

"My *brother* and I would like to sit here," Marley said.

"Come on." Cole tugged his sister's sleeve. "Let's find someplace else."

"What exactly are you saying?" asked Olivia.

"Marley." Cole's voice was quiet. "Let's go."

Suddenly, Cole's proximity no longer bothered me. Not when his sister was trying to coerce us into giving up our seats.

"We're not moving," I said. "We got here first."

Olivia sat up straighter. "You can squeeze onto the blanket next to us, but there's no room for chairs."

"I wasn't trying to get you to move," said Marley. "I was just making small talk."

I rolled my eyes. "Sure."

"No, really!" Marley protested. She grabbed her brother's elbow. "Cole loves talking to you."

"Marely!" Cole said, in a growly voice.

"There you are." A hairy arm snaked around Marley's waist, followed by Marley's boyfriend, Liam. I'll admit there was a time I'd thought Liam was deeper than he was. I'd incorrectly assumed that his skater haircut and vintage T-shirts meant that he had more than two brain cells to rub together.

He punched Cole's shoulder with his other hand. "I found seats for us with the rest of the lacrosse team." He leered at Marley. "Babe, you can sit on my lap."

"Um… okay." Marley stared at the space right next to my head as if I were invisible.

When Liam realized it was me his girlfriend wasn't talking to, he gave me a lecherous grin. "Hey, Ellie."

"Hey, yourself." I scooted back to my original spot. No way was I sitting next to Liam.

"I hear you're going to French Camp all summer." Liam licked his lips. Then he pulled Marley close and stuck his tongue in her ear. "I'm real good at French, aren't I, babe?"

Marley shook him off. "You're disgusting," she said. But she was smiling.

"Let's find someplace else to sit," Cole said in a clear voice.

Liam looked at the gigantic posters of Dean rimming the arena. "I don't care where we sit. I didn't want to hear this loser sing anyway."

Cole glanced at me for just a second and opened his mouth like he was going to say something, but then he turned to his sister. "I'm outta here." He strode back the way they had come.

"Cole!" Marley called after him. She grabbed Liam's hand, and the two of them rushed after him.

"Typical." Olivia shook her head. "Somebody needs to text Marley with the newsflash that she doesn't own the world."

"Why does—?"

An announcement drowned out the rest of my questions. *"Ladies and gentlemen, we ask that you turn off all cell phones and recording devices."*

"This is really happening!" Olivia squealed and pulled me to my feet.

"Let us remind you that this concert is a smoke-free zone." One announcement came after another. Then, the lights went out, whipping the crowd into a ginormous frenzy. A single spotlight lit up the stage.

"You first met him as the lead singer of the Heartacres. Two years later he embarked on a solo career that took the world by storm." The announcer's bass voice vibrated in my chest. Olivia held up her hands and hooted. *"America wants him. Australia loves him. He sold out stadiums across Europe. Put your hands together for Canada's nineteen-year-old superstar: Dean Mathews!"*

Dean leaped onto the stage into the spotlight wearing sparkly pants and a jean jacket with fringe on the sleeves. They might have put glitter in his hair because it caught in the light. The "Dean Pouf" was the most popular hairstyle for teen guys at the moment, but nobody wore it quite like him. I had a giant poster of Dean in my room.

"Girl," Dean crooned into the microphone. *"I've meant to tell you..."* The crowd erupted into screams of applause until Dean shushed them with one small wave of his hand. *"That you make me..."*

"Marry me, Dean!" a rogue fan called out.

"*…wanna melt,*" Dean sang. He smiled at the fan as the stage lights lit up in a burst of rainbow colors and six scantily clad dancers spun across the stage, flanking Dean on both sides. "*Helloooo, Seattle,*" he sang. Then with a drum solo leading him off, he dove into his hit single "Girl, You Make Me Wanna Melt" with so much enthusiasm that it was like everyone was hearing it for the first time.

Dean's performance was electric. He was tall and lean, muscled in all the right places. His blue eyes were so bright, they could light up the city. When Dean sang his next song, all of Emily Carr High clumped into a crazed mass of squirming dancers on the lawn, and I was right there in the middle, shaking my booty with the rest of them.

After twenty minutes or so, Dean left the stage and wandered into the audience. The music stopped, but Dean continued to sing a cappella into the mic. He slowly walked up the grass, getting closer and closer to me. Did Dean recognize me? I felt a zap of nerves. Was he moving up the grass to sing to me?

"*I want a girl who can listen,*" Dean crooned, "*to the things I cannot say.*" Dean was feet away. I looked into his blue eyes—the same ones plastered on the poster in my room—and my knees went weak. Hopefully Marley Evans was watching. These were the best seats.

But then Dean moved. He strolled farther up the field. Ten steps later, and he was singing to Marley. I hadn't realized she ended up so close to us. He finished the song to *her.* Dean got down on his knees for the last part. When he finally stopped singing, Dean kissed Marley's hand. "Can I have your autograph?" she asked. I could hear her all the way from where we sat.

"For sure." Dean pulled Marley's sundress down just a smidge to expose lace-lined cleavage. With a pen from his back pocket, Dean scribbled his signature onto her plump breast.

Marley giggled. Next to me, I heard Olivia squeak.

I wasn't jealous. I could care less if Marley flashed her boobs. But I was also confused. How could Dean pretend like he didn't know me? Or had he forgotten me for real? After all, we'd only seen each other that one time in my backyard. He'd been on a bunch of pain meds too. I hadn't known how he'd gotten outside in the first place. Narcosis patients are supposed to be locked up in their rooms on the fifth floor of the clinic for the whole three months. They're watched by nurses twenty-four-seven.

Had I misremembered?

I closed my eyes, grasping for solid memories. Dean started his next song and the intensity of the concert—the lights, bass, everything—became too much for me. I shouted at Olivia that I had to use the restroom. Then I left the lawn for a little clarity. I walked to the top of the field where I could look out over the scene. The sun had slipped below the horizon and everything appeared shadowy. I felt like I was being watched, and I looked up at a giant totem pole, the eagle's eyes looking right at me.

A sudden breeze swept my Mariners cap away, and I broke eye contact with the eagle to chase it down the path to the antique merry-go-round. It fluttered to a stop right in front of the ticket girl.

"Nice hat," she said, smacking her gum. "You know the Mariners suck, right?"

"Tell me about it." I fished out money from my pocket. "Ten tickets, please."

"Ten rides?" Her plucked eyebrows shot up. "But you'll miss the whole concert."

"I'm a Sam Anders fan," I lied.

"Whatever." The girl pocketed the money in her green vest and clicked open the metal gate.

Ten seconds later I sat on a wooden horse spinning into oblivion so fast that my hat flew off again. Painted ponies going up. Painted ponies going down. Mirrors and lights. Grab the brass ring. Up, down, round and round.

The ride was kind of like my life. My history was a blur, the memories hard to grasp. Two years at Remington Prep had ruined me. Something sinister had happened to me at boarding school, but my brain wouldn't let me remember what that traumatic event was. The carousel went faster and faster until I could no longer hear the din of music in the distance.

Nobody else was riding that night. Only me.

Whoever that was.

Who was I? Who'd taught me to ride a bike? What had happened in middle school? Why didn't Marley like me? What was that scar on my chest all about? Why was I afraid of water? How long could I live my life without remembering my past? Where were all my *details*? Mom and Dad were afraid of telling me anything because they wanted my brain to remember on its own, but so far that plan was crap.

When my tenth ride on the carousel was up, I was so dizzy that I could barely climb off the horse. I staggered around for a few seconds before I regained my footing. Then I zeroed in on the totem pole at the top of the field, peering down at me with its eagle eyes. I tramped up the hill across the damp grass.

"Hey," the merry-go-round operator called after me. "You forgot your hat!"

"Trash it," I said, not looking back. I felt like I was going to throw up, but not from nausea. Something sick clawed at my heart. It tore me up from the inside, begging to get out. Begging to be remembered.

When I got to the totem pole, I sank onto my knees. Tears streamed down my cheeks.

And I had no idea why.

CHAPTER FIVE: DEAN

8:45 P.M. | JUNE 3RD

The band struck the chords of the final set, and the spotlight roamed over me and the audience. In exactly two minutes and fifty-three seconds, exploding glitter bombs would blanket the whole stage, and I needed to have my eyes closed when they blew. (I learned that lesson the hard way at a concert in Pittsburgh.) Lyrics rolled out of me as I rotated through the dance steps. It was a good thing I could do the whole performance on automatic because whenever I could, I snuck a glance at the girl on the grass whose boob I had signed. She was curvy with tan skin and sandy-blond hair. I liked the way she wiggled in her short dress and cowboy boots. Maxine was right. I should be young and free. And the girl in the cowboy boots was as hot as they came.

I swung my hips in rhythm to the chorus. The spotlight darkened and then blazed on high. Dancing was easy. When I was on stage, everything clicked. It didn't matter how many hundreds or thousands or millions of people watched me. Performing to sold-out crowds was easier than talking. More natural than breathing. Music made everything better except the loneliness I'd felt since Pansy had left and taken my best friend with her.

I twisted on the balls of my feet and looked out into the mass of people one more time. There was cowboy-boots girl again. Her hands were in the air, and she was singing along. Her hips swayed in time to the music. Would it be so wrong to meet up with her after the concert? Maybe we could hang out tonight in the hotel hot tub. But how could I arrange that without talking?

One thing was certain; this concert was ending whether I was ready to approach that girl or not. I sang the last words to the song, squeezed my eyes shut, and counted.

Three.

Two.

One.

Glitter bomb.

When I opened my eyes, glitter fluttered down, obscuring everything. The audience erupted into a standing ovation. "*Goodnight, Seattle*," I sang into the mic. I looked out into the crowd straight at the spot where the girl had been dancing but couldn't see her. I raked my gaze across the crowd, searching for her brownish-blond hair and bare shoulders.

Shoot. She was already gone.

The band played my exit jingle, and the drummer launched into a solo that was my cue to leave. I leaped off stage faster than usual and flew to the dressing room, where Maxine was waiting with a gallon of makeup remover and a stack of heated washcloths.

"I found a girl," I whispered harshly. "Will you go get her for me?"

"What?" Maxine unscrewed the lid of solvent.

"She might already be in the parking lot." I grabbed a rag and started wiping off my face. "Cowboy boot-th mini thkirt. Hurry!"

"Since when did you get the idea I'd round up groupies for you?"

"Not groupies. Just one girl."

Maxine dipped a tissue in the makeup remover. "Sorry, buddy. That's not in my job description."

"But you thaid I should live a little."

"And I'm not stopping you. If you found a girl you like, go out and get her." Maxine blotted off my eye makeup.

"How am I thupposed to do that without talking?"

"Maybe you could whistle."

"That'th ridiculouth." I ripped the tissue out of Max's hand and wiped away the rest of my stage makeup. Then I did a final cleanup with one of the wet washcloths.

"Here, wear this." Maxine grabbed a zoo hat out of a paper bag and plopped it on my head. "I bought a set for the grandkids, but they won't mind sharing. Now you're incognito. Well, you will be once you change clothes."

I stared at myself in the mirror. The cap was covered with giraffe prints and made me look like an idiot. "I dunno."

"You'll never know unless you try," said Maxine. "But you better hurry if you want to find that girl."

Three minutes later I was changed into jeans and a blue shirt, wearing the dorky giraffe hat, and pushing myself into the crowd headed for the parking lot while Maxine distracted my security guards. The clusters of bodies surrounding me were intense, but so far, so good. My disguise was working, and nobody screamed my name.

But the girl in the cowboy boots proved difficult to track. I kept watching for her sundress and naked shoulders—but then I saw a girl in cowboy boots and a short skirt wearing a rattylooking lacrosse sweatshirt. Was that her? Two guys flanked her. One wore a letterman jacket, and the other shivered in short sleeves.

This was it. She was definitely the girl. Now what should I do? Whistle?

As I puckered up, two things happened. The guy in the letterman jacket wrapped an arm of ownership around the girl's waist, and cries of "OMG! It's Dean Mathews!" rang out into the night.

In a flash, a mob surrounded me. I was clawed at from every angle by hungry fans. Someone ripped off my giraffe hat, and it was torn to shreds. Long fingernails gouged into my biceps, and someone yanked my shirt from behind.

"Dean! I love you!"

"Marry me!"

"I have all your records!"

"For sure!" I called out. I smiled as wide as possible and waved both hands. Across the crowds, I saw security guards muscle their way across the field with Gary right behind them. Help would be here any moment.

I put my lips together and whistled "We're Off to See the Wizard" from *The Wizard of Oz*. A hush fell on the people closest to me, but not for long. By the time the burly security guards showed up and pushed people away, I was sweating bullets.

"What were you thinking?" Gary cursed me out so loud, they'd probably heard him in Canada. "Since when are you a moron?"

I let my middle finger do the talking.

But as I trudged along behind Gary in my circle of security guards, I was bummed. Couldn't go for a walk. Couldn't talk to a beautiful girl. This was no way to live. The sooner I went through narcosis, the better.

CHAPTER SIX: COLE
9:30 P.M. | JUNE 3RD

As soon as we got home and verified that Mom and Dad had left for their overnight *Royal Racer* run to Victoria, Marley handed me a cardboard box. "Pack up all the breakables from the living room—and hurry." She tucked a strand of hair behind her ears. "Then move the cases of soda in my closet to the bathtub."

"Anything else, Your Majesty?"

Marley rolled her eyes. "Hurry up! People will be here in an hour."

I grabbed a porcelain figure my grandma had painted and set it carefully in the box. The *Royal Racer*'s Emerald City People's Choice Award went right next to it. "Shouldn't Liam be helping set up? It was his idea to throw a rager, not mine." I added a few more items and scanned the room for more.

"I'm sure he'll be here soon." Marley whacked a throw pillow on the couch with her fist until it was artfully arranged to her liking. She and Mom were both obsessed with the Pottery Barn catalog. "He just had a few errands to run."

I tried not to jostle the cardboard box. For a bunch of knickknacks, they were heavy. "If this party had been my idea, you never would have agreed to it."

"Not true." Marley scattered some coasters on the coffee table as if any of our friends would use them.

"Doesn't it bother you that Liam can talk you into anything?"

"You're being unfair!"

"Am I, *babe*? Where'd you get the drinks?"

Marley tidied up a stack of magazines. "Liam brought them over this morning."

"For the record, I still think this is a bad idea." I paused a moment on the stairs, letting my words sink in. "And you can do a heck of a lot better than Liam."

At this, my sister looked up. "But he's on your lacrosse team!"

"That's why I know he's a dirt bag."

"Then why are you friends with him?"

"Because it's one thing to hang out with a dirt bag; it's another to watch him put his tongue in your sister's mouth."

Marley wrinkled her nose. "You're disgusting." She thumbed at her phone until music piped from the stereo system. "You know, it's still not too late to call up Ellie and invite her over."

My stomach dropped. "It'd be a waste of time. She wouldn't come."

"She won't come if she's not invited."

I started walking upstairs.

"How about I text her?" Marley suggested.

"No!" I paused mid-step. "She doesn't want anything to do with me, okay?"

"She'll never want anything to do with you unless you talk to her."

"I *have* spoken to her. She's not interested."

"That can't be true," Marley protested. "I'll just—"

"No!" I said, more sharply than I intended.

"Fine. Whatever." Marley spun on her heel and turned around.

I stormed upstairs to stash the box. If Marley knew what had happened between Ellie and me last June, she wouldn't be on my case all the time, but she would hate Ellie's guts. And that would make feel even worse.

CHAPTER SEVEN: ELLIE
9:55 P.M. | JUNE 3RD

I unlocked the front door and the alarm panel chirped. After I tapped in the security code, the humming stopped. As soon as I shut the door behind me, I typed in the alarm code again and locked the perimeter up tight. Nobody wanted to sleep for three months unprotected. Our high-tech security system was part of the Narcosis Clinic's appeal.

Moist air enveloped me when I entered the quiet lobby. The calming scent of lavender from the essential oil diffusers over-powered the smell of industrial-strength disinfectant. Glass, metal, and steel reflected dully in the shadowy half-light. My boots echoed on the concrete floor. The Narcosis Clinic was an architectural masterpiece of modern minimalism.

"Welcome home, Ellie," said Ursula, the head nurse. Her black hair was coiled into a tidy twist underneath her cap. Ursula was my parents' right-hand woman. Tonight she sat at the front desk with a switchboard of lights, most of which glowed green. "Was the concert fun?"

"It was a delight." I walked past the glass stairway that was for public use and slid open a hidden wall panel that revealed the private elevator to our third-floor residence. "Have a lovely evening," I called back to Ursula before hitting the button.

Mom and Dad were waiting for me in the living room, halfway through a second bottle of wine. A giant cheese plate on a silver platter, lined with grapes, figs, and crackers, rested on the ottoman in front of them. Cheese was my favorite, but normally Dad didn't let me indulge because dairy was bad for my skin.

"Look, Ellie. I bought Gorgonzola." Mom's red hair was a riot of curls and her green sweater matched her eyes. In the soft white lamp light, we looked more like sisters than mother and daughter. Mom had never done narcosis before, but Dad zapped her pores with the laser on a regular basis.

"Thanks." I reached for the cheese knife and cut off a small triangle. Dad handed me a flute of sparkling cider.

Mom watched me put the cheese and crackers into my mouth. She stared at me as I chewed. "So?" she asked. "Have you made a decision?"

Crumbs stuck in my throat. "Yeah, about that." I took a quick swig of juice. "I want to go for it."

Mom's face softened with a smile. "I'm so glad to hear that. Your father and I want what's best for you and recovering your memories in a safe way is paramount."

"I completely agree," said Dad. "Although I'm terrified of finding out what happened to you at Remington Prep that caused your retrograde amnesia. I hope you remember enough details that we can sue the pants off whoever did this to you."

"Yeah, me too." I sipped the cider.

"And I hope that this time we can rid your subconscious of nightmares once and for all," said Mom.

Icy cold water that could tear me to shreds. I shuddered.

"Narcosis will make the rest of your life easier," said Mom. She offered me a piece of brie, and I declined. My stomach already felt overly full.

"Olivia wants me to stay home this summer so she can give me swimming lessons."

Mom set the plate back down. "Olivia's a good friend, but she has no idea what you're dealing with."

"It's hard hiding the amnesia from everyone." I looked down at my ragged cuticles.

"All of our patients deserve the utmost privacy. Especially you. And—"

A buzzing sound stopped Dad short—the security system alerting us that somebody was entering the parking garage through the new patient entrance.

Mom gave Dad a sharp look. "Who could that be? You don't think it's..." She saw me watching and didn't finish her sentence.

"No," said Dad decisively. "Well, maybe. He wasn't supposed to arrive until tomorrow morning."

Mom sprang to her feet and smoothed out her skirt. "I'm sorry, Ellie. You'll have to excuse us. We'll come say goodnight as soon as we can."

"You better! I need to get a good night's sleep tonight. You know, before I sleep all summer."

"Ha, ha." Dad tousled my hair. "I can always count on you for sarcasm."

After Dad and Mom rushed downstairs to greet their new client, I headed to my bedroom suite for a quick shower, then blew my hair out straight and brushed on some lip balm. Thanks to narcosis, I didn't need makeup for my skin to look perfect. I slipped into my favorite green nightshirt, a button-up that concealed the scar on my chest. I tied my bathrobe around me tight and headed over to my window seat with my phone. The night was chilly, and I felt the cold press in through the glass.

Time for a picture. I held the phone up and snapped a post-concert selfie with the giant poster of Dean Mathews behind me. So what if he didn't sign my boob. Poster Dean and I were now an Instagram memory. I was scrolling through my feed when something in the yard caught my attention. A solitary figure stood below me in the starlight. I opened the blinds wide and looked down. Had a patient escaped?

The person had a T-shape to his shoulders that topped off a narrow waist whittled by exercise. His brown hair appeared casually tousled, and the cheekbones looked so chiseled they almost reminded me of… *Dean Mathews*? I did a double take, snapping my head from the poster on my wall to the person down outside.

Was Dean doing more narcosis too? Usually I didn't care who dozed away on the third floor. Patients like Katie and me, who needed help, were rare. About half of Mom and Dad's patients were housewives with deep pockets. The rest were famous people, who were usually boring. Politicians, anchormen, musicians only my parents could like. Snore.

But Dean was different. Suddenly three months of narcosis didn't sound so lonely with him sleeping in the room next to me. I only wished there was some way to spend that time with Dean awake instead of drugged to sleep ten feet away.

At the very least I could say hello. I tried to open up my window to wave, but the casement was stuck. When I finally jerked it upward, my nightshirt came up too, flashing more of my legs than I'd intended—plus my panties. I swooped my hands down to cover my boyshorts… and I lost my balance. Before I knew what was happening, I tumbled out the window and through the screen. Screeching, I threw my hands out and caught myself just in time by clutching the rain gutter. My slippers fell to the grass twenty feet below with a *thump*.

"Is thomebody there?" a voice asked. A voice I knew from the radio.

Shoot! All I had wanted to do was wave hello. Now I was hanging out my window.

The metal tube of ivy I clung to made popping sounds as one bolt after another ripped out, dropping me slowly toward the ground. Who knew when a whole section of gutter would come out and I'd fall. Frantic, I eyed the big leaf maple next to my window. It grew three feet away and would require a death-defying jump, but I had no choice. It was time to leap to safety.

I imagined going airborne and landing softly like a panther. Instead, I sounded more like a lumberjack. The tree groaned when I hit the branches, and twigs snapped.

"What's going on?" The voice sounded scared now.

"Nothing!" I hollered. I scrambled down the large branch I had landed on to the trunk, ignoring the stinging pain of a scratch along my shoulder, then jumped. When my bare feet hit the grass, Dean had his phone out, his panicked eyes telling me he was about to call or text for help. "No, wait!" I held up my hands. "Don't freak out! I live here. This is my backyard."

Dean looked me up and down. My robe was filthy and ripped, and my nightshirt didn't offer much coverage. There were leaf crumbles in my hair and blood trickled down my arm.

"You probably think I'm a crazy stalker." I scanned the darkness for my slippers and quickly secured my feet in the wool. "But this is where I live."

"For sure," Dean answered. He looked around the yard like he was checking for paparazzi.

With my slippers on I felt taller. "We've met before." I took a step closer to Dean. "Tonight at the concert and a couple of years ago, right here in this garden. My parents run the clinic."

Dean put his phone in his pocket and stared down at my face.

"Do you remember me?" I asked. "Because I remember you. But you meet thousands of girls, so it's highly unlikely that you would recognize me. Although, really, how many girls do you meet at the Narcosis Clinic?" I was totally rambling. Maybe that's why Dean tried to shut me up the one way he knew how.

He leaned in and kissed me.

It was my first real kiss, and it was perfect.

Okay, actually it was my fourth kiss, but I don't think the first three should count. Number one was one of my earliest memories after returning to Seattle—kissing Jimmy Nuremberg on our ninth grade field trip to the aquarium. (It was gross; he'd tasted like the clam chowder I'd posted a picture of on my Instagram account.) Number two was during the short three weeks I'd spent dating Zach Parker in tenth grade. (He was the one who gave me the striped tights.) And number three was (I hate to admit it)… Liam, in the back of his Jetta. Thank goodness Cole had interrupted us. We were supposed to be at a junior pep rally, but instead, Liam had lured me into the parking lot with flirting and a little attention. He and Marley had been "on a break," and I was being an idiot. Cole hadn't said one word to me, he'd just held the car door open and mumbled to Liam, "Coach wants you." It was humiliating.

But my kiss with Dean tonight? It was 100 percent perfect. I'm calling it my one-and-only true first kiss because it was the only one that counted.

Dean's lips were on mine, and he smelled like hair product mixed with soap. He even cupped my face with his hands. When Dean gently pulled us apart, I was speechless for about ten seconds. "So you remember me?"

"For sure." Dean pulled me in and kissed me again.

CHAPTER EIGHT: COLE

Okay, this is what happened last year between me and Ellie. It's a good thing she wasn't invited to the party tonight, because I don't know what I'd say.

Almost a year ago today I'd been hiking in Discovery Park when I came across Ellie standing on a cliff looking out across the water wearing a green dress, a khaki trench coat, and heels. Her high heels had sunk into the grass, and goosebumps stood out on her bare legs. The sun had been out, but it couldn't have been more than 50 degrees.

"Hey," I'd said, walking up next to her.

Ellie jumped. There were blackberry brambles caught in her coat, and she had a scratch on her left shin that was bleeding.

"Sorry!" I stuffed my hands into my pockets. "I didn't mean to startle you."

Ellie tugged her coat tight and double-knotted the belt. "My bad. I thought you were my parents."

I looked around for more people. "Are they here too?"

"I don't know. We were out to breakfast, and I ditched them." It was the most Ellie had said to me in years.

I felt around in my pocket and pulled out a tissue—hopefully a clean one. "It looks like you got cut. Can I help?"

Ellie nodded and lifted up her smooth leg. Perched on her other foot, she wobbled and grabbed my shoulder to steady herself. I crouched down and carefully dabbed at her injury. "You got scraped up pretty bad. That must have been one nasty blackberry bush."

She laughed ruefully. "It was worth it to get away."

"Away?" Adrenaline pumped through me. "Did someone hurt you?"

"No, nothing like that. I just needed to escape from my parents."

"Oh." I blotted up the last drop of blood, sorry to lose my excuse to touch Ellie's calf. I placed her foot gently on the ground and stood up. "All better."

"Thanks." Ellie turned back to the cliff and pointed across the water to the snowcapped Olympic Mountains. "Beautiful, aren't they? No wonder Stephenie Meyer set the Twilight series over there. If I were a vampire, that's where I would hunt."

I should have said something smart. Something witty. Or at the very least, something nice. But instead, I said the first stupid thing that came out of my mouth. "You read books?"

"Of course I read books. Don't you?"

"Yeah, for school." I burned beet red. I was saying one dumb thing after another. Time to move this conversation in a different direction. "I'm headed down to the shore. Do you want to come?"

"I'm not exactly dressed for it."

"I'll help." I offered her my arm.

Ellie teetered on her glittery shoes. She took a step forward, and we were so close that I felt the silkiness of her dress brush against my jeans. "I don't know if I'm brave enough."

Tingles broke out all over me. "Afraid I'll bite?"

She laughed and linked her arm in mine. "No, I'm terrified of water."

"I won't toss you in, I promise."

Ellie shivered and snuggled closer to me. "Lead the way."

The path down to the water started out paved but soon transitioned into woodchips. Ellie struggled in her high heels. Every time she leaned into me for support my pulse raced. The closer we got to the shoreline, the louder the waves became. I could hear whitecaps knock against driftwood. But it wasn't nearly as loud as my heart pounding in my chest. When the trail became steeper, I took a risk and swooped up Ellie in my arms to carry her the rest of the way down.

"I could get used to this," Ellie said, her breath hot against my ear.

I didn't set her down until we reached a gigantic bolder, worn smooth by water and time. A gentle spray of sea mist permeated the air. When I sat down next to her, Ellie jumped, which made me scoot away.

"Come back!" Ellie pulled the lapels of her coat up. "It's not you I'm afraid of—it's the water. I've had nightmares about swimming my whole life."

I slid my butt back next to her. "You don't have to worry. We're safe here." I picked up a rock and slung it at the waves. It bounced three times before submerging.

"That was pretty cool."

"What? Throwing pebbles? Anyone can do that."

"Not me. Afraid of water, remember?"

I reached down next to the driftwood and pulled up an oval stone. "It's easy." I placed the pebble in her hand. Then I slid my arm around her shoulder, grabbed her wrist, and helped her flick the stone off into the horizon. It bounced once, then twice before sinking beneath the waves.

"Nice." Ellie pulled her hand down as I hastily removed my arm. "Thanks for teaching me, although this is probably the closest I'll get to water for the next decade."

I wiped my palm off on the legs of my jeans. "I bet you'll get over it. Your water phobia, I mean. You did fine that time we went whale watching in fourth grade with Ms. Hatcher's class."

Ellie's face froze.

"Sorry," I mumbled. "I didn't mean to bring back bad memories."

"No," she said weakly. "That's okay."

In fourth grade, our class had gone on a field trip to Orcas Island. We saw a few sea lions, but no whales. Ms. Hatcher spent the whole time yelling at us to walk on deck and not feed the seagulls. Nothing exciting happened until Ellie dared Marley to snort chocolate milk up her nose. Marley did—quite successfully I might add, because I taught her that trick myself. Then Marley dared Ellie to eat her sunflower butter and jelly sandwich without using her hands.

Ellie stood on deck in a circle of a dozen kids like a ring master. "And now, ladies and gentlemen," she announced in a booming voice. "For my next trick, I'll eat this homemade, organic, gluten-free, trans-fat free, nut-free, sugar-free, and taste-free sandwich—without using my hands!" She waited while Marley held up the sandwich in position. "Drum roll please!"

All the kids banged on their legs to make a rumble. Up until this point, the field trip had sucked, but Ellie knew how to liven things up. She pulled back her hair and bent down to take a bite. It was nothing special until Ellie got a mischievous look in her eyes.

She ripped the sandwich out of my sister's hands and tossed it to a nearby seagull, who squawked his head off in delight. While most of the kids were watching the seagull devour the sandwich, Ellie reached into her backpack and pulled out two entire loaves of sliced white bread. She must have plotted this moment back at home. Ellie tossed the first bag of bread into the air. An enormous flock of seagulls materialized out of nowhere. Before we knew what was happening, the deck was consumed by flapping white wings.

"Don't feed the birds!" Ms. Hatcher cried, running up from the stern. "Ellie Savage! Put that bread away."

"But you told us not to waste food." Ellie chucked another piece of bread onto the deck and laughed.

Ms. Hatcher lurched for the bread bag, but it was too late. There were crumbs, feathers, and poop all over the deck. A giant seagull swooped down and pooped right in the center of Ms. Hatcher's bun.

It was the best thing that happened in fourth grade, but Ellie wasn't allowed back to school for a week.

"Sorry," I said again. "You probably don't like talking about getting suspended."

"I got suspended?"

"I love your sarcasm." I reached into my back pocket for some Juicy Fruit gum.

"Did we end up seeing any whales that day? I don't remember."

"No, I don't think so. I see them from *The Royal Racer* sometimes. Dad always has binoculars up on the bridge. When we come across a pod, we cut the engines so we don't disturb them."

"But what about the tourists and all their hotel reservations?"

I shrugged. "Dad says nature's more important. His precise words are, 'If tourists are too stupid to appreciate nature, they don't belong in the Pacific Northwest.' But really, most people love watching orcas—except when they're eating a seal."

"Wow."

"Speaking of seals, look over there." I pointed across the beach to a speckled lump leaning against driftwood. "Looks like a baby harbor seal."

"No way! Is it okay? Where's its mom?" She shifted positions, ready to leap up and investigate.

I placed a gentle hand on her shoulder. "We need to keep our distance, or we'll stress the little guy out. His mom's probably out hunting for lunch."

"What if she doesn't come back?"

"Orcas need to eat too. That's part of the reason that fifty percent of the baby seals don't make it."

"That's horrible." Ellie squinted, trying to get a better look. The baby was so camouflaged into the beach scene that he was hard to spot. "Hey, Cole," she said, suddenly changing the subject. "How long would you say we've known each other?"

I wanted to lie. If Ellie didn't remember me dragging my stupid purple dinosaur to preschool every day, that was fine by me. But I told the truth. "Since we were three, I guess."

She looked at me, her face the perfect deadpan. "And would you say I used to be a troublemaker?"

I laughed but then smoothed out my expression until it was as serious as hers. Ellie wasn't the only one who could be sarcastic. "No. Of course not."

She raised her eyebrows. "Good, because I wouldn't want to be a juvenile delinquent."

"I happen to like juvenile delinquents."

Bravery swelled up inside me. I swallowed my gum and kissed her.

Ellie felt tiny as a I wrapped my arms around her. Frail almost. Suddenly, I remembered she wasn't the renegade from our elementary school days, but the well-behaved girl who never talked to me in high school. And she wasn't kissing me back.

I pulled away. "Sorry," I mumbled.

All the blood had drained out of Ellie's face. "Too late. You can't undo it."

I stood up and pulled out my phone, pretending to check the time. "I better go."

"Wait!" Ellie jumped up beside me. "I only meant it took you long enough."

"What?"

Ellie threw her arms around me and kissed me fiercely. Her fingers dug into the soft hair behind my ears, her slim body pressed against mine. I slid my arms around her back and down the gentle curves of her hips. The cold shoreline of Puget Sound felt as hot as a Tahitian sunrise.

"I didn't think you liked me," Ellie whispered when we finally came up for air.

"Like you? Of course I like you. I've had a crush on you forever." I nuzzled her neck. "Didn't you notice all my lingering glances when you and Marley were best friends?"

Ellie uttered a soundless laugh. "What are you talking about?"

"Or how I always volunteered to bring you your class assignments whenever you got suspended?"

"Um, the truth is…" But instead of finishing her thought, she kissed me again.

Our hands were tangled, our arms were knotted, and our tongues played full-on tonsil hockey. This was the moment I'd been waiting for. I was making out with the girl of my dreams. Summer romance. Junior year. It all stretched out before me like a vision. Maybe we'd still be together by homecoming! During a breathing break, I leaned my forehead against hers. "Hey, Ellie, do you wanna go out sometime?"

"Yes," Ellie murmured. "Only here's the thing. I'll be gone all summer at French Camp." She pulled away, and the loss of her touch felt cold. "It's a total immersion experience, so I can't write letters or make phone calls."

"I'll learn French." I coiled a finger around a strand of her long red hair. "Then I can call you, and you'll still be immersed."

"I wish they allowed that, but they don't." Ellie shifted in my arms. "And I can't ask you to wait for me all summer."

"You don't have to ask because I'm already offering. Besides, I'll be working on *The Royal Racer* all summer. The time will go by fast."

"And then it will be September, and we'll be together."

"Yes, absolutely!"

"You better watch out." Ellie pressed into me hard. "I might never let you go."

"Intense much?" I kissed her without waiting for an answer.

Then, from somewhere off in the distance, I heard people call Ellie's name. Her name echoed down from the cliff. "Ellie, llie, lie, ie…Ellie, llie, lie, e…"

Ellie groaned. "It's just my parents. Ignore them."

"Ellie! Where are you?"

Ellie's fingertips traced my ribs. Her delicious touch blurred my vision.

"Ellie!" The voices grew louder. "Why aren't you answering your phone?"

Ellie paused. "My phone." She reached into her coat pocket and pulled it out. "Could we get a picture for my Instagram account? Please?"

"Of course." I was thrilled she wanted to document this moment. We posed, and she snapped some pictures.

"Ellie Irene Savage!"

"Shoot." Ellie looked up at the cliff. "I'm sorry, I better go. I'm in enough trouble as it is."

"What happened?"

But Ellie shook her head. "I'd rather not talk about it."

"Here," I said. "At least let me help you get up the path. Those aren't exactly beach shoes." I picked her up in my arms and carried Ellie up the steep part of the trail. My hands pressed against her thighs. When the path leveled out, I didn't bother putting her down.

"It's flat enough I can walk now," she whispered, her lips mere inches from my ear.

I tightened my grip on her legs. "I'll at least bring you to the pavement."

She didn't protest but looked back behind us to where the beach was shrinking. Ellie rested her cheek against the waffle fabric of my shirt.

When we finally emerged from the trail, trouble waited for us. Doctors Warren and Belinda Savage stood at the top of the cliff, shooting us murderous looks.

"I can explain," Ellie said to her parents as soon as she saw them.

"Put my daughter down this instant!" Warren shouted at me.

I readjusted my grip but didn't set Ellie down until she said, "It's okay, Cole. I'll be fine."

Ellie's mom looked like a ghost as she stalked toward us. Blotchy red marks spread across her cheeks from yelling. "I can't believe you!" Belinda yanked Ellie toward her by the arm. "We were in the middle of a conversation!"

"This is exactly what we were talking about, Ellie," Warren added. "You making rash decisions without thinking about how they impact your future." Ellie's dad cut me a quick glance and then looked at his daughter. "We'll discuss this when we get home."

"Ellie, wait!" I called as her parents pulled her away. "When do you get back from French Camp?"

Ellie lurched out of her parent's grasp. "September first," she said. "I'll call you as soon as I can."

I held up my hand to wave goodbye. "I'll be waiting." When Ellie blew me a kiss, I pretended to catch it.

And I did wait for her. All summer I savored that hour I spent with Ellie on the beach, looking forward to our reunion. I passed up parties and ignored cute girls who flirted with me. I stayed true to Ellie.

I didn't tell Marley what had happened because I knew my sister would be irate when she found out that I was dating her best friend turned frenemy. Instead, I spent summer softening Marley up. When I took my Vans off in the car and she told me my feet stunk, I apologized and put my shoes back on. When I found her iPhone laying around I put it back on the charger for her like a hero. I also started lifting the toilet seat up in the bathroom we shared instead of hosing the place down. By the end of summer, Marley and I were on such great terms that I hoped she would be okay with me dating Ellie.

But when September first came, Ellie didn't call me. I played it cool and waited. September first, September second, September third—still no call from Ellie. On the fourth day of September, which happened to be Labor Day, I called her myself and got her voicemail. "Hi Ellie," I said. "This is Cole. I hope you had a great summer. Um… I guess I'll see you at school tomorrow."

She never called me back. Instead, she deleted the picture of us she had posted on Instagram.

The next day when the doors opened at Emily Carr High, I hovered near Ellie's locker, waiting for her to arrive. When I saw her, she was more beautiful than ever—long red hair, creamy clear skin, a figure that begged to be touched.

"Hey Ellie," I called to her as she passed.

She looked at me, a total deer-in-the-headlights expression. Like she was trying to remember who I was or why she should bother with me.

"Hello," Ellie replied.

Then she walked right past me.

Marley was fooling herself if she thought that Ellie would come to our party tonight. Ellie had made it pretty clear that she wanted nothing to do with me or my sister.

It was a year later, and Ellie's brushoff still hurt.

CHAPTER NINE: DEAN

10:34 P.M. | JUNE 3RD

"So you remember me?" the girl in the yard asked.

I didn't. For a moment, I deluded myself into thinking the redhead in front of me might be cowboy-boots girl. Like wishing hard enough could make my fantasy come true. After our second kiss, I traced my finger down her chest, looking for ink.

"Um, no," the girl said, pulling away slightly. "You're thinking of my friend Marley, the one you sang to. I mean, I wouldn't exactly call her my friend, we're more like—"

Floodlights illuminated the grass from the door a few feet away, interrupting her chatter.

"Dean?" Gary called. "Are you out there? Stop fooling around and get your bony butt back here."

Fooling around? I couldn't have ten minutes of alone time to clear my head without that tool telling me what to do.

There in the shadows between moonlight and fluorescent light, the redhead looked at me with wide eyes. "Let's go back inside," she said. She took a step forward, but I pulled her back. Sure, she wasn't cowboy-boots girl, but her skin was creamy and clear, her green eyes were fringed by unnaturally full lashes, and she was a knockout in her own right.

"This isn't optional, Dean. It's in your contract!"

Screw Gary, and screw my contract. Here was a gorgeous, willing girl in my arms with soft-as-pillow lips. I deserved one night of fun.

"Are you pranking me?" Gary called. "Do you want everyone to know? Come on out, Dean. I'm your manager for a reason! You need me, buddy. This is for your own good."

"No way," I muttered.

"My parents are experts." The redhead looked up at me with an earnest expression. "I don't know what you're having done this summer, but I promise they can help."

"Time for that tomorrow," I murmured into her ear. "Tonight, me and you."

Her face flushed prettily, and she kissed me again. I was just feeling our tongues touch when a door slammed behind me with a *thud.* I lunged into the bushes, pulling the girl with me. We tumbled down onto the ground, with me breaking her fall.

"What's going on?" the girl whispered. A twig jabbed me in the elbow and her heart thumped against my own.

"Get me out of here!" I pleaded with her. Loud footsteps hit the deck, then crunched the gravel pathway of the yard. For a split second, I thought the girl might call out to Gary.

"You're so immature!" Gary shouted.

"I'll get you out of here," the redhead said, her forehead crinkled in annoyance. "Your manager is ticking me off. Doesn't he know patients are sleeping?" She crawled off of me and scooted to the edge of the fence, looking for the opening. The girl crouched along the perimeter of the fence, and I followed until we came to a hole hidden by a rhododendron bush on each side. She had plenty of room to slip under the boards, but I had to squeeze. Now we both looked scruffy.

"Okay, we're free," the girl said as we stood on the sidewalk. Her robe was shredded, and the cold night air hitting her nightshirt told me she wasn't wearing a bra. "Let's head back to the front entrance. My parents will put your manager in his place."

Here she was. My ticket to freedom. For one night, at least. Maybe wishing hard enough really did make dreams come true.

I stuffed my hands in my pockets and held out my elbow so the redhead could link her arm through mine and snuggle up next to me. "How about a walk in the moonlight?"

"With me?" she asked incredulously.

"For sure."

"Well… I'm not supposed to leave the house without telling my parents where I'm going."

"Come on." I grinned. "It'll be fun."

The girl chewed on her bottom lip a second before answering. "Okay," she said with a smile. "I guess a quick trip to the Space Needle and back wouldn't hurt."

Two beats later we were strolling down the street. If Maxine knew I was out and about with a real-life girl, she'd be thrilled for me. Or if I could somehow take a selfie of the two of us and send it to Pansy—that would be awesome. Maybe I could leak it to TMZ.

But the moment was ruined when the Narcosis Clinic lit up like a rocket. An alarm pierced the air, waking up every last comatose patient. It was a high alert signal.

I looked at the girl, and she looked at me. Then we both ran for it.

We bolted toward the Space Needle four blocks away. The Seattle Center has all of the famous tourist attractions—the Experience Music Project, Key Arena, and about a hundred places to sit on the steps and soak in the Emerald City. It was also where my tour bus was parked, across the street from the Hotel Great West. My plan was to slip in the back door and head up to my private suite.

But when I saw the crowds, I screeched to a halt, and the redhead slammed into me.

"*Oomph!* Sorry!" she said. She looked behind her toward the clinic. "Maybe we should head back to the clinic. My parents will be worried."

I tugged on her arm and pointed to the giant throng of girls camped out in front of my bus holding up their phones like portable lights.

"Holy crap!" the girl said. "Is that where you want to go?"

I violently shook my head. "No way."

Right then, as if some cosmic force laughed at us, thunder crashed and rain began to pour. Across the street, the fans screamed bloody murder. I thought it was because of the thunderstorm, but then I heard what they were yelling.

"Dean Mathews is over there!"

"Dean, I love you!"

"Marry me!"

There wasn't time to think. I grabbed the redhead's hand and pulled her along the sidewalk like she was a helium balloon. I didn't know where we were going. I fled the mob out of sheer terror.

"We'll never make it back to the Narcosis Clinic without that mob seeing us go in," the girl cried. "And as a patient, your privacy is our top concern." She surged ahead of me, tugging on my hand to lead me. "Let's go to the Duchess Hotel instead! We can call my parents from there." Looming ahead of us was our castle of protection, a Victorian monolith covered by climbing roses.

The doorman must have seen us barreling toward the hotel with two hundred teen skanks hot on our heels because he opened the doors for us before we crashed into the glass.

I pulled out my wallet and slapped down a credit card on the front desk. "Room. We need a room."

The desk man took one look at me and drooled. "Lock the doors!" He glared at the doorman. "Now!"

Just in time. The mob of rabid fans pressed into the glass. Thunder and lightning made them look like the living dead. Several had "LET ME BEAR YOUR CHILD" written in marker across their chests. I turned away with a shudder.

"Excellent, Mr. Mathews. My name is Michael, and I'm here to help. Would the Vice Regal Suite meet your needs?" He had a vise-like grip on my credit card.

"For sure."

Michael typed into the computer fast. "We heard you were booked at the Hotel Great West. I'm glad you realized we could better meet your needs. Here at the Duchess, every luxury awaits." Michael eyed our soggy clothing. "Do you and your guest have luggage our stewards can help you with?"

"No way." I shook my head.

"Should I send our porter to the Hotel Great West for your bags?"

"We won't be staying long," the girl said. "We just want some privacy." She looked innocently at Michael like she had no idea what she was implying.

Michael nodded discreetly. "Of course, miss. I understand completely. There's no need to retrieve luggage. Our boutique is fully stocked."

"Great." The redhead shivered. Her wet nightclothes were almost transparent.

"Shall I show you to your suite?" Michael held up the key card.

"For sure." I gave the girl's hand a squeeze. My stomach churned as we followed Michael into the elevator and up to the penthouse level. The elevator door slid open, and we padded down the hall across the soft carpet to the front door of the suite.

"Michael," the girl said, "do not, under any circumstance, tell the press that Dean is here."

I slipped the cash from my wallet—quite a wad—into Michael's hand. That was a trick I'd learned from Gary.

Michael kept his face neutral, but his eyes smiled wide. "Of course, Mr. Mathews." Then he unlocked the massive door and offered me the key. "Let me show you all of the amenities."

I shrugged. "No, thank you." I pulled the girl into the room, waved to Michael, and slammed the door shut. It wasn't until I locked the deadbolt and slid the chain that I breathed an enormous sigh of relief.

CHAPTER TEN: ELLIE

10:58 P.M. | JUNE 3RD

I should have gone straight for my phone and told Mom and Dad where I was. They were probably worried sick! Instead, I let adrenaline, angst, and hormones make me do something that I wouldn't have done under normal circumstances. At least Dean wasn't Liam, toying with my insecurities. My stupidity was all my own.

And there I was, dripping wet and shivering, with Dean in this fabulous hotel suite, in a living room graced by two velvet couches and a grand piano.

Dean stood in front of me and stared at my every bit. I folded my arms over my chest and looked him over just as appraisingly. His normally coifed hair was slicked down and dark. He stepped closer and slid his hands down my bare arms, giving me goose bumps. Then, with some super-suave playboy move, he was on me like an octopus. The dumb part was, I kissed him back. Because… well, because why not? Cole Evans might not think I was worth noticing, but Dean Mathews did.

Our lips were like suction cups. I felt my feet lift off the floor, and we were on the couch.

I don't know how far we would have gone if it weren't for that scratch on my left shoulder. During a particularly physical kiss, my shoulder rubbed up against Dean's shirt and started bleeding again. All over Dean.

The sight of my blood made me stop, back up a few inches, and think. Dean's eyes were closed, and his hands were up to my thighs. He had been kissing me deliciously along my neck.

I pushed the memory away. What did I think I was doing? "Your shirt, Dean! There's blood." I examined the stain on his blue silk shirt.

Dean opened his eyes and looked at me. For a moment I felt like he didn't know who I was. Then he looked down at the wound on my shoulder, blood mixing with the rain water and running down my arm.

"You're hurt." Dean pushed himself off of me. "I'm thorry. Let me get thomething." He rushed to the bathroom before I could answer.

"Thank you," I said when Dean came back with a box of tissues and offered them to me.

"For sure."

I held a wad gently to my shoulder and looked at Dean honestly for the first time. He stood there, jittery, like he might bounce away. The Armani shirt was splotched with blood and his tight black jeans had a rip in one knee. He was a typical nineteen-year-old boy. Sure, he was gorgeous, but lots of guys are.

"I don't know how I hurt you. I apologize."

"It's okay. It wasn't you. I nicked my shoulder when I climbed out of my window."

"I'm thuch a jerk." Dean's chest heaved faster than a jackrabbit. He circled the room a few times before he sat down on the couch next to me—three feet away.

My brain eventually processed what he had said, how he had been speaking, and I began to realize why he needed my parents' help.

"What'th your name again?" Dean looked at me sideways, embarrassment coloring his cheeks.

Dean not knowing my name stung worse than the wound itself, but he didn't need to know that. "I'm Ellie Savage." I smoothed back my hair. "My parents are Belinda and Warren Savage, your doctors."

Dean nodded. "For sure." Then he scooted closer and inspected my injury. He put his hand over mine and lifted up the tissues. "We should clean that out."

I followed Dean to the bathroom, which was more like a small palace complete with marble floors, a claw-foot tub, and a bidet. I had been to the Hotel Duchess before but had never seen an actual room. Last summer when I'd woken up from narcosis, my parents had brought me here to celebrate with high tea in the Regina Room. It was our end-of-summer tradition.

Dean took a fluffy, white bathrobe off a hook and wrapped most of it around me, leaving my shoulder exposed. He pulled down the top lid of the toilet so I could take a seat. Then he ran the faucet until the water warmed up. When he pressed a hot washcloth to my shoulder, I yelped.

"I apologize," he whispered.

"It's okay." I bit my lip a few seconds before I continued. "You don't remember me?"

Dean shook his head.

"No biggie," I lied. I waved my free hand at the bedroom. "You probably do *this* with a new girl in every city." I didn't mean to cry, but hot tears stung my eyes.

Dean brushed them away with his thumb. "I'm not normally a thleazebag." He looked back down at my shoulder. "Could you call the front desk for thome bandageth?"

"For sure."

Dean winced.

I marched to the bedroom and picked up the telephone. "Michael." I spoke clearly into the receiver. "Please send up a first aid kit and two sets of clothes."

"Of course, miss. Would you also like something from room service?"

I glanced at Dean, who stared out the window with his shoulders slumped. "Are you hungry?"

He looked back at me a nodded. "A hamburger," he whispered. "And thalad."

"Two hamburgers and something green, please."

"Something green? Of course, miss. Anything for Dean Mathews. Please express to him my deepest assurances that during his time here at the Duchess, his comfort will be—"

"Thanks, I'll let him know." I set the phone back into its cradle. Then I sat on the bed and stared Dean down.

The city lights peeping through the window illuminated his face. In his designer shirt and tight black jeans, Dean looked like a painting from the museum next door.

Several minutes passed in silence before I found the nerve to speak. "Tell me the truth, Dean." I glared at him, but he didn't move a muscle. "I'm going under narcosis tomorrow too. Whatever you tell me will be private."

That got Dean's attention. "Private?"

"Absolutely." I patted the quilt next to me.

"Why do you do narcothith? Ellie, you're perfect." Dean approached the bed, and for a second I thought he might have another make-out session in mind. But he sat down a safe distance away.

"I'm not perfect."

"But you are." Dean smiled. "For sure."

"Is that the only thing you can say without lisping?"

Dean swooped his head back like I'd smacked him. "What?"

"Your lisp." I looked down at my hands. "Sorry. That's rude of me to point it out."

Dean gulped. "'For sure' and 'no way.' I'm fine when I thing, but not when I talk. I have to do narcothith again. To fix my problem."

"Did it work last time?" I asked Dean. "Did narcosis make a difference?"

Dean nods. "For sure. I didn't lithp for over a year. But then it came back, and I curtailed giving interviewth."

"What about that interview in *GQ*?"

"They gave me the quethtionth, and I emailed them back. Gary, my manager, told them I had laryngitith."

Our conversation was interrupted by a sharp rap on the door.

"Maybe that's room service," I guessed.

"Or the bandageth." Dean lifted up the washcloth on my shoulder and wrinkled his forehead. "I hope."

I pulled my bathrobe on tight and went to open the door. When I held it open a crack, I saw Michael standing with two garment bags and a wheeled tray of food.

"It's me, miss. Our staff is very discreet, but I thought Mr. Mathews would prefer my personal attention."

"Thanks." I unlatched the chain and opened the door wide.

Michael pushed the cart into the room, and the luscious aroma of burgers filled the living room. Then he hung up the two garment bags in the closet and started to unzip them. "Would you like me to show you what I've selected?"

Dean shook his head and waved his hands. "No way."

Michael's face fell.

I smiled for both of us. "I'm sure it's terrific." I cut a quick look at the room service tray and saw a first aid kit lying next to an ice bucket of champagne.

"We're delighted you chose to stay here," said Michael. "I want you to know how much the Duchess appreciates your patronage."

Dean stood up and smiled broadly. "For sure." Then he walked Michael to the door and hurried him out.

"Great," I said when the deadbolt was locked. "Let's eat and then we'll call my parents."

"You need a bandage." Dean reached for the supplies and doctored me up right. When the last bandage was on, Dean leaned down and kissed it. "There," he said. "All better."

But it wasn't all better. There was still blood on Dean's shirt. I reached my hand up to the stain and pressed my hand against his shoulder. "I ruined your shirt. I bet that was expensive." Dean wasn't a big, beefy guy, but all of that dancing on stage meant he was tight and lean. My palm felt hot just touching him.

Dean took my hand and kissed it. "No biggie. We'll change clothes, and then we can eat. You're all wet."

I wasn't wet. At that point, I was only sticky, and my hair fuzzed up like a banshee's. I resisted the impulse to sniff my pits. My parents would hopefully understand that I brought Dean here to protect his privacy as a Narcosis Clinic patient, but if Mom and Dad collected me from the hotel looking like this, they would flip out.

"Dry clothes would be great." I walked over to one of the garment bags and reached inside. The first thing I saw was something red and lacy with strings. I held up a corset and blushed.

The hanky-panky lingerie on the hanger made Dean whistle loudly. I glared at him, and Dean smirked. Then I marched into the bathroom for some privacy.

Why couldn't the boutique have sent up a pair of bikini briefs? But it wasn't like I wanted to call down to the front desk and explain my preferences in underwear to Michael. I was creeped out enough that he knew what was in the bag. I washed my face in cold water and suited up in my new pornstar panties. The corset made my boobs stick out, which is remarkable because 32 As don't give you much to work with.

The dress I put on was short, violet, and strapless. The color complemented my red hair. In the mirror, I saw it was so low-cut that the faint scar on my chest showed. Luckily, the garment bag held a chain of tiny garnets. I arranged the necklace carefully to conceal my scar, then I slipped into a pair of black high heels.

When I came out of the bathroom, Dean had changed into jeans and a white shirt—not buttoned yet. It gave me the perfect view of his taut stomach muscles. I felt like I was in the middle of his *GQ* photo shoot, a tiny fly drooling on the wall.

Dean whistled again. Then he started singing. *"Do you know what I felt? Girl, you make me wanna melt."*

It was totally cheesy, and I rolled my eyes, giggling. "Does that work on girls?"

"I have no idea." Dean danced over to me, knelt down on one knee, and held out his hand. "Dinner, my lady?"

I tried not to smile, but it was impossible. "Okay, I'll call my parents after we eat." At this point, what was a few more minutes?

Dean led me through the living room, past the grand piano, and into the suite's dining room, where the mahogany table was set with the two trays of food and the ketchup and mustard were in silver holders. Dean pulled out a chair with a thick velvet cushion for me, and I sat down to the most expensive hamburger in America.

I had no business being hungry—it had to be past midnight—but I tore into that burger like a starving wolf. Then I felt skinned alive when I realized Dean was watching.

"Hungry?" Dean teased.

I wiped the ketchup off my mouth and nodded. "There's no need to worry about calories when you're going to be asleep for three months. The lipo doctor can just suck it off my bum."

"Fun."

"Gross!"

Dean smiled. "Theriously though, you don't need lipo."

"I know. That was sarcasm." I put down my hamburger bun and shrugged. "What about you? Why did you run away from the clinic?" I looked at Dean's beautiful face, the soft down of whiskers grazing his chin. His hair was brushed back, but it still looked perfect.

"I hate being forthed into anything. Gary ith a jerk."

"So tell him no. My parents would never operate on an unwilling patient."

"It'th not that I'm unwilling. I jutht wanted one night of freedom. I know I need to go back."

"There's nothing wrong with how you talk. The only bad thing is that you feel the need to be silent."

Dean's blue eyes looked down at his hamburger. "You don't think I need to be fixed?"

"Not unless you *want* to be different."

"I already am different."

"That's not what I meant," I said.

"I want narcothith to be my answer."

"My parents are brilliant," I said automatically. "If you want answers, they've got them."

"One more thummer. Your mom promithed."

I nodded my head. "It must be hard to keep a secret like that when so many people hang on your every word."

Dean nodded and looked down at his china plate. "People don't want the real me."

"And what is the real you?" I scanned the hotel room. "Serenading a new girl into bed every night?" I was joking, but Dean flinched like I'd hit him. "Look, I'm not judging. I'm just glad I came to my senses before we went too far."

"You didn't thay no. I would have thtopped if you thaid no."

"I'm not saying you wouldn't have stopped." *Or that I would have wanted you to stop.*

"What are you thaying then?"

I shrugged. "Nothing."

"You kithed me back."

"I did, but that's not the point. We were talking about the real you."

"I—"

"Is this what the real you does? Hooks up with strangers?"

"No. No way. I haven't kithed another girl since Panthy."

"Oh." Pansy Williams—the girl who'd run off with Dean's best friend. I wiped my mouth with a napkin. "Well, then, tell me about yourself. Who is the real Dean Mathews?"

"You're acting like a reporter." Dean guzzled his champagne.

"Fine. Forget about it." I looked for my phone before remembering that I didn't have it with me. Thank goodness for the hotel landline. "I'll call my dad to come get me."

"Why do you want to know about me anyway? Think you can make money from the tabloid?"

"Absolutely not!"

"Then why the third degree?"

"How is 'please tell me about yourself' the third degree?"

Dean didn't answer. He poured himself another glass of champagne and took a delicate bite of his burger.

"You don't know how to make conversation, do you? And not because of your lisp."

Dean didn't look at me. "I never go anywhere. I mean, I travel all over the world, but I never go anyplathe ordinary. Like to the grocery thtore, or out to eat, or to the mall."

"That's awful." I swallowed hard. Maybe I shouldn't have been so hard on him.

"I've been on tour tho long all my friendth back home have forgotten me." Dean rose from the table, crossed over to the window, and stared out at the skyline. "And the friendth who do remember would rat me out to the tabloidth if Gary didn't pay them not to."

"What about your friends in the business? Other singers or producers, people like that?"

Dean looked at me like I was clueless and I suddenly realized why. The memories of his legendary feud with Sam Anders clicked into place. The Heartacres had broken up after Sam ran off with Pansy.

"I only had one friend in muthic and he betrayed me." Dean flexed his jaw.

"Sam knew about your lisp?"

Dean nodded.

I dug my toe into the carpet. "At least he hasn't blabbed yet, right?"

"Not yet," Dean said ominously. "If my thpeech impediment became public, that would be all anyone would talk about."

I walked over to Dean and stood right by him, gazing out at the lights of the Chihuly Garden and Glass Museum and the monorail. Then I looked up into his clear blue eyes. "It must be lonely being you."

Dean nodded his head and then looked back out the window. I rocked back and forth on my feet, wondering what to say. "Well, I'm glad that my parents can help. Maybe we should get going. Hopefully your mob of crazed fans is gone by now."

"Wait!" Dean looked down at me. "You never told me. What's your treatment for?"

I rubbed sleep out of my eyes with the back of my hand. "I'm afraid of pools. And rivers. And lakes. And Puget Sound. And water in general. I have nightmares—intense ones. There's an icy cold river ripping me away from the shore. The water pulls me under, and I thrash around, trying to reach the surface." My breath sped up in a panic. Dean rested his hand on my shoulder to steady me, and I plunged on. "Mom fixes all of it with psychic-driving, and then slips in information that will help me with school."

I decided to not mention my amnesia and the mystery of what happened to me at Remington Prep. Or Dad fixing my acne—because who'd want to describe that? Or how my hairline had been lifted, my ears had been pinched back, my eyes had gotten Lasik surgery—I didn't want to overshare. Besides, all the changes were subtle enough that it was impossible to know how much my appearance had evolved over time unless I intensely analyzed my Instagram feed.

"Have you ever tried thwimming lessons?"

"What? You want me to go in a pool when I'm terrified of water?"

"I could teach you."

I shuddered. "No thank you."

"The hotel probably hath a pool. I could call Michael and have him find a life jacket—"

"No!" I said, gasping. "That would be horrible. I'd probably drown you or something."

"You wouldn't drown me. I'm a really good thwimmer."

I squeezed both hands into fists and considered. Dean offered exactly what Olivia wanted to give me. A way to conquer my fears—without narcosis. But I had just met Dean. Could I trust him with the scariest part of my soul?

"Ellie. About what happened earlier. I'm—" Dean was interrupted by the ring of the suite's doorbell.

I looked at Dean in confusion. "Michael knocked. Who's here now?"

"I'll find out."

I reached out to stop him. "No, I'll look. It might be one of your rabid fans." I walked across the room to the little hallway by the suite's front door. I almost tripped over the elaborate brass receptacle for umbrellas. Right when I reached the threshold, the doorbell rang again. I looked through the peephole and saw Liam. As in, back-of-his-car, major-jerk, Marley's-boyfriend Liam.

"Hey, Dean," Liam mumbled through the door. "I got your weed."

CHAPTER ELEVEN: DEAN
11:48 P.M. | JUNE 3RD

The guy who showed up at our suite with a plastic baggie of grass smelled like a Willie Nelson concert. He wore a gray hoodie and had a stringy ponytail.

"Hey." The guy nodded to me like we were old friends. "You ordered something green?"

"Salad," Ellie blurted out. "We ordered a salad."

Liam turned to Ellie, and his eyes went wide like he hadn't seen her when she opened the door. "Well, I'll be darned. I didn't know Ellie liked to party. I thought you'd become allergic to fun."

Ellie snapped back like she'd been slapped, but she kept her fierce expression.

"It's always the spacey girls who fool you," Liam said to me as he held up the bag. "Maybe this will help with her concentration."

"No way," I said. I stayed away from all types of narcotics. When I was in the Heartacres people offered us stuff like that all the time. Sam tried every last pill or joint he could. He'd always made a fool of himself to prove that he was two years older than me.

Normally, I didn't care when Sam got stoned. What he did in his room was his own business. But when he hadn't shown up for roll call the morning we were supposed to fly to Tokyo, I was the one Gary had sent to check on him.

I was the one who'd found Sam facedown in his own vomit on the bathroom floor.

I was the one who'd rolled him over, cleared his airways, and dialed 9-1-1.

Gary may have been the genius who'd kept it out of the press, but I was the one who'd saved Sam's life. When Sam had gone off to rehab for thirty days, I was the only person he'd asked to see during "friends and family" day.

But that was a long time ago.

"Look, Liam." Ellie wagged her finger. "I don't know where you got the idea that we need your services, but we don't." She looked up into my eyes to double-check, and I shook my head.

"Uh-uh. I got a specific request for something green." Liam sized me up from head to toe. "Are you sure you don't want this?"

"For sure. No way." I slapped Liam on the back and started whistling "Hit the Road, Jack," that old Ray Charles tune Maxine liked. Before Liam knew what was happening, I had shooed him out the door.

"Hey, wait!" Liam said, poking his head around the door jamb. "Marley's having a party tonight. You guys wanna come?"

Marley? As in the girl in the cowboy boots?

Ellie wrinkled her nose. "Do you think she'd want me there?"

Liam shoved his hand across the frame in one last desperate move to stay in the room. "She would if you showed up with Dean Mathews. Marley would be so happy, she'd probably give me—"

That was no way to talk about my girl in the cowboy boots. I fake-slammed the door, one inch away from Liam's knuckles.

Liam yanked his hand back. "Will you at least think about it?"

I gritted my teeth at the thought of Marley and Liam being together. I didn't want to spend one more second with this stinky butthead, but I did want to meet Marley. "For sure," I answered. As soon as I clicked the door shut, I rested my head against it, breathing hard. "That guy'th no good. How do you know him again?"

"How do I know Liam?" Ellie's eyes turned glassy. "I think my first memory of him is a chain reaction of kids vomiting on the bus in ninth grade. Liam leaped up on the vinyl seat shouting, 'I've been hit!' and then barfed all over me." Ellie picked up a chocolate-covered strawberry. "He's not worth getting mad over."

"What a jerk."

"Tell me about it."

"But what you were talking about earlier—about being normal."

"Yeah?"

"Maybe it would be fun."

"Huh?"

"To go to the party. One night of fun before narcothith." I put my hands over my face and rubbed it. "Darn it! I can't thay what I want to when it'th really important!"

"Maybe you could sing instead," Ellie suggested. "I'm sorry," she said a half-beat later, shaking her head. "That was a stupid thing to say, especially since my tone was flippant. Sometimes tense situations push my brain to the snarky response before I can think."

I stopped pacing and looked at her, my face brightening. "For sure." I eyed the grand piano across the room. "Come join me?"

Ellie's face softened. "I'd love to."

I pulled out the piano bench and took a seat, patting the place to my left. I felt comfortable when Ellie sat next to me. I reached to the low end of the keyboard and warmed up with my favorite chord progression. Once the music rumbled over me, I felt my whole body relax.

"*Ellie, you're brave. Ellie, you're kind. Ellie, you're a quick thinker.*" My words came out perfectly in song without one stumble. "*You're the first girl I've talked to in I don't know how long. I've bared my soul to you. I feel like I can talk to you.*"

Ellie elbowed me in the ribs. "Is this for real, or are you just trying to get me back in the bedroom?"

My fingers paused mid-melody, and I chuckled. Then I tackled the keys again. "*My bad. My bad. My bad. I'm sorry.*"

Ellie shrugged. "We're cool. I was your rebound kiss. Pansy sounds like a real piece of work."

My chest squeezed. "*The girl broke my heart.*" I poured my melancholy into the piano, not saying anything for a while.

"The weird thing is that making out with you wasn't as exciting as I thought it would be," Ellie admitted.

I fake-stabbed my heart. "*Ouch.*"

"We're being honest, right? There's this guy I like named Cole. That party Liam talked about is at Cole's house."

I kept singing and playing. "*Then who is Marley?*"

"Cole's sister. You signed her boob!" Ellie screwed up her face. "How can you forget a boob signing?"

"*Short skirt, cowboy boots; I remember Marley.*"

"She'll be there too."

"*Do you wanna go?*"

"To the party?"

"*Maybe I do. Am I crazy for wanting something I'm never gonna be?*"

"What's that?"

I stopped playing and looked right at her. "Normal."

Ellie froze. Her eyes welled with tears that she wiped away with her hand. "You and me both." Then she sat up straighter. "Well, why can't we go? We could say you have a sore throat and need to save your voice. That sounds plausible, right?"

The idea was too tempting not to consider, but there were so many ways it could fail. "*It would never work,*" I sang with a tickle of the ivory.

"You're probably right. I know I should be calling my parents right now. They must be freaking out. But…" She sighed. "I feel like having an adventure."

I jazzed up my accompaniment. "*I like the sound of that too.*"

"Really?"

"*Ellie, you're brave. Ellie, you're kind. Ellie, you're a quick thinker.*"

"Well, yeah." She grinned. "Everyone knows that."

"*You talk too much when you're nervous.*"

"Not just when I'm nervous. Sometimes it'll be a normal conversation, and I'll start—"

"*Rambliiing.*" I drew out the last part.

She blushed, and color hit her cheeks like a slap.

"*I think you use humor as a defense.*"

"Who, me?"

"*Ellie, you're brave. Ellie, you're kind. Ellie, you're a quick thinker. And I think we can do this.*"

"Me too!"

"*You'll get your guy, and I'll find my girl.*"

"Cole doesn't know I'm alive."

"*I'll make it all right. He'll see you tonight.*"

"Cole won't be able to ignore me if I walk in with you."

"*I want to be free. The world stares at me.*"

"You will be free! Tonight we'll party; tomorrow we'll sleep. My mom and dad will fix everything."

My fingers paused on the keys. "For sure?" I felt hopeful for the first time in a long time.

"My parents are miracle workers. 'Sleep for three months and make your problems go away.' It's not a slogan—it's the truth."

All of me wanted to believe her.

CHAPTER TWELVE: ELLIE

12:30 A.M. | JUNE 4TH

It was cloak and dagger all the way from the hotel to the party. The front steps of the Duchess were packed with fans waiting to catch a glimpse of Dean, so Michael arranged for us to borrow a florist van with a giant bouquet of red roses painted on the side. The only windows were up front. The back of the van was an enormous refrigerator with a bench seat.

Michael handed Dean the keys along with his private phone number. "If you need anything, please call." He smiled like a lizard on a warm rock. "The Duchess wants you to be happy, Mr. Mathews. We'll do whatever it takes."

I swiped the keys from Dean's hands. "I'll drive. You relax. This is my home turf."

Dean tilted his head to the side and shrugged. "For sure." Then he pulled down his Seahawks cap and slid into the passenger seat.

"You're coming back, right?" Michael tugged his collar. "I mean, the Duchess will be here, ready to make your stay in Seattle extra special."

I rolled the window down a crack and waved. "Thanks. We'll see you later."

Michael looked across me to Dean, who nodded, and then we were off. The gate to the service exit pulled up like slow giant teeth. I clicked on the headlights in time to see a teen girl with "WILL U MARRY ME?" written across her cheeks. And I don't mean the cheeks on her face. She turned at the sound of the gate opening, eyes wide.

"Oh my gosh!" My stomach turned into a barf factory as she dodged the service gate and threw herself against the van's driver window, butt first. Her cheeks smooshed against the glass, and I saw the dark hairs of an orifice I don't want to mention. "I think I'm going to throw up!" I moaned, trying not to gag.

"He's here!" the girl screamed to her friends. "It's Dean!"

Before I knew it—before I could even think—a small cluster of girls formed around the van. "The service entrance," one of them shouted. "He's over here!"

Dean locked the doors with a loud click. The service gate finished lifting.

"What should I do?" I gripped the steering wheel with white knuckles. My heart beat so hard, I heard the blood in my temples. Dean's psycho fan club streamed into the street and blocked my path. "Should I gun it?"

Dean's eyes widened in shock. "No way. You might hurt people."

I wouldn't have run anyone over intentionally. I mean, I don't think I would have. But the rabid fans rattled me. Who knows what I would have done if Dean hadn't been there? I was in kill-or-be-killed mode. I realized I was shaking and clenched the wheel harder.

Dean frowned and scanned the van. For a moment, I thought he was going to hide. Especially when he undid his seatbelt and climbed into the back. I was stuck up front with my foot on the brake and panic coursing through my veins, separated by throngs of screaming, mostly naked girls by a thin pane of glass. But then Dean came up front again with armfuls of roses.

"Get ready." Dean ripped the cellophane off the bouquets with a viciousness that surprised me.

When Dean rolled down the window, I was afraid we'd be attacked. Wiggling hands pushed into the van, and Dean leaned to the side so they wouldn't tear his hair.

What Dean did next was brilliant. He threw rose stems into the masses and started singing. *"Do you know how I felt? Girl, you make me wanna melt."*

The first recipients of Dean's offering cried in delight. "He gave me a rose! Dean Mathews gave me flowers!"

The crowd inched back a sliver, and it was just enough. Dean chucked roses out the window as far as he could fling them. The eager fans flew at them like pigeons, clearing the space for me to make the van crawl farther along the road.

"Dean, I love you too!" the girls screamed. Phones were up in the air catching every moment of Dean's performance.

He leaned out the window for the last line of the song and hurled a final bouquet.

"Ack!" a girl screamed "That's mine. Let go!"

In the melee, the road cleared further, and I floored it. In the side mirror, I looked back and saw a flock of girls tearing up roses, petals flying in the air like feathers.

"Holy crap!" The back of my neck felt sweaty. "How do you deal with this all the time?"

"Not very well." Dean looked out the window as we drove through the city, both of our breathing slowly returning to normal.

That's when the realization sank in. Three months of narcosis wasn't only a way for Dean to cure his lisp. It was also a way for him to escape. Three whole months of nobody hounding him, trying to tear him to pieces with too much love.

"Dean, I'm not sure if this is a good idea." I flexed my wrist against the steering wheel. "What if there are crazy fans at the party? Maybe we should go back to the Narcosis Clinic."

Dean adjusted his seatbelt. "There are crazy people everywhere. Thith ith my chance to be a normal guy for a few hourth."

But who were we fooling? There was no way either of us could ever be normal.

We drove for several minutes in silence, and my mind drifted to how much trouble I would be in at home. Would my parents understand why I was doing this? Did they even know I was gone?

Time to worry about that later. I glanced over at Dean's chiseled profile. He stared at the cityscape with eyes full of wonder, like he was a child gazing at a candy display. Mom and Dad always gave their celebrity clients the white-glove treatment. Surely they would want me to keep Dean happy. I mean, not *too* happy. Not like, back in the hotel room, peeling off my nightshirt happy. But keeping Dean content, and reassuring him that narcosis was the right decision, was important. If that meant giving Dean one night of freedom—and possibly getting Cole to *finally* notice me—then that was a win-win.

Somehow, I knew how to get to Marley and Cole's house. Capitol Hill. Millionaire's Row. Four houses down from Volunteer Park. Olivia must have pointed it out to me the last time we'd gone to the Seattle Asian Art Museum. I switched on the blinker to cross over the freeway and head for the Hill.

The Evans' house looked like a gothic mansion. Marley liked to brag about how it was featured in a home design magazine, but when I looked at it, I missed the cool modernity of my home. Plus, the gargoyles were terrifying.

Cars lined the street on both sides near the house. I'm horrible at parallel parking, and not being able to see out the van windows made it ten times harder. Picking a large spot a couple blocks away, I finally managed to squeeze in after a few attempts. Thankfully, Dean stayed quiet.

As we walked up the driveway, we could hear the bass boom, and the whole house seemed to sway to the music. "Here," I said, handing him the keys. "You're in charge of these. My dress doesn't have pockets."

"For sure." Dean had a bounce in his step like he was about to break into a dance move.

My stomach flipped when I saw the giant front door. Should we ring or knock? But then the door swung open, and Liam and Marley were both waiting, holding red plastic cups. Liam had changed into an Emily Carr High lacrosse jersey. Marley still wore the cowboy boots. Past her shoulder, at the back of the dimly lit room, I saw Cole dancing with a cheerleader. When he turned and our eyes met, I could have sworn he paused mid-step.

Liam stepped up to us, pulling Marley with him and breaking off my view of Cole. "See, babe? I told you." Liam grinned like the butthead he was. "Ellie and Dean Mathews, right here at your party."

Dean nodded.

"Of course!" Marley said, a little too brightly. "Ellie and I are old friends." Marley stepped forward and linked her arm in mine, dragging Dean and me into the house. "We were in pre-school together."

What the what? Of all the things to lie about, that seemed silly. Unless of course it was true. How was I to know?

Dean stepped into the semi-darkness of the party looking like an Abercrombie and Fitch model. The partygoers screamed as soon as they saw him, especially the girl dancing with Cole, but most seemed too drunk or high to do anything to drastic. Dean took one look at the crowd and scooted closer to me.

"Dean's saving his voice," I blurted out.

"No problem," said Liam. "Babe, get him a drink." Marley leaped to follow his request.

The golden light coming from the dining room chandelier made my brain hurt. There was something around me that seemed familiar...

"Want one?" Marley offered me a red plastic cup.

"No thanks." I noticed that Dean was already gulping his down. I wasn't sure what was in the drink, and someone needed to be the designated driver.

"I could use another." Liam handed Marley his empty cup. "Thanks, babe." He slapped her on the butt.

"Don't spank my sister." Cole appeared just outside our circle, his voice low and menacing.

"Dude, chill out."

"It's fine." Marley glared at her brother. "This is my brother, Cole." She rolled her eyes. "Sometimes he has trouble minding his own business. How do you know Ellie?"

Crap! We hadn't come up with a cover story. "Um…" I stalled for time. Before I could formulate an answer, Dean started whistling "La Marseillaise," the French national anthem. "French Camp!" I exclaimed. "I was in Paris and saw Dean perform."

"How romantic," Marley said without one ounce of sincerity.

"We're just friends," I admitted.

"Oh," said Marley in a happier voice. She looked at her brother. "Cole, do you want to show Ellie and Dean where the food is?"

Dean gave me a little push in Cole's direction.

I took a step back toward Dean with a little glare. "We just ate."

Dean whispered in my ear. "Let'th make sure Cole noticeth you." He guided me into the throng of people, and we started dancing. But instead of my basic head nod and side-to-side step, Dean twirled me around and pulled me close. I didn't know what the heck I was doing, but Dean made both of us look good.

Marley and Liam joined in, and from the periphery of my vision, I saw Cole watching me, another cheerleader bobbing next to him. The whole room danced around us with Dean as the nucleus. He was pulling me along with him into the spotlight of attention. The beat pulsed, the music grew louder, and I began to feel dizzy. But Dean guided me from one step to the next. His right hand led me out; his left hand brought me in. During the final bars of the song, Dean leaned me back into a low dip. When we rose, he smoothly pushed me into Cole's arms and stole Marley from Liam.

"Huh?" Cole snapped away from me like I was poison. The cheerleader who'd been dancing with Cole glommed onto Liam, and Dean led Marley in a two-step that matched the country western vibe of her cowboy boots. But Cole just stood there.

I pretended like Cole's lack of interest didn't hurt and kept dancing. Now that Dean's magical moves weren't washing over me in a vicarious glow, I reverted to my side-to-side shuffle. Hopefully, it was dark enough that nobody would notice my lack of skills.

"I guess you don't stay with any guy for long," Cole said loudly enough that I could hear him over the music.

"What's that supposed to mean?" I stopped swaying and stood still.

"You've got a lot of nerve coming here."

"Because Marley doesn't like me?"

"Well, yeah, that and—" Cole paused midsentence. People started glancing at us curiously. "Forget it," he muttered and stormed out of the room.

"Wait!" Without a backward glance at Dean or Marley, I followed Cole.

CHAPTER THIRTEEN: COLE

1:22 A.M. | JUNE 4TH

I pushed open the French doors and escaped to the deck. Our house was built into a hill, and my parents had spent major money landscaping the backyard. Plexiglass railings offered a translucent view of the gardens below, and spotlights lit up the rhododendrons and azaleas that lined our black-bottomed pool. Even though it was June, it was cold. I was the only partygoer who'd ventured outside until Ellie followed me out there.

"What's your problem?" Ellie demanded.

I spun to face her, fists clenched at my sides. "My problem? Are you kidding me?"

"I know your sister doesn't like me, but I don't understand why."

"And you think showing up with Mr. Superstar is going to make it all better?"

Ellie's lips trembled.

"Did you kiss him too?" I asked. "Tell him your sob story about being afraid of water?"

"What? No! I mean—yes." Ellie grabbed her forehead like she was trying to hold her head still. "How do you know about my hydrophobia?"

"Well, that's rich." I shoved my hands in my pockets, shaking my head. What was Ellie playing at? "Because you told me."

"What?"

"That day on the beach you told me all about it. Right after you promised to be my girlfriend."

"What?"

Something inside me ruptured. "Is that all you can say? *What?* That's all I get after you've spent this whole year ignoring me and pretending like that day on the beach never happened?"

"What day on the beach?"

Her wide innocent eyes made me even more furious. "Stop being sarcastic! I spent all summer waiting for you to get back from your camp so we could pick up where we left off and then you brushed me off without one word of explanation."

"This can't be happening." Ellie paced back and forth. "I'm not supposed to forget important things."

"What the frick are you talking about?"

"What are *you* talking about?" Ellie shouted right back at me. "I don't remember, okay? Not one single thing about the beach. And it's not my fault, so stop hating on me!"

I froze. "Huh?"

"Tell me," she demanded. "In simple words so I understand. What happened at the beach?"

My chest felt tight until I remembered to breathe. "You don't remember?"

"No, I don't. Please tell me?" She looked scared.

I stood there for a moment, too stunned to speak. Was Ellie for real or was she just messing with me again? "A year ago today," I finally said, "before you left for camp, we met up on the beach at Discovery Park. I told you I'd had a crush on you forever, and you told me the same, and we kissed… a lot and promised that in September we'd be together." My shoulders slumped forward. "You don't remember any of that?"

Two tears rolled down her cheeks, and Ellie's face crumpled up like broken pie crust. "No, I don't." Then before I knew what was happening, she threw her arms around my neck and buried her face against my chest. "I'm sorry, Cole."

My arms went around her on instinct, but I didn't let down my defenses. Whatever was going on was too weird. "How could you forget?"

"Something must be wrong. I need to tell my parents."

"You were running away from them that day I found you on the beach."

Ellie lifted her head and looked up at me in confusion. "Why would I run away from my parents?"

"I don't know. You were all scraped up from blackberry bushes."

Ellie breathed rapidly. "But my parents want to help me. They would never do anything to hurt me."

I didn't know what to say. Marley was the one who knew the Doctors Savage, not me.

"Cole." Ellie's tone was serious. "I want you to know that I like you too. I've always liked you but was too shy to say anything."

"You didn't use to be shy. You used to be the most outspoken person I knew."

"What?"

"There you go, saying 'what?' again." I searched her green eyes for mockery but only recognized pain and confusion. She really had forgotten, somehow. The wall protecting my heart from Ellie crumbled, and I hugged her tightly. "Hey, it'll be okay. We can start over. Because guess what? A whole year of you ignoring me didn't make my feelings for you go away."

"But I have to go to camp again."

"This time don't forget me."

Ellie wiped her tears away with the back of her hands and shivered in her strapless dress. "You said we kissed."

"We did." I lifted up her chin with my finger. "Care to try it again?" I didn't wait for a response. I leaned down and pressed her lips against mine, their pillow-softness as tender as I remembered them to be. She clung to me, and I bound us together in my arms. One kiss. One heartbeat. One tender reunion I would never forget. "Think you can remember this one?" I asked when our lips parted for a brief moment.

"I'll find a way to never forget."

I didn't know what she meant by that, but before I had the chance to clarify, a mob of party guests burst through the deck doors, spilling out of the house and surrounding us.

"Karaoke!" Liam shouted, holding up the stereo. He queued up a song and tossed Dean the mic. "Take this, Canada's homeboy!" The opening riff of "Something 'Bout Your Love, Lady" blared over the crowd—Sam Sander's most recent hit single.

Dean snarled, but a second later he plastered on a showbiz smile and twirled into the middle of the deck. "*My lady*," Dean crooned with a buttery voice. He held out his hand to my sister.

Marley beamed a smile so bright I didn't recognize her.

"*My lady*," Dean sang again. He didn't bother reading the words off the screen because he must have known them by heart. "*Your love is like a burning flame.*" Dean kissed Marley's hand before releasing it and leaped into the air in perfect imitation of Sam's iconic dance move. The party guests cheered as Dean tossed the microphone from one fist to another and moonwalked backward, belting out the lyrics. "*I said my heart would never be tamed.*"

"He's killing it!" Ellie squealed with delight.

I felt a pang of jealousy until Ellie snuggled closer. But she was right. Dean was reinventing Sam's most popular song right before our eyes in a fit of musical genius.

"*But...*" The music paused, and Dean froze until the beat boomed again. "*There's something 'bout your love, lady.*" Dean shimmied over the improvised dance floor to my sister. Then he twisted the lyrics. "*Something 'bout your love, Marley.*" With a sly wink, Dean dipped my sister back for a kiss.

The entire lacrosse team wolf-whistled—everyone, that is, except Liam and me.

"Hey, man! That's my girlfriend!" Liam's face was tomato red. "Babe! What are you doing?"

"My name's *Marley*," my sister said when Dean helped her up from the dip. "And you don't own my lips."

"Dude," Liam growled, "not cool." Liam passed his drink to one of the clingy girls standing next to him.

Uh, oh. Here comes trouble. Before I had time to step forward, Liam swung back his arm and punched Dean in the nose. It was so unexpected that the whole deck got quiet for a moment. Then Marley screeched in outrage and Ellie was letting go of me and running to Dean's side.

"Stay out of this, babe!" Liam shouted.

"What the heck?" Dean patted the bridge of his nose. A few drops of blood dripped from his nostrils. His words were nasally—but it didn't look like his nose was broken. Dean's next words were crystal clear. "Her name's Marley!"

"I'll call her whatever I want, and nobody kisses my girl and gets away with it." Liam pushed up the sleeves of his jersey.

"Liam." Marley's eyes bugged out like fish. "What are you doing? You can't hit Dean Mathews!" She shot a wild look at me. "Cole! Do something!"

"Yeah," echoed Ellie, eyes equally panicked. "Do something!"

What was I supposed to do? Heck if I knew. Before I could react, Dean broke away from Ellie and slugged Liam in the stomach.

"Fight! Fight! Fight!" people chanted. A circle formed around the two guys.

Dean and Liam circled each other. How did things go from okay to awful so fast? Liam threw another punch and Dean dodged it. Dean was quick on his feet, but I guess that made sense since he was a dancer. With his bulky frame and dense intellect, Liam was more like a drunken beach bum. The mob chanted louder and louder. I took my eyes off of the fight for one second and saw dozens of phones. *Great, what if this alerts paparazzi?*

Liam swung again and missed Dean by a wide berth. Dean bobbed and weaved around the circle, grinning from ear to ear. He didn't bother to punch back. "Her name's Marley!" Dean said again. "Marley. Marley. Marley!"

That was when I officially started rooting for Dean. Liam calling my sister "babe" had been aggravating me forever. "Show him you mean it, Dean!" I yelled.

Liam leaned low and plowed his head into Dean's middle. They both toppled over to the ground.

"A wrestling match?" Marley screeched from the sidelines. "We are *so* over, Liam!"

I edged my body in front of Ellie, shielding her from the action so she wouldn't get hurt. But she stepped around me so I wouldn't block her view.

Dean surprised Liam with a leg sweep that made him yelp. Then Dean pulled Liam down to the ground in a half nelson. "Her name is Marley," Dean hissed right into Liam's face. He rolled Liam over and pinned him to the ground.

"Babe," Liam croaked back.

He really shouldn't have said that. I was trying to stay out of it, but that was too much. I took two steps forward. "He told you, weasel. Her name's Marley." I bent down low and growled, "My sister can do a heck of a lot better than you."

Marley snapped her head to look at me. "Really?"

I rolled my eyes but smiled at her. "Well, duh."

Just then, a full Solo cup upended on Liam's face. Liam squirmed under the downpour, choking on the liquid sloshing down his throat and nose. I followed the shaking arm holding the cup to Ellie's surprised face. Now the cup was empty, she seemed frozen in place, stunned. "I can't believe I just did that."

Dean gave his neck another twist until Liam's eyes bulged.

"Marley," Liam sputtered. "Her name's Marley."

The whole room erupted in cheers. Dean let Liam go with a jerk. Somebody turned the music back on, this time to one of

Dean's biggest hits from last year. *"I'll fight for you, all night for you."*

"Karaoke!" Marley squealed, a desperate edge to her voice. Two seconds later she shut up when Dean leaned her back for another kiss.

Now I was the one wolf-whistling. But part of me felt guilty. It should have been me beating up my sister's dirtbag boyfriend.

"Best party ever!" somebody shouted.

"I agree," Ellie whispered in my ear. She tilted her chin up for a kiss, and I willingly obliged. Maybe it didn't matter who'd put Liam in his place. I had better things to do right now. We laced our fingers together, and euphoria washed over me. Everything was perfect.

Until the enormous *crack* and *crash* of snapping timber and shattering Plexiglass.

CHAPTER FOURTEEN: ELLIE

1:55 A.M. | JUNE 4TH

The firm pressure of Cole's hand tore away. My feet failed as the ground beneath them disappeared. Air swooshed over my head. We were falling.

Falling.

And falling.

The frigid pool hit me like a sledgehammer. I opened my mouth to scream, and icy cold water gushed in. I shut my mouth tight, but it was already too late. Water trickled down my throat, scorching my lungs, strangling my breath. In three seconds of terror, I was completely submerged.

Churning water surrounded me. Knees and elbows gouged my sides. Panic overwrought my nervous system and froze my hands and feet. I couldn't swim *or* fight. Blood beat a steady drum in my ears as I sank to my inevitable fate.

I opened my eyes to dark, thrashing water and prayed for a miracle. There, at the edge of death and the bottom of the pool, I saw a pair of green eyes. And I recognized them.

They were *my* green eyes. In shock, I flailed my legs and struck the concrete bottom of the pool. Instinctually, I pushed myself up with all my panicked strength and shot toward the surface. My arms reached out and propelled me higher until my face broke through into the clean night air.

I sputtered, vomiting out water and gasping for oxygen—and found my legs making neat bicycle circles, and my hands forming cups that pushed the water down. I was treading water. *Like I had swum all my life.*

I didn't have time to think about it. All around me was chaos—screaming dark figures, people thrashing in the water, half the deck hanging precariously above it all. "Cole!" I shouted. I couldn't pick him out of from the figures. A jagged piece of deck floated by and I kicked to avoid its sharp edge. Just past the broken piece, I saw a familiar patch of poufy hair floating in the choppy water. "Dean!" I screamed at the top of my lungs.

Sidestrokes. I needed to do sidestrokes. Somehow my arms slid across my body in perfect formation. I cut through the water, evading debris and other swimming bodies. When my hands reached Dean, I clawed at his shirt, turning his torso over in the water. I hooked my arm around his chin and towed his limp body to the side of the pool. At the edge, a muscular guy helped me pull Dean out of the water.

"Dean!" Anxiety lent a hysterical edge to my voice. "Breathe, dammit!" I tried to remember an ancient lesson from health class about CPR and pumped on his chest. Then the guy next to me took over so I could blow air into Dean's lungs.

It seemed both an eternity and just a few seconds before Dean was puking into my lap. He lay with eyes closed, but he breathed raggedly.

"You saved him!" said my helper. "Ellie, that was amazing. You swam through all that wood and rescued him."

I turned and realized that my assistant was Cole. He had a jagged gash across his forehead that dripped blood. "Cole!" I cried. "Thank goodness!" I threw my arms around him in a sitting hug.

"It's okay now." Cole's presence felt reassuring, but that didn't stop my teeth from chattering. "I thought you couldn't swim."

"I can't."

"But you just did. Like a freaking Olympian!"

"I don't know what happened." I looked down at Dean and wiped puke off his face with the side of my hand.

"Here they come," said Cole. "That was fast." Over my gushing rush of emotions, I heard the faint wail of sirens. "You should get him out of here before the cops arrive."

"But Dean needs an ambulance," I protested. "He almost drowned."

Dean's eyes shot open. "Marley," he sputtered. "Where's Marley?"

"Don't worry, man, I just saw her." Cole grabbed Dean's shoulders and helped heave him up. "Call me when you get home, okay, Ellie?"

"The police!" I heard Marley squeal. "Holy guacamole, Cole. Mom and Dad are going to kill us!"

A fleeing partygoer knocked into my shoulder in her haste to leave. She wasn't the only one racing for the gate. The backyard was a blur of escaping teens.

"See?" Cole said. "It's best if you hurry." He kissed me hard on the lips. "We're in enough trouble already without a celebrity being involved."

I surveyed the scene of destruction, feeling overwhelmed. Marley's pool looked like the log ride at a carnival, and it was only a matter of time before the rest of the deck collapsed.

Dean bent over and coughed hard, phlegm and water spewing to the ground. Then he grabbed my elbow. "Ready, Ellie?"

I kissed Cole one more time. "Let's go," I told Dean. I scanned the side of the house and pulled us toward the gate. "I gave the keys to you before we got here, right? Do you still have them?" Our path was empty, but as we crept along the side of the house, the police pounded on the front door.

Dean patted the pocket of his jeans. "Right here."

Thank goodness for his tight pants. "Good." I nodded to the florist van up the street. "Let's get out of here." We took off at a run.

"You there!" a cop shouted at us. "Freeze!"

We were only a few steps away from our ride. Dean and I both paused in terror. I slowly turned toward the cop and his partner, who were a hundred feet behind us.

"Hold it!" the cop shouted again. A piercing scream from behind the house changed his mind, and he and his partner sprinted toward Cole and Marley's house.

Dean fumbled for the keys and clicked open the locks. Miraculously, the key fob still worked, even after being submerged in water. We threw ourselves onto the front seat. Dean cranked the ignition and turned the van into the street.

Dean's hands had a white-knuckled grip on the steering wheel as he blew past a stop sign.

"Stop!" I screeched.

"What?"

"Slow down!" I scrambled for my seatbelt.

"Huh?" We ripped past a minivan that honked in aggravation—or fear, seeing that we were going sixty miles an hour in a neighborhood.

"You're going to get us both killed!"

"Oh." Dean eased up on the accelerator. "Thorry. I can't believe I'm finally driving." He reached for the blinker and accidentally turned on the windshield wipers. "Crap! Driving ith harder than it looketh."

"What do you mean? Haven't you driven a car before?"

"Sure. In a commercial shoot." Another horn blared at us as Dean squealed us into a left-hand turn.

"Maybe you should let me drive us home," I said diplomatically even as I clutched the arm rests. "You probably don't know your way around town anyway."

Dean grinned. "Where are we again? Montreal?"

"Very funny. But I've already faced death once tonight and don't want to do it again." I motioned to the side of the road, and Dean pulled the car over.

I turned to open my door but Dean's hand on my arm stopped me. "Ellie." I glanced at him in confusion. He looked at me with serious blue eyes. "You thaved my life. I would have drowned if it weren't for you."

Ice crept down the back of my neck and I looked at my red, freezing hands. "Yeah, only here's the thing. I don't know how I did that. I don't know how to swim. At least, that's what I've always believed." I squeezed my eyes shut. "I'm terrified of pools. I can't even use a bathtub without freaking out."

Dean's hand on my arm made me open my eyes. "Ellie, I'm theventy-five kilogramth. How did you rethcue me if you don't know how to thwim?"

I shook my head. "Adrenaline?"

"Are you sure you don't know how?"

I swallowed hard and put a hand to my forehead. "I'm positive I don't know how to swim. Unless…"

Dean waited a minute before prompting me. "Unleth what?"

"Well, let me start with this. Tonight, Cole told me about this day on the beach a year ago where we spent the afternoon together and," I looked sideways at Dean, "established a real connection." Dean whistled. "But the next day, I started a session of narcosis. And now I don't remember any of it."

Dean shrugged. "Maybe Cole was mething with you?"

"Or maybe," I said, feeling disloyal as soon as the words came out of my mouth, "I'm having a bad reaction to narcosis." I tugged up my strapless dress. The red corset was showing. "But why would my parents suggest I do another round if they knew it was making me forget things?"

"I don't know, but I have an idea how to learn more about your thwiming ability. When we get back to the hotel, let'th go to the pool."

"I can't ask you to do that! You almost drowned."

"Only because I hit my head." Dean reached up and brushed the hair away from his forehead so I could see the goose egg.

I cringed. "Ouch! We need to get ice on that."

"Later. After we thwim."

"How's your nose doing?" I asked, remember Liam's punch.

Dean gently pinched the bridge of his nose. "Tender, but not broken." He tossed the keys onto my lap. "If we're going to do narcothith tomorrow, we both detherve to know the truth about the thide effecths."

CHAPTER FIFTEEN: DEAN
3:02 A.M. | JUNE 4TH

Michael unlocked the double doors with a gigantic set of keys. "Technically the pool closes at ten P.M., but since you are priority guests, of course we're happy to make the exception." He threw the doors open, and the lights automatically turned on. He turned and leered at Ellie. "Do you want swimsuits?"

"No way." My head nod to Michael was returned with a lecherous grin. I shot my arm out and wrapped it around Ellie's shoulder. Her violet dress had dried tight, and her hair was crispy with chlorine. We stood barefoot on the floor of the changing room that opened into the swimming area, our shoes lost at the bottom of Marley's pool.

"Enjoy yourselves then. Our hot tub is perfection." Michael closed the doors behind us with a loud *click*.

The pool room was like a glass conservatory. The pool stretched out in a long rectangle. Aqua tiles lined the walls and floors, but enormous windows looked out into the Duchess's gardens beyond. At night, the windows turned into black mirrors. All I could see was me looking like I'd been in a bar fight, and Ellie in her wet, purple dress. But the room itself was quite peaceful, especially after the rowdiness of Marley's party.

"It's like staring at a coffin," Ellie said. She was shaking. "Or a graveyard. A watery graveyard. A watery graveyard with coffins and one of them has my name on it in big block letters saying, 'ELLIE SAVAGE, YOU WILL DROWN.'" She hugged her arms tight and dug her fingers into her triceps. "Are we doing this?"

"For sure we are." I stripped off my drenched shirt. "Come on, Ellie. You can do it. You owe it to yourthelf to find out the truth." I unbuttoned the top of my jeans and pulled down my pant so I could swim in boxers. I kicked my clothes to the side and walked over to the deep end. Then in one swift movement, I dove into the pool.

When I surfaced, I whipped my head around so my hair stood straight up. The water streamed down me in ripples.

"You could be a hair gel model." Ellie giggled.

"Huh?"

"The way your hair slicks down and then poofs again is like magic."

"My thtylitht Maxine would love that." I splashed the water next to me. "Are you coming?"

Ellie turned around and undid her zipper. I have to admit that the sight of her in that corset and thong took my breath away. She didn't have Marley's curves, but Ellie still managed to make me grateful for the cold water.

I whistled. "Thank you, Michael."

"Stop it!" Ellie placed her arms in front of her, immediately self-conscious.

"This was all an elaborate excuthe to get you in your underwear," I teased. "Now come on. We can begin at the shallow end."

Ellie picked her way across the cold pavement to the edge of the pool. "As long as I can remember I've been afraid of the water. When it rains, I wrap up in GORE-TEX and hide under a golf umbrella. When I shower, I'm a flash of speed. I don't even like to wash dishes in a tub of water. Rinsing them is enough for me."

I grinned at her. "Now for the thecond time in one night, you're going thwimming."

Ellie dipped her toe in the water and then yanked her foot back onto dry land. "I can't do it. This was a horrible idea."

"For sure, you can."

Ellie looked deep into my eyes and shook her head. "No. I can't."

"*Ellie, you're brave. Ellie, you're kind. Ellie, you're a quick thinker.*" The acoustics of the pool house were perfect for a cappella. "*And you deserve to know the truth.*" I held out my arms to offer help.

Her chest heaved up and down, constricted by the corset. "What's wrong with me? Why is this so terrifying?"

"*Ellie, you're brave. Ellie, you're kind. Ellie, you're a quick thinker.*" I walked through the water until I stood right below her. I reached up my hands. "*And you can do anything.*"

Slowly, ever so slowly, she leaned down and put her palms on my shoulders. I pulled her down into the water until her feet rested on the ground, the water at hip level.

"*Ellie, you're brave. Ellie, you're kind. Ellie, you're a quick thinker.*" I pulled my hands away. "*And I know that you can swim.*"

"Right. Swimming." Ellie held her arms above the water and tried to control her gasping breath. As her chest heaved, a faint line on her chest caught my attention.

I reached out my fingertip and traced the scar. "*What's this?*"

She shrugged. "A scar, but I don't remember how I got it."

"Oh." I felt embarrassed for asking. Mom had taught me to never point out oddities about a person's appearance.

I took a few steps back into deeper water. Here I was living the dream, hanging out with a wet girl in lingerie in the middle of the night—only it was the wrong girl. But also, maybe, the right one. "Show me how you thwam tonight. I don't remember anything until Cole thaid you rethcued me."

"Crap." Ellie shivered. "I guess I need to try." She sank into the water until it lapped against her neck. Ellie closed her eyes.

"Put your head under and hold your breath," I suggested.

Ellie screwed up her face. "Are you nuts? I don't think you appreciate how hellish this is for me."

"Try it."

"Okay. Here goes nothing." She gulped in air and pinched her nose and squeezed her eyes shut. Then she let out her breath and took another big one. After another ten seconds and another big breath, Ellie forced her body down until her head was underwater.

For almost a minute there was nothing but bubbles. I had no idea how she held her breath that long, and I was about to go over and pull her up when Ellie's head popped out of the water and screamed.

"Ellie!" I yanked her up by the armpits, most of her body coming out of the pool.

"Where did the girl go?" She frantically rubbed her chlorine-reddened eyes.

"What girl? Ellie, you were under there for a long time." Her skin felt clammy and cool as I steadied her on the pool bottom.

"The girl with burning eyes!" she blurted. "The one on fire."

Had Ellie gone bonkers? "Nobody'th here but you and me." I hoisted myself out of the pool and collected a stack of towels. "That'th enough for now. Let'th go retht up before we head back to the clinic." I reached down to help her out of the pool, but she was already scrambling up the ladder.

She clutched at my arm when I tried to hand her a towel, face panic-stricken. "You've got to look in the water and find her!"

"What?"

"The girl's drowning! And she's on fire!"

I shook my head. "That doethn't make any thenthe. How could thomeone burn and drown at the thame time?"

Ellie tugged me toward the pool. "Go back in the water and find her. Please!"

We both turned to look at the water, still choppy from our recent exit. "Ellie," I said, resting gentle hands on her shoulders. "There'th nobody here but you and me."

Ellie blinked in disbelief until realization spread across her face. She pulled away from me, hands to her forehead. "What? But I don't understand. Am I losing my mind?"

"You're tired, that'th all." I wrapped Ellie in a couple of warm towels. "Let's go order hot chocolate from room service."

"But what about the girl? The one with the melting eyes like burning coal?"

"There is no girl," I reassured her again, steering her toward the exit. "And you need to rest." Ellie's answers would have to wait for another day.

CHAPTER SIXTEEN: ELLIE

3:32 A.M. | JUNE 4TH

That ghost girl flipped me out. I didn't have a hallucination underwater, but I don't know what else to call it. A vision, maybe? A flashback? Right there in the Duchess's pool, I had an out-of-body experience. The pool had answers, and I was too chicken to stay there long enough to figure them out.

I was splashing in the water with my friend who wore a *Little Mermaid* tankini. The girl smiled when she saw me. She had tan lines and two braids of wet hair. We took turns doing underwater somersaults.

"Let's have a tea party!" I'd told the girl. She'd laughed with glee. Together, we'd held hands and pulled ourselves to the bottom. I'd opened my eyes, and she had too. Her eyes were the same color as mine.

Then her face changed shape, her skin melting off like wax. Her hair had caught on fire, and the water had boiled. The green eyes had turned bright red like burning coals. I'd screamed in terror and water had filled my lungs.

The whole ride up the elevator I pictured those burning eyeballs and felt tears course down my cheeks. I was crying! Over a stupid hallucination. Dean rubbed my back in smooth, calming circles. When the elevator doors opened, he led me down the hallway to the Vice Regal Suite. Inside our hotel room, two more garment bags of clothes plus a dumbwaiter with champagne and snacks waited for us.

Dean nodded to the bathroom. "Why don't you take a bath and warm up?"

I didn't have it in me to argue. A bath was certainly not going to happen, but a hot shower sounded, well, hot at least. I plodded off to the washroom.

The shower had five different heads and four different soaps. Instead of waking me up, the pounding hot jets soothed me into sleepiness. I massaged shampoo through my long hair, turned auburn from the water. When I stepped out onto the bathmat, I realized I didn't have anything to change into. The garment bags were in the living room. I wrapped myself in a fluffy, white robe. The complimentary body lotion stung when I slathered it onto my face, and I combed through my hair with my fingers.

Dean had an ice cold can of Sprite waiting for me that he must have scavenged from the mini bar. "Thirthty?" he asked me. "Or hungry?" He uncovered a silver tray. "Chocolate-covered berrieth."

"Awesome." I sat down at the table and pounded the pop in twenty seconds flat. Then I bit into the juicy flesh of a strawberry, bits of chocolate crumbling around my teeth. The chocolate tasted like heaven.

Dean cleared his throat. "I gueth I'll take a shower." He patted his hair. "Got to get the chlorine out." He grabbed one of the garment bags and headed into the bathroom.

I crammed four more strawberries into my mouth before the sugar and caffeine hit my blood stream, and I started to feel human again. I pulled the robe tighter, remembering my nudity. Hopefully Michael had sent clothes fit for a teenage girl rather than a stripper.

With a great deal of trepidation, I unzipped the second garment bag. Inside I found a pair of designer jeans and a cashmere sweater. There was also a silk camisole and matching boy shorts. Perfect.

I was still planning on going home tonight, so I slipped into the jeans and sweater and padded over to the bedroom. The pillow-soft duvet of the king-sized bed beckoned. I didn't want to fall asleep, but the bed looked so cozy that I climbed under the covers and clicked on the television. Since it was three A.M., my choices were news, static, or infomercials. I opted for CNN.

The story about trade embargoes with Russia had me nodding off. Maybe I would have been better off with the program about the microwavable cheesemaker. I settled into the feather pillow and closed my eyes. It wouldn't be long now, and Dean and I would go home.

"Stay tuned for breaking news about Dean Mathews."

I jolted upright and stared at the TV as the newscaster continued.

"Is he dead or alive? Shocking new footage shows he might have been a victim of what local authorities are calling a dangerous combination of an aging redwood deck and too many teens. We'll have more after a word from our sponsors."

"Dean!" I called. "Come out here." No answer—the fan and shower were still on and I could hear Dean crooning away. I leaped out of bed and raced to the living room, hunting for my phone. Dang it! This was the second time I'd forgotten it wasn't with me. I padded back to the bedroom and the television.

An ad for hemorrhoid cream ended and the program cut back to CNN. A newscaster with a helmet of platinum blond hair teased the headline of Dean Mathews and a near-tragic deck collapse. My entire focus was stuck on the grainy video of Marley and Cole's backyard.

The Barbie-doll newscaster was grim. *"Shocking footage tonight from Seattle. In a YouTube video going viral on the Internet, superstar Dean Mathews is allegedly one of over forty teens who was attending a party at a private residence when the deck they stood on collapsed into a pool below."*

Someone had shot video from above, like they had been standing on a second-story balcony. My skin went icy when I saw the blur of people plunge into the dark waters below.

"Just moments before this accident," the newscaster said, *"Dean Mathews was serenading this girl with Sam Sander's famous hit single 'Something 'Bout Your Love, Lady.'"*

There it was on international television for the whole world to see: Dean dipping Marley back for a kiss. The lip-locked couple next to them was Cole and me. I didn't need a mirror to know I was grinning like an idiot.

The camera cut to Liam wrapped up in a towel and talking to a local reporter.

"Yeah, um, the deck collapsed," he sputtered. *"We almost all drowned."* Liam had a dazed look that might have been from fatigue or fright.

"And can you tell us more about the girl Dean was kissing?" the reporter asked.

Liam's eyes turned fierce. *"She's exactly Dean's type, a real skank."*

"And what happened to Dean during the accident?"

"There Dean was," said Liam, *"floating facedown in the middle of the pool. I was just about to dive in there and rescue him—I'm on the lacrosse team, you know."* Liam gave a head-nod to the cameraman and flexed his muscles. *"When all of a sudden this girl named Ellie shoots through the water like she's part fish. I don't know how she did it, but she towed him to the edge like it was no big deal at all."* Liam puffed up his shoulders. *"But Ellie needed my help to pull Dean from the water."*

"Was Dean okay?" the interviewer continued. *"Did you ascertain his injuries?"*

Liam shook his head. *"I'm still not sure. He was pretty messed up. If I hadn't given him CPR, he'd be dead."*

"That's not what happened!" I yelled at the television.

CNN cut back to the reporter. *"Our newsroom has reached out to Dean Mathews's tour manager, and we have confirmation that Dean is still missing. All local hospitals have been notified. Authorities are worried that Dean might have a concussion."*

I heard the shower shut off in the next room, and I muted the program with the remote when commercials came on. There it was on national television—undeniable proof that I knew how to swim but had somehow forgotten my own ability. How could I not only forget to swim but develop a phobia of all water?

Dean appeared in the doorway wearing jeans and a black silk shirt.

"We were just on the nightly news," I told him.

"It happenth." Dean shrugged.

I twisted a lock of hair around my finger. "Did narcosis make you forget things?"

"I don't know, but I can't remember what happened a week ago. Half the time I don't even know what city I'm in, the tour'th tho crazy."

"What if three months from now, when you wake up, you don't remember me, or Marley, or any of this?"

Dean sat on the edge of the bed. "That would be awful. But I'm prepared to go through with it. Besides, I never forget a lyric." Then he sang to me again. *"Ellie, you're brave. Ellie, you're kind. Ellie, you're a quick thinker. You're the first girl I've talked to in I don't know how long. I've bared my soul to you. I feel like I can talk to you."*

Dean's song twisted me with sadness. "I feel like I can talk to you too, and that's why I have to be honest." I sat down next to him on the bed. "The truth is, in seventh and eighth grade my parents sent me to an elite boarding school called Remington Prep. It was my dad's alma mater and he had a great experience there when he was my age."

"And?" Dean tilted his head to the side as he listened.

My shoulders slumped. "Something bad happened there that I can't remember. When I came home all of my memories were gone. It's called retrograde amnesia."

"Oh my gosh, Ellie, how horrible."

I nodded. "That's the main reason I do narcosis. My mom hopes that if my brain can rest for three months, my memories will return on their own." It felt good finally confiding my secret into someone other than my parents.

"But you're still lothing memories?" Dean knit his eyebrows together.

"I think so." I scratched the pack of my neck. "I can't remember anything from before ninth grade, but I thought that all of my memories of high school were intact until Cole told me about us kissing on the beach last summer."

Dean's forehead wrinkled with worry. "Maybe you shouldn't do narcothith tomorrow after all."

"And you?"

Dean's shoulders slumped. "I've got to. It's in my contract."

I took a deep breath and let it out slowly, while I thought about my options. Would I remember Cole when I woke up in September? Would he forgive me again if I didn't?

Mom and Dad said narcosis was my decision. I could skip narcosis and spend all summer with Cole. But then I'd still have to deal with my forgotten memories.

I felt my face with my fingertips. Narcosis had given me a clear complexation and thick eyelashes. It had given me straight As in school. I let my hands drop and folded them in my lap. "I've seen narcosis work miracles a least a thousand times—on me included. Yeah, I've forgotten some things, but my parents are confident that this last round of narcosis will fix my retrograde amnesia in a safe way. I just need to figure out how to protect my memories from tonight, because it sounds likely that I'll forget them."

"Your mom and dad worked miracleth for me too," Dean said.

I nodded. "So I should be brave and do it one more time. Five more hours until check-in, right? Is your narcosis at nine A.M. too?"

"Yup. Do you want to go back to the clinic now?"

"Sure." I was about to stand up when a brainstorm hit. "No, wait! You watch some TV or take a nap. I want to jot down some notes first in case I do forget."

"Great idea." Dean yawned and laid down on the bed. He didn't bother reaching for the remote control. His eyes closed and soon as his head hit the pillow. Then he opened his eyes again and looked at me. "Do you think Marley might like me?"

"Maybe. I don't know."

"I know people got hurt and all, but I had more fun tonight than I've had all year."

"That can't be true."

"It is," Dean insisted. "I feel… I don't know. Happy, I gueth." A minute later Dean was snoring on top of the down comforter. It was a good thing he could trust me because that would have made a hilarious post on YouTube.

Sleep seemed like pure heaven, but my mind swirled too hard to rest. Writing notes about what happened tonight—like a cheat-sheet—was the perfect solution. But first, I had some recon to do. Feeling guilty, I swiped Dean's phone off the nightstand and snuck into the living room. The gratis bar had crystal glasses and a silver bucket of ice waiting. I poured myself some Perrier and sat down at the desk.

To start, I searched for "Narcosis Clinic" on Dean's phone. Wikipedia pulled up a reassuring article about how the Narcosis Clinic performed life-changing miracles on people who desperately needed help—everything I already knew typed up in a clear black font. But that didn't stop my nerves, so I tried Googling "burning eyeballs," and a gazillion sites pulled up, accompanied by disgusting pictures. I swiped the images away.

Frustrated about not finding answers, I called Mom. I wasn't sure she would answer, since it was an unknown number and the middle of the night, but she picked up after the first ring. "Dr. Belinda Savage speaking," she said in her clipped tone.

"Mom, it's me."

"Ellie?" Mom's voice softened and also contained a note of panic. "Where are you? Are you with Dean? Our team has been searching for him everywhere!"

"Searching for Dean, or me too?"

Mom's voice was muffled, like she was holding her hand over the receive. "It's Ellie," I heard her whisper.

"Ellie?" Dad's voice sounded in the background. "Thank God!"

"Keep her talking," said a third voice. Ursula?

"Why's Ursula with you?" I asked.

"She's updating patient logs," Mom answered. "A high-profile patient going missing is a big deal, and we needed our head nurse to help us process information. You didn't answer my question. Are you with Dean?"

"You didn't answer my question either." I sat up a bit straighter. "Were you searching for me too?"

I heard the receiver jumble, like it was yanked out of Mom's hands.

"Ellie, it's me," said Dad. "I'm so glad you're safe! Until we saw the news on TV about you being at that party, we thought you were asleep in bed. What happened?"

"I was keeping track of Dean." The phone felt sweaty in my palm. "His manager was harassing him and so we went for a walk. Then there was a mob of fan girls, so I helped him escape."

"You did?"

"Of course I did. Patient privacy is a Narcosis Clinic top priority, right?"

"That's right," Dad said in a louder than normal voice. "So you didn't run away? You were actually doing what you thought we would want you to do?"

Err... "Yeah. And Dean's all set to come in for narcosis this morning."

"Well done, Ellie. I'm glad to hear that. You are extremely trustworthy. Your mom and Ursula are working the public relations damage control for Dean."

"Um, okay. Is that why are you talking so loud? Are they being noisy?"

"Oh, sorry about that. Yeah, it's a zoo around here." Dad chuckled, but it sounded off. Strained. "All the excitement has got me keyed up. I'm just so proud of you, angel. You saved Dean Mathews and the whole world sees you as a hero. Way to go."

Way to go? Why was Dad acting so strange? I thought for sure he'd chew me out for going to Cole's party.

"Dad, I have a question about narcosis and my lost memories."

"And you're thoughtful, too," Dad said. He took a deep breath like he wanted to keep talking, but I butted in.

"Ah, thanks. Anyway, you probably saw on the news that when I fell into the pool, I swam. How is that possible when I'm terrified of water?"

He sounded relieved when he answered, "It's because your mother programed swimming lessons into your psychic driving. Wasn't that clever of her?"

"She did?"

"Absolutely. It was for your own protection in case you ever fell into water."

"Oh. That explains a lot. But I have another question too, about what I saw in the pool."

"What did you see, darling?"

"Burning eyeballs! I saw a little girl who looked like me who was in flames!"

Short pause, and then forced calm, like he was talking to a three-year-old. "Sweetheart, tonight was traumatic. Your mom's the psychiatrist, not me, but that the deck crashing and falling into that pool was a lot for your mind to process."

"Part of me was wondering if I should skip narcosis this summer and do traditional therapy instead."

Like a robot, he replied, "I one hundred percent support you whatever you decide."

"You do?"

"Of course I do. I just wish you didn't have to do therapy in the first place. I'll never forgive myself for sending you to Remington Prep." He sounded like himself again, finally. Tonight must have really stressed him out.

"Dad, whatever happened there wasn't your fault. You need to forgive yourself."

"Easier said than done, sweet princess. Your mother and I both want you to be happy."

"But what about my more recent memories? Tonight I learned that…" I paused. I didn't really want to tell Dad about kissing Cole. "Tonight I realized that I had gone to the beach last a June, a year ago today, and forgot about it."

"The beach? I don't remember the beach, but I do remember taking you and your mother out for Sunday brunch and you freaking out when you saw there was a water view."

"Oh. That sounds embarrassing."

"Don't be embarrassed. It was our fault for pushing your limits when you weren't ready. I felt horrible. I think—"

"You think what?"

"Well," Dad paused, "I can't be sure, but ever since that moment I've wondered if something happened at Remington Prep that involved seafood."

"Seafood?" My brow furrowed. What traumatic thing could have happened to me that involved seafood?

"Shrimp to be precise. That day at the restaurant you were doing fine—after we told the hostess we didn't want a window seat. But when the waiter brought out shrimp cocktail, you bolted. But I don't want to put ideas in your head. It's up to your brain to recover your lost memories without interference."

"You mean with narcosis."

"Or therapy," said Dad. "You're decision. You've proven yourself to be a wise and competent young woman." His voice was loud again, and in the background I heard shuffling papers.

"Thanks. I guess I need to think about it. Right now I'm thinking yes, I do want to do narcosis tomorrow, but I'll let you know for sure in the morning when Dean and I come in to the clinic."

Dad coughed. "You and Dean? Do I need to have a talk with this young man?"

"*Dad!* It's not like that. Dean and I are friends, that's all."

"Okay. Friends. Keep it that way, and I won't have to throttle him."

I laughed, anxiety leaving me. "That would ruin the clinic's reputation faster than the speed of Twitter."

"I can see the Twitter mob now—fangirls attacking me with pitch forks." Dad chuckled. "Stay safe, princess, and thank you for being so responsible, dutiful, and trustworthy. I know that I can count on your help to bring back our high-profile client."

"You're welcome. See you in the morning."

I hung up the phone, flush from Dad's praise. Our chat had clarified my decision. The simplest, fastest way to regain my lost memories was narcosis. I could fall asleep tomorrow morning and wake up in three months, remembering everything— hopefully.

Despite my parents' assurances, I didn't want to leave my post-narcosis self without a clear memory of tonight—just in case. The day-before memories were the ones I might forget. That's where my cheat sheet came in. I would leave my notes here at the hotel with Michael for me to read in September. That way I would definitely remember and Mom and Dad wouldn't have to know anything about it. The thought of Dad reading about me and Cole making out was too horrible to imagine.

I'd snap a selfie for Instagram too. Swiping open Dean's phone, I logged into my account and took a picture of me with the Vice Regal Suite behind me. Then I pulled open the desk drawer and found a stash of stationary. Per our tradition, we'd be due at this hotel for high tea when I woke up from narcosis. Tomorrow morning I'd insist that Mom make a reservation. During high tea three months from now, Michael would say he had a message for me and take me out of the dining room and up to this suite, where he'd give me this letter. Foolproof way to remember.

As the clock struck four A.M., I began to write every last thing that had happened tonight, starting at the concert.

Dear Future Me,

Ellie Savage, if you're reading this, wait until Michael leaves and lock the door before reading on. You know who I am, right? I'm you, Ellie. I'm the three-months-ago you. Past Me is writing to Future Me to verify the truth.

Okay, are you alone? Hopefully you'll remember everything written here without needing to read it, but if not, this letter will separate fact from fiction. I'll tell you what you need to know so that narcosis doesn't make you forget your precious night-before memories. I want you to remember the good stuff.

But first, when you wake up in September, search for the answers I couldn't find before narcosis. Find a pool and practice swimming—you're a natural. Remember kissing Cole Evans and how he wants to be your boyfriend! Review your Instagram account. Question Mom and Dad about your lost memories. Figure out the truth about your past, and why you can't remember. Whatever happened at Remington Prep to give you retrograde amnesia, I know you can overcome it.

I'm in our suite at the Duchess Hotel too, only it's three months ago. It's four A.M. Dean is asleep in the bedroom. Do you remember Dean? I hope so. In a couple of hours, Dean and I are both due at the Narcosis Clinic for a summer of treatment. It's been a long night, so pay attention as

I help our brain out by recording every last detail of what happened tonight...

BOOK TWO

NARCOSIS

CHAPTER SEVENTEEN: ELLIE
SUMMER

Your name is Ellie Savage. You are an obedient teenage girl who loves her parents. You never defy their wishes. Your parents want what is best for you. Mom and Daddy are brilliant doctors who are changing the face of modern medicine. You are lucky that they are your parents. You know that your parents make good decisions for you. You never speak out of turn or embarrass your parents in public. You get straight As and keep your room clean. Boys can wait until college because school comes first. You love your mom and daddy more than anything else in the world. You always do what they say. Your name is Ellie Savage. You are an obedient teenage girl who loves her parents. You never defy their wishes. Your parents want what is best for you. Mom and Daddy are brilliant doctors who are changing the face of modern medicine. You are lucky that they are your parents. You know that your parents make good decisions for you. You never speak out of turn or embarrass your parents in public. You get straight As and keep your room clean. Boys can wait until college because school comes first. You love your Mom and Daddy more than anything else in the world. You always do what they say. Your name is Ellie Savage…

BOOK THREE

AWAKE

CHAPTER EIGHTEEN: ELLIE

1:03 P.M. | SEPTEMBER 1ST

What the heck? My head throbs. I throw the stack of stationery onto the desk. The only thing I recognize is my handwriting. The rest of it—Marley's party, swimming in a pool, kissing Cole Evans… Was I on drugs when I wrote this? Seriously, I must have been hallucinating. I certainly don't remember writing it. Even if by some miracle I did run into Dean Mathews, it's not like I would care. I'm Sam Anders' number one fan.

I walk over to the balcony and fling open the French doors. The cool maritime air bites my cheeks. In the distance I see *The Royal Racer* take off for Victoria with another load of tourists. On the road below, a horse-drawn carriage clogs up traffic. Up here on the sixth floor, I'm on top of the world.

The Vice Regal Suite is tricked out. If I weren't so anxious to get back to Mom and Daddy, I could stay here all day. There's a full kitchen, a dining room, a living room with a grand piano, and the most gorgeous views of the Space Needle I've ever seen.

But nothing about this suite seems familiar. If I'd been here before, I'd remember it. My mind is like a diamond. This year I'll graduate as Emily Carr High's valedictorian. I'll crush my AP tests, and next year Harvard will be the perfect fit. Or maybe I'll head down to California and go to Stanford. My goal is to become a brilliant doctor, just like my parents.

The side pocket of my skirt rings with "Children Should Listen," Mom's favorite ballad from *Into the Woods*. This is the fifth time she's called since I've been up here, and I feel really guilty for ignoring the calls. I press the touchpad and accept the call.

"Where are you, darling? You weren't answering your phone. You've been gone forty minutes!" Mom's panic is contagious.

The back of my neck feels sweaty. I need to get back to my parents as soon as possible. But I don't want to disappoint them with the truth that I've snuck off.

"My bad. My phone was on mute. I got lost on the way back from the bathroom. Where are we eating lunch again? The Crystal Ballroom?"

"The Duchess Tea Lobby. Where are you right now?"

"Um… I'm at a window. I can see Lake Union."

Icy cold water that will rip me to shreds.

"Ellie? Stay right where you are. You father and I will find you. Can you see a room number?"

"A room number?" I look down at the credit-card key of the Vice Regal Suite. "I'll find an elevator. I'll be back for tea in five minutes." Before Mom can respond, I click off my phone.

When I step back into the living room, I see the massive stack of stationery sitting where I abandoned it on the desk. I swipe it into the rubbish on my way out.

The door closes with a *thud*, but the narrow hallway softens the echo. I walk across the hotel carpet woven with dogwood and rhododendrons. Pictures of Victorian ladies fill antique frames on the walls. They watch me with unspeaking eyes, judging my omission of truth. Should I tell my parents about the letter?

I step into the elevator and use six floors to think. Whoever the ingrate was who wrote that letter doesn't know what she's talking about. For one, I've never heard of this Remington Prep I'm supposed to find answers about. Maybe it was some sick joke from the hotel? Or Olivia? Though anyone's motivation for doing such a thing is beyond me.

But why was it in my handwriting? I push that thought away.

The elevators open into the bustling lobby. Doorkeepers in white gloves roll brass trolleys filled with suitcases. Action swirls around me, and for a moment I am lost. But then I see the sign for the Duchess Tea Lobby, and I rush to find my folks.

Mom sees me first. She flies over in a blur of red hair, enveloping me in a hug that smells like lavender. "Oh my goodness, you worried me to death." Mom's cheek feels smooth against my own.

Then Daddy is there, wrapping the both of us in a bear hug. "Remind me to put GPS chips in your shoes." His teasing doesn't hide his worried expression.

"Are you ready to eat?" Mom grabs my hand and leads me over to our sitting area. Brocade armchairs cluster together around a mahogany table laden with delicacies. The tea tray is three layers high with sweets.

Daddy pulls my chair out for me, and I take a seat. I place the linen napkin on my lap and cross my ankles, ready to enjoy the company of the two people I love most in the world. The waitress steps forward in a ruffled apron. She lifts a silver pot and pours me a steaming cup of tea.

"Do you remember how to strain the leaves?" Mom asks.

"Of course. How could I forget?"

Mom and Daddy exchange a glance, and then Daddy reaches out and squeezes Mom's hand. "Sometimes when patients wake up from narcosis," he says, "they have initial troubles readjusting to the waking world. We call it Post-Narcosis Stress Syndrome."

"But you've never had problems before," Mom interjects. "You're a pro."

I slather butter on a crumpet. "Of course I am. This is, what, like the third time I've done narcosis?"

Daddy smiles, but only with the bottom half of his face.

"You've been a regular patient," Mom explains. "Your mind is like a diamond, and it's polished to perfection."

With great care, I lift the tea leaves out of my cup and lay them aside. The fragrant taste of jasmine tingles my tongue.

Mom offers me a pink meringue. "Senior year will be a cinch for you. You'll barely have to study at all."

Numbers and functions flash through my head. "Calculus will be so much fun." I take a delicate bite of cookie.

"Exactly." Mom beams at me and then gives Daddy a pointed look.

"Ellie… About what just happened." Daddy twists his napkin.

I brush tiny crumbs off my mouth. "What do you mean? My narcosis?"

Daddy shakes his head. "No, I mean about when you got lost."

A bite of cucumber sandwich wedges in my throat. I take a deep sip of tea to push it down. "That was an accident. I got disoriented coming back from the bathroom."

"This *is* an enormous hotel," Mom adds.

"I know it." Daddy frowns. "But you need to be careful. Your brain needs time to rest after so much treatment. I'm not sure you should start classes next Monday. Maybe you should wait a few weeks until you've achieved more stability."

"Not go back to school with my friends?" I swallow hard.

"Warren." Mom's tone chides. "We've been over this. Ellie will be perfectly fine."

"That's what we said before she disappeared for forty-five minutes!"

Guilt scares me as I think about that crazy letter. "I'm sorry I got lost. I'll be more careful in the future."

Daddy reaches out and holds my hand. "It's not your fault, angel."

But he's wrong. I might be too cowardly to admit my guilt, but at least I can share other things in my heart. "I am so lucky to have you." Tears well up in my eyes. "I love you so much." I could say it a hundred times a day, and it still wouldn't be enough.

"Oh, darling." Mom reaches out for my other hand. "We love you too." She and Daddy exchange a glance again. This time, a look of relish.

At the table next to us, a middle-aged woman snaps a picture of the tea tray.

"I guess this meal is Instagram-worthy," says Daddy.

I harrumph. "Instagram is such a waste of time."

"That's what I've always thought too," says Mom, tapping her temple.

An hour later the three of us are standing on the front steps of the Duchess Hotel, waiting for the valet to bring the car around. "We have a surprise for you," Mom says.

"Maybe we should hold off on that right now. Save it for later." Daddy fiddles with his sunglasses.

"Don't be silly, Warren. We've waited all summer."

"Waited for what?" I ask.

"For you to wake up, darling." Mom reaches into her purse and pulls out a key ring. "So we could give you this."

"*Belinda!*" Daddy's tone is sharp, but Mom ignores it.

"It's only a few blocks. We'll be right there with her." Mom places the key in my hand at as the valet pulls up to the curb. "It's a Jaguar XK!"

When I see the convertible, my jaw drops. "Is this your new car?"

"No, darling. It's yours!" Mom links her arm in mine, and we skip down the steps. She traces her fingers across the forest green paint job. "It matches your eyes, don't you think?"

I'm too stunned to answer. Then I squeal so loud, I startle a gaggle of tourists a few feet over. The valet holds the door open, and I swoop into the driver's seat.

"Ellie!" Daddy shouts. "Belinda! I don't think this is wise." But Mom's already buckled up too. Daddy has to hop over the side to land in the backseat. "Do you remember the way home?"

"Don't be ridiculous." I adjust the rearview mirror. "Of course I know the way home. It's only a few blocks." But then I accidentally turn on the windshield wipers when I attempt to unhitch the parking brake. "Oops! Sorry." I flick them off and try again.

"Belinda…"

"Oh, stuff it, Warren." Mom ties an ivory scarf around her head and slides on her Chanel sunglasses. "Ellie's an expert driver. Aren't you, dear?"

I place my hands at ten o'clock and two o'clock. "I'm a defensive driver, and that's what counts." I glide the Jag out into traffic like it's an extension of myself. "Do we have to go home? Can't we drive to Edmonds and back? I want to take this baby out on the freeway."

"Well—" Mom doesn't get the chance to finish because Daddy interrupts her.

"No can do! We are driving straight home, young lady."

I pull to stop at a red light, right next to the Pacific Science Center. Dozens of totem poles stare down at me. I look up at an eagle that appears especially grim. "Okay, okay," I acquiesce. "Home it is. But next weekend we'll drive all the way to Portland."

"Next weekend we'll be busy," Daddy says.

"With what?" I glance at the walnut dash. This interior is gorgeous.

"We have a patient to release next Saturday," Mom says matter-of-factly.

"And both of you need to be there?" I whistle. "Must be somebody famous. Did you finally snag Beyoncé?"

"Ellie," Daddy reproaches. "You know better than to ask. Clients who come to the Narcosis Clinic deserve privacy."

"Sorry, Daddy."

When we arrive home a few minutes later, it's hard prying me away from the Jag, but it's worth it to retreat to the familiar comfort of my own room. I stare into a sea of Sam Anders posters. I love how perfectly shaped his head is under his buzz cut. If only I could run my hands across the stubble and feel our lips brush… chastely, of course.

"See?" Daddy pokes his head into my room, interrupting my daydream. "Nothing out of place. Your mom wanted to install new curtains, but I wouldn't let her."

Mom scowls at the windows. "They're frayed around the edges. I think it would have been fine."

Daddy crosses his arms. "You can replace them in a month or two. Environmental stability is important for Ellie after narcosis."

I walk over to the far walls and stare into Sam's paper eyes. "I have to admit, it *is* nice having my room exactly how I remembered it." I turn around and look at my father. An impulse makes me run into his arms like I was a little girl again. I kiss him on the cheek and then bury my head in his shoulders. "I love you, Daddy."

"Love you too, angel." Daddy gives me one last squeeze. "I need to check on the clinic. Belinda? Will you join me for rounds?"

"Of course. But I need some mother-daughter time first."

Daddy smiles and the skin around his eyes crinkles. He's volunteered for an eyelift before, but Mom vetoed it. She thinks the lines make him look sexy.

Yuck! Why do I know that?

As soon as Daddy leaves, Mom pulls me to the vanity and sits me down on the tufted cushion. "Are you ready for full disclosure?" She points to my reflection in the mirror.

My stomach flutters. "Sure. What's new about me this time?"

"Not a lot—with a couple of noticeable exceptions." Mom rolls my desk chair over so she can sit down next to me. Side by side, we look more like twins than mother and daughter. Mom spirals her fingers through a strand of my auburn hair. "I gave you a hair follicle regeneration treatment to add extra fullness."

"You mean I didn't always have Merida's hair from *Brave*?"

Mom rests her hands on my shoulders. "You did, but it wasn't so fluffy."

I grin like a Pixar princess. "Yeah, well, now I could sell shampoo."

Mom laughs. "That's a good fallback if your plans to become a surgeon don't work out."

I see the Sam Anders posters reflected in the mirror. My head starts to pound.

"And Daddy did a mitochondrial seaweed peel on your arms to minimize freckles while I switched you over to the vocabulary tapes in your psychic-driving."

I rub my temples. "I hope you didn't make me sound like a nerd."

Mom gives me a playful punch on the arm. "You've always been highly intelligent. The psychic-driving sessions are simply an added boost."

"Oh." I squint my eye, and the twinge of a headache disappears.

"Brains, beauty, and body; you're the perfect package." Mom irons imaginary wrinkles off my shoulders. "Your high school experience will be a thousand times better than mine." She pauses long enough that I stop admiring myself in the mirror to look at her. Tears glisten at the corners of her eyes. "They used to call me Crater Face. Did you know that?"

"That's horrible." I've never heard Mom talk about high school before.

"Nobody thought I was pretty enough or smart enough to amount to anything. I used to hide in the back of the classroom reading novels to tune out the world. I never went to dances or had friends to sit with at lunch. The teachers thought I was stupid and not capable of anything beyond their mediocrity, just because I was the daughter of a farm hand." Mom swipes a tissue off my dresser and wipes her eyes. She sniffs hard. "But that was a long time ago."

"You showed them, huh?" I twist on the bench to wrap my arms around Mom's slim frame and hug her tight, wanting more than anything to make Mom forget those awful people.

"Yes, well. It's not good to dwell on the past."

"Especially when the present is so wonderful." I rest my head on Mom's soft shoulder and breathe in the scent of lavender.

"Darling, what's wrong?" Mom asks when she notices my tears falling.

"You're the best mother any girl could ask for."

"Oh, darling." Mom hugs me again. Then she reaches into her pocket and pulls out four slips of paper. "I almost forgot. Here's one more present."

"Tickets to the Sam Anders concert next May!" I bounce up and down in my seat. "Oh my gosh!"

"You, Daddy, me, and Olivia."

I spring from my chair. "I can't wait to tell her. She'll be so excited. Olivia *loves* Sam Anders."

"She does?" Mom raises an eyebrow. "For some reason, I thought Olivia liked Dean Mathews." Mom's eyes are glued to mine.

"Dean Mathews?" I wince as pain shoots through my forehead. "Yeah, maybe. But Sam Anders is her favorite."

Mom smiles. "Thank goodness for that. Sam is in a different league, don't you think?"

"Totally." I clutch the tickets to my heart and sing "Something 'Bout Your Love, Lady," only I change the word "lady" to "Mommy," and my mother sings along too.

CHAPTER NINETEEN: ELLIE

4:10 P.M. | SEPTEMBER 1ST

"Ellie, stop napping and look at me." The girl stands before me with little boobs and a purple sundress. Her auburn hair is wet and shiny. A puddle forms on the carpet around her feet—she's soaking wet.

"What the heck?" I clutch the covers with one hand and reach for my phone with the other. That's when I notice the girl tucking my phone into her meager cleavage. A faint scar cuts across the top of her breastbone, and the top of her left shoulder is bandaged. Other than that, she could be my clone.

The girl takes a step closer to my bed. "You know who I am," she says with certainty.

Chills run down my spine. *Am I hallucinating*? I sink deep into my pillow and pull the blankets over my face. I try to remember what day it is, but I can't. "Go away," I mumble.

"I'm not going anywhere until you listen." She sits down next to me and the mattress sags.

"Please go." I hide under the covers like a little girl. When I don't move a muscle, my uninvited guest yanks the blanket down and slaps me across the face.

"Ouch!" I run my hand over my cheek and sit up. "Okay, I'm awake already."

"No, you're not," the redhead says. "You're asleep. As soon as Mom left, you laid down for a nap." She sighs. "I'm you."

"You mean like my subconscious? Freud or something?"

The girl shivers, her soggy dress plastered against her skin. "Not like Freud. Like you, Ellie. I'm *you*. I'm the Ellie who wrote the letter before Mom and Dad put us through narcosis."

"Whatever," I mumble. "Go away and stop bothering me." I roll over and prepare to drift off. The whole room feels heavy, like I'm weighed down by a blanket of sleep.

Ellie-Me grabs a pillow and whacks me across the head. "I'm not leaving until you listen!"

This is the weirdest dream ever. I scrunch up my eyes and glare at my ghost. "I already read your stupid letter."

Ellie-Me bolts from the bed. "It's not stupid!" She marches to the wall and rips down a Sam Anders poster.

"Hey! What are you doing?" I bolt upright. "Cut that out!" I throw my pillow at Ellie-Me but miss.

"Don't you understand what they did?" Ellie-Me's on a poster-shredding rampage. "These aren't supposed to be here. You only had one poster in your room last June, and it was of Dean Mathews."

"Weird." I shrug. I don't care what this copy of me says.

Ellie-Me points at my chest. I look down too—and realize I'm topless. *Where did my sweater go?* Ellie-Me jabs her finger right against my breastbone. "This skin is all new. What happened to your scar?"

"What scar? I don't know about any scar."

"You're darn right you don't know. Mom and Dad are messing with you. Don't you get it?"

"No!" I cross my arms over my naked torso. "*You* don't get it. Mom and Daddy wouldn't trick me like that."

"Daddy? You haven't called him *Daddy* in years."

"That's not true!" I scramble to wrap myself in the quilt and climb out of bed.

Ellie-Me shakes her head so hard that drops of water fly off her like a wet dog. "It *is* true! I don't understand what they're up to, but you've got to find out."

"No! You *don't* understand what they're up to. Mom and Daddy love me more than anything. I'm the luckiest girl in the world." I slam open the top drawer of my dresser and yank out a T-shirt. "Why are you even here?"

Ellie-Me sits down on my window seat, destroying the wood finish with her wet dress. "I don't know. Am I really here or are you only imagining me?" She trembles, and drops of water roll down her arm.

The way her shoulders slump elicits a little bit of sympathy in me. I pull out another hoodie and wrap the sweatshirt around her shoulders.

"Thanks." Ellie-Me zips it up, and the jersey changes color, soaking up water right before my eyes.

I sit down next to her, careful not to make contact. "Why are you dressed like this?"

Ellie-Me swipes a clump of hair behind her ear. "Because I went swimming. Don't you remember my letter?"

"Kind of."

Ellie-Me's face crumples. "You've got to remember. I'm your only hope."

I look down at my hands. "That's not true. You're probably a figment of my imagination. As soon as I wake up, you'll be gone. But Mom and Daddy will be with me forever. They're the best parents a girl could ask for."

Ellie-Me rolls her eyes. "*The best parents a girl could ask for.* Would you listen to yourself? You sound like a recording. How do you know they didn't psychic-drive that sentiment right into your head?"

"Mom and Daddy wouldn't do that!" I leap to my feet. "Maybe you should leave."

"I'm not leaving. Not until you listen to the truth. You can't believe a word they say. You can't even trust your own memory!" Ellie-Me reaches into her pocket and pulls out my phone. "Look up your Instagram account. Find the selfie you took at the Vice Regal Suite in June."

"Give me back my phone! What if it gets wet?"

"I'll give it back if you promise." Ellie-Me tugs up her strapless dress. "Look for that picture."

"I don't even have an Instagram account." I watch the phone vibrate in Ellie-Me's palm. "Social media's stupid."

"That's not true!" Ellie-Me declares.

The phone's ringtone gets louder and louder. "Girl, You Make Me Wanna Melt" floods the room with sound. I slap my hands against my ears to protect my brain. "I hate that song!"

The phone is deafening now. It reverberates inside my brain and rattles every bone. There's no possible way to ignore it.

"Girl, you make me wanna melt," Dean Mathews sings, louder and louder. If I hear him one more time, my skull will explode.

I jolt back to reality seconds before gray matter splashes across my room.

I'm awake.

And Ellie-Me is gone.

"Ellie? Are you there?" Olivia's voice on the phone sounds hazy in my sleep-addled brain.

I stifle a yawn. "Yeah, I'm here. I was taking a nap." *Where am I again?* Hazy twilight bathes my room. Sam Anders graces my walls from every vantage point. *Whoa. That was one crazy dream.*

"Oops. My bad. Your mom told me you had jetlag. I should have let you keep sleeping."

"No, I'm glad you woke me up." I glance over to my nightstand and see the clock. "Wow, I had no idea it was seven; I must have napped through dinner."

"I missed you so much this summer. I couldn't wait any longer to catch up."

The phone feels awkward in my hand. Mom and Daddy are right about cellphones being intrusive. I wish I could see Olivia in person and have a real conversation instead of relying on all this modern technology crap. "I've missed you too. How was the kayaking trip with your folks?"

"Fabulous. Mom got two whole weeks off from Microsoft as a reward for her last patent. We took the ferry to Orcas Island and paddled around from there."

"Cool." I struggle to remember what to say. It seems like I was supposed to remember something about my phone. It's right there on the tip of my tongue.

"So…" Olivia begins.

"Yeah…" *Who am I talking to again?* I shake my head and attempt to focus. *Olivia. My best friend.* The details are fuzzy.

"Jetlag must have really done a number on you. You don't sound like yourself."

"Sorry."

"Maybe we should stick to easy topics like clothes and stuff," says Olivia.

"Sounds thrilling."

Olivia giggles. "At least you still have your sarcasm."

"I'm sarcastic?" I grin, but Olivia can't see that over the phone. I climb out of bed and walk over to the window. I run my palm across the window seat and find it bone dry. Sitting, I stare down at the courtyard. *How long have I been awake? What did I do today?* I can't remember.

"Okay," says Olivia. "I'm going to be really careful what I say because I don't want you to turn psycho on me."

Turn psycho? I do that? "Thanks. I guess."

"I'm such a good friend," Olivia says, rushing on, "that if I had good news to share, I would tell you right away. I wouldn't, you know, keep it a secret and then make you find out on Twitter." There's a jagged edge to Olivia's tone that pricks my attention.

"What are you talking about?"

"Nothing." Olivia's end of the conversation sulks into silence.

Why is she so annoyed? What haven't I told her? Oh, right. The tickets! "Guess what?" I say. "I'm dying to tell you."

"What is it?"

I scamper to my nightstand and retrieve the concert tickets so I can admire them again. "You and I are going to the Sam Anders show in May. My parents bought us front-row seats!"

Olivia gasps. "No. Freaking. Way."

"I know, right?" I flop down on my bed and gaze at the ceiling.

"That's awesome. But what about…"

"What?"

"I wasn't going to talk about it."

"You can tell me. We're friends, right?" I stare at all of my Sam posters with adoration.

"Of course we're friends," Olivia says. "But I don't want to start an argument, especially since you just came home."

"Okay, now you're infuriating. Spit it out already."

"Dean," Olivia whispers. "What about Dean? Why didn't you tell me you knew him? Why didn't you bring me to that party too?"

Now I'm really confused. "Sam's musical arch nemesis? What are you talking about?"

"Duh, that party you two went to at Marley's house. The one that's all over the Internet. It looked like a lot of fun—I mean, until the accident. If I had been in your shoes, I would have, I don't know, called my best friend so she could come too. And how did you meet Dean Mathews?"

"Are you on drugs?"

"Of course not!" Olivia's anger transforms into worry. "Are you having one of your spacey moments again? Ellie, I really think you need to see someone about this."

My forehead clenches. A half-forgotten melody sounds in my ears.

"But I don't want to start an argument," Olivia continues.

"What?" I can't understand a word Olivia says. Memories prick through my brain like a chisel. *Cole. Marley. Liam. The lacrosse team. Karaoke singing at the party.* I jump up from my bed and pace the room. My head feels like a bomb went off. Shards of granite slice through my cerebral cortex. I rub my temples and try to make the pain go away.

"Ellie?" Olivia asks. "Are you still there?"

"Gotta go." I can barely get the words out because my head hurts so much. "Call you tomorrow."

The phone slips out of my grasp and falls to the floor. Images swirl around me. Colors, light, water, and darkness. Glowing red eyes and swirling goo. A giant orca leaps out of the water. A girl in a nightdress pulls a metal IV pole. The burning hot flash of fire. "Mom," I whisper. "Daddy." But I'm not sure the words leave my lips or if they simply float across my intention.

My brain shatters into a million pieces, smashed to bits, totally destroyed.

Or maybe that's me, lying on the floor.

In oblivion.

"Ellie? Ellie, angel? Can you hear me?" The pain still slams my brain like a hatchet, but Daddy's voice somehow slips through. "I don't like this, Belinda. I don't like this at all. Why won't she wake up?"

Somebody pulls open my eyelid, and I stare up at the plaster of my bedroom ceiling. "Bring me the flashlight." Mom's voice is clinical; she's in full-on surgeon mode. A flash of light assaults my vision. "Her pupils won't dilate. Let's get her to the narcosis room and hooked up to the monitors."

Somebody—Daddy?—lifts me with strong arms. My head flops back like a rag doll. *Wake up!* I issue myself instructions, but I can't follow through. I'm trapped between wakefulness and dreaming, that awful limbo where you want to snap out of it but can't. *"Girl, you make me wanna melt"* sings in the distance—Olivia calling me back on the phone.

My body sways as Daddy carries me to my closet. My ankle brushes against the wall and I feel my bedroom slipper fall off. I hear Mom moving stuff around on the floor.

"Open the trap door already," says Daddy. "I told you, Belinda. We shouldn't have risked it. No patient has survived this much narcosis without succumbing to Post-Narcosis Stress Syndrome."

"You think I don't know that, Warren? We didn't have a choice. Ellie was starting to remember. This is probably the migraine response to that Dean Mathews song."

"Why didn't I think to change Ellie's ring tones?" Dad carries me down a stairway into a dark tunnel.

"I wish there had been another way to extract those problematic memories," says Mom. "I'm just glad Ellie did narcosis willingly after your 'we'll support you no matter what you decide' crap. Watch her head!" Mom's hands cradle my neck, the aroma of lavender overwhelming my senses.

"There is *always* a choice!" Daddy adjusts my weight from one arm to another.

"She's going to be fine. Ellie's dehydrated, that's all." Mom removes my other slipper. "We'll bag her on the IV, give her fluids, and she'll wake up in the morning good as new. Better than new."

"That's the problem." Daddy's voice growls. "She doesn't need to be better. Enough is enough."

My head explodes in a fresh wave of pain, and there's no escape. I wish I really was unconscious like my parents assume so I could escape this agony.

I need to pay attention. That thought is a beacon of light in a torrent of pain. *I need to figure something out.*

But my eyes won't work and neither will my head. Mom and Daddy continue talking, but I can't decipher any words. The hammer of pain beats me senseless.

I rouse a smidge when Daddy lays me down, and Mom squirts goo across my arms. Tubes and sensors connect to my every ligament. *No!* I manage to think. *No more narcosis!*

But nobody hears my silent scream.

CHAPTER TWENTY: DEAN

The studio lights make my makeup melt and the arm chair I sit in smells like hairspray. Maxine hovers around me to do touch-ups with face powder. "It's fine." I pull away when she holds out the compact.

"It's not fine. You're all shiny." Maxine threatens to attack me with a powder puff.

"I don't want to look phony."

"Do I ever make you look phony?"

She has me there. "No, but I don't need makeup anymore. My skin is perfect."

"Perfect skin has natural oils that reflect back to camera lenses." Maxine leans in close and blots my cheeks with pressed powder before I can protest. "There," she says. "Now you're perfect."

"That's for sure!" A dark-skinned woman approaches us. She wears razor-sharp heels and a dress so short it looks like she has legs for days. "Taisha Fletcher. Nice to meet you." The *Hollywood Central* anchor holds out her hand to shake. "I've been dying to interview you ever since you toured with the Heart-acres."

"Touring has kept me busy, but I'm glad to meet you too finally." I pop out of my chair and shake her hand. Wikipedia told me that Taisha is old enough to be my mother. But Pilates, plastic surgery, and her low-cut dress make age seem irrelevant.

I don't know if the lady has kids, but she is definitely MILF material.

Taisha hangs on to my hand and pulls me in close enough that her husky voice can whisper in my ear. "How was your summer?"

I scooch back. "Fine. Bermuda was awesome. Have you been following my Instagram feed?"

"Your beach pictures were gorgeous." She flashes a toothy white grin. "The only way they could have been better is if I were there in my bikini."

"Or without your bikini."

"Oh, you naughty boy!" Taisha sits in her chair and crosses her legs. A golden ankle bracelet twinkles in the light. "I'm at least… ten years older than you." She looks across to the where the director is talking to Gary. "I'm ready when you are."

A hush falls across the set as the cameraman takes position and the director issues instructions. Gary gives me a thumbs up. "And we're live," the director calls.

"Welcome back to *Hollywood Central*. I'm your host, Taisha Fletcher. Tonight I have the great honor of interviewing the elusive Dean Mathews, whose talent, ability, and personal life have been capturing fans' attention for years. Dean, let's start off with the question people across the world have been dying to know: Why have you been so reluctant to give interviews in the past?"

Beads of sweat pool at the back of my neck. Hopefully, Maxine's last minute efforts with the face powder worked and I don't look like a human oil slick. "I haven't always skipped interviews," I say, "but, yeah, it's true that I've been avoiding the spotlight."

Taisha gives me an appraising look. "'Avoiding the spotlight'? That's a funny thing for someone to say who's been selling out stadiums across four continents."

"Music is one thing," I say defensively. "I'm paid to perform. But my private life is a different matter."

"Especially when your private life is full of heartache."

"Well, and seeing it plastered all over the tabloids just makes things worse."

"You're referring, of course, to your former girlfriend Pansy Williams and her new marriage to your Heartacres bandmate, Sam Anders?"

I nod. Hearing it spelled out right in front of me on national television hurts more than I expected. I should have had Dr. Savage slip in a cure for heartache in addition to my lisp fix.

"Is it true that their relationship caught you by surprise?"

"Totally. I had no idea any of that was going on until one day I boarded our tour bus before a concert and—" I stop myself from blabbing further. Just because I can finally talk doesn't mean I need to run my mouth about things that are nobody's business. "You get the idea. That was a rough day."

Taisha feigns an air of concern. "Which hurt more, losing your girlfriend or being betrayed by your best friend?"

"Honestly? I don't know because they both betrayed me. I lost two friends that night."

"How do you feel about their relationship now?"

"Fine, I guess. So long as Sam treats Pansy with respect, it's really none of my business."

"And you're young, single, and free, right?" Taisha's face brightens. "Tell me about this mystery girl you were spotted with in June that the Internet went wild over." Behind Taisha, a screen shows a picture of me kissing a girl in cowboy boots. She has sandy-blond hair and a pert little nose. The picture shows us doing full-on tongue hockey.

"A gentleman never kisses and tells." From the corner of my eye I see Gary smile, pleased that I am sticking to the script.

"It's been reported that this picture was taken the same night as the accident in Seattle where a deck you were standing on collapsed, and over thirty partygoers fell into a backyard pool." The screen displays a series of images—splintered timber, wounded teenagers, police and paramedics on the scene.

"I don't remember any of it."

"Any of it?" Taisha uncrosses her legs.

I shake my head. "I must have blacked it out. With good reason too, because that looks traumatic."

"It certainly does. Reports show that eight people were injured and over $50,000 worth of property damage occurred."

"Wow. That's awful."

When Taisha realizes I'm not giving up anymore, she changes topics. "Let's move on to happier topics. Before this interview started you and I were chatting about your summer vacation in Bermuda." My Instagram feed bursts into view, and photo after photo of beaches and palm trees taunt me with a holiday that never was. Hopefully whatever intern Gary sent on vacation in my place had a really good time.

"The pictures speak for themselves. I wish everyone had a chance to go there." Like me, for example.

"But it wasn't all sunbathing and relaxation, was it? Yesterday, you released a brand new song that's already topping the charts as the number one downloaded new single this year."

"Yeah. It just kind of came to me. We did one session in the studio, and it was good to go."

Taisha leans forward a smidge, away from the cameras and toward me so that I'm the only one who gets the view down the front of her dress. She's wearing a red lace bra. "Would you play your new single for us tonight on *Hollywood Central*?"

"I thought you would never ask." On cue, the spotlight rolls over to a grand piano waiting in the wings.

"Hollywood lovers," Taisha says in a delighted voice, "may I introduce you to Dean Mathews performing his new hit single 'Dream Girl' for the very first time on television."

As soon as I see the piano, relaxation takes over. My hands hover over the keys for a quick second, and then I began to play. *"Dream girl, you're brave. Dream girl, you're kind and you're a quick thinker. You're the first girl I've really talked to in I don't know how long. I've bared my soul to you. I feel like I can talk to you.*"

When the song is over, I look out across the studio and see Gary and Maxine beaming at me.

I am Dean Mathews. And I am back.

CHAPTER TWENTY-ONE: ELLIE

8:55 P.M. | SEPTEMBER 13TH

"**T**hey did it to you again, the bastards." Dripping wet, she leans over my bed. Her purple dress sticks to her skin, revealing an exoskeleton of corset. "I thought I could trust Mom and Dad to do what was best for me, but I was wrong. I see that now."

Where am I again? What happened?

"Listen to me carefully," the girl says. "You're on the fifth floor of the Narcosis Clinic. Mom and Dad have you so doped up on pain prescriptions, they're scrambling your brain. Which is pretty remarkable, considering you were already cracked." She sits on the edge of my mattress.

I feel moisture seep into my clothing. First my hips and then my thighs. Everything becomes soaked.

"Could you move?" My teeth chatter. "You're making me damp."

The girl shakes her head. "I'm not the one wetting the bed. You are." She points down to the covers. "The catheter isn't hooked up right."

A chirping sound starts and a door swings open. A woman in a white outfit rushes in and looks at the monitor. "Oh, dear," she mutters. Her dark black hair is coiled into a bun at the nape of her neck. "They really went too far this time."

"Who are you?" I ask the lady. She pulls up the quilt to examine my mess.

"That's Ursula, but she can't hear you," says the girl in the purple dress. "You're asleep."

I shiver. "Then why can you understand me?"

"Because I'm your subconscious and while you're in a coma, we're kind of sharing the same brain space, so I can hear your thoughts."

There's something familiar about her eyes.

"They should be familiar," she says, as if she heard my unspoken question. "My name is Ellie."

"Ellie?"

"Yes. And your name is Ellie too."

Her words make no sense. "How can we both have the same name?"

"Because we're both the same person."

I look down at my chest. I don't recognize myself.

"Your brain is trying to protect itself. That's why it made me. It can't handle any more narcosis and wants you to survive." Ellie-Me leans over and places a cool hand on my forehead. "You might not want to see what Ursula is doing."

"Why?" I feel my insides quiver.

Ellie-Me doesn't flinch. "That was the catheter. From now on you'll pee into a bag." Her eyes brim with unshed tears.

"Forever?"

Ellie-Me looks away. "I still think you can recover from this."

"How long have I been sleeping?" Then a faint thought occurs to me. "Am I under narcosis?"

Ellie-Me twists her wet hair into a knot and then yanks her hand away. "I think it's been a week. I'm not sure. But this isn't narcosis; you're only asleep. Dad wouldn't let Mom turn on the psychic-driving tapes again."

Next to the bed the nurse hums. I watch as she holds up a bag marked *urine*. My stomach feels queasy. *That's odd. I can't picture the last time I ate or drank.*

"Tea and sandwiches." Ellie-Me kneels down so that we're face-to-face. "At the Duchess Hotel. Remember?"

I strain to visualize the sandwiches. I try to taste the tea. But all I can grasp are wispy images like steam. For the first time, I feel afraid. Very afraid.

"You should be afraid," Ellie-Me says. "You should be terrified." She points to the cables and tubes that hook me up to computers. A monitor flashes hundreds of lights. "That box keeps you alive. Your brain can't operate its own body functions anymore." Ellie-Me glances away. "I mean, at the moment."

"Will I get better?"

Ellie-Me doesn't answer. The nurse who was attending me shuffles out of the room and closes the door with a soft *click*.

"I want to wake up." My words slur. I reach for Ellie-Me's arm but can't move a muscle. "Please help me."

Ellie-Me looks down at her wet feet. "I tried to help you before. I wrote the whole story down, and you threw it away."

"Yeah, I threw it away, and I'm sorry about that. But I did read it. Every last word."

"Tell me about Cole, then. Do you remember kissing him?"

Juicy Fruit, warm lips, strong arms around my back. And then pain—mind-numbing pain. "I don't want to think about Cole." My face contorts. "It hurts too much."

"Because they did this to you, and you ran back to them! Why didn't you stay in the Vice Regal Suite and be safe?" Ellie-Me pounds her fists on the mattress.

"Because that would have been crazy."

Ellie-Me spreads out her arms, encompassing to the whole room. "And this isn't nuts?"

I squeeze my eyes shut tight. "If you're going to yell at me, then go away and let me wake up on my own."

"Good luck with that," Ellie-Me mutters.

I tune her out. The sooner I can drift back to sleep, the sooner I can awaken from this nightmare.

CHAPTER TWENTY-TWO: COLE

11:30 A.M. | SEPTEMBER 14TH

It's just as I suspected. Instead of eating lunch with her friends, Marley is in the school library watching that segment from *Hollywood Central* again. Since Mom and Dad stripped us of our phones and changed the Wi-Fi password as punishment for that party, the school computers are our only ways to access technology. We also had to spend all summer aboard *The Royal Racer* working off the $6,000 insurance deductible for replacing the deck.

"How many times have you seen that now?" I pull up a chair next to her, and it scrapes on the carpet. When Marley doesn't flinch, I realize she's wearing earbuds. I tap her on the shoulder, and she jumps.

"Hey!" Marley pulls the white cords out of her ears. "You startled me."

"Sorry." I point to the screen. "Don't you have that memorized by now?"

Marley sighs and rests her chin in her hand. "Do you think there's any chance that song is about me?"

"Maybe. The only thing I know for sure is that I agree with Dean about women deserving to be treated with respect."

My sister shrinks in her chair. "Of course they do."

"So how come you let Liam treat you like crap for so long? You never listened to me when I said Liam was no good for you, but *poof,* Dean Mathews comes along for one night, and you're finally ready to dump your douchebag."

"You're just grouchy that Ellie's not back."

"Don't change the subject. You did the right thing breaking up with Liam, no matter what prompted you to do it. But now you need to own it. Stop hiding out in the library during lunchtime and go down the cafeteria. Dean's not here to help you face that loser, but I am."

Marley glowers. "You make it sound simple, but it's not."

"It *is* simple. Pretend like Liam doesn't exist. He's not worth your concern."

"I'm not worried about him. But this is my only chance to find out about Dean."

I roll my eyes. "Stalker alert."

"Cyberstalking is different. Besides, like you should talk. How many times have you looked at Ellie's Instagram account today?"

I pull out a stick of Juicy Fruit. "She deleted it."

"Weird." Marley flicks the mouse, and another picture of Dean pulls up. "He's going to San Francisco next."

"Forget about him. Dean's probably one of those musicians who has a different girl in every city."

"Probably." Marley gazes at the screen with sad puppy eyes before turning toward me. "No news on Ellie at all?"

Now I'm the one who slouches. "Nothing. Nada. Zilch."

"And she missed the first two weeks of school. I would have thought French Camp would be over by now."

"Are you guys talking about Ellie?"

We both turn to see Olivia Chen craning her neck toward us from her table a few feet away.

"We can talk about her if we want," Marley says.

Olivia sneers at her. Marley and Olivia haven't gotten along since Olivia replaced Marley as Ellie's best friend in the ninth grade. "It's not okay to talk about a person when they aren't there to defend themselves," Olivia snaps.

Marley slams the laptop shut. "We're not saying anything bad about Ellie. We were only wondering where she was."

"It's odd," I add. "The last time Ellie missed this much school, she didn't come back for two years."

Olivia bites her lower lip. She scans to the left and right to see if anyone in the library is listening. Then she pulls up a chair and sits down uninvited. "Do you think Ellie might not come back?"

Marley yanks her hair back into a messy bun. "It wouldn't surprise me. Leaving friends in the lurch is kind of Ellie's M.O."

"She wouldn't do that to me," Olivia argues. "We've been best friends for three years."

"Oh yeah? Well, Ellie was my best friend since preschool, but that didn't stop her from taking off in seventh grade and basically never talking to me again."

"You and Ellie were never friends," Olivia says.

"Um, yeah, we were." Marley looks indignant.

"No, you weren't. Ellie would have told me if you two had a history."

Marley's face becomes splotchy in a pattern I recognize. "Look," I interject before my sister explodes, "I don't know why Ellie didn't say anything to you, but my sister's telling the truth. Ellie and Marley were best friends for years."

"That's bizarre." Olivia furrows her eyebrows. "Look, I don't know why Ellie didn't share that with me, or what went on between her and Marley, but she must have had her reasons for finding a new best friend."

"There was no reason!" Marley shouts. The librarian gives us a stern look from her desk. "Sorry!" My sister waves at her. Leaning closer to Olivia, she whispers harshly. "One minute Ellie and I were inseparable. The next minute it was like she had forgotten everything about me and our friendship."

"She forgot about kissing me too," I blurt out. I feel color hit my cheeks as the two girls gape at me, and then a gigantic slap of epiphany turns into me face palming my forehead. "Oh."

"What?" the girls ask in unison.

"What if Ellie really did forget you, Marley?" The possibility makes some of the Ellie puzzle pieces fall into place, as if I found the edge pieces. I don't know why I've never considered it before. "She forgot she knew how to swim."

"Ellie doesn't know how to swim," says Olivia.

"Then how do you explain that video of her rescuing Dean from my pool?" demands Marley.

"Adrenaline?"

I shake my head. "She definitely knows how to swim, but Ellie told me she didn't know how. She forgot everything she knew about the water. Just like she forgot about kissing me last summer." I lunge for Marley's mouse.

"Hey!" she protests.

"We've got to look it up." I'm already jiggling the screen to life.

"Look what up?" Olivia demands.

"Narcosis!" I click to open a search engine and type in "DOCTOR SAVAGE." "What if Ellie's been put under narcosis?"

"Don't be ridiculous." Marley shakes her head. "Narcosis treatments only last three months, not two years."

"Yeah," echoes Olivia.

The Narcosis Clinic web page glows to life. "Then how else do you explain Ellie's memory lapse or changes in personality?"

"Maturity," offers Marley.

"ADHD," says Olivia.

"What?" asks Marley. "Ellie does not have ADHD."

"How do you know?" Olivia asks. "You're hardly around her. I'm with her all the time, and let me tell you, sometimes she zones out."

"You're making her sound like a zombie," I say. "I thought you were her friend."

"I *am* her friend," Olivia insists. "I've been trying to get her help, but she refuses to acknowledge that anything is wrong."

"What if she doesn't know something is wrong?" I suggest.

"How could you not know you did narcosis?" Marley grabs the laptop back and clicks the mouse. "Look, it says it right here: 'Narcosis lasts for three months of treatment.' *Not* two years."

"Do you think narcosis could treat ADHD?" Olivia asks.

"Enough with the ADHD," Marley says vehemently. "The Ellie I know, or knew, never had an issue like that."

"But she did have issues," I admit.

"What issues?" Olivia scoots her chair closer.

Marley looks at me, and I look at her. We weren't raised to be snitches. "She got in trouble a lot," Marley finally admits. "Like suspensions and stuff."

Olivia's eyebrows arch. "But Ellie never gets in trouble."

I shake my head. "*Now* she doesn't, but when we were kids Ellie was always mouthing off to teachers and cracking jokes when she wasn't supposed to."

Marley laughs. "This one time in fourth grade Ellie started an underground school newspaper where 'anonymous' reporters shared what they really thought of every teacher."

"She was suspended for three days, and our PE teacher sued her for libel."

"The newspaper claimed he was smoking in his classroom during recess." Marley looks pointedly at Olivia. "Which he totally was."

"The lawsuit was thrown out because Ellie's parents hired powerful attorneys, but it was all anybody could talk about for the rest of the year." I remember how relieved my parents were when Marley promised she wasn't involved.

It was Olivia's turn to shake head, disbelief written in the lines of her scrunched forehead. "The Ellie I know would never do that. Ellie always follows the rules. If I weren't her best friend, I'd say she was a goody two-shoes."

Marley and I exchange another glance. "We've noticed that change in her too," my sister says. "I always figured that maybe the reason Ellie ditched me was that she wanted a fresh start, free from trouble.”

“You weren’t the one getting Ellie in trouble,” I say. “If anything, it was the other way around.”

Olivia takes a deep breath. “This whole conversation is wacko.”

“And troubling.” I point to the computer screen. “I think we should go to the clinic and ask Ellie’s parents what’s up.”

Marley shakes her head. “It’s none of my business what happens to Ellie.”

“What do you think?” I ask Olivia.

She taps her fingers on the edge of her chair. “I’ve only talked to Ellie once all summer, and when I did, she didn’t sound like herself.”

“In what way?” Marley asks.

“She invited me to a Sam Anders concert.”

Marley snarls. “No way would Ellie do that to Dean.”

“I know, right?” Olivia says. “And how did she meet Dean Mathews in the first place? When we were at the concert together, she gave no indication that she knew him.”

“She said they met in Paris. Her French Camp went to one of his concerts,” Marley explains.

“And she never mentioned that to me that whole two hours were we watching his concert?” Olivia commandeers the computer and types in a blur of motion. Marley and I look at each other in confusion. “A-ha!” Olivia says a moment later, turning the screen to us. “There’s no mention of Dean ever performing in Paris. The closest he got was Marseilles.” Olivia nods at me. “I’m in. I owe it to Ellie to investigate.”

Anxiety buzzes inside of me. “So do I.”

Together, Olivia and I stare at Marley.

“Oh, all right,” she huffs. “I’ll come too.”

CHAPTER TWENTY-THREE: ELLIE
2:55 P.M. | SEPTEMBER 15TH

Still not awake. My stomach is raw, but I feel no hunger, only the steady drip of medicine into my veins.

Usually when I drift into semi-consciousness, I'm alone in my room, but this time, Ursula is wiping my legs with a warm sponge. I flex my calf, but my leg doesn't move. My foot lays heavy in her hand, like a dead piece of meat. "Too far," Ursula mutters. "This must be the point of no return."

"Save me!" I scream, but she doesn't hear. Nobody hears.

Ursula pats my limbs with a warm towel and then deposits the bathing supplies into a plastic bin. After a quick entry of data into the monitors, she glides out of the room.

That's when Ellie-Me appears in her wet, purple dress. "This is criminal. There's no one to speak up on your behalf."

"I want to wake up." My words clunk around like rocks. "I want to be normal."

Ellie-Me perches on the bed next to me and holds my hand. "Of course you do." She places her second hand over the first and squeezes. "Now tell me what you remember."

"Pain," I manage to whisper. "I remember pain when I tried to remember."

Ellie-Me takes a deep breath, and the scar across her chest stretches tight. "Neat trick that is, making you hurt every time you remember the truth." She reaches out and pulls a strand of hair behind my ear. "A migraine-bomb shouldn't go off in your head every time you think of Dean."

"Dean? Who's that?" But something stirs inside me as soon as I say the name.

"Dean Mathews." Ellie-Me holds out her phone and shows me a picture. I see myself in the front seat of a van. Dean's next to me holding a gigantic bouquet of roses. "Remember him?"

I shake my head.

"What about your best friend, Olivia?" Ellie-Me prompts. She pages through her phone and pulls up a picture of an Asian-American girl and me sitting on the grass. We're eating gourmet sandwiches.

"Is that the Woodland Park Zoo?"

Ellie-Me smiles. "It *is* the zoo. Look at that! You're making progress. Olivia and I took this picture right before Dean came on stage. I wrote all about it in my letter, which you foolishly threw in the wastebasket." She holds out her phone again, and I stare at the video. There I am in a fancy hotel suite scowling at a gigantic stack of stationery and chucking it in the trash.

"I don't know what to say. Sorry?"

Ellie-Me pockets her phone. "I'm done blaming you and I won't be mad anymore."

For some reason, that makes me happy.

"I *want* you to be happy." Ellie-Me tugs up her wet dress. "And guess what? While you were sleeping, I thought of another plan. You might have thrown that letter away, but I didn't." As if by magic, papers materialize on her lap. "I'm going to read it all to you again. Only this time, you're going to listen."

Ellie-Me stares deep into my eyes like she can control me.

And I let her.

"Are you ready? *This letter will separate fact from fiction. I'll tell you what you need to know so that narcosis doesn't make you forget your precious night-before memories. I want you to remember the good stuff.*"

Her peaceful tone hypnotizes me. It's so much easier to let her tell me what to do. I rest my head on the pillow and drift off again, focusing on the sound of Ellie-Me's voice.

CHAPTER TWENTY-FOUR: COLE

3:45 P.M. | SEPTEMBER 16TH

"It has to be you, Cole," Marley tells me from the driver's seat. I'm riding shotgun in the Jeep we share, and Olivia is in the backseat. We're illegally parked in the alley behind the Narcosis Clinic. "If I go in, Ellie's parents will recognize me. But it's been long enough that you might not be so noticeable."

"Maybe I should do it?" Olivia asks. "I've tried calling them a few times, and they never returned my calls. Their assistant, Ursula, keeps putting me off. If I show up in person, I could use the excuse that I've been trying to reach them."

Marley chews on her thumbnail. "It's worth considering, but I'm wondering if they would give you some sort of made-up story. Let's have Cole go in and scope the place out first."

"Like I'm a prospective patient," I suggest. "So what am I in for?"

"Annoying-brother-itis." Marley gives me a light punch on the shoulder.

"I'm pretty sure that's incurable." I look back at Olivia for ideas.

"Tell them you're a secret bed wetter, and you want to get help before college."

Marley erupts in laughter. "Good one, Olivia."

"Not going to happen. Give me something else to work with."

"How about coulrophobia?" Olivia offers. "That means the fear of clowns."

"Clowns *are* kind of creepy," I admit. "I mean, I'm not afraid of them or anything, but I wouldn't want to run into one in a dark alley."

"Yeah," Marley says, giggling, "they might make you a balloon animal, and that would be terrifying."

"Would you quit it?" I glare at my sister. "I need to have my game face on, and you're not helping."

Olivia sobers up, but Marley's still smirking. I look up at the backside of the Narcosis Clinic. It's a metal, glass, and concrete monstrosity. I'll never understand modern architecture. Give me a normal brick building any day.

I unclick my seatbelt. "It's now or never."

"Good luck!" Olivia calls from the back seat.

"Wait!" says Marley. "Pocket dial me from your phone so we can hear."

"Okay." I swipe open my phone and click on my sister's contact. Then I climb out of the car and slam the door shut.

I'm five steps away when I hear a creepy voice whisper, *"Clowns are everywhere!"*

"Shut up, Marley," I hiss toward my coat pocket. A tourist walking next to me jumps back like I'm a homeless person with mental health problems.

The steel handle of the clinic's front door burns cold in my palm. I swing it open harder than expected, and it bangs against the doorstop. The head nurse, a total hottie in a tight white nurse's uniform and black French twist, looks at me in disapproval.

"Sorry." I shove my hands into my pockets and glance around at the lobby before I step toward her desk. There's a sweet scent in the air that I can't identify. Maybe clean laundry? Ahead of me is a glass staircase leading up to the second floor. Next to me are hard-as-rock white leather couches. My shoes thud on the concrete floor as I approach the head nurse.

"Can I help you?" Her hands hover over a switchboard with dozens of blinking green lights. I look down at her shiny white nametag, which reads URSULA.

"Um… yeah. I was wondering if I could speak with one of the doctors."

"Do you have an appointment?" Ursula asks, flashing the whitest teeth I've ever seen.

I hesitate. "No, I don't."

"Too bad," says Ursula in a neutral tone. "I can schedule you for the future. Right now we're booked ten months out. What's your name?" She opens a leather-bound notebook and uncaps a silver pen.

"Cole. But I'm not sure I need an official appoint." I stuff my hand in my pocket for some Juicy Fruit before I remember the phone is there transmitting everything back to the car. I yank my hand out and continue. "All I really want to know is what narcosis is all about. Do you have some brochures or something?"

"Oh," says Ursula brightly. "Of course." She points at a screen across from one of the white couches. "We have a seven-minute documentary you can watch over there. Afterward, I invite you to inspect the sample narcosis room next to it."

"Thanks." I shuffle away, and she looks back down at her switchboard. As soon as I sit down on one of the couches, I confirm that they are every bit as uncomfortable as they look. But the video, which plays on loop, captures my attention.

"Doctor Belinda Savage grew up in Snohomish, Washington, a former logging town known for quaint antique shops and apple pies. As valedictorian of her high school, Doctor Belinda had her pick of any college. She chose a full scholarship to the University of Washington, where she later earned her MD and PhD with residences in both plastic surgery and psychiatry. Doctor Belinda is passionate about pushing the frontier of modern medicine as far as it can go. She has unbridled optimism in the power of surgery to reshape lives, and psychiatry as a means

of rewiring troubled brains to ensure that every person can lead a better life."

Pictures of Ellie's mom with various patients appear in rapid succession, each person smiling and looking grateful to receive her expert care. Then the footage transitions to Ellie's dad. *"Hailing from DePauw University in Greencastle, Indiana, Doctor Warren Savage met his wife Belinda while attending medical school at the University of Washington."* A much-younger version of Ellie's dad appears at a Huskies game wearing a purple U-Dub sweatshirt. Then the video cuts over to an interview clip.

"We were in a study group together," he says, *"and afterward I asked Belinda if I could take her out to dinner. She was so consumed with her flashcards, she didn't realize I was flirting with her."* He smiles conspiratorially. *"But once she finally looked up from her notes it was love at first sight."*

The documentary narration continues. *"As a world-renowned dermatologist, Doctor Warren can make any skin malady disappear."* Before and after pictures tell the story. *"From burns and scars to unsightly complexion problems, your skin is in good hands with Doctor Warren."*

"What we found in our early days of practicing medicine," says Ellie's mom, *"is that yes, we could work miracles. But the procedures themselves were intense, and the recovery period traumatic. Many patients came to us with the same wish: 'Can't you wake me up when it's all over?' That concept—to peacefully sleep while transformation occurs—prompted us to search the medical literature."* Ellie's mom fades off the screen, and black-and-white pictures emerge described by the official narrator.

"Narcosis rooms have been around since the 1960s, when Dr. William Sargant first used them in London to treat depressed housewives. Despite the dutiful attention of Nightingale nurses, Dr. Sargant's early experiments in narcosis sometimes caused death and insanity. But thanks to the pioneering work of Doctors Belinda and Warren Savage, narcosis is now safe. If

you struggle with any of a variety of health issues, the Narcosis Clinic can help. Patients wake up three months later thinner, happier, and with smoother skin. And they don't remember a single painful surgery."

The video pans across an ornate brass bed piled high with cushions. *"Sleep for three months and make your problems go away. At the Narcosis Clinic, dreams really do come true."*

I remain on the couch while the credits roll, but when the video loops back to the beginning, I stand up.

"Would you like to see the sample narcosis room?" Ursula asks from her desk. At my nod, she points to metal sliding doors. "It's right through there."

The doors slide open with a soft *whoosh*. There's the old-fashioned bed covered in cushions that I saw in the advertisement. Next to it is a collection of medical devices on wheeled carts. None of them appear to be on, but they look real. Tubing connects to an IV bag, and sensors hook up to a gray tower with a blank screen. On top of the tower is a set of headphones like you'd use to cancel out noise on the airplane or when your sister is playing the same Beyoncé song over and over.

"Long time no see." A booming voice makes me jump. I turn around and see Warren standing at the threshold. "You're Marley's brother, right?" He crosses the room with his hand extended.

I shake with a firm grip. "Yeah, I'm Cole."

"That's right. It's been a while, but I never forget a face. You look so much like your sister."

"It's the twin thing." I speak up, hoping our conversation is picking up on my phone so the girls can hear too.

"I saw you down in the lobby and thought I recognized you. What brings you to the clinic?"

I think about leading with the creepy clown phobia but decide to stick with the truth. "I'm looking for Ellie. Is she here?"

"Here in the first-floor reception rooms? No, she's not."

"But she is here?" I press.

Warren studies me for a moment, then smiles. "Ellie's at French Camp, Cole. She goes every summer."

"It's September. What type of summer camp goes into the school year?"

The smile disappears, and Dr. Savage's voice grows hard. "I don't like your tone of voice, Cole. It's none of your business where Ellie is."

"It *is* my business because Ellie and I had plans. I want to make sure she's okay."

At this, Warren's expression softens. "She's fine. I promise you. And you're right, summer programs don't usually spill into the school year, but this experience was different. Ellie got the opportunity to stay with a host family in the French countryside. Unfortunately, they don't have Wi-Fi, so communication has been spotty. But she's having a marvelous time, and my wife and I are letting Ellie make the decision when to come home." Warren extends his arm. "Let me show you out. I'm sure you have homework to deal with."

Maybe I should have stuck with the clown story because I have the feeling I was just sold a load of ding-dong. As I hurry out of the foyer, the head nurse smiles coolly and gives me a regal wave. I slam the front door shut on purpose.

"Did you get all that?" I ask as soon as I climb into the car. I jam my hand in my pocket, pull out my phone, and end the call to my sister.

"We heard every word," says Marley.

"No way would Ellie stay in France and not tell me," says Olivia. "When I talked to her on the phone she didn't mention it. I assumed she was in America."

I reach my hand in my other pocket and grab a stick of Juicy Fruit. Before I angrily shove it in my mouth, I think out loud. "We need to face facts. We'll be lucky if Ellie comes back to school at all."

In the rearview mirror, I see Olivia's face crumple. My sister reaches back to pat her hand. "Don't worry, Olivia. I lost Ellie once, but I'm not going to lose her again."

CHAPTER TWENTY-FIVE: ELLIE
11:32 A.M. | SEPTEMBER 17TH

We've read the letter at least a dozen times. At least, I think we have. I'm not sure what day it is, what time it is, or how long I've been here.

"Say it to me. 'Remembering my past is not painful.'" Ellie-Me marches around the room on bare feet, leaving puddles of water behind her.

"Remembering my past is not painful." I open my eyes briefly and look up into darkness. My eyelids flutter closed again. It's easier to watch Ellie-Me. She keeps me sane.

"Right," Ellie-Me repeats. "When you wake up, you'll figure out the truth."

"All by myself?" The narcotics make my voice shake.

Ellie-Me stops pacing. "I'll be here to help. You and I are going places."

"I thought I was trapped in narcosis."

"At least you're not stuck in limbo wearing a thong." Ellie-Me hops from side to side and tugs at her skirt.

"Wouldn't that look great with my catheter," I joke.

"Sarcasm!" Ellie-Me's eyes light up. "That's a good sign."

Somebody else told me that recently, but I can't remember who.

"Why are you wet?" I ask. "Don't get mad, but that's the part I keep forgetting."

Ellie-Me pulls a damp strand of hair behind her ear. "Because I went swimming. Don't you remember? You can swim!

Here, I'll read it to you again." Ellie-Me shuffles through the papers so fast, a small breeze forms. It's cool against my arm where an IV feeds into a vein. She reads the description of me rescuing Dean. "*Your brain holds the answers,*" Ellie-Me says. She cocks her head at the sound of footsteps.

The door opens a crack and Dad creeps inside. Ellie-Me melts into a corner of the room, even though Dad can't see her. He walks over to me instead and bends down to kiss my cheek. Then Dad examines the monitors.

"What time is it?" I ask. But Dad can't hear me, just like he can't see his duplicate daughter in the corner shivering like a drowned rat.

"Don't you mean, 'What day is it?'" Ellie-Me pulls up her wet dress, trying to hide the corset. Ellie-Me eyeballs Dad nervously before walking over to read the computer screens with him.

"Fine. What day is it?" I ask. "How long have I been asleep?"

"Two weeks." Ellie-Me spins to face me. "I had to check because I'm losing track of time too."

"So Dean is—"

"Already gone." Ellie-Me runs her thumb over her scar. "He probably left the clinic a while ago."

"But I'm still here."

"Yeah." Ellie-Me wrings out her hair and splatters water all over Dad's shoes. Dad shuffles his feet but otherwise doesn't notice.

I get a strong whiff of lavender, and Dad turns. Mom, her hair tied back into a curly bun, is in the doorway. She walks forward and puts a reassuring hand on Dad's elbow and stares at the flashing screens.

I fight to open my eyes, but they stay sealed shut. "Why won't Mom and Dad help me wake up?"

"It's not that simple," answers Ellie-Me. "They're not the one keeping you under."

"Huh? What about all these wires?"

Ellie-Me shrugs and wanders back over to me. "They keep track of your vitals—that's it. You're the one keeping you under. The computers only monitor your condition."

Mom tilts her head and glances over my sleeping frame. She purses her lips and then types something into her computer tablet.

I try to stretch out my hand and touch Ellie-Me to see if she's real, but my arms feel like cement.

"Your brain is protecting you." Ellie sits down on my bed. "Let's think of this as a mental vacation instead of a coma."

"A coma?" I shout. "Why didn't you tell me I was in a coma?" Sweat beads my temples.

"I did tell you," says Ellie-Me. "Don't you remember?"

"We need to face facts, Belinda." Dad rakes his fingers through his salt-and-pepper hair. "Ellie's been in a coma for sixteen days with no sign of recovering. We should have moved her to a hospital last week."

"Sixteen days?" I glare at Ellie-Me. "You told me it was only two weeks."

Ellie-Me raises her shoulders apologetically. "Two weeks-*ish*."

"This isn't normal," I say. "I've never heard of narcosis causing a coma before."

As if on cue, Mom says almost the same thing. "Is this unusual? Yes, it's unusual. Am I scared? Of course. I'm terrified. But we can't move Ellie to a hospital. ER doctors don't know about Post-Narcosis Stress Syndrome. Plus, the authorities would shut us down. The Narcosis Clinic is our life's work."

"Who cares about work? We're talking about our child!" Dad curls up his fist like he's going to punch the monitors but then releases his grip and lets his arms dangle.

"It's the same thing." Mom brushes a stray tear off her cheek. "Ellie and narcosis. Narcosis and Ellie. We can't have one without the other. If we took her to the hospital, they would have no idea how to help her. The doctors there would ruin everything and put us all in danger."

"What does Mom mean?" I ask.

Ellie-Me pulls her arms across her wet front. "I don't know."

"If we stick to the plan," Mom continues, "everything will be all right. Ellie will wake up, and we'll let her take the lead."

"No more mind games." Dad's voice is stern.

Mom sniffs and wipes her nose with a tissue. "Of course not, *Daddy*. You make it sound like this was all my fault when we both know that isn't true."

Dad grinds his teeth. "I'll admit, I have a major position of responsibility in this debacle, but for the record, I did voice my concern early on. Ten rounds of narcosis is seven treatments too many. We don't even know what Ellie is like without narcosis. Her personality has vanished."

My muscles tense.

"Defiance was not her true personality, and you know it." Spit flies out of Mom's mouth.

"Ten treatments?" My muscles burn. "Did Mom say I've done narcosis ten times? I thought it was only three."

Ellie-Me nods, eye makeup dripping down her cheeks. "I knew it was a lot, but I had no idea."

"Ellie was a handful, that's true," says Dad.

Mom presses her lips together in a tight line. "She wasn't a handful, she was a juvenile delinquent."

"I'd hardly call—"

"We spent eighty-five thousand dollars in lawyers' fees for that libel suit, Warren. All to keep our daughter out of juvie."

Dad waves his hand at me. "And now she's a vegetable."

"Don't call my daughter a vegetable!"

"I'd rather Ellie be a delinquent than a cucumber." Dad adjusts the quilt on my bed and covers up some of the tubes. "What do you suggest we do now?"

Mom twists the hem of her lab coat. "There's nothing we can do except wait." They both stand there together for several minutes, staring at me like I'll suddenly leap out of bed.

"Well, um…" Ellie-Me clears her throat. "Tonight we have an audience." She pulls out the stack of papers sitting on her lap. "But we shouldn't let them stop our progress. You need to memorize every last word. Are you ready?"

"What else have I got to do?" I attempt to scoot over on the bed to make room for my apparition, but I can't move one cell.

"I don't know, sleep?" Ellie-Me winks. Then she sits down and fans the papers until she comes to the right page. "*When you wake up in September, search for the answers I couldn't find before narcosis. Find a pool and practice swimming—you're a natural. Remember kissing Cole Evans and how he wants to be your boyfriend! Review your Instagram account.*"

"Wait!" This time I shake my arm so hard that my wrist jumps. "How do I know that's true? I mean, I've wanted Cole to notice me forever, but he doesn't. How do I know that this letter isn't wishful thinking?"

Ellie-Me blanches. "I don't know." Then she puts her finger to her lip. "Shh!"

Dad reaches for my hand with a clammy palm. "Belinda. We missed it. Ellie moved, and we were staring at the bloody monitors!"

"She'll move again. You'll see." Mom's voice is eerily calm.

"But what if she doesn't?" A tortured gasp escapes Dad's throat.

"Enough," Mom hisses. "You know we had no other choice."

"There is always another choice. We should never have let this happen."

"What are they talking about?" I ask Ellie-Me.

Ellie-Me stares at our parents, inspecting their every cell. "I don't know. Be still and let's listen."

I don't want to be still, I try to tell Ellie-Me with my thoughts, but she doesn't turn to look at me. *Can't you read my mind anymore?* I ask her. She doesn't answer.

I'm ready to wake up. The coma is drifting away. I'm ready to march down the hallway and away from here forever. Burn all my nightgowns; I'm never going to bed.

My eyelids feel like lead, but I manage to ratchet them open. The air hits soft tissue like a serrated knife.

"Warren," Mom whispers. "She opened her eyes."

Dad's voice is solemn. "I know, love. I saw." He squeezes my hand. "Ellie, angel, can you hear me?"

"Don't answer," says Ellie-Me. "I'm not done reading yet."

I close my eyelids and open them again.

"I mean it!" shouts Ellie-Me. "You're safer with me."

"Don't you want me to wake up?" I gasp.

"Of course we do, angel." Dad brushes hair out of my eyes. "We've been waiting."

"You can hear me?" My throat scratches; my tongue feels heavy.

"Yes, princess, and it's music to my ears." Mom holds my other hand, her face blotched with color. She laughs and cries at the same time.

"I don't think this is a good idea," says Ellie-Me. "Maybe the coma was better."

"How can you say that?" I ask.

Mom's smile vanishes. "Because I love you. Daddy and I have been waiting for days for you to wake up."

"Doesn't she mean weeks?" Ellie-Me bounds off the mattress and heads to the door.

"Where are you going?" I don't want Ellie-Me to leave. At least, I don't think so.

"We're not going anywhere," says Dad. "We're here to stay."

I shake my head and feel tubes pull. "I wasn't talking to you."

"You weren't?" Dad looks behind him to where Ellie-Me hovers by the door. "Who were you talking to?"

"Me," I sputter. "I was talking to me."

Mom and Dad exchange looks, the type that says, "Let's talk about this later in private."

Ellie-Me gives me one more pointed look. "Be careful." Then she's gone, leaving behind a puddle of water.

CHAPTER TWENTY-SIX: ELLIE
6:10 P.M. | SEPTEMBER 19TH

It's been two days since I woke up, but nothing seems familiar. My fork scrapes the plate in a pathetic attempt to pierce a carrot. Dad made sweet-and-sour stir-fry for dinner. Looking at the chopsticks on my placemat makes my brain fumble. I can't remember if I know how to use them or not. Even this fluffy white stuff is unfamiliar.

The word—I think it's right—comes to me. "Is this rice?" I pile it next to the chicken. "How can I not recognize rice anymore? What did you people do to me?"

Dad chokes on his tea.

"There's no need to be so dramatic." Mom neatly blots her mouth with a cloth napkin. "It's shredded cauliflower. Fewer carbs that way."

"I don't care about my waistline. I want to be *normal*. Not some freak-show Frankenstein you pieced together upstairs."

"Ellie!" Mom tosses her napkin to the table. "You know that's not what narcosis is like."

Dad looks away.

That's when Ellie-Me, wet and dripping on the dining room chair, appears. Based on Mom and Dad continuing to eat their dinner, I gather that the only person who can see her is me. "Nice work." She reaches over and grabs my chopsticks, helping herself to my dinner with expert skill. "I've wanted to tell them off forever."

"I didn't know you could eat," I mutter.

"Of course we can eat," Mom says. "Why would you ask that?"

"I wasn't talking to you," I tell Mom. Then I glare at Ellie-Me, who's standing between me and Dad. "This is all *your* fault."

"*My* fault!" exclaims Dad. "Well, if that isn't the hardest—" Dad stops midsentence, and tears pop out. "I tried to talk your mother out of it, I swear."

"That. Is. Unfair." Mom pulls her chair closer to the table, and the legs scrape the floor. "You know we decided together, Warren." She rests her elbows on the table and stares deep into my eyes. "We did what we thought was best for you. We didn't know another round of narcosis would cause you discomfort."

"Discomfort? Is that how you describe slicing me open and brainwashing me? How about *pain*, Mom? And the worst torture is not knowing the truth." Ellie-Me gives me the thumbs up. "What's my real name?" I demand. "Why did you delete my Instagram account? Where did my poster go? And why did you erase all memories of Dean Mathews from my brain?"

"Good," says Ellie-Me. "Finally."

"We…" Mom gulps. "What I mean to say is that…" She pulls her elbows off the table and folds her hands in her lap.

Dad stares at his plate. "Ellie is your real name. We erased your phone to help with environmental stability. And the poster is rolled up in your closet."

"Exactly!" Mom forces a smile. "I'm glad we got all that settled. More egg rolls?" She offers me the platter like the fact they have been lying to me my whole life is no big deal.

It's infuriating.

"What about Dean?" Ellie-Me and I say it together.

"Dean?" Mom plays dumb.

"I can barely think about Dean without getting a migraine, but I've been online, and I've found pictures of me rescuing him from Marley's pool." I squeeze my hands into fists. "You can mess with my memory, but you can't erase the whole Internet."

"Darling," Mom says, "we were only trying to help."

I turn my rage toward Dad. "Did you agree to this too? Wiping all traces of Dean from my memory?"

Dad pulls out a handkerchief and wipes beads of perspiration off his forehead. "I admit I had my doubts at first, but Dean was clearly a bad influence. Ten minutes in his presence and you ran away from home. And went to a wild party?" Dad pauses and twists the handkerchiefs into a knot. "Plus, I can't give you the details because of doctor-patient confidentiality. Let's just say that penicillin is a modern miracle, but there are certain STDs that stick with a person for life. Believe me—you're better off without him."

"What's that supposed to mean?" Ellie-Me shouts.

"What are you implying?" I ask Dad.

"You read the tabloids," Mom says matter-of-factly. "Do you really think you're the first girl Dean has seduced?"

"Seduced? What?" Ellie-Me tugs up her dress.

"Dean did not seduce me. It wasn't like that." But as soon as I say it, I second-guess myself. I have no idea if it's true or not. Would the old me sleep with Dean Mathews? How can I not know?

Mom's face is as smooth as marble. "Let's focus on getting you healthy enough to go back to school. Join your classmates! Have a fabulous senior year. There are lots of boys at Emily Carr High that would be a much better choice for you."

"Where did they get the idea that you like Dean?" Ellie-Me screeches.

"Shut up," I tell her. "Let me think."

Mom's pale face becomes ghostly.

"Ellie!" Dad frowns. "You don't speak to your mother like that."

"I wasn't talking to Mom." I point to my alter ego in her skimpy purple dress. "I was talking to her. She follows me everywhere I go."

"Who follows you?" The fear in Mom's voice makes me quiver.

"The other Ellie! She wants me to find out the truth."

Ellie-Me grins and scoops up a wonton. "You shouldn't have told them about me. Now they'll think you're nuts."

"I *am* nuts!" I push back my chair from the table and try to stand, but getting up so suddenly makes me dizzy. My head spins and all I see is white. Blood pools down my neck and my eyes flutter. "And I want to be normal!"

"Ellie!" Dad's at my elbow in two seconds flat. "Are you okay? Sit down and put your head between your knees. You look pale."

I collapse onto my chair until the spell is over. When I raise my head, it feels like lead.

"So you've been having hallucinations?" Mom pours me a cup of tea with a shaky hand. "How long has this been happening?"

I take the offered cup, and it feels hot in my hands. "Since before my coma."

"Yeah!" Ellie-Me pounds the table, and the dishes shake. "Say it again. *Coma.* Make them hurt."

"Let me handle this," I tell her. Across the table, Mom's and Dad's eyes are wide. I put down my tea and stare at them both. "You put me in a *coma.* You could have killed me. For all I know, I'll never get back to normal."

"Hallucinations are a symptom of Post-Narcosis Stress Syndrome." Mom pushes a bite of chicken around her plate. "They'll fade in time, assuming you get the proper amount of rest." She fiddles with her chopsticks.

My fists clench. "Why would you do this to me when you knew the risk?"

Mom twists her napkin nervously. "Because you're my daughter and I would do anything to make your life better."

I shake my head in disbelief. "How is my life better now? Stay out of my life. Stay out of my head. And stay out of my business!" This time when I rise from the table, I stand tall. And when I march out of the dining room, Ellie-Me follows.

"That was awesome," says Ellie-Me. "You showed them." She's crouched on the floor of my closet, picking through old shoes.

"What do you mean?" I step over the wet puddle Ellie-Me made in my carpet and examine the far corner of the closet next to my dollhouse. Dad said my old poster was in here, and I intend to find it.

"The way you yelled at them. I never had the guts."

"I find that hard to believe. You yell at me all the time."

Ellie-Me grins. "That's because you don't usually listen." She pulls on a pair of UGG boots and within seconds the suede stains from the water dripping off her dress. The whole closet smells like wet sheep.

"Hey, look," I say. "What's this bumpy place under the rug?"

Ellie-Me peers over to inspect the floor. "I don't know." She pulls back the carpet to reveal a trap door with an iron ring at the top. "It's stuck. Can you help me pull it?"

I bend over and place my hands over Ellie's wet ones. It takes a few tries, but the hinges creak open. With the trapdoor up, I peer into a cavern of darkness. "What's down there?" I hear a faint echo of dripping water.

"The Dean Mathews poster!" Ellie-Me reaches her hand into the depths.

"No, wait. Let me. You'll ruin it." I plunge my arm down and wave my hand around until it hits a cardboard tube resting on a metal surface. I pull it up and open the container. Dean's hair looks more enormous than ever.

I shrug. "Well, I found it." I place the poster aside and dip my arm back into the hole.

"What are you doing?" Ellie-Me asks.

"I want to see if anything else is down there. What do you think this place is?"

"I don't know. A maintenance crawl space? Or a shaft to the furnace?"

"It couldn't lead to the furnace," I say. "Not when I hear water. And there's some kind of shelving unit down there. Could you hand me a flashlight?"

"What are you going to do?" Ellie-Me jumps up and rifles around the other side of the closet where my sleeping bag and other camping stuff is stored in a crate behind my winter clothes. She produces a small black flashlight a moment later, flicks on the switch, and hands it over. "The batteries still work, but are you sure you're well enough for this? A half hour ago you almost fainted during dinner."

"I'm better now." I aim the flashlight down into the darkness and see stairs leading down into a tunnel. "This isn't a ventilation shaft; it's a secret passage!" I brace myself on my forearms, ready to lower my legs down below.

"Wait!" Ellie-Me yells. "Somebody's coming."

"Darling?" Mom's voice is muffled. "Can we please talk?"

Ellie-Me runs out of the closet into the bedroom. "Why didn't you lock the door?"

"I don't know!" I holler back. It was easier to communicate with Ellie-Me when I was in the coma and she could read my thoughts.

"Please, darling. I'm coming inside." I hear Mom jiggle the handle.

"Get out of there before she comes!" Ellie-Me rushes into my closet and pulls on my armpits. "Don't let Mom discover you know about this." She hurls me on my closet floor and stamps down the trapdoor.

"I don't care if she finds out," I mumble into yesterday's dirty laundry.

"Find out what?" Mom stands in the closet doorway, blocking out the light.

"That you were talking to me," Ellie-Me spits out. "Say it! Don't mention the secret passage."

I look at Ellie-Me, and then I look at Mom.

"Find out what?" Mom asks again.

"That I was talking to myself," I answer. "Ellie follows me around everywhere I go." I point to Ellie-Me lying on the carpet in her dripping-wet dress.

Mom swallows hard. "Darling… Princess… Why don't we get you back to bed?

"No!" I yell.

"It's been a long day," Mom says. "You'll feel better after a good night's sleep."

"Absolutely not." I leap to my feet and jab my finger against Mom's chest. "Get out of my room right now."

Only too bad for me, my sudden bolt upright makes me dizzy again. My eyes roll back, and I see stars.

"Oh, crap," says Ellie-Me. "Don't faint."

I fight to remain conscious. I stumble toward my bed. "I'm lying down," I tell Mom. "But only because I want to." As soon as I'm horizontal, I start to feel better.

Mom leans down and puts a cool hand on my forehead. "Would you like me to get—"

"No," I snap. "Just leave me alone. And lock the door behind you."

Mom winces like I've slapped her. Then she glances back toward the closet before offering me a sad smile. "Okay, Ellie. Whatever you wish. I love you."

6:33 P.M. | SEPTEMBER 21ST

Mom thinks me being trapped on a tour bus is the perfect time to call me, and since I'm bored out of mind I usually pick up. Okay, also I miss her, but that doesn't mean our conversations are any less annoying.

"I love hearing the sound of your voice," Mom says for the millionth time.

"So turn on the radio." I stretch out my feet on the couch in the dinette and stare out the window into traffic. We're a couple of hours away from San Francisco.

"You know what I mean. All that texting broke my heart. Plus, I could never find my glasses."

"I told you I'd pay for laser surgery."

"And risk going blind? No way! Anyhow, it's a relief now not to text."

"Texting is no big deal."

"Don't make light of your miraculous transformation. I was worried about you doing that narcosis thing, but now I realize you made the right decision."

"Thanks, Mom. I wish it was Thanksgiving already because I can't wait to see you."

"I've got a new pumpkin pie recipe I'm dying to try. I clipped it out of a magazine."

"That sounds delicious." I watch as Gary invades my lounge area, frantically waving his hands. "Sorry, Mom, I gotta go. I'll call you tomorrow, okay?"

"Love you, sweetie!"

"Love you too." I end the call and sit up straighter. "What's up?"

Gary slides onto the dinette couch right where my feet are. I slide them away a second before they're crushed. "All hell's breaking loose," he says as he reaches for the remote on the table and turns on the satellite television. His greasy hair is pulled back into a short ponytail that looks ridiculous with his receding hairline.

Hollywood Central blares to life and Taisha Fletcher fills the screen in a bright red dress and gold necklace. "*It's the shouting match heard around the world,*" she says, "*as newlyweds Sam Anders and Pansy Williams throw drinks, accusations, and more in this explosive footage caught by witnesses at a Miami nightclub last night.*"

Gary rips open a bag of potato chips with his teeth. "It's all over social media." He holds out the remote and cranks up the volume.

"*Please note that some words have been censored to protect sensitive ears,*" Trisha tells the audience. The footage cuts to a shaky video taken on somebody's phone.

"*You BLEEPing BLEEP! I can't BLEEPing believe you did that!*" Sam's usually smooth complexion is blotchy, and his blond hair flops out of control.

"*Well, if you weren't such a BLEEPing washout, none of this would have happened!*" Pansy screams back. Her fake tits bounce in a pushup bra that peeks out of her low-cut tank top. Bowser, her Chihuahua, hangs his head out of her designer purse.

"*You're accusing me of being a washout? Who pays the bills around here?*" Sam's hand twitches and the drink he's holding sloshes onto the couple sitting next to him.

"*Dean's had more downloads on his new single 'Dream Girl' than your last album got all summer,*" Pansy declares. I feel a surge of pride for a moment until—"*And that song was obviously written about me.*"

Huh? I have no clue where "Dream Girl" came from. I woke up from narcosis, and it was rattling in my mind.

"*Well, maybe you should go back to Dean, then, since he's obviously pining away from loneliness for you,*" Sam says snidely.

"*Maybe I will!*" Pansy shoots back. "*At least when I was dating Dean, I had a career.*"

"*It's not my fault nobody wants to hire you. Maybe you should have thought about that when you were acting like such a diva on your last shoot.*" Sam tosses back the remainder of his drink.

"Diva is right," says Maxine, crowding into the dinette.

"Shh!" Gary whispers. "This next part is priceless."

"*Bringing my Pilates instructor with me does not make me a diva. And it's not my fault that the hairdresser they hired was too stupid to care for my hair extensions properly.*" Pansy flicks her long locks over her bare shoulder.

"*Your Pilates instructor. It always comes back to your BLEEPing Pilates instructor. Is that where you were last night? With Tony?*" Sam points his finger at Pansy's voluptuous chest, and Bowser growls.

"*Tony's gay, you moron. How many times do I have to tell you?*" Pansy lifts Bowser out her purse and sets him directly on the bar. "*There you go, baby. Mommy's got you.*" Bowser immediately lifts his leg and pees on a bowl of salted nuts.

"*This is a bar, not a dog park!*" the bartender shouts, but both Sam and Pansy ignore him.

The television cuts back to Taisha Fletcher in her polished anchorwoman makeup. "Hollywood Central *has reached out to PR reps from both parties. Neither Sam Anders nor Pansy Williams has issued a statement.*"

Gary clicks off the television. "I guess we'll have to see if they board the plane together tomorrow." He heads out of the dinette muttering to himself about Anders' fan numbers.

"I hope she stays home," says Maxine. "I'd hate to be the poor person stuck on the airplane next to Bowser. That dog smells like urine."

"How do you really feel, Max?" I ask.

She gives me a saucy grin. "Eternally grateful that she's no longer my problem."

"Yeah." I smile broadly. "Me too."

"So," Maxine says, grabbing a can of Diet Coke from the mini fridge, "now that you're finally over Pansy—took you long enough by the way—have you given any more thought to dating?"

I stare out the window at the rainy commute. "Who am I going to date? We're in a new city every night." A weird sensation of déjà vu washes over me.

"Have a one-night stand. Wear a condom and it won't kill you."

I whip my eyes back to Maxine. "What?"

"You are a guy who needs to get laid." Maxine points at me and her armful of plastic bracelets rattle.

"I can't believe you're advocating sleeping around."

"You think like a monk!"

"You're old enough to be my grandma!"

"What's that have to do with anything?" Maxine asks, affronted. Her hair is dyed violet at the moment and teased up into a bouffant.

"I don't want to sleep around. Sex should be special."

"Then find a special girl to have it with."

"How am I going to do that when I'm stuck on this tour for the next ten months?"

"What about the girl you met in Seattle?"

"Which one?" My memories of that night are hazy, but I've seen the pictures.

Maxine pulls out her phone and does a quick search. "This girl," she says, holding her phone so I can see. "The one you sang to on that deck."

Maxine's phone case is hot pink and studded with rhinestones. It feels scratchy as I take it from her and stare at the image. There I am in full lounge-lizard mode, cradling the microphone and belting out a song. A beautiful girl with shaggy blond hair, a short skirt, and cowboy boots stands next to me with her hands clasped. I like that she has meat on her bones. I can almost feel what it would be like to slide my hand down the curvy backside of her miniskirt. The problem is, I've stared at her picture a hundred times, and I still can't remember who she is. I swipe the screen and find another picture of the two of us. This time I'm dipping her back for a kiss and her toe is extended in the air like she's enjoying it.

"Yeah," I mumble. "If I could go out with that girl, it would be awesome, but I don't know her name."

Maxine harrumphs. "Well, find it out, Sherlock."

"How am I supposed to do that?"

"Look up the news reports. Do some digging on Twitter." Maxine retrieves her phone and speed-types with both thumbs. "It says that the party took place at a house owned by the operators of *The Royal Racer*, some sort of tourist ship in Seattle. That's the place to start."

I retrieve my own phone from my back pocket. "What do I do when I find her?"

"Get her number. Text her." Maxine gives me a hard look. "You're an expert texter."

"I'm tired of texting. I want to actually talk."

"Well, why are you asking me for advice? Get her on the phone, and you'll be fine."

"I just thought of something. I don't need to be Sherlock Holmes. I'm Dean Mathews." I screenshot a picture of me kissing the mystery girl and post it on Instagram. WANTED, I type.

DREAM GIRL'S NAME AND PHONE NUMBER. Within seconds the comments section is flooded with profiles and digits.

Maxine looks over my shoulder at what's happening. "You might as well post an open invitation for the crazies to come out."

She's right. It's already total chaos. So I click over to the spyglass and search for *The Royal Racer*'s account. Duh! I should have started there to begin with. There she is twenty pictures back. It's a family shot of the owners on deck with Puget Sound behind them. I click on the picture and her profile pulls up.

"Woo hoo!" I shout.

"You found her?" asks Maxine excitedly. "What's her name?"

I hold out my phone so Maxine can see for herself. "Dream Girl is named Marley Evans."

Maxine whistles. "Go for it, kiddo."

And for the first time in years, I send a friend request.

CHAPTER TWENTY-EIGHT: ELLIE
3:20 P.M. | SEPTEMBER 27TH

The crispness of the September air contrasts with the yellow heat of sunshine. I sit down on the garden bench and wrap up in wool blankets to protect myself from the chill.

I'd like to say that I've been fierce and bold, that I've busted open the trap door and explored the whole house. But the truth is I've walked around in a fog of convoluted memories and migraine medicine. Every time I picture Dean my head explodes. The one time I checked out his Twitter feed my head hurt so much, I blacked out. Ellie-Me woke me up, a wet hand on my shoulder.

Now I'm resting in the garden like a human vegetable.

A little girl comes out into the yard, probably to enjoy the fresh air. She must be another narcosis patient. As soon as she sees me, the girl makes a beeline straight for me. "Hi, Ellie!" She wears jeans and a fleece, and her face is baby smooth.

"Who's that?" asks Ellie-Me, who materializes next to my elbow.

The little girl has beautiful brown eyes and thick eyelashes. "It's me, Katie," she says when I don't respond.

"Oh. Hi, Katie," I say in a friendly tone. I cut a glance to Ellie-Me for help.

"I have no idea who this girl is, but it seems like she knows you," Ellie-Me responds.

"Don't worry," the little girl says. "I already checked, and there aren't any raccoons here. But if there was, I'm not afraid anymore."

"That's awesome."

The girl's nurse comes out and seems surprised to see me. She hustles the girl back into the clinic before I can talk to her some more.

"Are raccoons something we're supposed to be worried about?" I ask Ellie-Me.

She shivers. "I don't think so. But hey, can I have one of those blankets?" Her dampness seeps into the stone bench and leaves a dark mark. "It's almost October."

"Were you saying something, Ellie?" Ursula, my nurse shadow, arches an eyebrow. Her white dress feels out of place in the garden. Slivers of grass blades stick to her shoes.

I look up at Ursula's patient face. "You don't need to watch me."

She clears her throat. "Your parents want me to stay with you to make sure you're safe. But if you'd rather have some space to think, I could observe you from the rose bushes."

"How about the patio instead?"

Ursula wrinkles her forehead. Dad must not have given her any Botox. "How about the hedge?" She glances backward to the halfway mark between the patio and roses.

"Deal." I pull my blankets tighter.

"Come on." Ellie-Me's teeth chatter. "One blanket? Pretty please?"

I look at Ellie-Me quiver in her strapless dress and take pity. "Of course," I whisper. Then I hand her one of my blankets. I eyeball the nurse nervously to see if she notices.

"You want me to go away," says Ellie-Me. "I get it. But that's not going to happen."

"Why not?" If Ellie-Me would go away, I could be normal again. Or whatever scummy normal my parents have cooked up for me. "You're ruining my life."

"I'm not ruining your life, I'm here to help."

"They think I have some sort of syndrome," I whisper. "Because I keep talking to myself."

Ellie-Me reaches through the blanket and places a soft hand on my elbow. "I'm not the enemy. Mom and Dad are." She looks up to the third floor of the clinic, where the shutters are closed.

"I know I can't trust Mom and Dad. Okay? But what you don't seem to understand is that I want to go back to school and have a normal life, but I can't do that with you messing me up."

"I'm here to help!" Ellie-Me pulls her blanket closer.

"Then stop talking to me when other people are here." Despite my best intentions, my voice carries. I look up and see the nurse staring at me from the hedge.

"Did you ask me a question?" Ursula asks.

"Oh, sorry." I think fast. "I was singing a song to myself."

Ursula smiles benignly in return. But two seconds later I see her scribble something in her pocket-sized notebook.

"Great." I look at Ellie-Me and fume. "Thanks to you, everyone thinks I'm nuts."

Ellie-Me looks down at her wet feet and frowns. "You are nuts. But it isn't my fault."

"So go away and leave me alone."

"That's just it!" Ellie-Me's green eyes glow with temper. "I can't leave you alone with these people. That would be criminal. Until you find out the truth, I'm the only true friend you've got."

"That's not true, and you know it. What about Olivia?"

"Olivia doesn't know about your narcosis. That's why we need each other." Ellie-Me digs her bare toe into the grass. "Together we can remember everything."

"I doubt it." The wool blanket starts to itch. I wish I were wearing a soft fleece like that girl named Katie instead of the freshly ironed blouse Mom insisted on when she dressed me this morning.

"That's another thing," Ellie-Me says. "You're seventeen years old, for crying out loud. Mom shouldn't pick out your clothes. I never let her do that."

"You didn't?"

Ellie-Me rolls her eyes at me. "Of course not. See what I mean? You *need* me."

I look away and consider for a minute. Then I turn back and stare at her with my most earnest look. "Okay. I need you. But can we at least strike a deal?"

"What type of deal?"

"From now on, I'm only talking to you in private," I declare. "We're not having a conversation like this in public ever again."

"But—"

"But nothing. And in return, I promise that when you do appear to me—in the sanctuary of my own room—I will listen to what you say and take your advice into serious consideration."

Ellie-Me twists the edge of her blanket but doesn't respond for a while. Finally, with a steady tone, she answers. "It's a deal." Then her face brightens. "Will you look at that? Up in the tree?" She points to the big leaf maple that stands sentinel next to my window.

The turning leaves—green, red, orange, bronze—whisper in the wind. I glance up through the branches and see a tuft of brown. A bald eagle examines me from his perch. Am I predator or prey? Then he extends his long wings and flies away in a rush of silence.

When I glance back to share the moment with Ellie-Me, my hallucination is gone.

CHAPTER TWENTY-NINE: COLE

"Why are you so secretive all of a sudden?" I ask Marley. "This is the third day in a row you've let me drive to school. You *hate* my driving."

"You're a fine driver," Marley says without looking up from her phone. "You just need to leave more space between our Jeep and the car in front of us."

I pump the brakes real quick.

"What the?" Marley looks up from her phone and shrieks. Then she slugs me in the shoulder when she realizes we're in an empty parking lot. School doesn't start for thirty minutes.

"Who are you texting this early in the morning anyway?" I ask.

Marley blushes. "Nobody."

I reach for her phone, but she pulls her arm away. "Someone from student council?"

Marley giggles. "Nope."

"From your French class?"

"No, sir."

"It's not Liam, is it? Because if you go back to Liam, I'm gonna—"

"No," Marley says, cutting me off. "I've learned my lesson."

"Then who is it?"

Marley shoves her phone at me. "Take a picture of me, and I'll tell you. A *good* picture," she clarifies.

"What's wrong with selfies?"

"Nothing," Marley says defensively. "But he wants a full body shot." She opens up the Jeep door but leaves her backpack inside.

I grab both of our bags and follow. "I don't know if I like the idea of you sending your 'full body' to some guy I don't know."

"Don't worry so much. You've met him." Marley bends over and fluffs up her hair. Then she frames a shot with her fingers as an imaginary camera. "Over here with these trees behind me. The vine maples are turning." Marley poses while I take a few pictures. "Now over here on these steps," she says. "Hurry, before it gets too crowded."

It takes fifteen minutes for Marley to be satisfied with one lousy picture. Cars pull into the student parking lot left and right. "So who's the mystery guy?" I ask as I hand her back her phone.

Marley takes a deep breath. "Okay, so you're not going to believe me. I didn't believe it myself until I did some investigating and made sure it was legit. I didn't want to be catfished or something."

"What?"

"But he has seven million followers and is only following thirty-two people. *And* there's a verified blue check, so I think it's really him."

"Spit it out already."

"Dean Mathews! From our party. He sent me a friend request last week, and we've been texting and talking every day."

"No way!"

Marley grins. "He wants to take me out on a real date."

"That's awesome." I open the front door of Emily Carr High for my sister. "When's Dean coming to Seattle?"

"Um…" Marley scratches her head. "He's not. Dean's tour schedule is super tight. He's in a new city practically every day.

Right now he's in Vegas, for example. But on Saturday he'll be in Portland, and I'm taking the train down to meet him."

I stop in my tracks. "You're what?"

"You won't tell Mom and Dad, will you?" Marley looks at me with puppy dog eyes. She holds out her pinky finger. "Promise?"

"You know I can't resist puppy eyes." I pinky swear back. "But I'd feel better if I was coming with you."

"On my date? Not going to happen."

"What if it turns out you *are* being catfished, and a psychopath meets you at the train station?"

"That's why we're meeting in a public place," Marley says as the bell rings. "And telling you where I'm going makes me responsible."

"He's older than you."

"Only by a year," Marley protests. "I'm eighteen, same as you, and I can do what I want."

"Yeah, well." I pull Marley in for a hug and whisper in her ear, "Be careful."

"You worry too much," says Marley before she takes off for French.

In second period I'm sitting in Calculus and my phone buzzes. It's a text from Marley, and I think it's going to be more about Dean Mathews, but it's not. My nerves electrify as I read, HEADS UP. ELLIE IS BACK. A moment later the classroom door swings open and Ellie walks into the classroom. It's like I'm watching a movie in slow motion. The plaid skirt of her school uniform swings with each step, offering tempting views of her thighs. Her navy sweater hugs soft curves, and auburn hair frames her face. Every muscle in my body twitches for her attention, but she doesn't notice me.

"Ellie!" Olivia exclaims. She jumps up from her desk and encircles Ellie in a hug. "You're finally here!"

Twenty pairs of eyeballs stare at Ellie, especially mine. Calculus starts in a few minutes, but she's the main topic of study.

"It's nice to have things back to normal," Ellie says loudly enough for everyone to hear. "And to speak English again."

Olivia giggles. "Only you would say that. Anyone else would have been thrilled to spend so much time in France."

"You wouldn't say that if you knew how many snails I had to eat." Ellie sits down in the seat next to Olivia and takes out her binder.

"Hey, Ellie," I call across the aisles. "Welcome back."

Ellie looks over her shoulder, sees me, and blushes. "Thanks." She turns her attention to the problem written on the corner of the whiteboard.

Thanks? That's all I get? My stomach drops. But I don't have time to rehash what happened because class is starting.

Mr. Dunsmuir enters the classroom holding a steaming cup of tea. "Okie dokie, folks, let's get started. Please open your books to chapter three, 'Applications of Differentiation.'" He pushes his glasses up the bridge of his nose and stares out into the audience of students. "Well, well, it seems we have a new student." He looks down at the attendance register. "Miss Savage?"

Ellie nods.

"Welcome to Calculus. I told Headmaster Griffin it would be flippin' hard for a student to miss a whole month of school and still function in my classroom." Mr. Dunsmuir chuckles. "Get it? Function? Gosh, I love puns. Anyhoo, I tried to warn him, but apparently your parents insisted you'd be fine."

"Ellie's most definitely fine," Liam blurts. He adds an extra emphasis to the word "fine," and the guys in the class holler like testosterone-crazed animals. I contemplate throwing my pencil like a javelin at Liam's thick neck. How did Liam place into

Calculus in the first place? His parents must have donated a bundle.

"People!" Mr. Dunsmuir wrinkles his nose. "Settle down. Now, Miss Savage, if you feel like this class is a mite too difficult for you, I can—"

"It'll be fine," Ellie says with confidence. She looks past Mr. Dunsmuir to the white board behind him. "In fact, I'll solve that problem there for you if you'd like."

Mr. Dunsmuir turns to look at the board. "My challenge problem? It's a function of several variables from the last chapter of the book. I only put it up there for inspiration."

"Now she thinks she's brilliant," says Liam in a stage whisper.

"Shut up, Liam," I mutter.

"Well, Miss Savage?" Mr. Dunsmuir polishes his glasses and then rests them back on his nose. "Shall we get on with it? With class, that is?"

"Yes," answers Ellie. "I mean, no." She leaps to her feet. "First I'm going to solve that equation." There's a feverish gleam in Ellie's eyes, like she'll be physically sick if she doesn't do math. Ellie stalks down the aisle between desks, her attention zoned in on the board. My eyes drift to the exposed part of Ellie's thigh, where the knee socks stop and the plaid skirt doesn't begin.

Ellie selects a marker off the tray and uncaps the tip. With one swipe of the marker, Ellie draws the function symbol. Then quickly, magically almost, she fills the board with tidy numerals.

Mr. Dunsmuir clears his throat. "Well, I'll be a monkey's uncle! Miss Savage, I stand corrected. I thought this class would be too difficult for you, but perhaps you should consider taking a course at the University of Washington instead."

Ellie drops the marker into the tray with a clink and strides back to her seat.

What the eff was that? Ellie's always been smart, but she's never been showy about it. Now all of a sudden she's a math prodigy. Is that what her parents were doing to her this summer?

An hour later Ellie bolts out of Calculus as soon as the bell rings. "Ellie, wait!" I sling my backpack over my shoulder and hurry after her. "Stop!"

She's already halfway down the hall on the way to the cafeteria. Olivia catches up to her first and tugs on her sleeve. Ellie pauses, just long enough for me to catch up. "What do you want?" She turns a pretty shade of pink.

I open my mouth, but nothing comes out. There are so many things I want to say. A billion questions flood my mind. But I can't speak one word because I don't want to blow it. Plus, Olivia's right there next to us. I tug my necktie, which is already dress-code-infringing loose. "Um… Can I eat lunch with you?"

Ellie hugs her binder to her chest. "Sure." She glances at Olivia. "If that's okay with you?"

"The more, the merrier," Olivia says brightly. "Marley can join us too if she wants."

Ellie shuffles backward. "Marley? Why would she want to sit with us?"

Olivia elbows Ellie in the ribs. "Maybe it's time to let bygones be bygones."

"Huh?"

"Don't worry," I add hastily. "Marley has student council today." Before I forget, I reach into my pocket and pull out something dark and sparkly. "Here's your necklace." The garnets sparkle in the fluorescent light. "This is yours, right?"

Ellie threads the necklace through her fingers. "Um… I think so. Where did you get it?"

"I found it on the patio the day after the accident."

"How'd you know it was mine?"

"I remember you wearing it that night; plus, I saw it in the pictures." I lightly touch her elbow and steer her toward the cafeteria. "I'm hungry. Let's eat."

"Great idea." Olivia flanks Ellie's other side.

Ellie slips the necklace over her head and arranges it under her tie. "Thanks for bringing this for me. But how did you find out I was returning to school today?"

"I didn't. I've been carrying it around for a while waiting for you to come back."

Her pink cheeks turn red then and she doesn't answer, but she smiles a little, and that's a good start.

A few minutes later, after the gauntlet of the lunch line, the three of us sit at a corner table. Ellie picks at her hamburger without eating it. Olivia pulls out a massive sandwich. That girl eats like a trucker.

"So," Olivia asks Ellie, "have you heard from Dean?"

Ellie spreads mayonnaise on her bun with studious precision. "No. He was in Bermuda all summer, and now he's on tour."

"Oh." I dip my french fry in gravy. "Probably he's busy." *Texting my sister.*

"I guess." Ellie takes a sip of water and the ice rattles.

"At least we have the Internet." Olivia whips out her smartphone and holds up the screen so that Ellie and I can see. There's that picture again, the one that was plastered all over the Internet. Dean's leaning Marley back for a kiss, and behind them, I have my arms wrapped around Ellie in a circle of protection.

Ellie colors but doesn't look at me.

"That was a fun night." I glance at Ellie sideways. "Except for the near-death experience."

"I think I've blocked a lot of it out," Ellie admits. "It was pretty traumatic, after all."

"It was a miracle," I blurt.

"What?" Ellie asks.

I clear my throat. Here goes nothing. "I mean, I know that sounds crazy, but that's what I've been thinking all summer."

"What was a miracle?" Olivia asks. She gives me a smile of encouragement when Ellie isn't looking.

I try to sound like this whole speech isn't rehearsed. "Ellie rescuing Dean Mathews in the pool," I say. I look at Ellie pointedly. "You can't swim, right? You're afraid of water?"

Ellie nods.

"And yet you were freakin' amazing," I continue. "You were like Dean's guardian angel."

"You make me sound like Wonder Woman or something."

"But this was real." I lean forward against the table and my chair squeaks. "I saw you with my own eyes."

Olivia whistles. "Ellie Savage, miracle worker."

"It wasn't a miracle," Ellie says. Her forehead furrows, and she rubs her temples.

"Then what was it?"

"Yeah," says Olivia. "You told me you couldn't swim."

"I can't swim," Ellie declares. "At least..." Her shoulders slump.

"If it wasn't a miracle," I say, "then what was it?"

"I don't know." Ellie shrugs, then crosses her arms. "It doesn't even feel like that was me."

"Ellie, where were you this summer?" Olivia asks pointblank.

"I told you," Ellie answers defensively, hugging herself tighter. "I was studying French."

"I believe you." I scoot my chair closer to Ellie. "But were you awake for that?"

"What's that supposed to mean?" Ellie crumples up her napkin.

"What we want to know is," Olivia whispers, "have you been doing narcosis?"

"Are you both out of your mind?"

"No," I say in a quiet voice. "But we're worried that somebody has been messing around with yours."

"How would you know?"

"We're concerned about you," says Olivia. "Ditching your friends, that bizarre performance in math just now—it's not like you."

"I don't know what you're talking about." Ellie stands up and takes her tray with her. "I thought you were my friend," she says to Olivia. Ellie's eyes brush over me with disdain. "But I guess I was wrong." She pivots on the heel of her foot and marches off.

"I *am* your friend!" Olivia jumps up. "Ellie, wait!" She chases after Ellie, not bothering to clear her own tray. I slide it over and stack it under mine.

Shoot. That conversation did not go as planned. Maybe we shouldn't have dumped all our suspicions on Ellie her very first day back. But now I'm more concerned than ever.

I take out my phone and text Marley. `ELLIE'S ACTING WEIRD.`

CHAPTER THIRTY: ELLIE
4:03 P.M. | SEPTEMBER 29TH

"They're on to me," I tell Ellie-Me as soon as I get home from school, head to my room, and close my bedroom door. "All I want is to be normal, but my friends are making it difficult."

"What do you mean?" The September day is chilly, and Ellie-Me sits next to the radiator making a cloud of steam.

"Olivia and Cole. They asked a bunch of questions about where I was all summer."

"Well, why wouldn't they? You told them you were studying French, right?"

"Yeah." I unthread my necktie and toss it on my dresser. "But they didn't believe that I was at French camp. They asked me if I had done narcosis."

"Oh my goodness! What did you tell them?"

"Nothing. I promised Mom and Dad that I wouldn't tell anyone so they'd let me go back to school. Plus, I don't want everyone knowing I'm crazy."

Ellie-Me tugs on her violet dress, trying to conceal the red corset. "You're not crazy. You're as sane as I am."

"That doesn't make me feel better. I don't want everyone to know the strange things I've been through. Olivia and Cole will think I'm a zombie." I pull off my blouse and reach for a T-shirt. Right when I'm about to tug it over my head, Ellie-Me squeals.

"My necklace!" Her damp hands yank at my throat. My windpipe constricts and the world gets dark. Her clammy fingers dig deep around my neck.

"Ack! Let go!" I use all my muscles to shove her away, and Ellie-Me stumbles to the floor. Topless and panting, I glower at her in disbelief. "What, now you're attacking me?" I pause a few seconds, and then I slip the cotton shirt over my head, covering the necklace.

"I'm sorry." Ellie-Me trembles. "I didn't mean to choke you. That was an accident."

"Was it?" I step back without breaking eye contact.

"Really," Ellie-Me whispers. "You caught me off guard with the necklace. That's all." She looks down at her dripping dress. "It belongs with my outfit. Do you have the black heels too?"

I shake my head slowly. "This was all Cole found."

Her green eyes spark when I say that. "Cole? How did he get my necklace?"

I pull out a dresser drawer behind me and remove the first pair of yoga pants I find. I keep my gaze focused on Ellie-Me, even when I pull the pants on under my skirt. "Cole found the necklace next to the pool. He thinks you rescuing Dean was a miracle."

"It *was* a miracle." Ellie-Me creeps back to the radiator. "I don't know how I did it." She shivers like a wet rat. "You're supposed to figure that out. *Your brain holds the answers*, remember?"

"I remember nothing, and I'm still not sure if anything you say is true."

"How can you say that?"

"Because you're a figment of my imagination, that's why." I take the long way around the room to avoid her and then flop down on my bed. With a click of the remote, I turn on the television.

"So what if I am?" Ellie-Me asks.

I turn up the volume to tune her out. The five o'clock news is on.

"I'm trying to have a conversation!" Ellie-Me raises her voice.

But I pretend to be engrossed in a local story about a granny in Spokane who beat up a would-be purse snatcher. If I really want to be normal, then normal starts now, and that means making my hallucination go away.

"Pay attention!" Ellie-Me shouts. She moves to block my view of the TV.

"No!" I yell at the pathetic creature in front of me. "You just tried to choke me. Now leave me alone!"

"I won't go a—" Ellie-Me pauses midsentence, her attention caught by the newscaster.

The woman has helmet hair and a plastic smile. "*Dean Mathews continues his tour of America with sold-out concerts in Las Vegas.*" Behind the newscaster is a video of Dean in a fringed jacket with ten thousand girls screaming his name. The image cuts to an interview with Dean in front of the MGM Grand. Dean sits on a camel with the hotel behind him. A flock of teenage girls flank Dean and let out ear-piercing shrieks.

"*Of course I love America,*" Dean says in the next shot. "*For sure. I love connecting with fans everywhere, but there's something especially exciting about performing in the USA.*"

"It's Dean!" Ellie-Me rushes toward the television.

Blood pounds in my temples and my forehead throbs.

The video switches back to the newscaster addressing the teleprompter. "*Dean's next stops are Reno, Sacramento, and Portland. Then he flies west to Honolulu before embarking on a tour of Asia. His newest hit single 'Dream Girl' is already rocking the charts as the number one most downloaded song.*"

Three bars of music. That's all the news plays before they cut to weather and traffic. "*Dream girl, you're brave. Dream girl, you're kind and you're a quick thinker.*" Three bars are all it takes to make Ellie-Me turn sheet white.

My hallucination appears more ghostlike than ever.

I click off the television. "What's the matter?" I approach Ellie-Me with hesitant steps as the left side of my brain splits open with a migraine.

"That song." Ellie-Me gasps. "It's so familiar."

"I've never heard it before." I rub the back of my neck.

"I'm positive it's important."

"Really? Maybe if you hear the whole song, it'll jog your memory."

That suggestion perks Ellie-Me up. She rakes through her wet hair and pats her dress. Then she eyeballs me and the computer. "Well, what are you waiting for?" she asks. "Turn on the computer."

I mutter under my breath about literature homework and a calculus problem set due tomorrow, but I log on to my laptop anyway. The truth is, I'm equally curious to find out what secrets Dean's lyrics might reveal. I swallow some ibuprofen while the song boots up.

Ellie-Me hovers by my elbow, making me nervous. "Would you mind not standing so close?" I trace my throat and finger the garnets. Maybe I should give the necklace back to her. But I don't have time to explore that thought further because "Dream Girl" is ready to play. "Here we go." I click on the button.

Dean's buttery voice emanates from the speakers. *"Dream girl, you're brave. Dream girl, you're kind and you're a quick thinker. You're the first girl I've really talked to in I don't know how long. I've bared my soul to you. I've got a crush on you."*

Ellie-Me grasps my arm and digs deep with her fingernails. Her eyes are glued to the screen, even though there's no video, only a picture of Dean on stage. I can't look at it without feeling nauseated.

"Dream Girl, you're brave. Dream girl, you're kind and you're a quick thinker. And you're beautiful, the most beautiful girl I've ever seen. So make it okay. Please tell me your name."

There're some guitar riffs after that, but mainly the chorus repeats forever. It's a lame song if you concentrate too hard on it. Sam Anders lyrics are a lot more complex. At least I think so. That could be the narcosis talking. Or the migraine.

"How did you meet Dean in the first place?" I keep my tone casual; Ellie-Me's annoying, but I don't want her to go psycho on me again.

"I don't know," Ellie-Me answers. "Maybe we could meet up and ask him."

"Huh?"

"He might have answers or more information about what narcosis did to us," Ellie-Me explains. "Let's find him."

"No." I shake my head. "No way in heck."

"Why not?"

I massage my scalp with stiff fingers. "I can barely handle school right now. I don't need anything else on my plate."

"What?" Ellie-Me's shrill voice pierces my nerves like an ice pick.

"Not so loud. I have a headache."

"Sorry." Ellie-Me steps behind me and kneads my shoulders. "Is that better?"

"Mmmm." I close my eyes as the pain melts away.

Ellie-Me whispers in my ear. "Dean might be able to tell us more about that night."

"Even if that was true, does it really matter? I want to be normal and move on with my life."

Ellie-Me's cold hands freeze on my shoulders. Then she chops at my back like she's tenderizing meat. "You'll never be able to be normal until you figure out your past."

"Maybe so, but every time I hear Dean's name my head hurts."

Ellie-Me's fingers wrap around my throat like a vice. But instead of strangling me, Ellie-Me swoops the garnets off my head in one swift motion. When I spin around to confront her, they're already wrapped around her neck.

"That's mine!" I shout through my headache.

"Is it?" Ellie-Me's teeth chatter.

"Cole gave it to me, not you."

"Cole. Cole. Cole." Ellie-Me's voice is sing-song. She puts her hands on her hips. "How will you ever have a normal relationship with a guy like Cole if you can't even remember kissing him?"

"I don't know," I say. "I'll figure it out."

Ellie-Me grabs the laptop off my desk and shoves it in my face, so all I can see is the picture of Dean. "He might know clues that could help us."

I brace myself with weak arms but the migraine blares. I'm trapped between Ellie-Me with the laptop, the desk, and the wall.

"Look at him!" Ellie-Me yells. "Stare at Dean until you're desensitized to whatever psychic-driving tape Mom rammed into your brain."

"Stop." I whimper pathetically, trying to turn my head away. "It hurts."

"Keep. Looking," Ellie-Me hisses into my ear. She keeps the laptop in front of my face.

"No!" White-hot pokers stab my gray matter.

"Dean, Dean, Dean."

"When did you turn into a crazy fangirl?" I whimper.

Ellie-Me flinches like I've struck her. "I'm not. But I'm positive that Dean is part of this puzzle."

"Darling?" Mom's voice calls to me from the hall. She raps on my door with quick knocks. "Is everything all right?"

Thoughts of Dean contaminate my thinking. I'm paralyzed by pain.

"Ellie?" Mom rattles the doorknob handle. "Are you okay?"

"Fine," I call back with my last reserve of strength. "Everything's fine."

Ellie-Me clicks on another picture of Dean and crams my face toward the screen. My migraine doesn't worsen, but I don't know if that's proof her desensitization torture is working.

Worn out, I twist out of her grasp, crumble to the ground, and look up at my imaginary tormentor. "I don't care about the truth," I moan. "Keep the necklace and go away. You're not welcome here anymore."

Ellie-Me twirls the chain of garnets around her fingers. "You can't keep me away," she hisses. "I'm part of you forever."

"I don't believe you." I declare it proudly, but my words sound false to my own ears. There's nothing I can do but hug my knees as Ellie-Me plays Dean's song on repeat and forces me to look at every last picture of him she can find online.

Your brain holds the answers. Those words float across my mind when I wake up at 3 A.M. in an eddy of migraine medicine and slumber. I rest on my elbow while my pupils dilate. Shadowy shapes in the room solidify. My desk. The antique dresser. The rocking chair in the corner. My stomach growls. Mom and Dad must have let me sleep through dinner.

At least there's no sign of my former self, dripping wet and hurling accusations. I shudder under the covers, remembering Ellie-Me's abuse. I fell asleep with her shouting Dean's name in my ear. Now I'm trapped in the dark, about to pee my pants, and afraid that my hallucination will reappear. The quicker I race to the bathroom, the better. I fling the covers away and rush to the toilet. Then I tiptoe through the gloom of my room. But a foot away from my bed I pause. I hear a tinkling sound coming from my closet. Almost like the drip of flowing water.

I twist the side of my T-shirt in knots trying to decide what to do. If I turn the light on to investigate, will Ellie-Me come back? I don't want her help. I never want to see Ellie-Me again. But do I have enough courage on my own to face my closet?

Get a grip. There're no such thing as monsters. I flick on my nightstand lamp for good measure, and it casts a circle on the carpet. The sound in my closet drips louder, tinkles turn to drops, and drops morph into roars. Scuffing my feet into my slippers, I throw on my bathrobe. Then I cast open the closet door and flip the light switch. *Water. I hear water.* The sound is coming from the floor.

I snatch up my flashlight and turn on the light. Then I pull back the loose carpet and yank open the trapdoor. My flashlight shoots a small beam through the gloom. Dusty steps lead down and then up into a narrow tunnel. When I stretch my arms out, my fingertips brush the wall. My slippers swish through cob-webs for a few feet, but then the path becomes cleaner. I climb up steps, and ahead of me, the sound of rushing fluids grows louder and louder. Only up close, I realize it's not water I'm hearing, but the gurgling hum of a computer.

In the center of the room at the end of the tunnel, a hospital bed is hooked up to a collection of medical devices used for nar-cosis. Next to the IV tower is a mobile workstation, the type you stand at without a desk chair. The large monitor has a bright blue screensaver, and the huge tower beneath it hums in the si-lence. Across the room, I see another door that's shut. Its relative distance from my room leads me to believe it connects to my parents' master suite.

I stretch out my hand and shake the mouse. The monitor wakes up and reveals a desktop full of folders.

"What are you doing?" The shrill voice startles me, but thankfully, I don't scream. Standing next to me, dripping wet, is Ellie-Me.

"Shh!" I point at the door leading to Mom and Dad's bed-room. This is the worst possible place to argue with my messed-up vision. I chew on my fingernail and look back at the screen.

"What is this place?" Ellie-Me asks.

It's easy to ignore her. Especially since another word has captured my interest—an audio file with my own name and the first day of summer. I click the play button and Mom's calm voice fills the tiny chamber with sound.

Your name is Ellie Savage. You are an obedient teenage girl who loves her parents. You never defy their wishes.

Frantically, I pound the mute button until I adjust the volume to a quiet murmur. I stare up at the door to Mom and Dad's room, but thankfully, it hasn't budged. I press play again and prepare to concentrate.

Your parents want what is best for you. Mom and Daddy are brilliant doctors who are changing the face of modern medicine. You are lucky that they are your parents.

"What is this?" asks Ellie-Me. Her flimsy dress sags against the boning of her corset. The garnet necklace coils around her throat like a snake.

I ignore Ellie-Me and keep listening, even though the words on the screen are already etched into my mind.

You know that your parents make good decisions for you. You never speak out of turn or embarrass your parents in public. You get straight As and keep your room clean. Boys can wait until college because school comes first. You love your Mom and Daddy more than anything else in the world. You always do what they say. Your name is Ellie Savage. You are an obedient teenage girl who loves her parents. You never defy their wishes.

"I told you so. I told you not to believe anything Mom or Dad said was true," Ellie whispers.

I pull my robe around me like a hug. Tears stream down my cheeks, and I don't know why.

"It's because you know I'm right," Ellie-Me says.

"Who am I?" I question out loud. "Am I me, the girl in the pajamas? Am I you," I glare at Ellie-Me, "my crazy hallucination?" I point to the computer. "Or am I this perfect person my parents want me to be?" A wretched sound escapes my vocal chords before I can stop it. Half cry, half stab-to-the-heart. "Where's the real me?"

Ellie-Me's face softens, and she encircles me with wet arms. "It'll be okay," she says soothingly. I rest my head on her shoulder and allow myself to be consoled—until she yanks me back to the monitor and shoves my face toward the screen. "Once you start fighting for yourself and demanding answers."

Against my better judgment, I scurry the mouse across the desktop. There are dozens of files with my name on them, all with different dates.

"My whole existence is on this computer," I say. "This hard drive knows more about my life than I do."

"Let's see." Ellie-Me tears the mouse away from my hands and starts clicking. "Look! There's one that says DEAN MATHEWS. Was he a patient too?"

"You're getting the computer wet!"

Bedsprings squeak from the direction of Mom and Dad's room.

"Crap! They heard us." I look at Ellie-Me's face, but she's too intent on trying to wrest information from the mainframe. "I don't care if Dean was a patient or not. I'm leaving," I whisper. But Ellie-Me doesn't answer. So I flee down the hallway back up to my room. I scramble through the trap door, toss my flashlight into the laundry hamper, and turn off my bedside lamp.

A few seconds later when I'm safely under the covers, I hear my bedroom door creak open. My heart beats like a snare drum. Heavy footsteps approach my bed. I don't know if they're Mom's or Dad's. But whoever it is must be satisfied that I'm asleep. After a minute of what I imagine is scrutiny, they depart.

Your brain holds the answers. I find myself whispering those words again when I wake up the next morning. But why are they so important? Because of some letter? The real answers are on that computer, and I would have found them if my crazy-nutter sidekick hadn't messed things up. I peer over the covers and see no sign of Ellie-Me. With a breath of relief, I toss back my duvet, race to the closet, and throw myself down on the floor. But when I tug with both hands, the trapdoor won't budge. Somebody locked it from the inside. If I want to find answers, I'll have to break in.

Or maybe, I can't help thinking, *I can figure this out on my own.* "It all seems to start with swimming," I mutter to myself. "Would water help me remember?"

"That's a great idea." Ellie-Me stands behind me, a hot mess of wet. "You could go back to the Duchess."

"Go away." I barge past her on the way to my dresser. I slip on my underwear and pray that she disappears.

"All you'd have to do is rent a room, and then you could use the pool." Ellie-Me hands me my plaid skirt.

I tear it out of her hands. "I'm never going back to the Duchess."

"The Duchess is nice. You know it is." When she sees my frown, Ellie-Me tries a different tactic. "Or you could talk to Cole and see if he'd help. It's been four months since the deck crashed. His pool is probably fixed."

"That's not going to happen." I throw on my blouse and rush through the buttons.

"What do you mean?" Ellie-Me calls after me. "Cole likes you. He wants to be your boyfriend. It said so in the letter."

"Go away and leave me alone!" I glare at Ellie-Me one more time and then open my bedroom door, only to discover Mom standing at the threshold with her fist poised to knock.

Mom's face is ripe with questions. "I'm sorry, darling, I was just bringing you this." She holds out a cappuccino.

"Thanks." I smooth out my expression and try to ignore Ellie-Me yelling obscenities behind me, all of them directed at Mom, who doesn't notice. I take the offered cup. "This is great, Mom. Thank you."

Mom smiles and wraps her arms around me in an impromptu hug before I can stop her, and she squeezes the breath out of me. Mom pulls back and adjusts her lab coat. "I'll be in the clinic all day," she says, "but I'll be here when you get home from school. Okay?"

I fake a smile. "Great. Looking forward to it." *Shoot!* Mom hovering is going to make it a lot more difficult to break into that secret passage. I push past Mom into the front living room, where I left my backpack and car keys on the side table. "See you tonight."

"Ellie, wait!" Mom rushes to follow me but then stops, her two feet glued to the parquet wood floor. "Don't you want any breakfast?"

"I'll stop at Starbucks on my way to school," I mumble. I don't need eyes in the back of my head to know that she watches me all the way to my car.

CHAPTER THIRTY-ONE: COLE

"**A**re you going to wait there all day?" Marley asks me. "Class starts in ten minutes."

"I know what time is. I can read the clock same as you." I shift from one foot to the other. Standing in one place for half an hour is no fun. "I'm surprised you noticed the hour. Your phone keeps buzzing so much, it sounds like it's alive."

Marley giggles. "It's Dean. He wakes up two hours early so he can text me before school starts."

"Aw. That's sweet," I say with a mocking tone.

"Jealous much?"

"I'm not jealous!"

"Are too. And you've got a mopey look that's pathetic." Marley slips out her phone from her skirt pocket. "I'm posting this on Instagram."

"Don't you dare!" I hold out my hand to block her.

"Gotcha!"

I can't tell if she's actually taken the picture or is only teasing me. "Would you quit it? I need to tell Ellie I'm sorry for bombarding her with questions yesterday. I really screwed up."

Marley rolls her eyes. "Impossible. If anyone screwed up, it's Ellie for not making her claim on you as soon as she came back to school."

"You make me sound like a homestead."

"More like a tree that a dog should mark."

"Cut it out!"

"What? There's a word that means female dog that I could have used but didn't." Marley looks down at her phone. "Ooh! That's a good one. I'm editing that into the Instagram comments."

"Gimme that!" I lunge for Marley's phone right when she swings her hand away.

"Kidding! Gosh, Cole, you've got it bad." She scrambles away, but not before I catch her and tickle her under the armpits until she squeals.

"Is something the matter?" asks a familiar voice. And there she is: Ellie, standing in the hallway beside me with light from the frosted windows pooling around her.

"Ellie." Marley giggles. "Hi."

I let my sister go and unconsciously brush back my hair. "Nothing's the matter." I lean casually against Ellie's locker. "I was hoping to speak to you before schools starts is all."

Ellie shifts her gaze from Marley to me. "Oh. Good. I wanted to talk to you too," she tells me right as the bell rings.

"You're going to be late," Marley says, picking up her backpack and walking away.

"Why does your sister hate me so much?"

I rub the back of my neck. "Are you joking or do you really not remember?"

"Um…"

She might be playing up the sarcastic bit—I can't tell. But I decide to dive bomb with the truth anyway. "You two used to be best friends. But when you came back from the two years you spent at prep school, it was like you forgot all about her. Marley cried for months—that's how harsh you were."

"What?" Ellie's face becomes pale. "Marley and I were best friends?"

I guess that answers my question about whether she was sarcastic or not. "For years, Ellie. You'd been best friends since preschool."

"Oh. My. Gosh." Ellie leans back against the nearest locker, rattling the door. "Cole," she says, lifting her heavily-lashed eyes to mine. "Will you do something for me?"

I rest my arm on the locker next to her and lean in. "Anything."

Ellie closes her eyes, and for a moment I think she wants me to kiss her. I move in closer until our lips are inches apart. "Would you take me swimming?" she asks, popping her eyes open.

I jump back. "Of course. Tomorrow's Saturday. I could pick you up in the morning, and we could go out to brunch first."

Ellie shakes her head. "No, I mean, will you take me swimming right now?"

"But…" I look down the empty hallway. Any second now a teacher is going to come by and yell at us. If I get caught ditching, my lacrosse coach will rip me a new one. But when I look back at Ellie, her eyes say, *Who cares if we get in trouble?* Maybe the rebel deep inside her is fighting to be reborn. "Of course." I take her by the hand. "Let's go."

We race down the hall, buzz by the office, and almost run into a freshman who's scrambling to beat the tardy bell. It's a good thing I drove today because the keys to the Jeep Marley and I share are in my coat pocket. When we reach the parking lot, I click the remote to unlock the doors and the lights flash hello.

Ellie reaches to open the passenger door, but I shift my body in front of her and place my free hand on her waist. "Wait a sec." I pull her toward me. "First things first." I kiss her quickly before she knows what's happening. Our mouths press together and our lips part. Any question over whether or not Ellie wants to kiss me back is answered when her tongue searches for mine. Ellie wraps her arms around my neck, clinging to me like I'm the only thing holding her steady.

"It's true," she whispers when we finally pull apart. "You do like me."

"More than any other girl I've ever met." I cup her face in my hands, troubled by her confused expression.

"And you want to be my boyfriend?"

"Yes." I kiss her behind the ears, down her neck, and back up to her lips again. "And this is the third time we've had this conversation."

Ellie breathes in sharply. "Because I keep forgetting."

I nod. "You need to tell me the truth, Ellie. I'm on your side. Have you been doing narcosis?"

Ellie's head collapses onto my shoulder. "Yes," she whispers into my neck.

"But why?" I ask. "You're perfect."

"My parents want what's best for me."

"How can that be true if narcosis messes with your memory?"

"I don't know. I can't remember what exactly I've forgotten." Ellie pulls away and stares up at me. "But I know that one of the things I've forgotten to remember is that I can swim. That's why we've got to go to your pool."

I rub her arms briskly against the September chill. "It's 51 degrees today, and besides, my backyard is still a construction zone after the accident. Let's go to my parents' club instead."

"Okay."

"And Ellie?" I hold open the door for her. "Thanks for finally telling me the truth."

"I wish I knew all the truth to tell you." Ellie smiles ruefully before sliding into the passenger seat.

CHAPTER THIRTY-TWO: ELLIE

10:03 A.M. | SEPTEMBER 30TH

The harsh light of the dressing room hits every square centimeter of skin. I glow like an alabaster freak show. Wiggling into my bikini bottom, I try to make the sparse fabric cover more than its design allows. The pro shop in the club lobby didn't have many offerings. I shove my belongings into a locker and clamp the padlock shut. My make-out session with Cole has me all kinds of confused. Telling him about narcosis was probably stupid, but it's not like I told him about the secret room I found last night. Should I tell him? Crap! I don't know.

Your brain holds the answers, I repeat to myself. Right now I need to focus. The important thing is to put my head underwater and see if I can remember something critical.

From my backpack, my phone buzzes. I pick it up to find a text from Olivia. WHERE ARE YOU? WHEN YOU DIDN'T SHOW UP AT SCHOOL, I GOT WORRIED. HEADED TO YOUR HOUSE RIGHT NOW.

Shoot! I probably should have told her about some of this at least. TAKING THE DAY OFF, I text back. COLE IS TEACHING ME HOW TO SWIM. I wait a sec, but she doesn't answer. Maybe she's in the car. I stash my phone and bag in the locker and pin the key to my top.

When I step out of the dressing room into the cavernous pavilion, the humidity is so thick, my lungs chew air. The door swings shut and echoes behind me. Across the pool, heads turn in my direction. Old people, moms, men in speedos, and toddlers in swim diapers. I twist the edge of my beach towel into a knot and keep my eyes on the ground as I walk over to a lounge chair.

I kick off my flip flops and see in my periphery a pair of feet walking toward me. When I look up, Cole's there, his Adam's apple bobbing.

"Wow." Cole's blond hair is darkened by water. "Just when I thought you couldn't look more beautiful."

I try not to notice the driblets of water glistening on his tanned shoulders. "Thanks," I mumble. "I hope you haven't been waiting long."

"Nah. I swam a lap or two is all." Cole rubs the back of his neck.

Suddenly, Ellie-Me pops up at my elbow. "I told you Cole liked you!"

I blink rapidly, trying not to shift focus to my hallucination. Then I realize that I'm fluttering my eyelashes like a vamp, so I peel my eyes open and don't blink.

Cole stares back at me like it's a contest. He smiles, and I feel heat rush to the tips of my toes.

"Get in the pool and let's figure this out," Ellie-Me demands.

I chew on my thumbnail and look toward the pool. A squad of old men ogle me from the deep end.

Cole sees where I'm looking and grimaces. "Dirty old men." He steps in front of me and blocks their view. "Let's get started. I thought we'd begin in the shallow end with a kickboard. You can get your feet wet first."

"That sounds like something our Calculus teacher would say," I say before I can think.

Cole grins. "Okie dokie then." But then his smile dissolves when he sees how nervous I am. "You can do this, Ellie. I've seen you do it before. Don't be scared."

I walk to the edge and dip a cautious toe into the water. *I've done this before.*

Cole splashes in ahead of me and holds out his hands to guide me down the steps. When I touch them, his palms feel hot against my icy skin. His fingers clamp down, gripping me tight before I lose my nerve and pull away.

"Come on." Cole's voice is deep and soothing. "You can do this."

"Be careful!" Ellie-Me yells. "If you die, I die!"

It's easy to ignore her when Cole's hands are wrapped around mine. I glide after him into the water, moving faster than I ever thought possible. Before I know it, I'm up to my waist. A few steps later, and I can barely touch the bottom. My breaths come faster. "This was a bad idea. I'm not so sure—I think I should—"

"Relax." Cole's grip is tight. "You're doing fine. Try putting your face in the water."

Up close, Cole's breath smells like Juicy Fruit. I close my eyes and relive our kisses in the parking lot. Warmth rushes over me, and my teeth stop chattering. I let go of Cole's hands and focus on my deep desire for the truth. Taking a deep breath of air, I plunge under the surface.

I hope to see something. Feel something. Have my memories illuminate in an instant. But all I sense is darkness—and I'm tired of darkness. I'm sick of people never telling me the truth. When I finally surface, my lungs burn and anger ripples over me like waves. Across the room, Ellie-Me is screaming. "Are you okay?" She paces the concrete edge, frantically tugging at her dress.

"I'm fine," I announce.

"More than fine." Cole grins. "That was awesome! I bet you're ready for the kickboard." While I gasp for breath, Cole moves over to the side of the pool and retrieves a blue piece of foam. "This won't hold all of your weight, but it'll help."

I can still touch the bottom of the pool, but barely. Cole holds out the kickboard, and I grab it. Then he pulls the kickboard forward, and I'm forced to follow. The balls of my feet lift off the floor, and I stretch out into the water with long kicks. "That's it," Cole murmurs. "You're doing great." He leads me into deep water in a wide circle, pulling the board in front of him with one arm and swimming with the other.

I'm too focused on swimming to think about anything. Every nerve is focused on not drowning. I stretch my arms out long, holding on to the edge of the kickboard with my fingertips. When I put my face in the water and blow bubbles, I can't hear anything. But when my lungs burst for oxygen, and I lift up my head, I hear Ellie-Me's shrill voice screech, "Be careful!"

"Great. You're doing it," Cole says calmly. He lets go of the kickboard, and I float forward under my own propulsion.

"Did you remember anything yet?" Ellie-Me asks. When I don't answer, she yells louder. Then, from the corner of my eye, I see Ellie-Me slip. Her slim body arcs out across the water and her arms flap. There's a splash and screams of terror as she flails in the water, fighting for life. "Help me!" she screams.

I look at Cole, whose face doesn't flinch. The only one who can hear my hallucination drown is me.

"Help me," Ellie-Me shrieks. "Please! Before it's too late."

For half a second I hesitate. With Ellie-Me out of my life, I could be normal. Sort of. But then I see the mass of red hair trailing across the surface and recognize it as my own. The pale face goes under and I see my own features. When bubbles rise to the surface, I know they're my last breaths.

So I take a giant breath and pump my lungs so full of air, they're bound to explode. I let go of the kickboard and dive down into the water, shooting forward with strong kicks. When I open my eyes, the chlorine stings. But I see Ellie-Me's purple dress. She's floating, lifeless and blank, already unconscious. I link my arm around her waist and shoot for the surface, pushing off from the bottom to give me momentum.

When I break through the water Cole cheers next to me. "Are you sure you've never taken lessons?" he asks. "You're a natural."

My heart pounds fast as I gasp for air. I look at my empty arms and sputter. "What happened? Where is she?"

"Where's who?" Cole wrinkles his eyebrows.

Shoot! Did I really say that aloud? I pat the water all around me, searching for Ellie-Me with tiny splashes. "I thought—I mean, I saw…" But I don't know how to continue. My alter ego is gone, and if I mention her, Cole will think I'm crazy.

Cole splashes me back like it's some sort of game. "Maybe it was your reflection," he suggests. "I'd dive after you too."

I pull my head back underwater and open my eyes one more time, searching for Ellie. But all I see is a cloud of blue and the white hot burn of the pool light glaring back at me.

Then I see something else.

Burning flesh. Boiling water. Churning white froth.

Nerves course across my body like lightning. When I pop back up in the open, I feel like I'm on fire.

"What's the matter? Why are you shaking?"

Did I just see boiling water? I rub my hands up and down my arms, trying to stop the tingling. My circulation is all messed up. "I think I'm getting a fever." The water glows around me.

Cole places a cold hand on my forehead and wrinkles his eyebrows. "You're definitely hot," he says, more loudly than he probably intended. The dirty old men who're watching whistle their enthusiasm and Cole blushes. "Let's get you home." His hands touch the back of my elbow and help steady me as we step out of the pool.

As soon as I climb out of the water, the heat dissipates like steam.

"Ellie?" Cole asks. "Are you okay?"

I pick up my beach towel and wrap it around me. "Yeah," I answer. "I'm perfect."

My head clears, my pulse rate slows, and the woozy feeling goes away. I take a deep breath, relieved, and turn around for one last glimpse at the pool.

A memory flashes through my mind.

A memory of something I wish I could forget.
The memory of being burned alive.

All I want to do is find Ellie-Me. If I could see her, standing wet and dripping in her purple dress, it would all be okay. I need to tell her about the burning. That's what I remembered in the pool today.

When I was thirteen, I was almost burned alive.

Burned alive.

I was standing by a pool of water, having an argument with an unknown man. There was a flash of light. The world lit on fire. For a moment I was safe, underneath the water, but when I finally surfaced for air, there was no escape. My hair burnt to my scalp and my skin melted. I crashed around in agony until I was nothing.

Ellie-Me would be able to explain it. She would calm me down and tell me I'm not crazy. Compared to her, I'm the sane one.

But when Cole drops me off at home, confused that I don't want him to stay, Ellie-Me isn't there. I look in my closet and under my bed. I poke my head into the secret passage. It's like she doesn't exist. Finally, I resort to calling her.

"Ellie! Are you there? Come out so I can see you. I need to tell you something."

A startling thought grabs hold and refuses to release. *Did Ellie-Me drown? Is she dead?* "Ellie!" My cries become desperate. "Where are you? Come out so we can talk."

Frustrated that I can't find her, I head downstairs and go out into the garden. I zip up my fleece jacket to keep out the chill, and poke around the courtyard looking for any sign of Ellie-Me. The big leaf maple is starting to turn and crinkled yellow leaves flutter to the moist grass.

The soft sound of footsteps captures my attention, and I turn to see Mom and Dad standing on the patio, pale but smiling.

"Honey, are you okay?" Dad asks. "Why are you home early?"

"The school called and said you didn't show up. Who were you talking to?" Mom wrinkles her eyebrows—or at least tries to through all the Botox.

"Olivia," I bluff. "On the phone. We hung up a second ago."

"Oh," Mom says, like she doesn't believe me for one sweet minute. "That's nice."

"We've brought a present for you." Dad nudges Mom in the ribs with his elbow. "Show her, Belinda. It was my idea, but your mother picked it out."

"Dean Mathews tickets?" I'm as surprised as they are when it pops out of my mouth. But maybe Ellie-Me forced it out of me—she did tell me Dean was important. Maybe she isn't completely gone.

Mom wrinkles her nose, like she's smelled bad cheese. "No, not concert tickets. Something better." She reaches behind her and pulls out a tiny, green, leather box. "Open it and see what's inside."

I take the offering and sit down in my desk chair. When I pull open the lid, I see sparkles.

"It's a diamond bracelet!" Dad exclaims. "Because you're our diamond."

"Polished to perfection." Mom winks.

"We're so proud of you and all your accomplishments," Dad gushes.

I can't keep back the bitterness. I feel like my parents and I live on two different planets—on their world, I'm a perfect daughter, and on mine, I'm their science experiment gone wrong. "What accomplishments?" I ask. "Surviving a coma?" I hold the diamonds up to the sunlight. "Or surviving the fire?"

Crap! Why did I blurt that out? I don't want Mom knowing about my swimming hallucinations.

Mom blinks. "What are you talking about? What fire?"

There's a rap on the sliding glass door that connects the garden to the Narcosis Clinic. Ursula stands inside, holding up a tablet and trying to get my parent's attention.

I snap the box lid close. "Returning back to high school," I bluff. "It's a gauntlet. But I'm surviving."

"Of course you are," Dad says with force.

"Polished to perfection," I add with a wavering smile.

"Absolutely." Mom smiles back. And I know that she knows that I know.

Dad places a gentle hand on my forehead. "You're burning up. You shouldn't be outside in the cold. Let's get some ibuprofen into you, and you can sleep it off."

"No." I push away Dad's hand. "No drugs. But I will take a nap."

"Ellie," Mom begins, "your father and I—

"No, Belinda, it's okay. How about some orange juice instead?"

"Sure." I take another look at my diamonds and get an idea. "And thanks for the bracelet. It's just the pick-me-up I needed."

Twenty minutes later I'm back in my room. I snuggle under my duvet and try to decipher the thoughts swirling around in my head.

I drift off to sleep quickly and sleep like the dead. I don't wake up until ten hours later in the middle of the night. "Not the water!" I murmur. "Save me!" Only there's nobody there to help. I'm drenched in sweat, and every pore of my skin cries out in agony until the sensation passes.

With nightmares, you at least have the comfort of knowing they're untrue. But there is something about this nightmare that seems real.

Because it's not a nightmare; it's a memory.

I swing my legs over the side of the bed. I have to get out of here. Where can I go? Cole would help me; I know that in a heartbeat. But all he could offer is moral support and frustrating conversations about how I blew him off. I need more answers than that.

Maybe Dean Mathews could help, especially if Ellie-Me's right and he was a narcosis patient too. I don't know where Dean fits into all of this, but maybe talking to him will jog my memory. At least I can think of him now without getting a migraine. But is going to all the trouble of seeking out Dean worth it, or am I grasping at straws?

I consider this for a moment and decide that I'm definitely grasping at straws, but I owe it to myself to uncover every clue.

I dress in the dark, not risking the light. Jeans, boots, and an emerald-green sweater cut low at the V. I add some gold earrings that dangle like chandeliers. The last thing I gather is the diamond bracelet. I lay it across my thigh like it's a sparkly snake. Three karats set in white gold. I don't bother putting it on because it's a ticket, not an accessory. A ticket to find out the truth. I'll pawn the bracelet at that shop near Pike Place Market, gas up my car, and drive off to the next stop on Dean's tour. I'm not a diamond expert, but I know Mom has exquisite taste in gems—this bracelet is worth a fortune.

Dean Mathews, here I come.

CHAPTER THIRTY-THREE: DEAN

This hat was the worst idea ever. I don't know how I let Maxine talk me into it. Nobody wears a fedora anymore. I stick out like a sore thumb, and this trench coat isn't helping. When I said I wanted a disguise so I could go out in public without being mobbed, I meant a wig or something. She has me dressed up like Frank Sinatra.

"You don't look like Sinatra," Maxine said as she shoved me into the town car. "You look like a hobo. That coat is three sizes too big for you. Keep your sunglasses on, and you'll be fine."

Now I'm standing on the train platform fiddling with the handle of my umbrella. A steady drizzle of rain makes the day look grim. Everything about this morning seems doomed to fail. Like this bouquet of red roses I'm holding for example. Once I give them to Marley, where will she put them? The limo? I should have asked the driver to get a vase of water. Otherwise, these roses will wilt in an hour. And then what will Marley do—carry droopy roses home with her tomorrow on the train?

I should chuck them now in the trashcan before it's too late.

"Excuse me," says a voice behind me. "You dropped your umbrella."

I turn around and a girl about my age hands over my umbrella. "Thanks," I mumble as she walks away. Maybe this getup was a better disguise than I gave Maxine credit for.

My phone sings the opening chords to "Dream Girl," and I rush to answer it before the ringtone gives me away. "Marley?" I ask, trying to tamper down the eagerness in my voice.

"We're pulling into the station right now. I'm on the Empire Builder."

"I see it!" The engine is coming closer now, slowing down as it approaches the platform. "Do you see me? I'm holding a bouquet of roses."

"I don't see anything," says Marley. "Hang on; we're getting closer. Yeah, I do see someone holding flowers, but it looks like a homeless person."

"That's me!"

"What?"

"I'm wearing a trench coat and fedora."

"Why?"

"So we're not mobbed by crazy fans."

"What crazy fans? This train is packed with old people."

"Maxine told me—"

"Who's Maxine?" Marley asks, sounding panicked.

"My stylist."

The train arrives, and the doors automatically unlock. The first few passengers disembark. I clutch the phone closer to my ear.

"How do I know it's really you," asks Marley, "and not a weirdo? You could be catfishing me."

"I'm not," I promise. I crane my neck, trying to get a glimpse of her. I see a blond head pop out of the window, watching. "Here, I'll prove it." I throw my hat down on the ground and shimmy out of the coat, which is tricky to do without dropping the roses. The blond head vanishes inside the train.

When Marley races down the steps onto the platform a minute later, I'm holding the roses so tightly, the cellophane wrapper feels sweaty. I pretend like they're a microphone and all my nerves vanish.

"Dream girl, you're brave. Dream girl, you're kind and you're a quick thinker." It's a cappella, right there in the middle of the Amtrak station. *"You're the first girl I've really talked to in I don't know how long. I've bared my soul to you. I feel like I can talk to you."*

Marley rips the roses out of my hands and throws her arms around me, crushing her lips against mine. The weight of her against me steadies my nerves. The curve of her hips in the palm of my hand is every bit as magical as I imagined it to be.

"Put your coat back on," she advises when we finally part for air. "People are staring."

"Let 'em look." I dip Marley back for a kiss.

"I bet this is beautiful in the summertime." Marley pulls her stocking cap down over her ears. Then she links her arm in mine as we stroll through the International Rose Test Garden in Washington Park.

When I Googled "First Dates in Portland" the famous rose garden was top of the list. Unfortunately, I hadn't considered that it was October and everything looked dead.

"I'm sorry I was too stupid to realize the flowers weren't in season."

Marley snuggles closer to me under the umbrella. "Don't say that. This is perfect. I love walks in the rain."

"I love walking with you," I say before I stop to think how dippy it sounds. But Marley lifts her face up for a kiss, and I willingly oblige.

"I'm so happy to get the chance to really know you," Marley says. "That night at my house we barely got the chance to talk."

"I wasn't much of a conversationalist."

Marley grins. "You made yourself heard just fine."

I feel empty inside, not knowing what she's talking about.

"I wish we had longer than one day together," Marley says wistfully.

"Me too. I'll be in Hawaii for three nights, and then I leave for Asia. Maybe you could fly to Singapore in a couple of weekends and visit."

"My parents would never agree to that."

"You never know. They let you come down here to Portland to see me."

"Well…" Marley pulls her collar up. "I might have told them I was at Ellie's house."

"Who's Ellie?"

"What do you mean?"

I wrinkle my eyebrows. "I'm sorry. I've been trying to pay attention. Remind me again who she is."

Marley pauses, and we both come to a halt underneath a Victorian arboretum. "Ellie Savage?" she says in a reminding tone.

"You mean like the doctors Savage from the Narcosis Clinic?"

"How do you know about the Narcosis Clinic?"

"Everyone knows about the Narcosis Clinic. It's famous."

The expression in Marley's hazel eyes is hard to decipher. "How did you meet Ellie again?"

"Um… I still don't know who you're talking about."

"Ellie Savage," Marley says, "the girl who brought you to my party."

"Ah, I see." I grind the toe of my shoe into the grass. "The thing is, I'm kind of hazy on that night. That dunk in the pool must have given me a concussion or something."

Marley's face fills with concern. "Of course. I'm so sorry." She tugs on my arm, and we continue walking down the path. "Ellie's the one who rescued you. Then she disappeared all summer."

"Oh." Unknown facts click into place somewhere in my brain. "Ellie. Savage. From Seattle," I repeat like a robot.

Marley twists her lower lip like she's thinking hard. "You were gone all summer too." She looks up at me.

"In Bermuda," I say on reflex. My stomach feels sick lying to her.

"Bermuda." Marley pulls her arm away. Every nerve I have screams for me to follow.

"Wait." I reach for her hand. "That's not true. I wasn't really in Bermuda, and I don't want to lie to you."

Marley lets me take her hand in mine. "Where were you really?" she asks in a way that makes me think she already knows.

"I wath—" Shoot! My free hand flies to my mouth, trying to stop the lisp.

"At the Narcosis Clinic?" Marley supplies for me. "With Ellie?"

I close my eyes and count to ten. *I can say what I want to say. I can say what I want to say; Silly Sammy sees a seashell.* I open my eyes back up and concentrate on every syllable my mouth forms. "The thing is, I don't remember Ellie, and I don't know where she was this summer. But yeah, I was at the Narcosis Clinic."

"For what?"

"My lisp."

"You don't lisp."

"Now I don't. Thanks to my treatment. But that night at the party? I don't have to remember any of it to know that I barely talked to anyone. Am I right?"

Marley looks down at the wet grass. "But you sang to me."

"Singing's easy." I take a step closer. "Especially when it's to the girl of my dreams."

"Shut up," Marley whispers. "I bet you say that to everyone."

"But I don't." There, in the middle of the rainy garden, I tell Marley everything. "I was in speech therapy for eight years. When you're a little kid and you sound different, everybody thinks you're cute. But then you grow up, and people think you're stupid."

Marley stares into my eyes, listening intently.

"Relatives would make fun of me. Teachers told me to try harder. My mom fought the school district to get me more help. But they wouldn't do anything for me until third grade. By then I felt like garbage."

"Oh, Dean," Marley says.

"I did everything the speech therapists told me. I could make the sounds they wanted me to if I really tried." I puff out my cheeks and click my teeth together. "*S-s-s-s-s-s-s-s,*" I hiss. "Silly Sammy sees a seashell."

"So you could make the sounds under controlled conditions, but you couldn't do it all the time?"

I nod. "I remember the first time I could say my own name clearly. *Dean Mathews.* I was in fourth grade and felt proud. But it took years before I could articulate well all the time. When I was tired or worried, my lisp was awful."

"What about when you were with the Heartacres?"

"I let Sam do most of the talking. By then I had enough therapy that I could for the most part articulate clearly. Then when Pansy ran off with him, I was devastated. Ellie's mom explained it was like brain trauma that triggered my articulation problems all over again."

"Stress made you forget everything you had learned in speech therapy?"

"Exactly. And not feeling stressed by the whole world watching is impossible. So you see?" I tell her. "At any moment my lisp could return."

"It won't come back," Marley says soothingly.

"But it could."

Marley places her palms on my chest. "It won't because you're in a good place now. And even if it did, you're a different person now. Instead of hiding, maybe you could share your struggles with the public. You could end up helping a lot of people."

"I'm not that brave."

"You *are* that brave," Marley insists. Her eyes shine with conviction. "To do everything you've already done—that took courage. What I want to know is, who's been taking care of you? Who's been making sure you're okay through all of this?"

"My mom is the best, but she's in Toronto with my little sisters."

"You're paying people to help you, right? So who's helping you? Your manager?"

I shake my head. "Nah. Gary only cares about his next paycheck.

"What about that Max person you mentioned?"

I smile with affection. "Maxine absolutely has my best interest at heart."

"And what did she say about all of this?"

"Maxine always tells me to be myself."

"I like her already."

I grin. "Don't say that too fast. The other thing Maxine tells me is to go out and get laid."

Marley steps nearer, pressing our bodies so close together that our hearts beat as one. She looks up at me coyly. "Maybe it's time to start following Maxine's advice."

CHAPTER THIRTY-FOUR: ELLIE

10:03 A.M. | OCTOBER 1ST

With each flick of mascara, I look more awake. I left Seattle at 6 A.M. and arrived in Portland late this morning. It took me a while to find a pawn shop that was open—the one by the market didn't open until nine—and another twenty minutes to build up my courage to actually enter the store and pawn the bracelet, but now I'm two thousand dollars richer. It's better this way. Mom and Dad could trace my credit card in ten seconds. Now they won't have any idea where I am. Let them suffer from confusion for once.

I stare into the hotel mirror and line my lips with the pencil. Lipstick smears and creates the perfect pout. I stole this tube, Crimson Revenge, from Mom's purse. Well, actually I stole her whole purse. She won't notice it's missing until it's already too late.

When I dip my kabuki brush into the powdered foundation, my temples twinge. I squeeze my eyes shut and the pain passes. When it does, it leaves a memory.

"Go to your room!" Mom yelled at me. "And stay there!"

I had gotten in trouble at school again. Something about walking on my hands in the middle of P.E. when I was supposed to be doing something lame like running around the track.

That's all I can remember. I coil my red hair into a French twist and jab in pins. Then I finish the style off with a coat of hairspray. I shiver despite the warm room. Am I really better off remembering?

"Of course you are," says Ellie-Me. "You deserve to know the truth about your own life." She sits on the marble counter wrapped up in a fluffy bath towel and then casts it aside for a new one as soon as it becomes wet.

"You're alive!"

Ellie-Me sniffs. "Kind of."

"I thought you drowned in the pool."

"And leave you to solve this mystery on your own?" She shakes her head. "Never!"

"But where were you? Where did you go? You missed me figuring out that I was burned alive!"

Ellie's clammy skin pales. "I don't know where I went. I was just gone. But now I'm here again and I remember the same things you do."

I pull on Mom's white lab coat and adjust the collar. "DR. BELINDA SAVAGE" is embroidered on the front in purple thread.

"I'm proud of you for coming up with this plan all by yourself." Ellie-Me snuggles deeper in her towel. "You called Dean's tour and said Mom needed to check up on him?"

"Yup." I slip the VIP backstage pass that was waiting for me at the front desk into its clear plastic holder and tie the cord around my neck. "And that confirmed Dean was a former narcosis patient." I pull out my mom's phone and text Dean's manager. DR. BELINDA SAVAGE: PLEASE SEND A CAR FOR ME NOW. MEDICAL EXAM SHOULD ONLY TAKE FIFTEEN MINUTES.

"How long do you think it will be before Mom realizes it was you who stole her purse?" Ellie-Me asks.

"I don't know. Probably she'll cut off the number any second, or trace the phone or something." I slip on Mom's sunglasses and adjust them on my nose.

"You could be twins," says Ellie-Me. She turns around so we're both looking in the mirror. "You look more like her than you do me."

Chills ripple up and down my spine. "I'm not so sure that's a good thing," I answer.

Ellie-Me squeezes me in a side hug. At her clammy touch, another memory splashes me.

I was sitting on a pleather chair in a school office, and people were yelling.

"We do provide discipline," Dad shouted. *"Ellie knows that there is a consequence for every action."*

"Are you really going to suspend her for making a dumb joke?" Mom asked.

"Maybe this school is too small for a child with Ellie's intelligence," Dad insisted. *"It's iconoclasts like her that change the world."*

"Exactly!"

"If your curriculum was more engaging, our daughter wouldn't seek out entertainment by breaking your draconian rules," said Dad.

Ellie-Me gasps. "I remember it too. Cole was right about the getting-in-trouble thing."

I feel a sharp pang of guilt thinking about Cole. He's texted me ten times this morning and left five voice mails. Now that I'm safely in Oregon I guess it's okay to return his call. I dial the number and he picks up on the first ring.

"Ellie! Where are you?"

"In Portland. Sorry I didn't return your calls earlier, but I was driving."

"Portland? Why are you in Portland? Is everything okay?"

I escape into the bathroom stall and close the door. "Yes. No. Maybe…"

"Did your parents take you away?"

"No, the opposite. I ran away."

"You what?"

"I'm here to see Dean Mathews. I think he might know something about my narcosis."

"Why would Dean have anything to do with it?" Cole asks, confused.

"Because he was with me my last night of summer and—"

"—because he might do narcosis too," Cole says, finishing my sentence. "I get it. I can't believe I didn't think of that before. Hey, is my sister there yet?"

"Marley? Why would she be here?"

"Because she and Dean are—friends. Look, I know you don't remember that party, but she and Dean really connected."

"Um… okay. That's really none of my business." I look at the time. "But I've got to go. Dean's expecting me and my parents might be tracking this phone."

"Wait!" Cole says. "I'm coming to Portland. I don't want you there by yourself."

"I'm not by myself."

"Who's with you?"

I look at Ellie-Me, who makes a buzzing noise and pretends to slice her neck. "Sorry, Cole! You're breaking up. I gotta go."

"We're not breaking up! Tell me where you are!"

I click off the phone. "I feel horrible," I tell Ellie-Me.

"He'd just get in the way," she says. Ellie-Me pulls a wet strand of hair behind her ears. "You can do this."

I step out of the crowded bathroom stall and look one last look in the mirror. Ellie-Me is right. It is time to find answers.

The old guy who opens Dean's dressing room door appraises me from head to toe. "Wow, Dr. Savage." He whistles. "I forgot you were so hot."

I whip off my sunglasses and give Dean's manager a scorching look. "Are you high?" I peer at his pupils like I'm checking for dilation.

The man jumps back like I've caught him. "No. Sorry. Where are my manners?" He wipes a sweaty hand on the back of his jeans and holds out his hands. "You probably don't remember me. I'm Gary, Dean's manager."

I lower my voice to the soothing tone Mom uses when she's trying to get her way. "Of course I remember you. Is Dean here? As I explained over the phone, it's imperative to his health that I stop by and monitor his treatment."

"Maybe this time the narcosis will stick," Gary says.

My smile could freeze water.

Gary opens the door wide, revealing a reception room. We walk through a tasteful collection of furniture, including a small table laden with food, to the bedroom door. Gary bangs his fist on it roughly. Without waiting for an answer he pushes it open and we step into a dim living room.

"Dean?" Gary asks. "Are you awake? The doc's here for your checkup."

"I didn't mean to wake him up," I say, feeling intrusive.

"Dean needs to get going now anyway. He has hair and makeup in thirty minutes." Gary raps on the doorframe with his knuckle. "Dean. Get up!"

A poof of hair bolts upright from the couch. "What the heck?" Dean yells. A girl with dirty-blond hair sits up too. "Get lost!" Dean tosses a pillow at Gary and smacks him in the face.

"I'm so sorry." I step backward, wobbly in my stiletto shoes. But then I see a glimpse of hazel eyes I recognize. "Marley?"

"Ellie?" Marley smooths out her rumpled shirt.

"Who's Ellie?" Gary asks.

I whip my head around and give him my meanest look. "You heard Dean. Get out of here."

"You've got three seconds until you're fired," says Dean, throwing the last remaining pillow.

"A threesome," Gary says, leering. "I never saw this coming."

"Out!" I shout, slugging him with my purse. As soon as Gary leaves I rip the pins out of my hair and take off Mom's lab coat now that my disguise is no longer needed. Dean and Marley have moved to a couch by the window.

Dean rubs his eyes. "Hey," he says when he sees me. "Do I know you?"

I sit down next to Dean on the couch and smell hair product mixed with soap. My head twinges only slightly. Dean's eyes are bluer than on camera and his cheekbones appear every bit as perfect as the magazines portray. "We've met before," I say. "But the only time I can clearly remember is a year or two ago in my backyard."

"What are you doing here?" Marley demands. She throws her arm across Dean's chest like she's marking her territory. "And why were you pretending to be your mom?"

"I need to speak to Dean privately if that's okay."

"No," Marley says, "it's not."

"This isn't really a good time," Dean says, nuzzling the back of Marley's neck.

I squeeze my hands together. "I'm sorry to interrupt, but I drove all the way down here to get answers."

"Answers to what?" Marley asks. "Narcosis?"

"What about narcosis?" I say defensively.

Marley rolls her eyes. "I'm not an idiot, Ellie. I know you did narcosis."

"Did Cole tell you?"

"No, I figured it out myself." She pauses. "Finally."

"What did you do narcosis for?" Dean asks.

"I don't remember. That's why I was hoping you could tell me."

"Sorry," said Dean. "I don't remember you at all, but I've seen pictures of you and have been told you saved my life. Thanks for that."

"Are you unhappy you did narcosis?" I ask.

"I'm not lisping anymore, so your mom's psychic-driving tapes worked. I can say whatever I want now and it's a huge relief." Dean brushes his hair back and the pouf morphs from bedroom-sexy to casually tousled in three seconds flat.

"Do you have blank spaces that you can't explain?"

"Just that one night." Dean gazes at Marley. "And I desperately wish I could remember it."

They kiss, and I feel like a conspicuous intrusion. Right when I'm about to make my escape Marley puts me on the spot. "Do you have memory gaps that you can't explain, Ellie?"

I take a deep breath and stall for time. Should I lie? Should I tell the truth? I didn't come here to confide in Marley; I came here for Dean. But if I'm to have any chance of spending more time with Dean and hoping that he jogs my memory, I need Marley on my side.

"I have huge memory loss." I look directly into Marley's eyes, which are the same hazel color as Cole's. "Your brother told me that you and I used to be best friends, and I don't remember any of that."

Marley gasps.

"The truth is, I don't clearly remember anything until ninth grade." Unbidden tears come to my eyes and I wipe them away.

"But…" Marley's mouth falls open. "That's when you came back from Remington Prep."

"Remington Prep?" I raise my eyebrows. "Huh?"

"The boarding school your parents sent you to for middle school," Marley says.

"Before you left, we were inseparable."

My shoulders slump. "I'm sorry. I don't remember anything about our friendship—or Remington Prep. I didn't even know I went to boarding school."

"Retrograde amnesia," says Dean. "I bet that's what you have."

"Huh?" Marley and I ask at the same time.

"I remember reading about that in the fine print before my treatment. It's a possible side effect of narcosis."

"If your parents knew that was happening to you, why did they keep having you do more narcosis?" Marley asks.

"I have no idea." I nod my head at Dean. "But thanks for the insight. At least I found one answer today." I grab my purse and stand up. "I better go. I've used up enough of your time."

"Wait!" Marley jumps up. "You shouldn't drive home by yourself."

"I'll be okay. It's only a four-hour trip."

"No." Marley grabs my shoulder. "We'll drive home together tomorrow morning."

"That's a great idea," says Dean. "That way you won't have to take the train all by yourself tonight, Marley. You can both stay for the concert and crash here at the hotel after I leave on the redeye for Honolulu."

"Are you sure you don't mind?" I ask Marley. Dean is already heading out to the other room to arrange things with Gary.

Marley shrugs. "No big deal." Then a bright smile spreads across her face. "Besides, we always used to dream about going on a road trip."

"I'll have to take your word for it."

"You better," says Marley. "And also, you always promised that I could drive, and I'd love to try your new Jaguar."

The Keller Auditorium is packed with fans, all of whom are shrieking. Marley and I have front-row tickets for Dean's concert, but nobody sits down. Everyone is on their feet, phones in the air, screaming Dean's name.

"This is so exciting!" Marley yells.

"What did you say?" I call back.

"Exciting!" Marley hollers.

The lights dim and a deep voice echoes across the auditorium. *"Ladies and gentlemen, we ask that you turn off all cell phones and recording devices."*

"I can't wait!" Marley squeezes my hand.

"Let us remind you that this concert is a smoke-free zone," the announcer continues. The lights black out, and when a single beam of light hits the stage, the whole auditorium erupts in cheers again. It takes five minutes for the frenzy to die down.

"You first met him as the lead singer of the Heartacres," says the announcer. *"Two years later he embarked on a solo career that took the world by storm. More gold records than Sam Anders."* The announcer pauses for dramatic effect. *"America wants him. Australia loves him. He sold out stadiums across Europe. Put your hands together for Canada's nineteen-year-old superstar: Dean Mathews!"*

The curtain rises, and Dean is front and center. *"Girl,"* Dean sings into the microphone, *"I've been really meaning to tell you."*

As soon as he sings that my forehead erupts in pain.

"That you make me…" Dean winks at both of us and points directly at Marley, *"wanna melt."* Rainbow lights speckle the stage, and dozens of dancers leap into view, surrounding Dean with writhing, half-naked bodies. "Helloooo, Portland!" Dean shouts. A drum solo kicks him off, and then he's crooning "Girl, You Make Me Wanna Melt."

But I can't hear one word because my head is exploding.

Déjà vu washes over me like nausea. In fact, I *am* nauseated, and the room spinning around me doesn't help.

I squeeze my eyes shut trying to make it all go away.

"Are you okay?" Marley asks in my ear.

"Fine!" I manage to answer. "I'll be right back." I push my way past the other people in the front row and race to the emergency exit. The music is so loud, nobody hears me bang open the doors.

Oh my gosh. Oh my gosh. Oh my gosh. I rush out onto the street, and the cold air hits me like a freezer. I crumple into a heap underneath a lamppost in the alley.

"What's the matter?" Ellie-Me asks, materializing beside me.

"I don't know." I massage my temples. "But something about that was really familiar."

"You've been to one of Dean's concerts before." Ellie-Me rubs the back of my neck. "That night in Seattle."

I take three deep breaths and focus on the present. The crowds. The announcer. The lights. The music. "Yes!" I gasp. "The only thing missing is the merry-go-round."

Understanding lights up her face. "Yes! The merry-go-round. You left the concert early that night too."

Oxygen fills my lungs, flooding my brain with lucid thought. "Because I felt overwhelmed." I stare at Ellie-Me in her dripping-wet dress. "I remember it," I say with relief. "I remember the concert."

"That's a mighty good start."

Ellie-Me hugs me, and she's as cold as ice.

CHAPTER THIRTY-FIVE: COLE

"Cole?" Mom calls as she raps on my bedroom door. "Can I come in?"

I stare at my alarm clock with bleary eyes and groan. "It's Sunday morning," I holler. "Let me sleep in!"

She swings the door open anyway. "Sorry, hun, but this is important." She sits down on the edge of my bed, and the mattress squeaks.

I bet this is about Marley. She texted me a picture of her and Ellie at the concert last night. Ellie's not turning on her phone because she's worried her parents might be tracking her. But she and I talked on Marley's phone while Marley said goodbye to Dean at the airport. The girls didn't get to the hotel room until the middle of the night. Hopefully they sleep in before they hit the road this morning.

I scooch up in my bed. "What is it, Mom?"

Mom's brown hair is tied up in a ponytail, and she's got a warm-up jacket over her yoga outfit. "Do you know a girl named Olivia from school?"

"Yeah, why?"

"Her parents called. Olivia's been missing since Friday morning."

I sit up straighter, suddenly alert. "That's weird. Where do they think she went?"

"That's the strange thing. She texted them from school on Friday and said she was going to Ellie's house."

"Oh," I say noncommittally.

"But when she didn't come home yesterday Olivia's parents called up the Savages, and they said that Olivia wasn't there and that she couldn't have possibly spent the night because Ellie had the flu."

"Wow."

"But then that makes me worried because your sister told us she was at Ellie's house too."

Uh, oh. I see where this is going.

"So part of me is wondering if Marley and Olivia are off having an adventure or something. That seems less strange than your sister patching things up with Ellie after all these years."

"Um…"

Mom's hazel eyes bore into my own. "Spill it, mister. I know you're covering for her. Where is your sister?"

"She's safe," I blurt out. "I promise."

"That's not good enough."

"She's on her way home. Marley will be here in a few hours, and you can question her yourself."

Mom narrows her eyes. She reaches into her jacket pocket and pulls out my car keys. "Recognize these?" she asks. "I don't know what Marley is up to, but she's not going to be driving the Jeep until Christmas. If you want to keep your own privileges intact, you better tell me what's going on. Otherwise, you'll be riding the bus."

Marley would hate riding the bus. Me fessing up is clearly for her own good.

"I don't know where Olivia is, or why Ellie's parents lied about her having the flu, but Marley and Ellie are on their way home right now from Portland." I grab my phone so I can show Mom the picture. "They went to a Dean Mathews concert last night."

"Unbelievable." Mom stares at the picture of Marley, Ellie, and Dean all hugging backstage. "This is just like the old days of Ellie getting your sister in trouble."

"It's not like that, Mom."

Mom hands me back my phone. "It's exactly like that. No wonder Belinda and Warren lied about Ellie having the flu. They were probably too embarrassed to admit they didn't know where their daughter was again."

"What do you mean, 'again'?"

"You know what Ellie was like when she was younger. Ditching school, mouthing off to teachers, always in trouble. If I didn't know Belinda, I'd be like every other mom in our group, blaming her and Warren for being bad parents. But they honestly did everything they could. Ellie's a strong-willed kid who saw consequences as a challenge to push back."

"Ellie's not like that anymore. She never gets in trouble."

Mom points to my phone and raises her eyebrows. "Oh really?"

"This was different."

"Running away to see a boy band is precisely something Ellie would do."

"Dean's not in a boy band; he's a solo artist," I say, defending him for some reason. "And Ellie didn't drive down there to go to a concert. She went to get answers." My ears feel hot.

"Answers to what?"

"About her narcosis," I say, completely betraying Ellie's trust. But I need Mom on my side so she doesn't blab to the Savages about where Ellie is.

Mom gasps. "What are you talking about?"

"That's where Ellie was these past summers. She was asleep."

"Belinda wouldn't treat her own child. She'd lose her license."

"You don't know Ellie's parents as well as you think you do. They really effed up Ellie's brain."

"I can't believe that."

"But it's true! Ellie can't even remember that she and Marley were best friends."

"Good! Marley's better off without a friend like Ellie."

"How can you say that?"

"Because it's the truth!"

"Well, guess who I'm dating, Mom? So you better get used to her."

Mom's shoulders sag. "It's not that I don't like Ellie. She has plenty of excellent qualities. But she's impulsive."

"Quick thinking," I counter.

"She doesn't think things through."

"Ellie's a risk taker. She saves lives."

"One life." Mom glares. "And do you really want to bring up that party again?"

I look at my nightstand. "No."

"Look, I know you and your sister have been in and out of Ellie's life for years. You should be able to see the truth about her as well as anyone. Ellie gets in trouble because she challenges authority."

"She doesn't anymore. That's what I keep trying to tell you."

"Then why did she run away?"

"Because she can't trust her parents!"

Mom throws up her hands. "Exactly!" Mom leaps to her feet. "I'm calling Belinda right now. She and Warren will be relieved to know that Ellie is safe and on her way home."

I groan. *Shit.* "What about Olivia?" I ask, trying one last distraction. "It doesn't bother you that she went to Ellie's house and never came back?"

Mom glares and for a second is the spitting image of Marley. "Who knows if Olivia even went to Ellie's house? I'm sorry that she's missing, but Olivia isn't my problem. Your sister is."

I crash down into my pillows. Nuts. Marley's going to kill me.

◆◆◆

When Marley pulls Ellie's Jaguar into our driveway a few hours later, I'm pacing on the front porch. Wind swirls orange-red leaves across the yard, and my hands are chapped from cold.

"Uh oh." Marley slams the car door. "Looks like we're both in trouble." She looks at Ellie and laughs. Both girls giggle and link arms as they walk up the path to the front door.

"Is this a dream or a nightmare?" I ask. "Have you guys made up?"

"We had a long talk in the car," says Marley.

"*You* had a long talk in the car," Ellie corrects. "I mostly listened." She grins. "I should have recorded it all on my phone in case I forget again."

"That's not a bad idea," says Marley. She glances between the two of us. "I'll leave you two alone. It's time for me to be grounded."

"I hope you like riding shotgun," I call after her as she marches through the front door. "So," I say, turning my attention to Ellie. "Did you find what you were looking for in Portland?"

Ellie shakes her head. Then she looks through the living room window, where Marley and Mom are launching World War III. "But maybe I found something better."

"Ellie." I reach out and smooth a red curl behind her ear. Then I pull her toward me into a hug. "Next time you take off, bring me with you. I want to help."

"I know." Ellie's lips find mine, and she drowns me in kisses.

My hand slides behind her waist, and relief surges over me to have her safe in my arms. I press our foreheads together. "I'll come with you to your house, so you don't have to face your parents alone."

"Thanks, but I'll be okay. There's a conversation my parents and I need to have that's long overdue. Marley and I talked a lot, and she made me realize that my parents are the people who should be giving me answers, not anyone else."

"That makes sense. But I hope they don't ground you for Portland. I've got big plans for us."

A devilish grin lights up Ellie's face. "Oh, you do?"

"This Saturday. You and me. Top of the Space Needle."

"It's a date," she promises.

I walk Ellie to her car and steal a few more kisses before opening the door for her. "By the way," I say as she slides into the driver's seat, "you should probably check your messages and see if Olivia's contacted you."

"Why?"

"She's been missing since Friday."

"What?" Ellie fumbles with her keys. "Oh my gosh!"

When I see the concern on her face I feel lousy for giving Ellie one more thing to worry about. "Forget I said anything. They've probably found her by now."

"But—"

I kiss the top of her head. "Go home and get some rest. That's the best thing you can do for anyone right now."

Ellie turns the ignition. "You're probably right." She blows me one last kiss. "I'll call you tonight."

CHAPTER THIRTY-SIX: ELLIE
10:03 A.M. | OCTOBER 2ND

Mom and Dad aren't in our third-floor residence when I get home, so I search for them downstairs in the clinic. I find them in their joint office reviewing patient files with Ursula.

"Oh," Mom says nonchalantly. "You're home." She glances up from her charts. "Did you have fun at your sleepover with Marley?"

"What?"

Dad ignores my confusion. "Definitely check on room fourteen," he tells Ursula. "I want his glucose levels strictly monitored." He hands her the paperwork and escorts her out the door, shutting it softly. When Dad turns around, his face is white with rage. "How could you? Do you know how worried we were?"

"We woke up, and you were gone! And then to discover you stole my purse?"

Dad shakes his head. "Stealing from your own mother. I never thought you capable of something so heinous."

"Heinous? You want to talk heinous?" Ellie-Me pops up behind me, spitting mad. "How about—"

"It's okay." I hold up my hands to stop her. "I can handle this."

"It is certainly *not* okay, young lady." Dad paces the room. "And to run off to Dean Mathews of all people after I specifically told you what he was like."

"You told me nothing," I snarl. "You rerouted my memory so I barely knew my own name."

Mom rolls her eyes. "Don't exaggerate."

"I'm not exaggerating, and I want answers."

"We told you," says Dad, "there was no guarantee that narcosis would bring back your memories. Retrograde amnesia is difficult to treat."

"Yeah, except narcosis isn't treating my memory loss. It's causing it. And you're doing that to me on purpose."

Mom sinks down onto the edge of the couch. "Ellie, traveling has worn you out and you're tired." She rummages through her desk. "I'll give you something to help you calm down and take a nap and then we'll talk about this when you wake up." Mom pulls out an orange pill bottle.

"Not going to happen." I cross my arms. "If you try to give me one more drug, I'll scream for the police."

Mom rattles the bottle. "Darling, it's only melatonin. It's over the counter. They sell it at the supermarket."

"No. Freaking. Way."

"Language, Ellie." Dad wrinkles his eyebrows. "That's no way to speak to your mother."

"I can speak to her however I want."

"No," Dad says decisively, "you can't."

"Don't listen to him." Ellie-Me drips on the white carpet.

"You lost all rights to demand my respect when you tricked me."

Mom and Dad exchange a look before Mom speaks. "We haven't tricked you, darling." She puts the pill bottle away in her purse.

"Then why can't I remember being best friends with Marley? Or my entire childhood? Or Remington Prep?"

"Retrograde amnesia," says Dad, who stands next to the office door.

I want to scream. They've deluded themselves as much as they've deluded me. "Liar. Narcosis makes my amnesia worse."

"Good," Ellie-Me murmurs. "Keep going."

"You're not my parents. *You're monsters.*" I take a step closer to Ellie-Me and feel her cold embrace. "I can't remember anything that happened before the treatment."

"You can't remember anything that occurs before treatment?" Dad echoes me in a booming voice.

"But you keep putting me under again and again. You're not my parents. You're criminals." Tears course down my cheeks, but they don't cool off the fiery intensity of my rage.

Mom emits a whimper, like that of a dying animal. "Stop! Oh, Warren, I can't bear it." Before I understand what's happening, Mom's crying every bit as hard as I am.

"Do you see what you're doing to your mother?" Dad glares at me sternly before crossing the room to Mom and tenderly embracing her hair. "It's okay, Belinda."

"No," I growl. "It's not okay. I want the truth."

Mom nuzzles her face into Dad's shoulder. "Is she listening?"

"Of course I'm listening. If you don't tell me the truth about my life, then I'll reveal to the press everything you've done to me. At least everything I can remember." I mentally count how many steps there are between me and the door in case I need to escape in a hurry. If I have to, I'll run straight to the police. "What do you think your patients will think when they find out you put me in a coma?"

Dad shudders. "That was an accident."

"Does it matter?" I take a step backward. "Tell me everything, or I'm gone for good."

"Darling, you don't understand." Mom's nose is red from crying. "We're trying to protect you."

"You're not protecting me, you're protecting yourself, and you're ruining my life in the process."

"Ruining your life?" Mom gasps. "Well, if that isn't—"

"Enough!" Ellie-Me and I yell at the same time. Dad and Mom both startle.

"Enough," I repeat. "I deserve the truth."

"No. I won't do it." Mom sticks her chin out defiantly.

"Belinda…" Dad hugs her once more. "Maybe—"

"Never!" Mom fishes out tissues from her purse and dries her eyes.

I swallow hard. "In that case, you leave me no choice." I take another step backward, preparing to scramble for the door.

"Ellie, wait!" Dad jumps up and points something toward me. "Don't move." Full of terror, I freeze—until I see that Dad is holding up his phone. "Everything you want to know is right here."

"You can't make me look at those pictures, Warren. Not after all we've done to move past them." Mom takes a wet wipe out of her purse and wipes her face. She stands up straight and fixes the label on her spare lab coat. "I have patients to see, and staff to supervise." She gives Dad a meaningful look.

Dad doesn't swipe on his phone until she's left the office. "Your mother's right. These pictures are brutal. Are you sure you want to do this?"

I nod, curiosity pumping my heart like a machine gun. The wait for Dad to open the protected file is excruciating.

"This is what you looked like as a baby." Dad displays the first photograph, and I see a chubby mini-me with a tuft of carrot hair sticking up wildly from my forehead. "We had you late in life," Dad says, "because it took so long to build our careers and establish the Narcosis Clinic. Dad scrolls through more pictures and the baby ages before my eyes. *Is this me?* I feel prickles of recognition.

Me as a toddler. Me taking my first steps. Me covered in spaghetti. Then there's one of me on the first day of preschool standing in the center of a group of children. Off in the corner, I see a boy and a girl, both blond with hazel eyes.

"Why don't we have photo albums or pictures in our living room?"

"We're scientists," Dad answers, as if my question is nonsensical. "You want us to scrapbook?"

"Not even one picture? Like in a frame or something?"

Dad coughs. "We didn't think it would be a good idea."

"That doesn't make any sense." I look across the couch to Ellie-Me to see her reaction, but she has eyes only for the pictures.

"It will." Dad sighs and pulls the phone close as if he wants to shield me from the next images. With trembling fingers, he swipes the screen, and I see a picture of our family standing on a white sand beach with turquoise water behind us. "When you were twelve years old we traveled to Mexico on what was supposed to be a work vacation." Dad scrolls through several more photographs, and I see pictures of myself lounging on the beach, licking an ice cream cone, and sitting in a restaurant with a sand floor.

"It looks like fun." From the corner of my eye I see Ellie-Me nod in agreement.

"It was fun—for a while." Dad's hand begins to shake until he steadies it with the other. "Your mom and I had work to do at the clinic of course, but we did tourist things in the evenings and weekends. You spent your days swimming—"

"Swimming?"

"Yes, swimming—at the beach or in the pool of our private hacienda. It was a secure building and we had every reason to believe you were safe on your own."

A chill creeps up my spine. "But I wasn't?"

Dad takes a deep breath and shakes his head. "Are you sure you want to know this?"

No, I think. "Yes," I say.

"Your mother and I never found out what happened. Our suspicion is that fireworks were involved." He looks at me intently. "We told you to stay away from the fireworks for sale at the local market, but you weren't one who always followed instructions."

I swallow hard, thinking of the stories Cole and Marley told me about my wild past. The memories that have been surfacing confirm what they've told me. *Maybe I don't want to know this after all.*

"You *do* want to know," Ellie-Me says. "You've got to."

Dad continues. "We're still hazy on the details, but there was a horrible accident. A Roman candle exploded on the patio instead of in the air and the house caught on fire. The blaze was so bad that the local firefighters were unable to save the property."

"And me?" I whisper.

"You jumped into the pool." Dad's voice is soft as a tissue. "That's what spared your life." His hand hovers over the touchpad of his phone before he continues. "Although I'm not sure what type of life it would have been without narcosis."

Ellie-Me sees the image first, and her scream is a double assault on my system. There, in front of me, is a face I would be unable to recognize except for the emerald green eyes and one patch of red hair. Everything else looks like hamburger. Or perhaps peeling paint would be a better description because it looks like part of my skin was stripped off in ribbons.

"The pool saved your life, but it didn't spare you from being burned." Dad rests his hand on my back, and then, before I can stop him, he kisses the top of my head. "Everyone said you would die. If it hadn't been for the Narcosis Clinic, maybe you would have. But your mother and I had hope. We knew our clinic had the best medical facilities the world had to offer. We had used our methods a thousand times to help heal other patients, and we had every reason to believe we could save you too. The great irony was that I had spent part of my residency studying burn patients, and there you were—my own daughter—in need of my best efforts."

I take the phone from Dad, and it feels warm in my hand, as if the fire that burned my face is emanating through technology. "Are there more pictures?"

"Yes. Hundreds." Dad touches the screen again and again, and more gruesome images pop up. "Your pain was unbearable, so we put you under for three months. By the time you woke up from your first round of narcosis you looked like this. Luckily, not all of your body was burned, and the doctors had enough healthy tissue from your legs to use for grafts."

"Why weren't you working on me?"

"Doctors aren't supposed to operate on their own family members."

Ellie-Me lets out a scoff of derision.

"But you and Mom do narcosis on me all the time," I reply.

"Yes…" Dad hesitates. "That's different. Your mother and I are narcosis pioneers. There *is* no one else to help you. But when it came to burns, we flew in the best professionals we could find."

Dad rushes through more pictures, and I see my face get pinker, smoother, paler, and more normal-looking. My hair grows back and my nose reforms. After a hundred pictures I look less freakish—and older. I'm not good at judging ages, but I'd guess by the final photos I'm thirteen or fourteen.

"Why don't I remember any of this?"

"Because it was too horrible. Yes, the surgeries were successful, but no matter how much we recovered your features, we couldn't heal your soul. Even with the medication, you endured horrifying pain. Your nightmares tormented you. Narcosis was your only relief. Your mother revisited Dr. Ewen Cameron's research into psychic-driving in earnest. She was convinced we could rewrite your memory so that you would no longer be tormented by any of it."

"And narcosis worked."

"Yes," Dad nods. "Too well. At first, we tried inserting happy memories into your subconscious, some real like your fifth birthday party, and some fake, like traveling to Paris when you were thirteen years old instead of undergoing your twentieth surgery. But what your mother found, after years of attempts, was that those positive memories didn't stick—no matter how many times she drove them into you. Vocabulary, math facts, languages—those were easy because they were neutral facts. Happiness was harder to impart."

I rub my eyes, struggling to take it all in.

"We made up the story of you going to Remington Prep to make it easier for your brain to forget the bad things that happened to you."

"So I didn't go to boarding school?"

"No." Dad shakes his head. "But saying you were in Connecticut helped protect your privacy. We didn't want you to become the poster child for burn victims."

"I see."

"Well?" Dad asks. "Do you hate us?"

I don't know how to answer, so I don't say anything. But I do manage to give my head a little shake before I rush out of the room.

CHAPTER THIRTY-SEVEN: DEAN

10:03 A.M. | OCTOBER 4TH

"Do you think Marley would like pearls?" I ask Maxine. I stare down at the glass jewelry case in the gift shop of The Polynesian Queen, our Honolulu hotel. Rows of creamy pearls reflect the light, and black pearls gleam in platinum settings.

Maxine sniffs. Her hair is dyed pineapple yellow, in honor of our tropical location. "Pearls seem a bit formal for an eighteen-year-old. Why don't you just send her flowers? Girls love that. Or if you wanted to be really romantic, you could send her a dozen roses."

"Gotcha." I make a mental note to order Marley roses every day for a month. But I also tap on the glass case. "This one," I tell the saleslady.

She pulls out a pearl necklace with a golden lobster clasp.

Maxine whistles when she sees the price tag. "Ten thousand dollars! Are you out of your mind?"

"I'm completely out of my mind." I whip my credit card out and the salesgirl drools.

"And I want to buy some postcards for the grandkids," Maxine tells the clerk. She looks up at me. "When are you going to give the necklace to Marley? Maybe the hotel should mail it for you."

I run my fingers through my hair. "I want to give it to her in person."

"Don't mess up the poof! You're on your way to the stadium in an hour, and I don't have time to fix it."

Feeling guilty, I stuff my hands in my pockets. No way do I want to go back into the styling chair.

"I have a plan, but I haven't told Gary yet because he'll be pissed."

Maxine's eyes light up. "I love pissing off Gary."

"This Saturday morning when I'm supposed to fly to Miami, I'm going to fly to Seattle instead. I'll take Marley out for a date that night and take the redeye out to Florida. I'll still be in Miami in time for my concert on Sunday."

"Gary's going to hate that. What if you miss your redeye?"

"Then I'll spend another day with Marley." I grin, hoping for bad luck.

"See how happy you are when you follow my advice? You should listen to what I say all the time."

"You're right." I throw my arm around Maxine's shoulder and squeeze her. "Thanks for being in my corner."

The salesgirl hands Maxine and me our bags, and we're heading out into the lobby when a tiny blur of fur races past us. Sharp teeth dig into my ankle, and I yelp.

"Bowser, no!" says a high-pitched voice. A rail-thin figure in open-toed boots, short shorts, and a midriff-bearing sweater blocks our path. Pansy's waist-length hair is filled out with pink extensions, and her lips are plumped with collagen.

"Oh, crap." Maxine nudges the Chihuahua. "Get off him, you little rat!"

"What are you doing here, Pansy?" I shake Bowser away and grab my ankle. Maxine hands me a tissue to stanch the bleeding.

"I'm here to see you!" says my former girlfriend. "Sorry about Bowser. You know how he likes to play."

Maxine wags her finger. "Why would you think Dean has anything to say to a skank like you?"

"It's okay, Max. I can handle it."

"It's not okay." Maxine jabs her finger at Pansy's saline-filled chest. "You leave my boy alone, and go back to that traitor husband of yours."

"Chill, Maxine," says Pansy. "Don't you need to buy a box of Kool-Aid to dye your hair with?"

"You little—"

I pull Maxine back before she can do any damage. "I said I'd handle it. I'll see you in the limo in ten minutes." I hand Maxine the bag with Marley's necklace in it. "Hold on to my girlfriend's present, will you?"

Maxine simmers down. "I'll go tell Gary about your change in flight plans," she says. "It'll be my pleasure."

"So," I ask Pansy as soon as Maxine's left. "What do you want?"

"Can we go someplace more private than a hotel lobby?" she asks. "Everyone's staring."

"I thought you liked it when people stared. Isn't that why you dated me in the first place? For the attention?"

Pansy scoops up Bowser and clutches him under her arm like a purse. "It wasn't like that." Her long fingernails are claw-like and painted hot pink. Sam's twenty-karat diamond wedding ring twinkles on her finger.

"Look!" a girl screams. "It's Dean Mathews and Pansy Williams!"

"Oh no," I mutter.

"Dean Mathews!" another fan screams. "In the lobby!"

The front desk man picks up his phone. "Call security!" he yells, but it's too late.

A swarm of people surrounds me, holding out scraps of paper for autographs. Some of the fans ask Pansy for her autograph too, and she graciously obliges.

"Hold Bowser," Pansy says to a little girl, and then she hauls out a stack of glossy photographs from her purse. "There's plenty for everyone."

Twenty minutes later, the autograph hounds have dispersed, but there are still people wandering around, not-so-casually filming us with their phones.

"And now a selfie!" Pansy holds out her phone.

I hold up my arms to block the photo. "No way!"

"That better not be Dean," calls a voice from the elevator. "You've got to be kidding me."

Pansy drops her phone like it's a burning ember. "Dammit!" she swears as she stoops to pick it up, cleavage threatening to bust out of her tight sweater. "The screen cracked."

Bowser growls as Sam approaches. He wears a turquoise Hawaiian shirt with a shark tooth necklace. Sam's skin is so tan that his teeth appear peppermint white.

"How could you do this to me?" Sam demands. "Hooking up with Dean while I was on a diving trip?"

"What the eff?" I hold out my palms. "We just ran into each other."

"You can't stop true love!" Pansy throws her arms around me and plants a kiss on my cheek.

"Get off me!" I wrench away from Pansy's claws.

"Pretending you're innocent won't help." Sam pounds his fist into the palm of his hands. "I know about your affair."

I hear gasps from the tourists milling around us. Cameras flash, and people murmur.

"We're not having an affair," I say to the audience at large. "I seriously just ran into her twenty minutes ago."

"It's okay," says Pansy, putting Bowser on the floor. "We can't hide our love forever, Dean. Stop trying to protect me."

"I don't know what you smoked this morning, Pansy, but there is no way we are ever getting back together," I say loudly enough for the whole lobby to hear.

"Are you dissing my wife?" Sam asks as Bowser pisses on the marble floor.

"I am! Get away from me, the both of you."

I push my way through the crowd of onlookers to where my limo is hopefully waiting outside. But right before I enter the revolving door I hear Pansy ask someone. "Did you get all that?"

"This will be perfect," Sam adds. "What a way to kick off our reality show!"

Crap! I spin around. "What?" Anger fills my senses like the smell of Pansy's saccharine perfume. "No way am I going to be part of your effing reality show!"

"Sorry, dude." Sam grins like the prick he is. "Gary already signed the waiver."

"What?"

Pansy entwines herself in Sam's arms and runs her hot pink fingernails across his chest. "See, sugar bear? I told you this would be guaranteed drama." Bowser yaps at her feet.

That's when I take out my own phone and go live on Facebook, making sure the video encompasses Sam and Pansy behind me, plus part of the enormous crowd that has grown in the hotel lobby. It's a good thing Maxine already did my hair and makeup. "This is Dean Mathews," I begin, "and I want to say right now, October 4th, that there is no possible way I would ever want to get back together with Pansy Williams ever again. She and my former best friend Sam Anders deserve each other."

"What are you doing?" Pansy screeches.

"Telling the truth."

"Dude," Sam warns.

But I keep going. "They are both narcissistic, lying, manipulative egomaniacs who only think of themselves and their own careers." I'm revving up now, and it feels good. "They say that the truth will set you free, so here's the truth."

"Stop!" Pansy lunges for my phone, but I pull away.

"The time I spent with Pansy was the worst year and a half of my life. I thought I was in love. I was wrong." From the corner of my eye I see Maxine and Gary hurry through the revolving doors. When Gary sees what I'm doing his face turns as red as an exploding tomato. "Really, I was being exploited."

"You can't say that about my wife!" Sam throws a punch that I dodge with ease.

"My best friend was using me too, and I didn't realize it. The Heartacres leeched off my talent every day. No wonder Sam's solo career is in the toilet."

"Why don't you *thtop*," Pansy says with a nasty expression. "You've always been jealous of *Tham*."

I take a deep breath and aim my phone right at Pansy and Sam. "These two people are so despicable that their actions caused me psychological trauma and made me afraid to talk." I point the camera back at me. "I was in speech therapy for years because I had—I have—articulation problems that include a lisp." Blood pounds in my head so hard, I can barely hear. "But none of that is my fault, and I'm through being silent because other people don't like how I talk or are afraid of what I might say. A really wonderful person taught me that. Marley Evans from Seattle, if you're watching this, will you go out with me on Saturday? You're my Dream Girl."

I hit stop on the recording. There are a hundred people around me by this point, but the normally bustling entry of The Polynesian Queen is still as a tomb. Then, from her place at the edge of the crowd Maxine starts clapping. "Bravo!" she cheers. Her encouragement ripples across the audience, and everyone joins in. The applause is contagious.

"You're going to pay for this," hisses Pansy.

"No," I say. "You're the one who's toast." I storm off to fire my manager.

CHAPTER THIRTY-EIGHT: ELLIE

"I still can't believe it." Cole strokes my cheek. "Your skin is perfect; I don't see one scar from the burns. Your parents really are miracle workers."

I spear lettuce with my salad fork. "I've seen them help other patients too. That's why they've always been my heroes. But I never knew that I was one of the people they saved." From the corner of my eye, I see Marley enter the cafeteria too. "I told your sister."

"Did you? I didn't share anything with her because I wasn't sure you wanted her to know."

"I figured that I owed her the truth about why I abandoned our friendship." I raise my hand and wave.

Marley joins us a couple of minutes later, after she's survived the lunch line. "I've got five minutes to eat before I have to run off to the student council meeting."

"About that…" I rustle around in my backpack and retrieve the flier I made that says, "Missing! Olivia Chen of Seattle. Last seen on September 30th. If spotted, call 9-1-1." "Would the student council consider helping in the search for Olivia? I'm headed to her house this afternoon to help canvas the neighborhood."

"That's a great idea." Marley places the flier carefully in her binder. "I'll ask."

"The police will find her soon," Cole says in a reassuring voice.

"I hope so."

Marley's phone buzzes and she gives it a quick glance before continuing to wolf down her lunch.

Cole winks at me and then says innocently to Marley, "So, have you heard from your Canadian boy toy today?"

Marley rolls her eyes. "Don't be a jerk."

Cole smirks. "I can make fun of my sister's boyfriend if I want."

"He's not my boyfriend. I mean… I don't know for sure or anything. We haven't made it official."

"It seemed pretty official on Saturday," I comment.

"What's that supposed to mean?" Cole asks, eying Marley.

"Nothing," Marley and I both say at the same time.

"Jinx!" she says, and we both grin.

Cole shakes his head. "I don't want to—"

"Marley!" a girl shouts.

"You're all over the Internet!" screams another.

A ripple of commotion rolls across the cafeteria. Several of Marley's friends rush over, holding out their phones. "Oh my gosh!" a girl cries. "Dean Mathews wants to go out with you!"

"What?" Marley turns beet red.

I'm already Googling it on my phone. A second later Cole and I are watching a gif of Dean, having a heart-to-heart with the camera. "*Marley Evans from Seattle, if you are watching this, will you go out with me on Saturday? You're my Dream Girl.*" He says it again and again on endless repeat.

Cole whistles. "Looks like it's official now."

Marley emits a girlish giggle. "I guess it is." But then she notices the time. "Shoot! I'm supposed to be at the student council meeting."

She pushes her chair back—right into Liam wearing his letterman jacket with a greasy man bun and sneering down on us. "What are you, a groupie now? American guys aren't good enough for you?"

"Not if they're Neanderthals," I blurt out.

Liam glares at me. "Nobody asked you, weirdo."

"Hey!" Cole jumps to his feet.

"It's okay," says Marley, holding out her hand to calm Cole and me down. "I can handle this." She slides out of her chair and faces Liam. "Get out of my face, Liam. We're through. And in answer to your question, Dean is ten times the man you'll ever be, and I mean that in every sense of the word."

Beside her, Marley's friends laugh. They must not have liked Liam either.

"You are such a cow." Liam sneers.

"Don't you dare call my sister that!" Cole lunges at Liam, and before I know what's happening he's pounding his face with both fists.

"Cole!" Marley shouts. "Stop! You'll be grounded too."

"I don't care!" Cole shouts as he ducks a punch from Liam. "This feels too good!"

A massive feeling of déjà vu creeps over me, and I place my hand on the table to steady myself. My stomach twists and turns.

Adults rush on the scene to intervene, but not before Cole gets one last jab in that cuts Liam below the eye.

"Ellie? Are you okay?" Marley puts her hand on my shoulder as the teachers pull Cole and Liam apart.

"Sure," I lie. "Never better." Puzzle pieces click into place in my mind.

"I'll explain to Mom!" Marley shouts to Cole as he's escorted out of the building.

"Me too!" I holler.

"Wait until Dean hears about this."

Dean! That's it. "Marley?" I ask. "Did Dean get in a fight with Cole? I kind of remember that."

"You're close. Dean beat the crap out of Liam."

The déjà vu melts away, replaced by a memory of Dean, nose bloody, dodging a punch from Liam's meaty fist. "Oh yeah," I say. "I knew I liked him for a reason."

"Say, do you want to come to the student council meeting with me and tell them about the search for Olivia?"

I think about the stack of missing fliers in my backpack. "That's a great idea."

CHAPTER THIRTY-NINE: COLE

6:06 P.M. | OCTOBER 8TH

"I feel guilty going out tonight since Olivia is still missing," Ellie says, clutching her satin purse. The glass elevator up to the top of the Space Needle is packed with tourists, but I muscle them out of the way so that Ellie can have a spot up front and see the view.

I kiss the top of her head. "After all you've been through, you deserve a night off stress. I don't know where Olivia is right now, but I'm sure she wants you to be happy."

"I'm just glad you were able to come at all. I thought your parents would ground you after that fight with Liam."

My knuckles ache with bruises. "Lucky for me, Dad has his own sense of justice. Mom wanted to ground me, but Dad offered to take me fishing."

"You were pretty awesome." Ellie snuggles next to me in the elevator. The Experience Music Project Museum glows below us like a giant guitar, and in the distance, the globe of the old *Seattle P-I* is a lit up piece of history. The forty-five-second ride is over much too soon.

But when we step off the elevator and into the lobby, I get sweaty. Maybe this "tourist in our own town" thing is a bad idea. After all, SkyCity restaurant is kind of gimmicky. The reception desk is stationary table, but the dining area rests on a revolving platform with a glass floor. Every sixty minutes it makes a complete orbit so that diners can enjoy 360-degree views of Seattle no matter where they sit. What if Ellie thinks coming here is corny?

"It's perfect," she whispers into my ear, bringing instant relief to my self-doubt. "I've wanted to eat here forever, but my parents never wanted to."

"Wish granted." I lead us to the hostess desk and check us in.

"Did you know your sister was coming too?" Ellie asks.

"Huh?" I turn around in time to see Marley and an old man walk off the elevator.

"What are you doing here?" Marley demands. The man she's with wears a trench coat and coffee-brown hat.

"Dean?" Ellie whispers. "Is that you?"

The guy grins and pulls off his hat, revealing a luxurious head of hair. "At your service."

"Would you like a table for four?" the hostess asks brightly.

"Um…" I stall and look at Marley.

"Fine," she huffs. "Let's do this." Marley hooks her arm through Dean's. "If Cole gets to know you," she tells him, "he can help talk my parents into liking you too."

"Anyone would be better than Liam." I grin. Ellie holds my hand as we follow the hostess, who warns us to be careful as we step onto the rotating glass floor. Our table is by the window. Right now our view is of Lake Union, but it changes every minute. I hold out a chair so that Ellie can have the window seat on our side of the table.

"My lady," says Dean, pulling the chair out for my sister. She rewards him with her puppy dog eyes. They gaze at each other as if they're the only two people in the room.

Ellie gives a little cough, reminding them of our presence. "Would you like me to take your picture?" she offers.

"I'd love that." Dean sits down and hands Ellie his phone. "Is it okay if I post it on Instagram?" he asks Marley.

"Sure." Marley strikes a pose with Dean's arm draped around her.

"Pull up your dress," I tell her. "That's way too much cleavage."

As Marley reaches down to tug her neckline, Dean stops her with a nibble at her neck. "I like your curves," he growls.

Ellie snaps the picture while I throw up a little in my mouth.

"Now one of you two," Marley says. I hold out my phone so she can take my picture with Ellie. "Do you still have your Instagram account, Ellie?" Marley asks after snapping a few shots.

"I've meant to ask you about that." I retrieve my phone and post the picture to my own account. "You used to post a new picture every day, but your account was deleted this summer."

"What did I used to post?" Ellie asks.

I think back to Ellie's account. "Ordinary things, like what you ate for breakfast or places you went."

"Like you were documenting your life," Marley adds.

"I know that my parents think Instagram is a waste of time, but that's strange that they would delete my account," Ellie says. "Maybe I only forgot my password or something."

I read the concern in her expression, which is a total buzzkill. Tonight was supposed to be fun.

"Look at the view," I say. "It's already changing."

Ellie turns to the window and gasps. "It's breathtaking."

Dean turns away from my sister with reluctance. "I wish I knew what I was looking at. There are so many lights."

Marley taps on the glass as it slowly moves past us. "Over there is Gas Works Park." She picks up a slip of paper on the windowsill. "Cool, someone left a picture."

"Huh?" Ellie asks.

"It's a Space Needle tradition," I explain. "The tables slowly revolve around the platform so that in the course of an hour we see the whole view. But the windows are stationary, right? Diners leave pictures and notes on the windowsill that other people can read as the tables move past."

"Normally it's kids scribbling stuff." Marley unfolds the note and reveals a family of four underneath a rainbow. "But sometimes people leave jokes or messages."

"That reminds me." I pull a flier out of my pants pocket. "Not to bum everyone out, but I brought one of Olivia's missing posters." Ellie gives me a grateful smile.

"Can I see?" Dean takes the paper from me and stares at Olivia's picture. "Should I know her? Did we meet at your party?"

"Olivia wasn't there." Marley places the paper carefully on the windowsill, and we all stare at it as it glides past.

Ellie sighs. "The not knowing is the hardest part."

Underneath the table, I squeeze Ellie's hand. "Try not to think about it. The authorities are doing everything they can to find her."

After the waitress takes our order, Dean brings up a difficult subject. "Marley told me what you learned about why you did narcosis. Ellie, I'm so sorry. Burns are the worst."

Ellie pauses in the middle of buttering a dinner roll. "The thing is, I barely remember any of it, including the pain."

"That's why your parents are miracle workers," says Dean.

"Yeah," agrees Ellie. "I mean, I think they should have told me the truth upfront, but I've seen them help so many patients over the years that I still believe in them. There's a reason their practice is so successful."

"And you never actually went away to boarding school?" Dean asks.

"No." Ellie shakes her head. "Remington Prep was a cover story for me doing narcosis for my burns."

Marley shudders. "Awful. Just awful." Then she glares at me. "Cole, stop hogging the bread basket."

"Didn't our mother teach you to say please?" I hold out the bread basket to my sister. As I do my elbow hits Ellie's water goblet. It tumbles over and showers her with icy liquid. "Frick!" I drop the basket and scramble for my napkin. "I'm so sorry!"

"It's okay." Ellie dabs at her dress with the linen. "It was an accident."

"You must be freezing." I look down at my long-sleeve shirt with disgust. "I should have worn a sports coat like my dad told me to so I could give it to you, Ellie."

But then I'm the one who gets chills as I watch Ellie's eyes glaze over and her neck twitch.

"Are you okay?" Marley asks.

"What's the matter?" says Dean.

I reach out and hold Ellie's shoulders as she rocks back and forth in her chair. My touch seems to steady her, and Ellie's eyes regain their focus.

"I think I need some air." Ellie stands up abruptly, and her napkin drops to the floor. "You guys stay and enjoy your date," she tells Marley and Dean. "Cole, could you please take me home? I'm not feeling well."

"Sure." I reach for my wallet to leave money on the table.

Dean stops me with a scornful look. "Don't worry about it." He points to Ellie, who's already rushing away. "Just make sure she's okay."

"Ellie, wait!" I chase after her. She's already halfway to the line for the elevator before I catch her by the elbow.

"Can we take the stairs?" she asks the hostess. "Where are the stairs? I need to leave right now!"

The hostess looks at me like I'm poison. "Is this young man bothering you?"

Ellie glances over her shoulder as if she's surprised to see me. "No, of course not. But I need to get down to the ground floor right now."

"The line for the elevator is over there." The hostess gestures to where diners are queued up waiting to depart.

Ellie pounds the desk. "I can't handle a line. I need to leave right now."

"Please, miss," I say. "Isn't there another way out?"

The woman wrinkles her eyebrows. "We have a fire escape, but that's for emergencies."

"This is an emergency!" Ellie shouts, startling the people standing next to us.

"Please," says the hostess. "Lower your voice." She fiddles with her nametag. "I'll get you out of here." She guides us over to the front of the elevator line and whispers to the operator. A minute later we cut in line and are plunging down to safety.

Ellie doesn't bother looking out the glass windows at the view this time. "What's wrong?" I ask as she buries her face in my chest. I wrap my arms around her, feeling helpless.

"I remembered something," she whispers. "Something important."

As soon as the elevator opens and the people pour out into the lobby, Ellie takes off at a run. Her high heels click on the pavement. "Ellie!" I call after her. "Wait!"

Totem poles tower over us. A street performer plays a mournful song on a saxophone. I catch up to Ellie at the entrance to the Pacific Science Center. The iron gate is locked shut, but that doesn't stop Ellie from shaking the bars like she's a prisoner trapped in a jail cell.

"What's going on?" I place a gentle hand on Ellie's shoulder, and she flinches. I pull my hand away. How did our first real date get so screwed up? "Ellie, I'm sorry. Please tell me what I did wrong."

Ellie spins around, tears streaming down her nose. "It's not you; it's me."

"I don't understand."

"I remember, Cole. I remember why I forgot."

CHAPTER FORTY: ELLIE

7:24 P.M. | OCTOBER 8TH

I don't want to keep secrets from Cole, but some secrets are best left unsaid. Standing there in the moonlight with the mid-century modern architecture of the Pacific Science Center behind me, I worry that if I don't confess what I remembered to somebody, I'll forget it forever. When I gaze up into Cole's hazel eyes, I see worry and concern. I take a step closer and rest my head on his chest. He envelops me in his arms, and that comfort gives me the courage to tell him my story.

I'd just finished sixth grade and was looking forward to a summer of hanging out with Marley, playing video games, and sleeping in. Mom and Dad were pissed with me because the last week of school I got suspended—again—for back-talking a teacher. They were super stressed anyways because the American Medical Association was investigating the clinic. The Food and Drug Administration was involved too because of the nutrient and narcotic packs patients drank while they were asleep. Without proper medical licensing, the clinic would close.

All month government officials came and went. They toured the operating rooms, poured over medical data, and interviewed former patients. That part really ticked Mom off because to her, patient privacy was paramount. Dad was worried that if too many people understood how narcosis worked, there would be copycats everywhere. He didn't want competitors sucking away the Narcosis Clinic's profit or prestige. Mom was concerned about the science behind it. Every time copycat doctors failed to recreate Mom's work, patients at the false clinics suffered.

One night that June before seventh grade, Mom gave me a hideously ugly dress to wear. It was turquoise with black ruffles and made me look like a troll. I pitched a huge fit, but she said I had to look "presentable" at dinner that night when we went to eat at the top of the Space Needle with some prospective business partners.

"I'm not wearing that stupid dress, and I'm not hanging out with your annoying friends," I said. "Why do you need me for a business dinner anyway?"

Mom threw the dress down on my bed. "Because they want to get to know all of us before they decide to help or not."

I rolled my eyes and shrugged.

"Please, Ellie." Mom sounded desperate. "These people can make all our legal troubles disappear."

"What legal problems?"

Mom sat down on the corner of my bed. "The government wants to shut us down. The FDA says we didn't follow proper protocol to prove that narcosis is safe."

"That's crap!"

"Language!" Mon said on instinct. Then she softened. "But yes, it's discouraging because we did conduct extensive trials during our research and development phase. Now it will take a whole army of lawyers to protect what we've built—unless these new partners agree to help." She held up the polyester nightmare of a dress. "Please, darling?"

I gave in, and that was the worst decision of my life.

An hour later I was at the top of the Space Needle eating dinner with my folks and a couple of suits. I don't remember what they looked like. A man and a woman, I think, dressed in pinstripes and blazers. I carved my dinner roll into butterflies while the adults rambled on about things I didn't care about.

"The Agency has been interested in psychic-driving ever since the 1950s when Dr. Ewen Cameron first invented it in Canada," the man said.

"But that turned out to be a disaster," added the woman.

Mom raised her chin. "We've made considerable advancement since then, and I can give you my personal guarantee that our methods are safe."

"And efficient." Dad rapped on the table for emphasis. "We can teach someone Russian, Korean, or Mandarin in three months."

"With perfect accents," Mom bragged.

The man sat back in his seat. "That *is* interesting." He folded his arms. "But what we want to know about is your ability to remove memories."

"You see," said the woman, "when a person is no longer of use to the Agency—"

"Call it retirement," the man interrupted.

"Right. When an agent is ready to retire, they're full of secrets."

"Classified secrets," said the man, "that we wouldn't want to fall into the wrong hands."

"What our superiors want to know is whether or not your methods could help give our retirees a fresh start."

"Absolutely." Dad's eyes were hungry. "We can help you with your situation if you can assist us with ours."

"We have a deal," said the man.

"I believe we do," added the woman. She lifted her arm to pull a strand of black hair back into her neatly coifed French twist. As she did, her elbow knocked over her cocktail, spilling alcohol all over me.

"Hey, lady!"

"I'm so sorry," said Mom, apologizing for my outburst. But their guests laughed it off.

"Sorry," said the woman, offering me her napkin.

"She's a feisty one."

"That's for sure," Dad replied.

I gave Dad the stink eye. I couldn't believe he didn't defend me. If I had spilled my drink on someone, Dad would have flipped out.

When dinner was over, all I wanted to do was go straight home. But the man and woman were from out of town. They insisted on walking past the Pacific Science Center.

I pointed to the "CLOSED" sign. "It's ten o'clock at night. The place isn't open."

The woman raised her eyebrows. "Rules like that don't apply to us." A sick smile plastered on her face as the man typed a code into the lockbox and the gate clicked open.

"Ellie's right," Mom said with a shaky voice. "It's late. We should go home."

"Not yet," said the man. "We have unfinished business." When he held open the gate, I saw a flash of gunmetal where his suit jacket gaped.

"Great," Dad spoke with false confidence. "Let's get this deal settled and then we can all go home." He charged into the courtyard of the Pacific Science Center like we had every right to be there. Mom grabbed my hand and pulled me to follow.

The twisted arches of the 1960s architecture cast lacy shadows. The gate clanged shut behind us, and I shivered. The night had moved from boring to weird. I slowed, keeping a few step behind to let the adults finish their business. Concrete paths snaked between giant pools of water. One of the pools had a giant orca statue leaping out of the water. In the moonlight it looked like a sea monster come to life.

I heard footsteps behind me and spun around to come face to face with the man from dinner. How did he get behind—

"If you can really do what you claim," said the man in a booming voice, "prove it. Make your daughter forget this ever happened." He threw something at me, and the next instant, the whiskey on my dress flashed to life.

I was on fire! White hot, shrieking nerves, screaming terror, singeing skin. Agony crested over me. My hair lit up, hair-sprayed bun igniting. I was burning alive.

Stop, drop, and roll, I thought, but before I could try that, the woman pushed me into the pool of water. The icy water stung me like knives. My lungs choked with water. Sinking to the bottom seemed like my only escape. The next thing I knew, strong arms pulled me to the surface.

"Ellie!" Mom shrieked.

"You bastards!" Dad rammed into the man head first and knocked him over to the ground. Dad's fists flew and he got in several punches before the man twisted away.

My hands shook as I tried to peel off my burnt dress, the source of all my pain. *"Take it off."*

"I can't." Mom cradled me in her lap. "The dress is fused to your skin!"

"I'll murder you!" Dad shouted, but his voice sounded weird. I turned my head and saw that he was pinned to the ground.

"Why?" Mom screamed in between sobs. Every ounce of her professional cool was gone. "Why'd you do this to her?"

As pain blurred out to black, I heard the woman speak with a stiff, clear voice. "We're the CIA. We can do whatever we want. Prove that you can erase your daughter's memories, and we have a deal."

Cole rubs my back in soothing circles as I finish my story. I spoke as quietly as I could because there was no way I wanted anyone to hear. The white arches of the Pacific Science Center tower over us, making my memories as clear as the night sky. I let myself get lost in Cole's embrace, trying to put the memory out of my mind. For a few minutes, we stand in silence. But I know this moment of calm can't last.

"What do you want to do?" Cole finally asks. "Confront your parents?"

"I think I have to." I shudder.

"I'll come with you."

"No! That would put you in danger."

"I'm not sending you to confront your parents all by yourself. I'll text Marley so she knows where I am."

My shoulders slump. "This was supposed to be our first date, and all my problems came out and ruined it."

Cole cups my face in his hands. "One thing about you that never changes is that you make life interesting." His lips brush mine gently until I pull him against me hard and crush my mouth to his.

On our short walk to the clinic, neither of us says anything. The weight of what's about to happen is too heavy. What will my parents say? Will they try to deny it? Will they insist on putting me back under narcosis for my own protection? Icy chills creep down my spine as I consider the possibilities. I'll never forgive myself if I put Cole in danger.

When we reach the massive front doors of the Narcosis Clinic, I punch in the security code and wave to Ursula as we walk past the front desk to the secret panel that conceals the elevator. Ursula's control panel is green tonight, which means upstairs on the fifth floor the patients are quiet.

"I can do this, right?" I ask Cole right before the elevator doors slide open to our residence.

"Absolutely."

I kiss Cole for good luck and brace myself for what's to come.

CHAPTER FORTY-ONE: COLE

8:45 P.M. | OCTOBER 8TH

Belinda looks just like Ellie, but taller—and curvier in a way that makes me feel guilty for admiring how gorgeous my girlfriend's mother is. It's Saturday night, but Belinda still looks professional in slacks and a cashmere sweater. Ellie's dad is more laidback. He's in jeans and a polo shirt. Both of them are holding stems of wine, and from the look of the empty bottle on the coffee table, these aren't their first glasses.

"We need to talk," Ellie blurts out as soon as we walk in.

"Darling, you're home early." Belinda sets her drink on the end table next to the velvet sofa. "Hi Cole."

I nod, and shove my hands in my pockets.

"Is anything the matter?" Warren removes his glasses and rubs the bridge of his nose.

"*Everything* is the matter!"

Belinda sighs. "What now?"

"I remember!"

"What?" asks Warren calmly. "What do you remember?"

Ellie stalks into the living room, and I follow, but she doesn't bother sitting down. "You're working with the CIA."

Belinda eyeballs me. "Patient privacy is confidential," she says primly.

"A CIA agent lit me on fire!"

Warren fumbles with his wineglass and almost drops it. "Don't be absurd."

"You wiped my memory to prove that you could do it!"

"Ellie, it's late." Belinda stands up. "Why don't you say goodbye to Cole and we'll discuss this in the morning."

The tension in the air makes my shoulders cramp up. I hate conflict, but I'm not going to let Ellie face her parents alone. "Your daughter deserves the truth," I say quietly.

"The truth?" Belinda's eyebrows shoot up. "The fact is we've done everything we can to help our daughter, but she never listens."

"Belinda," Warren says in a warning tone.

"You have it so easy." Belinda points a finger at Ellie. "Private school. Nice clothes. The right address. You've never had to work for anything in your life."

"That's not true." Ellie's face is white.

"It *is* true," Belinda insisted. "But were you grateful? Were you respectful? No!"

"Do you know what your mother's life was like growing up in Snohomish as the daughter of a farm hand?" Warren stands up from the couch.

Belinda puts her hands on her slim hips, eyes hard and bitter. "I grew up with nothing. We didn't even have heat in the winter."

"Mom,'" Ellie says sternly, but Belinda doesn't notice.

"Nobody told me I was smart, or special or beautiful—and why would they? I was the girl who woke up at four A.M. to milk cows every day. I showed up for school in dirty jeans and secondhand hoodies."

"This isn't about you," says Ellie, louder now. "It's about me."

"Everything's about you." Belinda holds her arms out wide. "My whole life is about you."

"I was set on fire!" Ellie shouts. "Stop changing the subject!"

"You have a nice life because your mother and I work hard for it," says Warren.

"You're darn right we do," Belinda adds.

"Everything you have," Warren tells Ellie, "is a gift you don't fully appreciate." He sounds like a teacher talking to a child, and I want to roll my eyes.

"You never appreciated it," Belinda snaps, "and that was a huge problem."

"So you decided to turn me into a perfect child using narcosis?"

Warren shakes his head. "It wasn't like that."

"We didn't want you to be perfect," says Belinda. "We wanted you to be happy."

"And have a future that didn't involve expulsion or parole," added Warren.

"What?" Ellie looks at me with watery eyes, and I know with every heartbeat that she doesn't know what to believe.

"You make Ellie sound like an animal and she wasn't." I put my arm around Ellie protectively. "Sure, she got into trouble sometimes, but Ellie was the queen of merry mischief. She made people laugh. Ellie didn't put up with lousy teachers, and whenever she refused to do something at school, it was because the assignment was dumb."

"None of the other kids got in trouble like Ellie did," says Warren, wrinkling his forehead.

"That's not true," I say patiently. "There were over twenty kids in our class. Everyone got in trouble at one point or another. Ellie just did things on a grander scale. She was a leader." I hug her tighter. "You tried to turn her into a mindless drone."

"That's ridiculous," declares Belinda. "Parents have every right to expect their children to be obedient."

"I was a kid!" Ellie shouts. "Not your robot."

Belinda's eyes flash fire. "You were a constant source of drama. You never made smart decisions."

"Oh, so I'm one big disappointment?"

"Of course not," says Warren. "We love you, and you could never be a disappointment to us."

"It sounds to me," Ellie says, "that you took the CIA's challenge to erase my memory of the fire one step further in order to rewrite my personality and make me easier to parent."

Belinda squares her shoulders defiantly. "Maybe we did, but only after we tried everything else to help get you in line."

"Parenting classes," Warren adds, "new discipline techniques, reward charts, bribes… you name it, we tried it."

"But you'd never listen!" Belinda closes her eyes and takes a deep breath in through her nose. "Every time the phone rang I thought it was the school calling to tell me you were suspended."

"So why didn't you take Ellie to a new school?" I ask shakily. "Find a better fit for her? Our preppy elementary school wasn't for everyone. Maybe Ellie would have been happier someplace else."

For once Belinda is speechless. Her lower lip trembles.

"I suggested homeschooling," Warren whispers, "but your mother didn't think it would be a good idea."

"And what about putting less pressure on her?" I ask. Defending Ellie is giving me confidence. "You could have celebrated Ellie's strengths instead of obsessing over her discipline record."

"I was bold," Ellie says timidly.

"You were fierce." I squeeze Ellie tighter. "You were funny, witty, and a true leader." I stare at Belinda. "Just because you weren't popular in school doesn't mean you should have punished your daughter for being successful."

Belinda looks taken aback. "Ellie wasn't successful. She was on the verge of being expelled."

"Because the school administrators had sticks up their butts! Ellie was popular. She had loads of friends and everyone looked up to her as the brave girl who didn't care what the adults thought."

"You've always cared what people thought," Ellie tells her mom, "especially what they thought about me."

"No." Belinda shakes her head. "That's not true."

But Ellie wasn't done, and as she spoke I saw her old fierceness ignite. "Mom, it's like no matter how much money you make, or how famous you become, or how many celebrities come to the Narcosis Clinic and call you their doctor, you're still that little farm girl with the mud-splattered jeans. Nothing is ever enough for you. *I* was never enough for you."

"That's not true!" Belinda reaches her arms out to hug Ellie, but her daughter jerks back.

"I had to be perfect for you to love me," Ellie says accusingly, "and perfection meant erasing who I was. You never loved me at all."

"Darling, that's not true!" Belinda cries.

"We had to erase your memory to protect you," says Warren. "The CIA made us. They said if we couldn't prove that we could erase your memories, we wouldn't have a contract."

"So you should have told the CIA to go screw themselves," I say.

"But Ellie was already burnt." Belinda tugs at her cashmere sweater. "We had to heal Ellie no matter what, and without the CIA's help the Narcosis Clinic would have been shut down."

Warren puts his arm around Belinda's waist, a gesture of solidarity. "Our contacts in the CIA saw you as a loose cannon, Ellie, because you knew so much about narcosis but couldn't be trusted to stay quiet or follow basic instructions."

"We were protecting you from yourself," says Belinda.

"No," Ellie spits out, "you were erasing me."

Warren shakes his head violently. "That wasn't our intention. We were trying to bring you peace."

"It's too late for peace," says a voice in the corner. "This situation has gotten dangerous, and I don't like a mess." A woman with pale skin and gleaming black hair stands behind us, aiming a pistol straight at Belinda.

"Is that the head nurse?" I whisper.

"Ursula?" Warren asks. "What are you doing?"

"What I should have done a long time ago," the woman says distinctly. "Dispose of assets that no longer have value." She eyeballs Ellie. "Especially now that they're blabbing." Ursula crosses the room in quick steps and digs the barrel of the gun into Belinda's temple. "The CIA doesn't need you anymore, Dr. Savage. I've learned all your tricks."

"No!" Warren clasps his hands together and drops down on his knees to beg. "Take me instead!"

Ursula flashes Warren a chilly smile. "Don't worry. You get to come too." Ursula grabs Belinda's arm and yanks her forward. "You all get to go on a little vacation." Ursula nods her head at Ellie. "Lead us to your bedroom."

"Dad?" Ellie asks, seeking her father's approval.

"Do what she says." Warren's voice quakes with fear. "Ursula, please. Do what you want with me, but don't hurt my wife and daughter. Give them a chance. I'm begging you."

"What about Cole?" Ellie asks. "Don't hurt him either."

"It's okay," I murmur. "You come first."

"Enough!" Ursula shouts. "And give me your phones. Put them on the ground, and kick them over."

It's when I drop my phone to the ground that I become afraid. Did Marley get my text before we came here? Will she know where I am?

"Start marching." When no one moves, Ursula twists Belinda's arm so painfully that Belinda screams. "Start *marching*."

We shuffle to Ellie's room and then to the entrance to her closet.

"Open it," Ursula tells Warren, who crouches down to reveal a trap door in the floor. "How convenient that you built a soundproof room right here where I can hide you all."

"You're not going to kill us?" Belinda asks breathlessly.

"Not yet. I might need you for technical questions in the future." Ursula kicks Warren, urging him down the hole. "Get down there, people. I have phone calls to make." Her gun glints in the lamplight, the barrel still pressed into Belinda's neck.

With obvious regret, Warren climbs through the secret passage.

"You next, lover boy." Ursula sneers at me.

For a half second, I think about attacking her, swinging my leg out and knocking Ursula off her feet. But could I do it before she shot Belinda? But if Belinda dies, Ellie would never forgive me, and I can't risk that. So I climb through the hole too. It's cold and dark and I hear a faint humming sound in the distance. I wait at the bottom of the short ladder for Ellie and her mom, who cry when we hear the trapdoor deadbolt slide shut behind them.

"Mom!" Ellie screams.

"Darling, hurry, there's no time. Let's see if the other door is unlocked."

Belinda leads us through the dark passage into a small room with a hospital bed and medical equipment. Warren is already there, switching on lights and shaking his head. "I already checked. The exit in our room is locked too."

"The key," Belinda says. "Do you have it?"

Warren shakes his head. "The secret key is missing too. We're trapped."

"What about this computer?" asks Ellie, referring to a standing desk with a monitor. "We'll message someone for help."

"It's not connected." Warren sits on the edge of the hospital bed and throws his head in his hands. "This room is designed to be hidden."

Belinda tears up but doesn't bother to wipe her eyes. "It's where we kept you," she tells Ellie. "So the rest of the staff wouldn't know you were enduring two years of treatment."

"The only nurse we let assist us was Ursula, our contact with the CIA." Warren reaches out for his wife's hand, and Belinda joins him on the edge of the bed. "Nobody else knows this place exists."

"So that's it?" Ellie asks. "We're doomed?"

"No," I say. I point to the rumpled sheets. "Someone's been sleeping here."

Warren jumps to his feet. "That's not possible." Then he looks at the smashed pillow. "I don't understand."

Belinda leans down and sniffs the sheets like a bloodhound. "These don't smell fresh. Cole is right. Someone has been here."

"Who?" Ellie asks. "You said this room was for me."

Belinda nods. "Yes, and later we used to it to treat high-profile agents from the CIA."

"Ursula helped with that too," Warren adds.

"Don't worry," I tell Ellie. "There's got to be a way out. I'll inspect every inch of this narcosis room if I have to."

She runs into my arms, and we melt into an embrace. I close my eyes and start praying. What we need now is a miracle.

CHAPTER FORTY-TWO: URSULA

9:22 P.M. | OCTOBER 8TH

The only reason I took this assignment was because of Larry. He was five feet five and had a bald spot the size of Alaska on his shiny head. Larry worked out at the gym, but you'd never notice his muscles. His wardrobe of pleated khakis and navy blue polo shirts was designed to make him look average. If anyone asked, Larry told people he worked at Best Buy. In reality, he had a PhD and invented biological weapons for the government.

Larry was the most ordinary, extraordinary man I'd ever met. He was also my first partner in the CIA. Once, when we ran a research trial in Bogotá, Larry killed two cocaine dealers and a taxi driver who'd tried to kidnap me. I took out a couple of narcs too but was grateful that Larry had had my back.

Larry was also a big kidder. He rubbed his PhD in my face every single day, but it was all in fun. I'm a doctor, not a registered nurse like the Savages assume. I've got an MD from Cornell University.

Larry and I spent five years together conducting secret medical experiments all over the world with HN-914, a strain of influenza infused with probiotics. It would have been the most brilliant bioterrorist weapon our government had ever created—if the new president hadn't replaced the agency's director and axed our funding.

Larry threw a huge fit when our bosses terminated our program. He threatened to give the bureaucrats in Washington a taste of the program they had destroyed. Our managers responded by firing Larry and stripping him of his badge.

Unfortunately, with the CIA, you can't just quit or be fired. A lifelong agent like Larry was a walking book of information.

"Ursula," he told me over the phone ten minutes later. "They're coming for me. I know it. Don't let me die in vain. Find a way to keep HN-914 going."

The newspapers reported it as a drunk driving accident. The headline said, "BEST BUY EMPLOYEE DIES IN FATAL DUI." But I knew the truth. Larry had known too much.

With HN-914 on the chopping block, I scrambled to find a way to apply my medical skills to the agency in a way that would both keep my job and honor Larry's legacy. When the Savages claimed to have revived Dr. Ewen Cameron's pioneering work in psychic-driving, everyone was intrigued. I jockeyed my position and was assigned to the case. If psychic-driving worked, agents like Larry would still be alive.

I've played the game. I've worn the white nurse's uniform. I've done my time in Seattle. A lot of agents owe their lives to me—or at least their retirements. But bringing psychic-driving to the CIA was only one part of my goal.

I made a promise to Larry to finish what we began with HN-914.

That little minx who came snooping around the Narcosis Clinic last Friday was the perfect test subject. One look at her skinny frame and I knew she had the perfect metabolism for probiotic research. I'd heard Warren joke about his daughter's friend being a calorie-torcher before, and seeing was believing.

"How long have you worked here?" Olivia asked. "I'm writing an article for my school newspaper." Nancy Drew should have kept her mouth shut.

Now she's stuffed in the trunk of my car. We're on our way to Sea-Tac Airport. The drugs shouldn't wear off until we're already on the plane to Bogotá. I still have friends in Columbia who'll set up a clinic for me.

More importantly, I've got one last strand of HN-914 to play with and lots of contacts who want to buy it.

I'm done being other people's puppet.

This special agent has gone rogue.

CHAPTER FORTY-THREE: DEAN

12:30 A.M. | OCTOBER 9TH

All I can say is I'm glad that limo had a privacy screen. It was a half-hour drive from downtown Seattle to Sea-Tac Airport, and Marley and I took pleasure in every last second. Even now, standing here at the gate, with her pressed next to me, I can barely stop myself from sliding my hands up her dress. Since I'm wearing my old-man disguise, that might cause unwanted attention.

"I can't believe you bought me a ticket to Miami and I don't get to use it," Marley says.

"An extra hour with you is worth the added expense. I didn't want to have to say goodbye at the security gate."

Marley looks at both tickets. "Hey! Your ticket is in first class and mine is in coach."

I grin. "That's why you need to stay in Seattle. If I encourage you to ditch school and run off with me, your parents will hate my guts."

Marley sighs. "They're already going to be pissed. My curfew is midnight, and it's almost one in the morning."

"What time will the limo bring you home, do you think?"

"I don't know. Two maybe? Hopefully Cole can sweet-talk them. He texted me to say he was going to Ellie's house, but he should be home by now."

"Marley—" I start to say, but she stops me.

"I know. I'm going to miss you too."

"I'm in the middle of a tour, and I need to hire a new manager, but as soon as all that gets worked out, I'm coming back to see you. Every chance I get."

Marley smiles, and her hazel eyes are joyful. "And I can fly out to see you too on the weekends."

"And we'll talk every day on the phone."

"Every day."

My voice is choked with emotion. "Talking with you has been everything."

Marley squeezes my hands. "I'm going to miss you so much."

"*Flight 784 is now boarding for Miami.*" The woman's voice blares over the loudspeaker. "*First class passengers, please step forward.*"

"I'll wait and board with coach."

"You do have two tickets, after all." Marley lifts her face up for a kiss.

It's when we pull away that it happens. I notice a girl in the crowd who looks familiar. So familiar, in fact, that my heart stops thinking about Marley and my brain kicks into action.

"That girl," I say urgently, "the one with dark hair over there. Could that be the girl from the missing poster?"

Marley spins around to look where I'm pointing. "It is!" She bolts away from me. "Olivia!" Marley shouts at the top of her lungs.

"Security!" I call. "Police!"

Ahead of us, the woman shepherding Olivia through the crowd breaks into a run, dragging the girl, who looks half asleep, along by her arm.

"Stop!" Marley cries.

I run so fast that the fedora flies off my head.

"Is that Dean Mathews?" I hear someone ask.

"Olivia!" I shout. "Security!" Marley is two steps behind me as TSA agents swarm into the terminal. "Over there!" I point to the duo that's rapidly getting away.

"Freeze!" an officer shouts.

All around us, the crowds go silent.

The woman turns around with both hands in the air. She has smooth skin, raven black hair, and a defiant gleam in her eye. "I'm Agent Ursula Harper with the Central Intelligence Agency, and I'm going to reach into my pocket and pull out my badge."

"No, she's not!" calls Marley. "She's kidnapping Olivia Chen, who's been missing from Seattle for over a week!"

"Quiet!" the officer in charge barks. He's a beefy guy with a thick mustache.

Agent Harper pulls out her badge and hands it over.

The officer inspects it and grunts. Then he looks at Olivia, who's wearing yoga pants and a sweatshirt. She stares into the distance, a bit of spittle dripping down her cheek. "Olivia Chen?" the officer asks her. "Is that you?"

"You're interfering with federal business," Agent Harper says with authority.

"The last time I checked, I worked for the government too," says the TSA officer. "Agent Ursula Harper, you're coming with me."

I don't board the plane, which means tomorrow night will be the first tour date I've ever missed. Refunding those concert tickets will probably cost a boatload of money, but there was nothing I could do. All of the flights were delayed, and it took four hours before the TSA cleared everyone to leave. By that point it was almost five A.M., and I didn't want to send Marley home to face the wrath of her parents all by herself.

Now we're standing on the porch of her house, an enormous gothic mansion, stealing one last kiss.

"Your front door looks vaguely familiar. I think it's the gargoyles."

"Wait until you see the deck."

"Maybe your parents won't be angry about you breaking curfew. You did find Olivia, after all."

"*You're* the one who rescued Olivia." Marley rises on her tiptoes so that her mouth is closer to mine.

I'm just leaning down to kiss her when the front door flies open.

"Where have you been, young lady?" a man shouts. He has shaggy, blond hair and a scruffy beard.

"Uh… hi. You must be Captain Evans." I hold out my hand to shake. "I'm Dean Mathews. Pleased to meet you."

Captain Evans ignores my hand and glares at his daughter. A lovely woman in a pink bathrobe squeezes into the door frame next to him. Her hazel eyes are the exact same shade as Marley's.

"Is your brother with you?" Mrs. Evans asks.

"No," Marley answers, shooting me a confused glance, "he's not."

"What did you do with my daughter?" Captain Evan's voice rumbles low and fierce.

Nervousness takes hold. "We went to the Thpace Needle," I say. Marley squeezes my hand, and I take a deep breath and focus on my tongue. "We went to the Space Needle. Then we went to the airport so I could fly back to my tour. That's when we spotted Olivia being kidnapped."

Mrs. Evans gasps. "Olivia Chen? You found her?"

"Dean found her." Marley smiles. "And then the authorizes got involved, and nobody could leave for hours. Otherwise, I totally would have been home by midnight."

Captain Evans looks me up and down and grunts. Then he turns his discerning gaze to his daughter. "Why didn't you call?"

"I texted Cole about it. I figured he would tell you."

"Cole's not here." Mrs. Evans holds the door open. "Come into the house so we can talk. I don't need the whole neighborhood seeing me in my nightgown."

"I'd say welcome to my house, but you've apparently been here before," says Captain Evans.

"Uh, yeah." I sit down next to Marley on a navy blue sofa in the living room.

"When was the last time you saw your brother?" the captain asks Marley.

"Tonight—er, last night at SkyCity restaurant," she says. "Ellie wasn't feeling well, so Cole took her home." Marley holds out her phone and scrolls through texts. "My last message from him was at 8:30."

Mrs. Evans throws her hands up in the air. "See, Gerald? He's probably fine." She gets up in a huff. "I'm going to make some coffee. Dean, I hope you like pancakes."

"I love pancakes. Do you need any help?" Mrs. Evans seems like a lot better company than her husband.

"Not so fast," says the captain. "You and I have things to talk about."

Marley's phone buzzes, and I swallow hard.

"I love your daughter, and I respect her very much, and I would never want to come between her and her education," I ramble.

"You love me?" asks Marley with a squeal.

I feel the back of my neck turn red. Love? Where did that come from? But I turn to Marley and own it. "Yeah," I say. "I do."

Marley tosses her arms around me and nuzzles my neck while Captain Evans makes choking noises. "I love you too," she whispers in my ear.

"Are you going to answer that?" Captain Evans demands as Marley's phone buzzes again. "It might be Cole."

"Sure." Marley pulls away and swipes open her screen. Her eyes go wide. "It's the federal agent at the airport asking me to call him back." She steps into the foyer, but before I can think of something to say to her father, she's back, her expression grim. "He wanted to know if I'd seen Ellie or her parents. I told him no, but that the last place we knew they were headed was Ellie's house. The police are securing a warrant to enter the Narcosis Clinic right now."

"Coffee, anyone?" Mrs. Evans re-enters the living room holding a tray.

"The police don't know where Ellie and her parents are?" the captain asks.

"Oh no!" Mrs. Evans rattles the tray and almost drops it.

"Cole and Ellie are probably together," I say.

Marley looks back at her phone. "The last place Cole told me he went was the Narcosis Clinic."

"The police might need the warrant to check that place out," I say, "but we don't."

Captain Evans raises one eyebrow at me. "Thanks, Captain Obvious."

We take our coffee with us on the road.

CHAPTER FORTY-FOUR: ELLIE

6:56 A.M. | OCTOBER 9TH

Cole's fingertips are bleeding from his failed attempt to pry the baseboard off the wall. Mom finds some bandages and antiseptic and tends to the wounds while Dad chides him.

"I told you there was no way out. I designed this room myself." Dad looks at me with love that I can't say I feel in return. "I spared no expense to make it perfect because my daughter's safety was at stake."

"Yeah, because you're so concerned with my wellbeing," I mutter.

"Of course we are." Mom applies the last piece of gauze to Cole's finger. "Ursula might think she knows everything she needs for the CIA to recreate narcosis, but she doesn't. Sooner or later they'll need my help. Our only hope is that Ursula will come back to release us."

"Why was Ursula here in the first place?" Cole asks.

"That was part of the deal we cut with the CIA," Dad explains. "They gave us the money and protection we needed to make our legal problems go away. In exchange, we helped treat whomever they wished."

Mom sits back down on the bed next to Dad. "Ursula stayed on as our liaison. Whenever an agent was being treated, she was that person's private nurse. She tried to prevent us from knowing what the agents knew, but it was impossible to do to our jobs properly unless we knew what memories we were supposed to erase."

Dad pats Mom's hand. "Over time, we learned more and more information about CIA operations."

"At first, we didn't realize the danger that placed us in. We were so focused on your recovery." Mom squeezes her eyes shut like she could make the memories disappear. "And once our problems with the FDA went away, we became famous. The Narcosis Clinic was more successful than ever."

"But then things got weird." Dad shakes his head. "Ursula monitored us twenty-four seven. She had to know where we were at every moment of the day, and if we didn't clock in with her, or did anything to displease her, she'd make us pay."

"How?" Cole asks.

Mom chews her fingernail a second before answering. "She'd freeze our bank accounts, stop checks, change our passwords."

"File bogus anonymous tips with the FDA that would appear and disappear depending on how pleased she was with us," Dad added.

"Her favorite tactic," Mom says, looking straight at me, "was to text us pictures of you at school or in your room."

"Huh?" My stomach drops.

Mom bites her finger nail again and Dad explains. "Ursula would constantly remind us that if we didn't do what she wanted, she'd hurt you."

Mom drops her hand to her lap. "Once she left a lock of your hair tied with a black ribbon inside the pocket of my lab coat."

"How'd she get my hair?"

"Ursula had access to anything she wanted," Dad says and shudders.

"For the past few years we've had to do what she said or else. But I'm done with that now." Mom leans her head against Dad's chest. "I won't give them one bit of assistance until they let the rest of you go."

"I'm not leaving without you, Belinda."

"Oh, Warren, this is a nightmare."

"I know, darling.

"We should have gone to the press or the FBI. Anything would have been better than getting entangled with the CIA."

"I'm the business side of this operation," says Dad. "If I could go back and do things over, I never would have returned their first call."

"It's not your fault. I would have done anything to make the Narcosis Clinic successful."

"That's not true," Dad says reassuringly. "You never would have let them hurt Ellie if you had known what was going to happen."

"No," Mom sobs. "Never!"

Cole and I watch this exchange with wide eyes as Dad strokes Mom's hair. I've never heard them talk like this, like they know they made mistakes and regret it.

Dad turns and looks at me. "It was wrong of us to interfere with your memory and personality, Ellie. I wish I could have a do over on that too."

"Do overs are what narcosis is all about." I cross my arms in front of me. "You can't do over a do over."

"We should have left you exactly the way you were," Dad says, trying again.

"I'd rather have a daughter who was expelled than dead," says Mom.

"Ellie wouldn't have been expelled," Cole says. "You guys are blowing her discipline stuff up all out of proportion."

"You aren't her parent, Cole, so I don't expect you to know what it was like. I don't know what Ellie would have become without narcosis." Mom shrugs her shoulders. "The only thing I'm certain of is that we were always butting heads and it was awful."

"There is no justifiable excuse for taking away my free will. I can never trust you again. And you haven't even apologized! That's the worst part. You're just going on about how much messing me up has ruined *your* life. I don't get a measly 'I'm sorry, Ellie, for screwing you up'?"

"I'm sorry," Dad says quickly, but it seems sincere. He crosses the room to give me a hug. "If I could take it all back, I would. You and your mother are the most important people in my life, and I would never do anything to intentionally harm you."

"Thanks Dad."

When Mom doesn't say anything, Dad sits down next to her, and elbows her in the ribs.

Moments pass before Mom speaks. "I'm sorry things between us were so difficult. I let my pride and ego get in the way of accepting you for what you were."

"And loving her because of it," Cole says. "There was nothing wrong with the old Ellie." He grips me by both shoulders and stares into my eyes. "Ellie, there was nothing wrong with you. The old Ellie was brilliant and I loved her just as much as I love you."

I gasp. "You love me?"

"I mean, I might as well say it. It's the truth, and we could die in here. It's been love at first sight for me ever since you walked into my kindergarten."

Warm, fluttery hearts fill up my insides like emojis dancing over my phone. I throw my arms around him. "Cole, I'm not sure about many things anymore, but I think I most probably, most definitely, love you too."

For a wondrous minute there is only the softness of Cole's lips and the secure feeling of his strong embrace. When Dad fake-coughs I ignore the intrusion. So what if me making out with my boyfriend makes my parents uncomfortable? I no longer care what they think. Mom just admitted she didn't even like me.

And she didn't apologize for changing my personality either.

It's that thought that finally makes me pull away from Cole's kiss. I look over my shoulder and glare at Mom. "You said you were sorry that I was difficult, not that you were sorry for changing my personality or destroying my memoires."

"That's not what I said," Mom insists.

"Then say it. Apologize again," I demand.

Mom starts to protest and Dad stops her. "We were wrong to do what we did, Belinda, and we both owe our daughter an apology."

Mom comes over to join me where Cole and I sit in the corner. "I just wanted us to get along." She sits down next to me on the linoleum. "And I became desperate."

"You should have loved me through it instead of obliterating me."

"I had good intentions."

"That's no excuse."

"You're right, it isn't."

"And you haven't said sorry for changing me yet."

Mom closes her eyes and in the fluorescent light her normally flawless skin reflects age spots and wrinkles I've never seen before. She's no longer the mother I know—calm, clinical, and in charge. Instead, she's a woman who's trapped and at the end of her rope.

Mom opens her eyes and looks at me. "I am deeply sorry for all the hurt I have caused you. I have tried so hard to be a good mother." At this she tears up. "And I love you more than life itself."

I'm not sure if that's enough, but with a cold feeling, I realize that it's all I'm going to get. "I love you too, Mom. Maybe someday I'll be the real me again, and we can be friends."

When she leans over to hug me, I let her, but my arms are slack, and my heart isn't in it. I escape to the warmth of Cole's embrace as soon as I can.

"This isn't over," he whispers in my ear. "I'll rest my eyes a bit so I can think clearly, and then I'm going to try again on that old computer. There must be a way to connect to the outside world."

"Yes," I agree. "There must be."

"And next year you'll go off to college, and you and your parents will have some space between you. You can see them on your terms, not theirs."

"Right." From the corner of my eye, I see my dad, who gives me a sad smile. He seems less defiant than Mom about all of this. Maybe there's still a chance for our father-daughter relationship.

Cole and I share space on the floor in the corner. I sit up straight so that I'm tall enough for Cole to rest his head against my shoulder. "Let's get some sleep." Cole yawns.

Terror… exhaustion… fatigue… It washes over us all. Cole falls asleep within seconds, and my parents drift off too. But my head is too full of thoughts for sleep just yet.

Am I a victim of my own bad choices, like Mom says? Was I so defiant and awful that I deserved what happened to me? Or am I what Cole says—a leader? Someone my peers used to look up to? I wish I had the answers. My memories seem to be returning, but I'm still scrambled.

"Ellie!" I whisper. "Are you there?" I squeeze my eyes shut. When I open them, I don't see her. "Ellie," I try again in a louder voice. "I need you!"

"That's for sure." Ellie-Me materializes before me in her purple dress. She shivers in the small room, her bare feet making wet marks on the concrete floor.

"How do we get out of here?"

"I don't know."

"You have to know. You said you'd help me if I was in danger."

"I said I'd be here when you were in danger. That's different."

"And here you are." I reach out, and she squats next to me and lets me take her clammy hand in mine.

"I wish I could help you, but I don't know how."

"I wish I could help you too," I tell her.

"You've come a long way. You learned to swim. You're dating Cole. You confronted your parents. You've come too far to die trapped in this room."

"You don't need to be the girl in the wet dress anymore. You deserve peace."

Ellie-Me looks in my eyes. "Maybe so, but I can't leave you like this."

"So don't. Find a way to get us out of this mess."

Ellie-Me takes a deep breath and then adjusts her strapless dress. "Well, there is one thing I might be able to do, but I don't know if it will work."

"Anything, Ellie; I'll take anything."

"I'll have to be brave."

"You can do it."

"And it might make things worse."

"You and I, we take risks."

Ellie-Me smiles and looks at Cole. "That's because risks are worth it." Ellie-Me takes off her garnet necklace and places it around my neck. "You think you're scrambled, but you're not. I see your memories coming back one by one. I know that you make good choices. Ellie, you're on the path to a good life. I can see it for you! All you need to do is get out of this room." She kisses me on the cheek. "Goodbye," she says, "it's been interesting."

CHAPTER FORTY-FIVE: DEAN

7:22 A.M. | OCTOBER 9TH

Police have swarmed the front of the Narcosis Clinic, which is why Marley leads her parents and me in through the garage.

"How did you know the security code?" I ask.

"I guessed." Marley smiles. "4-1-1 SLEEP AWAY CAMP. It's the same code as when we were little."

"I don't feel right about snooping around Belinda's house uninvited," says Mrs. Evans. "She and Warren are very private people."

"We're finding Cole and dragging his scrawny butt out of here," says Captain Evans. "That's it. But you can stay here if you want, Sandy."

Mrs. Evans bristles. "If my son's in trouble, I'm going to find him."

"That's my girl." Captain Evans pecks his wife on the cheek.

Marley takes us to the stairway. "Let's not use the elevator," she says. "Less obvious that way."

The stairwell is dimly lit and smells like bleach. Captain Evans leads the way up three flights until we reach the locked door to the residence.

"Now what?" asks Marley's mom.

"Turn around," orders Captain Evans.

"Gerald!"

"I'm serious. I don't want my wife and daughter to witness me breaking and entering." Captain Evans pulls out a small collection of tools. "You too, Fluffy Hair," he tells me.

Mrs. Evans looks embarrassed. "He learned a lot of skills on the water," she says by way of explanation.

"Done!" the captain says a minute later. "I've still got it, Sandy!"

"Nobody says you haven't, Gerald."

Marley rolls her eyes and blows through the door into the kitchen. "Follow me," she orders.

The whole place is still as a tomb. Daylight seeps in through closed blinds, but none of the lights are on.

"Look at this!" exclaims Marely's dad.

We follow the sound of the captain's voice into the living room, where we discover two glasses of wine tipped over.

"Ouch!" Marley stumbles. "Turn on the light; I tripped on something."

I reach for the nearest switch, and an electric glow illuminates the room.

"Cole's cell phone!" Mrs. Evans cries. "And some others."

"Don't touch anything," orders the captain. "We need to get the police."

Ten minutes later there are officers everywhere, taking pictures, dusting for fingerprints, and asking awkward questions about how we got inside.

"What I want to know," says a young sergeant, "is how freaking Dean Mathews got involved in all of this. Can I get your autograph for my wife?"

"Find my friends, and you can have all the signatures you want," I tell him.

"Get back to work!" his superior hollers.

"They'll find Cole, right?" Marley asks me.

"Of course they will," I say reassuringly.

"But what if they don't? What if he's with the CIA or something?"

"Why would the CIA want Cole?"

"I don't know," Marley says worriedly. "But that woman had Olivia."

"Marley?" Mrs. Evans calls from across the room. "The detective would like to see your phone."

I use the opportunity to wander away from the hubbub in the living room and down a hallway that the police have finished searching. One of the doors swings open and I enter into the master bedroom, which smells sweetly of flowers. It's eerily quiet in the bright daylight. Gauze netting billows around the four-poster bed like a poufy white wedding dress. In the Narcosis Clinic, Dr. Belinda Savage is every inch the scientist. In her own private sanctuary, she appears to be a gooey romantic. A dozen lace pillows litter the bed, including several shaped like hearts. I don't know how Dr. Warren Savage can sleep here.

Even the windows are decorated with ivory lace curtains. I walk over and enjoy the view of the Seattle Center in the distance. Was it really last night that Marley and I were enjoying dinner at SkyCity? A sleepless night later, it all seems like a memory.

"Dean?" says a voice behind me, interrupting my thoughts.

When I turn around and see who's there, I about lose it.

"Don't be afraid," the guy says. "I'm not here to hurt you." He's wearing True Religion Jeans and a white buttoned shirt that's drenched with water. His slicked-back hair looks bedroom-sexy.

"Who are you?" I demand.

"You know who I am."

I take a step back toward the wall. "No. I'm exhausted, that's all."

"For sure," Dean-Me says, "you are exhauthted, but you're altho theeing me."

"This can't be happening." I bunch up the lace curtains in my hand, as if crawling up the wall would help.

"I need you to lithen. It'th important."

"What do you want from me?"

"We need your help," says another voice. Beside my apparition, a second one appears. In front of me is Ellie, dripping wet in a violet dress that looks painted on her skin.

Dean-Me and the ghost girl clasp hands. "Follow us," she says, "and we'll lead you to the missing people." Together, they point to a full-length mirror next to the dresser.

The ghostly version of Ellie curls her wet fingers around the mirror's edge. "The lever's here."

I step toward the mirror and let my fingers explore the crevices. My pinkie hits the lever first, and with a small *pop*, the mirror swings open.

"Thee?" Dean-Me says. "We told you."

"Ellie?" I call through the hole. "Cole? Doctor and Doctor Savage? Are you down there?" I turn around and shout for the police. "I found something!"

"Dean?" says a faint voice from inside the passageway. "Is that you?"

Within seconds, the room is flooded with people. Police officers, Marley, her parents, and Narcosis Clinic staff pack the room just in time to see Dr. Warren Savage step out of the passage looking rumpled but otherwise safe. He holds out his hand to help his wife out. When Ellie comes next, Marley hugs her. Then Cole emerges, and his mother begins to cry.

"It's a miracle!" says Dr. Warren. "You found us."

"I thought we'd be in there forever," says Cole as Mrs. Evans strangles him in a hug.

"How did you find us?" Ellie asks me in a voice so low that only I can hear.

"If I told you, I don't think you'd believe me."

Ellie adjusts the sparkly necklace that coils around her neck. "I would believe you," she says. "I totally would."

Cole stumbles back and shakes my hand. "I owe you, man. I really owe you."

Marley latches on to her brother with one arm and me with the other. Cole grabs Ellie, and I do too so that we're in a four-person hug.

"Somebody get a camera," Ellie demands. "I want to remember this moment forever."

A flash blinds us as a police officer snaps our picture.

"I can see the headline now," says Marley. "'DEAN MATHEWS TO THE RESCUE.'"

"I'm pretty sure it was a collective effort," I say as I look around at all four of us. "I came to Seattle for a miracle and I got one. But narcosis didn't make my problems go away; you all did."

Ellie nods her head in agreement. "I don't know what would have happened to me without you guys." She snuggles next to Cole.

"I'm exhausted." Marley yawns. "Sleeping for three months sounds perfect."

"Don't you dare fall asleep on me now," I tell her.

Marley winks. "I'd love to fall asleep on you."

"Gross!" Cole blurts out as I pull Marley in for a kiss.

As I enjoy Marley's lips, I hear Ellie in the background say, "I don't know about the rest of you but I could use a cup of coffee."

NEXT: OLIVIA

"I made you a sandwich, sweet plum," says a man as he enters my room holding a silver tray. "It's turkey pesto on a French baguette—your favorite." He sits down at the edge of my bed. "Wouldn't it be nice to eat some solid food for a change?" The stranger holds the sandwich to my lips. "Just one bite?"

I try to open my mouth but accidentally close my eyes instead.

"You're sleepy?" The man pulls the sandwich away.

I struggle to open my eyelids and end up jerking my head.

The man sighs. "I see. Well, this sandwich will be right here waiting for you when you wake up. Until then, the IV will keep you nourished."

My arm prickles at the mention of the IV. I feel the wetness seep through my veins. I can't remember the last time I ate a real meal.

"It was in September," says a familiar voice. "You had lunch at Emily Carr High and then took off for the Narcosis Clinic to find out why Ellie wasn't at school."

My eyes pop open. A petite girl stands beside the bed with silky, black hair and a sunburnt nose. Her plaid skirt is cinched in at the waist as if her school uniform is a size too big.

"Who are you?" I ask.

The man gasps. "Who am I? I'm your father, sweet plum." He kisses both of my cheeks, and his tears mingle with my own. "Betty," he calls out to the hallway. "She's awake!"

"The poor things," says the girl. "Mom has been working from home for the past two weeks, and Dad's made so many uneaten sandwiches, he could start his own deli."

"That's Dad?"

"Of course I'm your dad," the man says. "It's me, your father." He turns away for half a second. "Betty! Get in here."

"Tell me the truth." I attempt to scoot up in my bed, but my muscles are creaky.

"Let me help." My father rushes to adjust my pillows.

"Olivia!" A tiny woman in a cashmere sweater flies into the room. "You're finally awake!" She embraces me in a warm hug.

"I *am* telling you the truth," says the girl. "My name is Olivia, and that's your name too. You've been in and out of sleep for a long time."

"Why aren't I in a hospital?" I push the woman away.

"You were in a hospital," says Dad, "but we decided to bring you home to recover instead."

"You've had round-the-clock nurses," says the woman defensively. "The very best care."

"That's Mom," says Olivia-Me.

"Oh." I look at the sandwich. "Can I have lunch now?"

Mom and Dad exchange a hurt glance.

"Absolutely," Dad says with forced enthusiasm. "You can have anything you want."

"Anything," Mom echoes.

"Well," says Olivia-Me with a sly grin, "almost anything." She picks up my kayak paddle and spins it like a weapon.

"What do you mean?" I ask.

"A new car. A trip to Alaska. A whole new wardrobe." Dad rattles off incentives like he's a game show announcer.

"A new phone," Mom adds, "or a double kayak. Anything you want."

Olivia-Me snort-laughs. "You can have anything you want, all right." She slams the paddle onto the wood floor. "Anything but the truth."

AUTHOR'S NOTE

The Narcosis Clinic is an imaginary place, but narcosis rooms were real. I first learned about them while researching brainwashing for my book *Genesis Girl*, published by Month9Books in 2016.

Dr. William Sargant worked at the Royal Waterloo Hospital in London during the 1960s. Ward 5 was Dr. Sargant's domain for treating psychiatric patients, and yes, there was a room devoted to narcosis, or "deep sleep therapy."

Over the course of ten years, Dr. Sargant treated more than 500 patients, most of whom were women. Families would come to the hospital desperate to help their daughters, wives, and mothers, many of whom suffered from postpartum depression. Dr. Sargant promised that narcosis was the answer. He put women on a steady diet of barbiturates and had Nightingale nurses wake them up to use the restroom or be fed. Doctors conducted electroshock therapy, which caused many patients to suffer from memory loss.

"It was like being buried alive," a former patient recalled to *The Daily Mail* in an article titled "The Zombie Ward: The chilling story of how 'depressed' women were put to sleep for months in an NHS hospital room—leaving mental scars that remain 40 years on." What happened in Ward 5 was an open secret at the hospital, but nobody intervened. There were rumors that the American CIA might have been involved.

In fact, the CIA was keenly interested in another prominent psychiatrist of the time, Dr. Donald Ewen Cameron from Canada, who had the distinction of serving as the president of both the American Psychiatric Association and the Canadian Psychiatric Association. In the 1950s and 1960s, Dr. Cameron's research into brainwashing was secretly sponsored by the CIA as described in the book *In the Sleep Room: The Story of the CIA Brainwashing Experiments in Canada* by Anne Collins.

Like Dr. Sargant, Dr. Cameron also experimented on women suffering from postpartum depression. He placed helmets on their heads and forced them to listen to recorded messages that looped for weeks, and sometimes months, at a time. This treatment, combined with electroshock therapy, LSD, and other barbiturates, destroyed the lives of many patients, who woke up with shattered memories and trauma.

With the compassion and sensitivity of modern thinkers, we can see that what Doctors Sargant and Cameron did was obviously wrong, especially considering they did not always have their patients' informed consent. However, at the time they were conducting experiments, these two men continued to receive funding, privileges, and acclaim from their peers in the psychiatric world.

Another aspect of Narcosis Room that is important for me to address is Dean Mathew's lisp. I do not know what it is like to be a nineteen-year-old with an articulation issue, but I did spend nine years of my life with a speech impediment. In addition to a lisp that was originally much more severe than Dean's, I was also unable to pronounce the "R" sound. This meant that for a good portion of my childhood, I could not accurately pronounce my own name: Jennifer Williams. All the feelings and emotions Dean expresses about his lisp are my own.

When it comes to my articulation disorder, I was lucky for two reasons. The first was that I had parents who advocated for me to get help. The second was that I grew up in California at a time when public schools were quicker to offer services to children with speech disorders than they are now. I had an Individual Education Plan for speech therapy before I began kindergarten and was pulled out for speech therapy all the way until fourth grade.

Later, when I became an elementary school teacher in California public schools, I fought special education departments on several occasions to provide speech therapy to students who needed help. Every single time I was told that the student might grow out of it and that there was nothing the school district could do until third grade.

I believe that if I had not received early, immediate intervention, I might still struggle with articulation today. Sometimes even now, my lisp comes back if I'm tired or under stress. That's proof to me that I did not outgrow my speech impediment. Hard work and speech therapists helped correct it.

ACKNOWLEDGEMENTS

Every journey begins with the first step, and writing a book is no exception. I begin writing *Narcosis Room* when my daughter started preschool. I would drop her off in her classroom, and then find a quiet place in the community center where her school was located, to write. Six years later, that book is finally in your hands.

I owe a huge debt of gratitude to my literary agent, Liza Fleissig of the Liza Royce Agency, who is one of the smartest, kindest, most honest people in the business. Thank you also to the team at Owl Hollow Press, editorial director Emma Nelson, acquisition editor Hannah Smith, publicity manager Caroline Geslison, and my top-notch editor Olivia Swenson. I truly value their integrity, flexibility, and passion for literature.

My critique partners Amy McNulty and Sharman Badgett-Young read early versions of *Narcosis Room* and provided invaluable feedback, as did Ginger Everhart and Carol Williams. Jeff Garvin suggested the name "Heartacres" for Dean's boyband, and that was a winner.

Thank you to authors Benjamin Alderson, Joshua David Bellin, Alessandra Clarke, Nicole Conway, Jennifer Anne Davis, Jennifer M. Eaton, Tobie Easton, E.M. Fitch, Melanie McFarlane, Laura Moe, Derek Murphy, Shaila Patel, Jenetta Penner, Julie Reece, Leigh Statham, and Penelope Wright who have given me their wisdom and friendship. I am also grateful for my membership in The Sweet Sixteens, the Nine Lives Authors group, the Author Support Network, and An Alliance for Young Adult Authors.

When I'm not writing books, I pen a column called "I Brake for Moms" for *The Everett Daily Herald*. My editor, Sara Bruestle, is a pleasure to work with and an excellent journalist. Thank you to all my "I Brake for Moms" readers who have stuck with me on this journey from stay at home mom, to published author.

My husband, Doug, makes all things possible, and my children, Bryce and Brenna, add excitement to every day. I love you with all my heart. I would never want to sleep for three months because I'd miss out on too much fun.

Louise Cypress believes in friendship, true love, and the everlasting power of books. She has never met a nefarious plastic surgeon but has eaten dinner at the top of the Space Needle. Louise lives near Seattle, Washington, where the air is misty, and summer is short.

Do you want to know a secret? Louise's alter ego is Jennifer Bardsley. Her Facebook page, The YA Gal, is one of the largest privately-owned Facebook pages dedicated to young adult books.

You can follow Louise on Instagram as @the_ya_gal, on Facebook as The YA Gal, and on Twitter as @JennBardsley. Find out more at: www.louisecypress.com.

#NARCOSISROOM

www.ingramcontent.com/pod-product-compliance
Lightning Source LLC
Chambersburg PA
CBHW062022190726
48284CB00014B/1813